DATE DUE

APR 05 '94	FEB 04 2009
APR 16 '94	2342
MAY 10 '94	FEB 04 2009
1 '94	SEP 1
1 '94	
5	

I've travelled the world twice over,
Met the famous: saints and sinners,
Poets and artists, kings and queens,
Old stars and hopeful beginners,
I've been where no-one's been before,
Learned secrets from writers and cooks
All with one library ticket
To the wonderful world of books.

© JANICE JAMES.

BLUE DRESS GIRL

When She-she is sent as a concubine to the household of Li Hung, her parents impress upon her the honour of her position. However, the reality proves to be far from honourable, for She-she finds she is to be a blue dress girl — little better that a prostitute — whose task is to pleasure visiting foreign traders. This stirring tale of adventure, and a moving and tender love story, is played out against the exotic background of China in 1857, at one of the most turbulent periods in its history.

E. V. THOMPSON

BLUE DRESS GIRL

Complete and Unabridged

CHARNWOOD
Leicester

First published in Great Britain in 1992 by
Headline Book Publishing Plc
London

First Charnwood Edition
published January 1994
by arrangement with
Headline Book Publishing Plc
London

British Library CIP Data

Thompson, E. V.
    Blue dress girl.—Large print ed.—
Charnwood library series
I. Title II. Series
823.914 [F]

ISBN 0-7089-8746-X

Published by
F. A. Thorpe (Publishing) Ltd.
Anstey, Leicestershire
Set by Words & Graphics Ltd.
Anstey, Leicestershire
Printed and bound in Great Britain by
T. J. Press (Padstow) Ltd., Padstow, Cornwall

This book is printed on acid-free paper

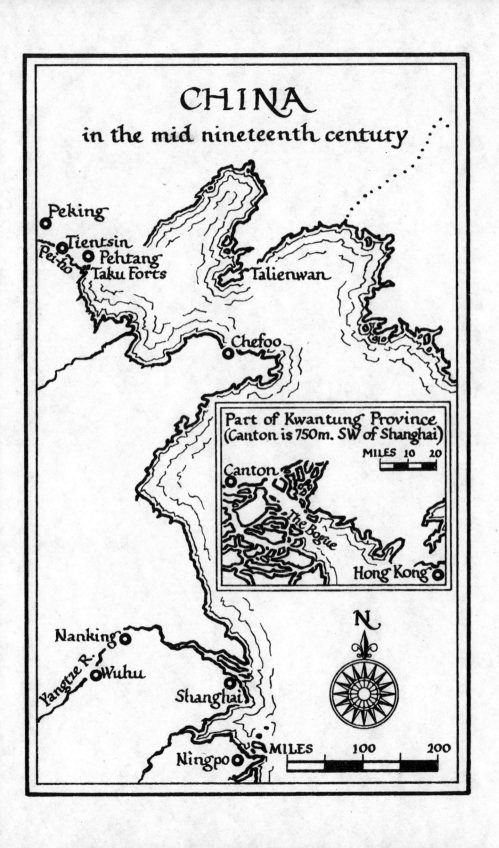

CHINA
in the mid nineteenth century

Peking

Tientsin
Pei-ho Pehtang
Taku Forts Talienwan

Chefoo

Part of Kwantung Province
(Canton is 750m. SW of Shanghai)
MILES 10 20

Canton

The Bogue

Hong Kong

Nanking
Yangtze R. Wuhu

Shanghai

N

Ningpo MILES 100 200

Book One

1

"KEEP still, She-she! You're wriggling about so much it's a wonder I haven't stuck every one of these pins through your skin."

"Perhaps Li Hung will send her back thinking the rash of pin pricks is something he may catch."

"I doubt it. If all that's rumoured of Li Hung is true he'll waste no time inspecting She-she's body for spots. They say he takes as many as six of his concubines every night, peeling the clothes from them as he would the skin from an orange. After savouring the fruit he casts it aside and reaches out for another."

"*Ai-yah!* This must be why he is such a small man and always looks as though he is about to fall asleep."

"Surely he must have forgotten what sleep is? How are you going to keep such a man happy, sister?"

"Enough of such talk! Have you no shame?" The mother of She-she and her two sisters entered the room on slippered feet, unnoticed by two of her three daughters. "Out you go, or the dress will become as ugly as your thoughts. I'll finish pinning it myself. Go!"

As her two unrepentant sisters were driven from the room, She-she remained balanced precariously on a stool in the centre of the room. She said nothing, but her shoulders sagged despondently.

Closing the flimsy bamboo door firmly behind the two giggling girls, She-she's mother returned to the centre of the room. Walking in a full circle about her eldest daughter, she nodded approval of the sheath of bright blue silk that was pinned tightly to accentuate the body beneath.

Her expression became one of loving concern when she looked from the slim, silk-clad figure to a face that reflected none of the brightness of the unfinished dress.

"Take no notice of your sisters, She-she. They are young and know nothing. They merely echo the crude banter of the fish-market. Li Hung is the *Hoppo*, the chief customs official of the Canton district. He was appointed by his Imperial Majesty. Li Hung is a very important man. As one of his concubines you too will have importance. Not at first, of course. The older women must take precedence. But he is rich and as he takes more concubines they will look up to you as you look up to the others. You will see."

"But . . . Li Hung is *old*!"

"Age brings wisdom and distinction. Have you ever heard of a young *Hoppo*? He has much power. Because Li Hung has taken you for a concubine your father has become head boatman on this part of the river. A girl who can find a place in a wealthy household and improve the lot of her family too should be filled with happiness and gratitude at such good fortune."

The stern expression left the mother's face as

4

swiftly as it had appeared. Taking hold of one of She-she's hands, she squeezed it in painful affection.

"All will be well with you, She-she. I know it will. As for me, I will swell with pride whenever someone mentions Li Hung's great house by the river at Canton, knowing you are living there."

Unwanted tears suddenly sprung to her eyes. "But I will miss you, child. I will miss you more than any mother has ever missed a child that was born of her body."

For a few minutes mother and daughter clung to each other in a rare display of emotion. Then She-she's mother pulled away with a sudden exclamation. "*Ai-yah!* You are a porcupine . . . but what are a few scratches?"

As she spoke her critical eye followed the line of pins that drew the silk dress together on one side of She-she's body. She realigned three of them with a deprecatory clicking of her tongue. "Those sisters of yours! I pity the man who takes either of them into his household. Their minds are like a butterfly's wings."

She-she's mother stood back from her daughter and as her glance went from dress to face, her expression softened once more. "Your heart is closest to my own, She-she. Yet you are the greatest dreamer of them all, your mind forever travelling far beyond this village and the great river on which we live."

"That is because your own brother taught me to read and allowed me to bring home his books. There is much to be learned of far away places in books. You know so. You most of all would enjoy it when I read aloud to you and the girls."

"It is not good for a girl to learn to read when so many men and boys cannot. It is fortunate you are going to the house of a learned man, or your knowledge might have caused you trouble. A man does not like his wife to know more than he."

"I'm not to be a wife to anyone." There was a note of wistfulness in She-she's voice as she added, "I wonder what life will be like as a concubine of Li Hung?"

"That I do not know, although I once spoke with the concubine of a great Tartar war lord. He came through this very village when I was a girl, and I was ordered to take food to the women of his household. I asked one of them the very same question. She told me it was an honour to be the concubine of such a great man — and so it is. All the women in the village are envious of you, while the men wish they had a daughter with beauty enough to attract the attention of a high official like Li Hung. Then they too might be given an important post, like your father."

"Where is he? I had hoped he would be here to give me his blessing before I leave."

"You will not be going until late this afternoon. He should be home by then, although his work keeps him very busy. But unfasten your dress carefully and step out of it. We must have it finished by the time Li Hung sends for you."

6

O-hu, head eunuch in the household of the Canton *Hoppo*, arrived at the door of the small house in the riverside fishing village as the sun was sliding gently towards the distant western hills. Such surroundings as these were not to the eunuch's delicate tastes. He grumbled at the time She-she took to say farewell to her family, viewing the simple furnishings of the hut with disdain.

A curtained carrying-chair had been brought to the door to take She-she to the *Hoppo*'s boat which was waiting alongside the river-bank. As she stepped inside the brightly painted conveyance, She-she tried hard to hold back the tears which threatened the make-up so assiduously applied by her mother.

The other three women had no such reason for controlling their own emotions. As She-she was carried away she parted the curtains that hid her from the view of villagers she had known all her life. The last glimpse she had of her mother and sisters was of three faces contorted with grief, their cheeks wet with tears.

For She-she, the pain of parting was made far worse by the absence of her father. His quiet strength and wise words had always been available to her when they were most needed. She wondered whether he had deliberately stayed away. His way of telling her that things were different now she was about to become a woman in another man's household.

She dismissed the thought. Her father was

hard at work in the service of Li Hung, earning the promotion she had brought him. He would probably be waiting for her at the river.

She-she's father was not at the river and, minutes later, she was being borne away by boat, in an enclosed cabin. Drawn curtains prevented her from looking back at her family and the village that had been her home since her birth, sixteen years before. She would never see either again.

* * *

Twenty-four hours later She-she was carried from the boat and borne along a dirt road in the carrying-chair to enter the cobbled yard of Li Hung's impressive residence. She risked a glance from behind the curtains of the cramped and hot carrying-chair, but there was time only to observe an abundance of flowering, climbing shrubs before the chair was lowered to the ground. She raised one hand to her hair, but then the curtains were drawn aside and the *Hoppo*'s senior eunuch said, "Come."

It was the moment She-she had been secretly dreading. She had dismissed the stories told about Li Hung by her two younger sisters, bringing to bear upon them all the scornful authority afforded by her few extra years. Now she wished she had allowed them to tell all they claimed to have heard. What if the rumours were true? Would Li Hung be awaiting her in his room . . . the bedroom? If so, what would he do? What would be expected of her?

"Come."

This time there was impatience in the eunuch's voice and She-she put her fears aside, hurriedly stepping from the carrying-chair. All the gossips, family and otherwise, were agreed on one point: the senior eunuch in an important official's household wielded great power, albeit assumed power. It would be foolish to upset such a man before she had even set foot in Li Hung's house.

As she straightened up, She-she tried to apologise, but the eunuch ignored her. He walked away and passed through a doorway hung with bamboo curtains, to which were attached many tiny bells. They continued their soft music after the eunuch had passed through. After a moment's hesitation, She-she followed.

The door led to an enclosed garden. Following her guide, She-she caught a sudden, unexpected glimpse of a number of young women, perhaps a dozen or more. They were gathered about a small dog to which were attached a number of squirming, teat-hanging puppies, each hardly larger than a man's closed fist.

One of the girls glanced in She-she's direction and nudged a companion. As She-she followed the eunuch from the garden she could hear giggling behind her. It sounded very much like the merriment of the two sisters she had left in the village that was her home no longer.

"Are they concubines too?" She-she spoke to the eunuch politely, but he ignored the question as he had ignored her attempted apologies. She wondered whether he was being deliberately rude, or was merely hard of hearing.

When they reached the far side, She-she followed the eunuch through a doorway that opened into the house itself. She found herself in a corridor that was part of an awesomely rich world. Here were silk drapes and huge items of intricately carved camphor-wood furniture. Wall paintings depicted birds, cloud-capped mountains and men and women dressed in the style of the ruling Manchu dynasty.

The eunuch pushed aside a silken curtain that served as a door for a room off the corridor, saying, "This is yours. You will keep it clean and tidy. When a gong sounds once it is time to eat. If it sounds many times you will assemble with the other girls in the room at the end of the passageway."

With this brief information, the eunuch turned — and was gone.

Left alone, She-she stood in the room and her feeling of bewilderment grew with each silent passing moment until it bordered on panic. She had been left with so many unanswered questions. This was not how she had imagined life would be as a concubine of the *Hoppo*, Li Hung. She had thought she would be surrounded by other concubines and servants. Yet the eunuch had told her she was expected to keep her own room clean and tidy!

"Welcome!"

She-she turned to see a girl of about her own age standing inside the curtained doorway. She had entered the room quietly, her small feet making no sound on the heavily carpeted floor.

10

"I am Kau-lin. We heard from the eunuchs that a new girl was expected today. What's your name? Where are you from?"

She-she introduced herself eagerly, greatly relieved to have found someone in this vast and unfamiliar place who was at least prepared to speak to her.

Kau-lin proved to be both friendly and informative. She, like She-she, was a Hakka girl and she went about the room opening cupboard doors and pointing out the clothes that had been provided for She-she. There were slippers to wear about the house — and a light, silken robe she must wear when she went to bed.

This latter piece of information was accompanied by heavy innuendo. She-she felt emboldened enough to ask the question that had been uppermost in her mind since first being told she was to become a concubine of the great *Hoppo*.

"When I am dressed for bed will the master come to my room? Or will I be summoned to go to him? And . . . will it be tonight?"

"The master? You mean Li Hung?"

She-she nodded, puzzled by the other girl's evident amusement.

"Li Hung will not send for you. You're a Hakka girl. A peasant, the same as me. Look at us — at our feet. They were never bound when we were children, as were the feet of the wives and concubines of Li Hung. He would not so much as look at us."

She-she's mouth dropped open at Kau-lin's

revelation, "I thought . . . I was told . . . "

"You thought you had been brought here to be a concubine for the *Hoppo*?" Kau-lin laughed, but seeing She-she's bewildered distress, stopped quickly. "Never mind, you are not the only girl whose family has been fooled by such a tale."

"But if I am not to be a concubine, why am I here? Why are you here?"

Kau-lin reached out and touched the dress worn by She-she. It was the same colour and material as her own.

"This shows everyone why you are here. You are a 'blue dress girl'. Foreign devils like blue. It is the colour of their eyes."

"Foreign devils? I still don't understand."

She-she's eyes showed her fear. She had never met a *Fan Qui* — a 'Foreign devil'. It was the term given to Europeans. They were so fearful that the Emperor of China restricted them to only a few ports around the coast, never allowing them inland. Canton was one of such ports. She-she had not thought about this in the excitement of her changing life . . . but Kau-lin was talking again.

"After an evening spent drinking with the *Hoppo* and his officials and a night sharing a bed with a blue dress girl, the 'Foreign devils' are less inclined to question Li Hung's customs dues. Don't worry, She-she, the 'Foreign devils' are not as frightening as they are said to be. Once you have become used to their hairiness and their smell, you will find that some of them are not too bad . . . "

12

2

SHE-SHE'S tears flowed for much of that first night in the house of Li Hung. It was almost daylight before she eventually drifted off into an exhausted sleep. Mercifully, the nightmare of the day was not carried into the night. During the brief sleep her troubled mind conjured up no disturbing dreams.

Leaving her family and the hard but familiar life she had always known had been deeply distressing to her. Yet even at the moment of parting she had her pride to sustain her. Pride in the belief she had been chosen by the *Hoppo* to become one of his concubines. It had brought honour to her family, recognition to the Hakka village, and given her father a new importance in the community.

Now the pillar of her pride had been toppled, it had brought the world she thought she was entering crashing down about her ears. Far from being an honourable concubine of a high Imperial official, she had become a 'blue dress girl', virtually a prostitute. Even worse, she was a prostitute whose body was to be provided for the pleasure of the *Fan Quis*, the 'Foreign devils'. It was a prospect that filled her with unspeakable horror.

During the sleepless hours, She-she wondered whether her father had known what Li Hung intended for her. Could this be the reason he had not put in an appearance when she left home? She had been deeply hurt by his failure to say goodbye to his eldest daughter.

She immediately dismissed the thought that he could have known anything of the life to which he was sending her. There had always been too much love in their family. He would not knowingly have done such a thing to her. There must have been something else to keep him away. The pressures of his new duties. He did not know — and must never know — of her place in Li Hung's household. He would not survive the shame.

★ ★ ★

In spite of her unhappiness, life was not unpleasant in the *Hoppo*'s house during that first day. There were ten blue dress girls and they passed the hours talking, playing mah-jong, or walking in their part of the extremely beautiful gardens. The garden used by the blue dress girls was separated by a wall from that used by the concubines, but the official mistresses could be heard calling to each other, and at midday they had musicians to entertain them.

The concubines were scornfully dismissed by Kau-lin as foolish, empty-headed dolls filled with jealousy of one another. She declared they spent their days tottering awkwardly on bound feet, telling tales about each other and squabbling about the favours bestowed upon them by their lord and master, Li Hung.

Kau-lin, like She-she, was a Hakka. Their

14

feet had been left unbound because few Hakka families could afford to have a girl in the household who was not able to work to earn her keep. Kau-lin, in particular, was fortunate to be alive. As she told She-she, every other girl born in the village in her birth year had been consigned to the Canton river.

During She-she's first, unhappy week, Kau-lin became her constant companion. She did her best to keep the new blue dress girl's spirits from sinking too low. Kau-lin was a bright and cheerful girl and her efforts met with success during the day. She could do nothing to help She-she at night, when loneliness closed in.

Yet She-she found the night-time solitude in her room preferable to the alternative offered by her new way of life, and reminders of her place in Li Hung's household were never far away.

This was 1857 and Canton was a busy trading port. Relations between China and the Western nations were currently under considerable strain, but many sailing ships, flying the multi-coloured flags of Great Britain, France, America and Portugal, were constantly being towed upstream from Whampoa by multi-oared 'dollar boats'. An occasional sea-going steamer was also to be seen, owned by one of the faraway sea-faring nations.

Not built to battle against the currents of great rivers, the paddles of the steamships threshed the water to foam and black smoke poured from tall, thin funnels as the craft struggled against the tide to reach their assigned anchorages. Unseen in the dark oven-like caverns of the boiler-rooms, near-naked lascars were driven to the limits of endurance in order to meet the constant demand for more power. Frequently they collapsed from a combination of heat and exhaustion.

Standing at a window of the great house, which was set well back from the water in order to avoid the odours of the river, Li Hung would watch the bustle of commerce with great satisfaction. Each ship arriving at Canton brought to China broadcloth, chintzes, tin, Bengal cotton, rice — and opium. Such cargoes meant revenue for the Imperial coffers, with a considerable sum from each siphoned off into the account of Li Hung.

When the holds of the ships were emptied they would take on cargoes of silk, Sycee silver, satins and tea for the return voyage to Europe. An even larger percentage of the revenue from such exports would also find its way to Li Hung. It was a most satisfactory arrangement.

Li Hung was not greedy by Chinese standards and no official complaint had ever been received from the foreign traders who made use of Canton's facilities. Indeed, traders and ships' masters were always eager to avail themselves of the Canton *Hoppo*'s world-renowned hospitality. Food was plentiful on his tables, the wine flowed freely and, for those who wanted it, there was a ready-warmed bed to help a man forget the uncertainties of navigation and commerce, while he recalled what he had left at home.

Hoppo Li Hung enjoyed such simple pleasures as much as he delighted in offering them to others, although the women who shared his bed were dainty-footed Chinese girls from good backgrounds.

For the 'Foreign devils' he had his senior eunuch gather in peasant girls. True, they were the pick of the countryside, but they were Hakkas, the daughters of fishermen or peasant farmers. Girls whose feet were like those of men. The traders and sea captains seemed not to care. Such lack of taste served only to increase Li Hung's carefully concealed contempt for the barbarians whose commerce had made him a very rich and powerful man.

'Foreign devils' came to the quarters of the blue dress girls nightly during She-she's first week there. All were regular traders who had their own established favourites among the girls. Nevertheless, each night she lay awake as the heavy and unsteady footsteps of the *Fan Quis* came along the corridor. They were accompanied by the soft-walking eunuchs with their high-pitched voices, and only a flimsy curtain separated her from the men she feared so much.

On one occasion Kau-lin received a visit from one of the traders. When she appeared the next morning she looked pale and tired.

She-she offered the other girl her sympathy. "I heard the *Fan Qui* being taken to your room. Was it very bad?"

To She-she's surprise, the other girl smiled. "Bad? No. He was young — and almost sober. I lay back and imagined he was a man from my village. The one I would have married had

17

I not come here. It was almost enjoyable. I would have enjoyed it more had he drunk an extra glass or two of Li Hung's wine. Then he might have allowed me some sleep. Do I look awful this morning?"

She-she was taken aback by the matter-of-fact manner with which Kau-lin was able to talk of a night spent being made love to by a 'Foreign devil'. She lapsed into silence.

"Was there no one in your own village you hoped to marry, She-she?"

The girl thought hard. There were a number of young men of whom she was fond, but she could think of no man she would like to have shared a bed with. "No. Is it really what you do? Think of someone else while it's happening?"

"Sometimes. But last night was not too bad. The *Fan Qui* was not like the others. He has learned a little of our language and tried to speak to me. He likes to talk, that one . . . when he is not doing other things."

★ ★ ★

When O-hu, the senior eunuch, came into the garden a few days later, his glance fell upon She-she and she immediately knew the purpose of his visit. The other girls had fallen silent at his approach, but She-she never noticed them. She had eyes only for the eunuch. He stopped in front of her, inclining his head slightly before speaking. It seemed to her there was malicious delight in his expression.

"Good evening, She-she. You will be pleased

to know you are at last to have the privilege of repaying Li Hung for the honour he has brought upon you and your family. You will go and bathe, using sweet herbs. When you return to your room you will put on the silk robe laid out in readiness on your bed. The *Fan Qui* who will come to you tonight is a most important man. You will ensure he has a night of great pleasure."

"Who is this 'most important *Fan Qui*'?" Kau-lin was the only blue dress girl who dared question O-hu. He was usually quick to take offence, but he seemed to find only amusement in Kau-lin's cheekiness.

"It is the trader, Courtice. He is both important and wealthy."

"Why is he to go with She-she? Trader Courtice has always been Che'eng's man."

Che'eng was the oldest of the blue dress girls. There had long been speculation about the length of time she would remain in the household of Li Hung. Now O-hu put an end to such speculation.

"Che'eng is too old to remain as a blue dress girl any longer. Tomorrow she will leave the house of Li Hung."

"But she has nowhere to go. What will become of her?"

"Arrangements have been made for her future."

"What sort of arrangements?" Kau-lin persisted. Li Hung had a reputation for ruthlessness from which ageing blue dress girls were not immune.

"She is to go to a flower-boat tomorrow. It has been agreed with the flower-boat owner."

There was a gasp from the listening blue dress girls and the unfortunate Che'eng put her hands to her face and fled inside the house. The flower-boats were curtained sampans that plied the Canton river. Bedecked with flowers and manned by prostitutes, they found their customers among the ships anchored in the waterway. Catering for sailors of all nations, the girls were despised by their fellow-countrymen, and women.

"Why give She-she to Trader Courtice? Why not some other girl? Me, if you like. She-she doesn't know enough to please an important man like him."

O-hu showed She-she the malicious smile once more. "You are right, of course, but I think perhaps the *Fan Qui* will enjoy teaching her."

"The Trader Courtice is a pig. A fat, *Fan Qui* pig."

"You will watch your tongue, or Che'eng will have company when she goes to the flower-boats." O-hu responded to Kau-lin with a sudden flash of venom that showed his patience was not inexhaustible, even with her. "Come, She-she. You will ready yourself now."

"I'll come and help her."

O-hu inclined his head once more, "As you wish, but be quick or you will both feel the bamboo cane tomorrow."

As the eunuch walked away, She-she discovered she was shaking. Kau-lin noticed it and took her friend's arm. "Take no notice of O-hu. The only pleasure he will ever have in life is frightening blue dress girls."

"Have you seen this Trader Courtice? What is he really like?" She-she was still trembling uncontrollably.

"Huge and hairy, but don't let that frighten you. Don't let *anything* frighten you. While you bathe I'll tell you what you can do to make it easier . . . "

3

AS the lights went out one by one in the quarters of the blue dress girls, She-she's hopes began to rise slightly. She had been waiting for Trader Courtice for many hours. Perhaps he would not come. He was an important man, O-hu had said. It might be that he had business elsewhere.

As the sounds of Li Hung's household faded and died she relaxed even more. It was very late. Surely he would not come now?

It was peaceful in this part of the house and she must have dozed off. It could not have been for more than a few moments, but she awoke with a start to see O-hu standing in the entrance to her room, an expression of disapproval upon his face. He was holding back the curtain and through the opening behind him a man entered. A *Fan Qui* man. He was so tall he needed to stoop in order to pass through the doorway.

The man came across the room somewhat unsteadily and She-she looked up at him with horror. Trader Courtice was more than a big man. He was *huge*. He must have weighed at least three times her own weight — and he was old. Older than her father. It was difficult to see much of his face, hidden as it was behind a huge, bushy beard, but above the hair his skin was blotchy and laced with thin, purple veins. Signalling for the eunuch to leave the room,

22

Trader Courtice stood swaying beside the bed for many moments, gazing down at She-she. His blue, bulging eyes reminded her of those of one of the great carp that swam in the waters of the pool in Li Hung's garden, eyes blue-blind with age.

Trader Courtice stood swaying above She-she for what seemed an age. Then he grunted and began to undress. Pulling his shirt over his head he revealed a chest that was almost as hairy as his face. Her heart racing alarmingly, She-she closed her eyes, unable to look any longer. She knew she *had* to make an effort to control the revulsion she felt, but this Courtice was more animal than human. He reminded her of a drawing of a huge ape that had filled a page in one of the books belonging to her uncle.

What was Li Hung thinking of, entertaining such a creature? This *Fan Qui* should be caged. Instead, he had been brought to her room so he might make love to her . . . No, *love* was not involved. He was here to use her.

She-she opened her eyes when the clothes were pulled back from the bed. She averted her gaze again immediately. Courtice stood over her, gross in his nakedness, a huge belly sagging over the parts she tried hard not to look at.

The trader spoke one word. It was the only word she would hear him utter, and it made no sense to her. He said it again and it sounded more like the noise made by an uncertain dog: "Off." This time the word was accompanied by a gesture and She-she understood. Courtice wanted her to remove the sleeping robe she wore.

She obeyed as though she were acting out a dream. A nightmare. Then she lay back and the trader stood looking down at her, studying her from head to toes.

She-she still averted her eyes from his ugly body, but she was aware that the sight of her nakedness had stirred him.

Courtice sat down heavily on the side of the bed and the stout bamboo frame protested noisily. The trader ran a hand over her body and she closed her eyes once more as her skin recoiled in revulsion from his touch.

His hands roamed her naked body, feeling, pressing, probing. She-she moaned in abject despair, but Courtice took it to be a response to his crude explorations. He lay down beside her for a moment and then rolled over upon her. As his huge flabby body sagged on top of her, enveloping her, the mass of hair on his chest covered her nose and mouth. She found difficulty in breathing.

She-she fought hard to free her face but Courtice again misinterpreted her response. He grunted as he fumbled in an attempt to force himself inside her.

Suddenly something in She-she's mind snapped. It no longer mattered that this man was one of Li Hung's honoured guests. It counted for nothing that he was a wealthy and powerful trader. She began a frenzied attempt to break free of his embrace.

Finding a strength she had never known before she beat at the huge trader, punching and gouging. When this proved futile she seized the hair of his head with both hands and forced it back. She even sank her teeth into the loose, flabby skin of his revolting, hairy chest.

Taken by surprise, Trader Courtice let out a bellow of pain. He heaved his chest clear of her face but as She-she sucked in great gulps of air he raised his fist to strike her.

The blow never fell. A frightening, deep gurgling sound filled Trader Courtice's throat and for a few moments there was a terrible conflict deep within his body. The sounds ceased as suddenly as they had begun and his body sagged to envelop She-she once more.

This time she had her face turned to one side. Although the smell of him threatened to choke her, she could at least breathe — but she had not stopped fighting him. Making a supreme effort she pushed Trader Courtice away.

The large man rolled off her and crashed to the floor. Gasping for breath, She-she swung her legs from the bed, steeling herself for a beating from the gross *Fan Qui*.

Trader Courtice remained where he had fallen, lying on his back on the floor. Arms akimbo and mouth open, his eyes looked more like those of Li Hung's carp than before.

She-she stared at the prostrate figure for almost a minute, until horror took the place of revulsion. Trader Courtice was dead. Her resistance to his advances had killed him!

★ ★ ★

She-she's screams wakened the other blue dress girls and brought O-hu hurrying to their quarters. He was accompanied by two lesser eunuchs.

When the eunuchs entered the room the blue dress girls crowded around the doorway. They tittered and made immodest comments as each sought to catch a glimpse of the body of the huge trader.

Pushing her way between the other girls, Kau-lin ran to She-she's side and put her arms about her friend. While O-hu kneeled beside the dead trader, uncertain of what he should do, Kau-lin spoke angrily to the giggling girls.

"Be quiet! This is no time for such foolishness. Can't you see She-she is upset?"

"Why upset?" One of the girls spoke maliciously. "She should be proud. She has killed a *Fan Qui* — and on her first time too! What will she do when she has some experience?"

As the ribaldry gained new momentum, O-hu stood up and glared at the blue dress girls in the doorway. "Yes, he was a *Fan Qui* — and a very important one. This could cause trouble — big trouble, for everyone. Li Hung must be told immediately."

Ordering the two eunuchs with him to dress the dead trader, O-hu ushered the girls from the room, telling them to go to bed and remain silent.

Kau-lin remained comforting her friend. By the time the two struggling eunuchs had succeeded in dressing Trader Courtice, She-she

26

had regained some of her composure.

The two girls were talking quietly together when the curtain in the doorway was pushed aside and Li Hung entered the room, followed by O-hu.

Both girls stood up and bowed low, but Li Hung impatiently ordered them to stand up and face him.

"Which one is She-she?"

"I am, Master." She-she bowed again.

"You . . . go!" The order was given to Kau-lin. At the same time the *Hoppo* waved a hand at the grovelling eunuchs and said to O-hu, "Tell them to drag the body of the *Fan Qui* outside. We will send it back to his ship and say it was found beside the road near the house by one of the servants. Trader Courtice was a very big man. Too big for his heart. It will be thought it finally failed him."

Turning to She-she, the *Hoppo* said, "You will say nothing of this to anyone. Should you be questioned you will deny any knowledge of the trader Courtice. Is this understood?"

"It is understood, Master."

"Good!"

Li Hung had reached the doorway before She-she's voice brought him to a halt.

"Master . . . O-hu must order the other girls to remain silent also. They saw the body of the *Fan Qui* lying on the floor of my room."

Li Hung was silent for a few moments and She-she thought she might have gone too far in telling the *Hoppo* what he should do. Then he

27

nodded his head. "That was well thought. O-hu will tell them."

Li Hung's gratitude extended beyond words. The following morning O-hu came to the quarters of the blue dress girls bearing a gift for She-she. It was a heavy bracelet of gold and jade, on which was worked the Chinese symbols for 'Happiness', 'Long Life' and 'Good Fortune'.

4

DESPITE the dire warnings of Li Hung, the true story of Trader Courtice's death did not remain within the walls of the *Hoppo*'s house for very long. Within a week the story was circulating in the market place of Canton and rumours had reached the European business quarter alongside the river. The *Hoppo*'s spies brought him disquieting rumours that an 'investigation' was being demanded into the matter, fuelled by jealous traders and merchants who had never been invited to enjoy the delights of Li Hung's hospitality.

He found such rumours extremely disquieting and was anxious they should go no further. But discovering the source was not a task for the District Collector of Customs. Distasteful duties of this nature were always passed on to Li Hung's secretary, who also happened to be his nephew.

Small and insignificant, Secretary Po was a pinch-faced young man with a diffident manner and a voice pitched almost as high as one of his illustrious uncle's eunuchs. His appearance was deceptive. Po was one of the most ruthless and ambitious young men in the employ of the *Hoppo*. He would stop at nothing to help further his career, as many men had discovered to their cost.

Po came to the quarters of the blue dress girls accompanied by an unusually agitated senior eunuch. O-hu's own position was in jeopardy. Should it be proven that one of the girls in his care had been indiscreet, the eunuch would be flogged and demoted and would suffer permanent disgrace.

Unannounced, Secretary Po pushed aside the curtained entrance to She-she's room and with O-hu in his wake, entered to find her and Kau-lin seated on the carpet playing a game of chess.

"Stand up in the presence of Secretary Po!"

O-hu barked the order even though the two girls were already rising to bow to their visitor.

"Which of you is She-she?" In asking the question Secretary Po made no attempt to hide the distaste he felt at having to question blue dress girls. He considered them to be prostitutes. Whores kept by his uncle for the gratification of the *Fan Qui*.

"I am She-she."

Secretary Po looked at the neat young girl, but did not allow her beauty to diminish his contempt. "You were with Trader Courtice when he died?"

She-she shuddered as the secretary's words brought back the events of that night.

"Answer Secretary Po when he speaks to you!" O-hu's voice rose to new heights.

She-she nodded.

"And who have you told of what happened here in this room?"

"Only Li Hung. Who else is there to tell?

There have been no traders since that night and we see no one else."

Behind the secretary's back O-hu nodded his approval of her words. He had already informed both Li Hung and Secretary Po that the blue dress girls had spoken to no one outside the *Hoppo*'s house. Since the death of Trader Courtice all *Fan Qui* traders and merchants had been kept away.

"You'll not find the one you seek here."

Kau-lin spoke the words nonchalantly, seemingly unimpressed by the importance of the visitor to the quarters of the blue dress girls.

"Silence! You will speak only if Secretary Po addresses you." O-hu squeaked his displeasure once more.

Irritably, Secretary Po waved the eunuch to silence, "If this girl has something to say on this matter I wish to hear it. What is your name?"

"Kau-lin. The one you seek, the girl who told of the death of Trader Courtice, is no longer here. She left almost a week ago. You're too late."

Secretary Po frowned. "Your words make no sense to me. Explain what you know."

"I *know* nothing, but it isn't hard to work out who passed on details of the *Fan Qui*'s death. It was Che'eng. She had entertained the Trader Courtice for as long as she had been a blue dress girl, yet the night he died he was brought to She-she's room. The next day Che'eng was sent to a flower-boat. She lost much face and would have gone away from this house with no love for Li Hung in her heart. I have no doubt she enjoys repeating the story to all who have time to listen — and it will lose nothing with each telling."

Secretary Po swung around to confront O-hu. "Is what the girl says true?"

A glimmer of swiftly disguised smugness was visible in O-hu's eyes before he bowed his head. "It is true, Honourable Secretary. The order to send Che'eng to the flower-boats was signed by yourself. I was pleased to carry out Your Excellency's orders as swiftly as possible. Che'eng was sold to Ah King, owner of the flower-boats, the day after the death of Trader Courtice."

There was an embarrassed silence after O-hu had spoken. This information placed Po in a difficult situation. Selling ageing blue dress girls to the flower-boat owner had been his own idea. Originally he had intended carrying out such transactions without Li Hung's knowledge, or approval. In view of the outcome it was fortunate that fear of what the *Hoppo* would do if he found out had outweighed the prospect of immediate monetary gain. Nevertheless, Li Hung would not forget it had been his secretary's idea. Po would be held responsible for the ex-blue dress girl's indiscretions. Action would need to be taken — and quickly.

"Come, O-hu. I have work for you to arrange."

"You do not wish to speak to any of the other girls?"

"Kau-lin has told me all I wish to know. I need waste no more time here. You should have

32

thought of this Che'eng yourself. It would have saved me much time, and Li Hung a great deal of trouble."

When Secretary Po and O-hu left the room, the two girls returned to their game, but She-she found it difficult to concentrate now.

"Poor Che'eng. She must be very unhappy."

"Don't waste your pity on her. She didn't care about the trouble her loose tongue would cause us — you in particular."

"All the same . . . What do you think will happen to her?"

Kau-lin looked at She-she sharply, uncertain whether or not the question was a serious one. Deciding that it was, her reply took the form of a gesture, one finger tracing a line across her throat.

"You don't really believe they'll *kill* her? Not without finding out for sure first?"

"What else can they do with her? Her words might already have cost Li Hung his post as *Hoppo* of Canton. She can't be allowed to stay around to prove the stories are more than mere rumours."

"You knew this and yet told Secretary Po about her?"

"Would you rather we all suffered torture because we could not tell Secretary Po something we do not know?"

"What about me? I know the truth of the *Fan Qui*'s death better than anyone."

It was clear the thought had not crossed Kau-lin's usually quick mind. She frowned, then her expression suddenly cleared. "They know you wouldn't say anything. You're not like Che'eng."

Kau-lin's confident assertion did nothing to allay She-she's fears. Li Hung was a very powerful man, with much to lose. He would not hesitate to dispose of another blue dress girl if he believed she posed a threat to him — and he had a like-thinking henchman in his nephew, Secretary Po.

★ ★ ★

She-she would have been even more concerned had she been aware of the stir Trader Courtice's mysterious death was causing among the European traders in Canton. More serious for Li Hung, a garbled version of the story had also reached the nearby British colony of Hong Kong. The missionaries here, ever eager to castigate the low morals of the traders, had called for an investigation to be instigated immediately by the colony's governor.

Such a clamour suited the immediate purposes of Governor Sir John Bowring, but for other reasons. In a stern letter to Viceroy Yeh, head of the Chinese province of Kwangtung, in which Canton was situated, he demanded a full explanation of the death of Trader Courtice.

On such occasions it was customary for the Chinese authorities to prevaricate. A reply would be delayed in the hope that the incident in question would fade into insignificance — unless the tone of British reminders suggested their exasperation might no longer be contained.

34

Surprisingly, the reply to the Hong Kong governor's letter was swift — and brief to the point of political rudeness.

"His Excellency the Provincial Viceroy can accept no responsibility for the death of a foreign trader on Chinese soil. He would point out that no evidence has been offered by the British authorities to suggest either violence or foul play. The body was returned to the British enclave at Canton with all speed and they will no doubt have ascertained that the trader's death was due to natural causes. I repeat, therefore, that this is not a matter for official Chinese concern. If foreigners do not wish to die on Chinese soil the remedy is surely apparent to all."

The insulting tone of the last paragraph of Viceroy Yeh's letter proved to be the final straw for the Hong Kong governor. Announcing that he was sending two top diplomats to Canton to investigate the matter, he demanded that Viceroy Yeh afford them every facility to carry out their inquiries.

The request received an equally swift and categorical refusal from the Chinese Viceroy. The diplomats would not be welcome. There would be no investigation.

Governor Bowring had not fully recovered from a bout of malaria and he appeared tired and gaunt as he read the correspondence aloud to a gathering of senior British staff and naval and army officers, assembled in his office, called there by special messengers.

"Well, gentlemen, there you have it. It would

35

seem Viceroy Yeh is determined we shall not learn the truth of poor Mister Courtice's mysterious death. May I have your views, please?"

Admiral Sir Michael Seymour responded immediately. "I think it's high time Viceroy Yeh was taught a lesson. He's been thumbing his nose at the British government, not to mention the French and Americans, for far too long."

His words brought murmurs of agreement from the others in the room. Loudest of all were the naval and military men, but it was to a churchman, the Reverend Michael Porrett, that the governor turned.

Reverend Porrett had been appointed by the Bishop of Hong Kong with special responsibilities for all the missionaries. Currently restricted to only a few areas, they were straining at the leash to enter China as soon as the treaties could be clarified.

"What are your views, Michael? If we begin a military operation your missionaries are likely to be in some danger. What do you think?"

"Since the recent execution of a French Catholic missionary I have anticipated military action in some form or another. I sent out orders recalling the missionaries. Most refuse to forsake their stations and those who rely upon them. Many of them are outside my jurisdiction, of course. However, they are all well aware of the risks of their calling. They are prepared to accept them in the Lord's name."

"Send them another warning — and couch it in the strongest possible terms. I want them to be in no doubt of the risks they are running — and I want you to inform them the Church is not looking for martyrs. There will be no troops available to save their skins when action is taken."

"Does this mean you've made up your mind to teach Yeh the lesson he so richly deserves, Governor?" Admiral Sir Michael Seymour's voice betrayed the eagerness he felt at the prospect of impending action.

Governor Bowring sighed and shook his aching head wearily. "I have no alternative. As you know, there has been a virtual state of war between Britain and China since the misunderstandings of last year. If I allow Yeh's arrogance and contemptuous attitude to go unchecked now, the situation for the European in China will be quite impossible. I need to consult with my French and American colleagues, of course. But yes, gentlemen, I intend taking punitive action against the Chinese on behalf of Her Majesty's government."

5

AN invitation to have dinner with Viceroy Yeh was a great honour indeed, but Li Hung entered the palace of the provincial governor with a feeling of deepening apprehension. Yeh was not a man who entertained because he enjoyed meeting people. The Viceroy must have a reason for issuing the invitation — and *Hoppo* Li believed he knew what it was.

The evening went much as Li Hung had anticipated. Over dinner Yeh passed on the latest information obtained by the Viceroy's spies in Hong Kong. The news was alarming. The British and French, with the tacit approval of the Americans, were gathering a fleet with the intention of blockading the approaches to Canton, and preventing any movement of Chinese shipping.

Li Hung had known for some time that something must be seriously wrong. Not a single European ship had come upriver to Canton for more than a week. It was a certain indication that a hostile act was planned. Yet he could not believe the *Fan Qui* nations would carry out hostile actions on such a scale. It was inconceivable that the natural death of one *Fan Qui* trader should trigger off acts of blatant aggression against a nation such as China.

Viceroy Yeh shrugged off Li Hung's incredulity.

This particular incident was far less serious than others that had gone before. The truth was that the British and French had for some time been seeking an excuse to use their might against China in a bid to gain more trading concessions. If it had not been the death of Trader Courtice it would have been something else.

However, Viceroy Yeh had a warning for his *Hoppo*.

"As you are aware, I find the arrogant attitude of the *Fan Qui* distasteful. I am convinced they are encouraging and supporting the Taipings, the long-haired rebels who are causing so much trouble in the north-east of my province, and who threaten the peace of China itself. It will give me much pleasure to inflict defeat upon the *Fan Qui* in battle, especially the arrogant British.

"Yet it would be unwise to underestimate the fighting capabilities of any enemy. It is possible that in the early days of battle our own army will suffer reverses. Should these occur it will be necessary for me to assure our esteemed Emperor that the war has been sought by the *Fan Qui*, without any justification. I have informed the British that their trader died in a natural manner whilst returning to his ship after a business discussion with you. There is, therefore, no reason for there to be an inquiry. My report to the Emperor repeated this view. You will ensure that should *Fan Qui* armies march on Canton, they will find no one to contradict my words. I trust I make myself perfectly clear, *Hoppo* Li Hung?"

★ ★ ★

Li Hung acted upon the Viceroy's warning without delay. Less than forty-eight hours later She-she and the other blue dress girls, together with O-hu and four lesser eunuchs, were en route for the home of Li Hung's brother, a powerful District Magistrate at Foochow, in the province of Fukien, a few hundred miles along the coast to the north.

It would have been far too much of a threat to Li Hung's future career to have kept the girls at Canton with the French and British threatening a hostile move against the Chinese trading port. However, Li Hung had no intention of disposing of them altogether. They had proved their worth in his dealings with *Fan Qui* traders and merchants in the past. They would do so again when the latest political storm had blown over.

For She-she, the move came as a tremendous relief. Unaware of the strained relations between the *Fan Qui* and the Chinese, she had dreaded each new night, fearing that another repulsive and hairy *Fan Qui* would be brought to her bed.

★ ★ ★

Standing on deck with Kau-lin, She-she breathed in the air of the great river. She was a fisherman's daughter, more at home on the river than she would ever be in the household of Li Hung. She felt a contentment she had not known for

40

many weeks. Even the movement of the deck beneath her feet was comforting as the vessel was caught in the wake of a passing, multi-oared war junk.

She-she automatically shifted position to maintain her balance. The sailors on board the war junk shouted across the water, but there was a stiffish breeze blowing. It was impossible to tell whether they were attempting to impart information, or merely calling out to the two girls, conspicuous on deck in their blue dresses. Kau-lin did not share She-she's love of the water. Maintaining her footing with great difficulty, she announced her intention of joining the other blue dress girls below deck.

"You'll feel much better staying up here in the air," declared She-she, sympathetically. "The movement will be much worse down in the hold, with nothing to take your mind off the way you feel."

Kau-lin groaned, "I could feel really ill right now if I thought about it too much. All right, I'll stay with you — but only if you stop being so cheerful."

She-she smiled as the junk changed direction to avoid one of the many islands that made navigation on the river dangerous.

"Remain on deck until we pass those forts up ahead. It looks as though we'll be in the estuary soon afterwards. I'll come below with you then."

The Bogue forts guarded the entrance to the river where it was about two miles wide from bank to bank. Low and menacing, the forts had cannon capable of reaching any enemy ship attempting to force its way upriver to Canton.

One of them boomed out as the *Hoppo*'s junk passed by, but this was not a shot fired in anger. It was a salute to the scarlet and gold pennant flying from the junk's mast, proclaiming that the vessel was employed in Imperial service.

★ ★ ★

Other, less friendly eyes witnessed the salute. On board H.M.S. *Sans Pareil*, an eighty-four gun man-o'-war hove-to on the seaward side of the forts, seventeen-year-old Second Lieutenant Kernow Keats of the Royal Marines had a telescope to his eye and watched the gesture of courtesy with great interest.

Turning to the captain of the *Sans Pareil*, he said excitedly, "The forts are keeping a sharp look out, sir. They've just fired a salute to a junk flying an Imperial pennant."

Without saying a word Captain Hamlyn took the telescope from the young marine and put it to his own eye. Skilfully adjusting the eye-piece, he spent some minutes studying the junk.

"Hmm! It's not a fighting junk, Mister Keats. The only armament appears to be a small cannon on the upper deck. It's possibly an Imperial despatch boat. We'll close on it and you can take a boarding-party to search the vessel. You might find something of interest to us."

"Thank you, sir! I'll go and organise the boarding-party straight away."

42

Excitedly, Second Lieutenant Keats clattered down the ladder to the first gun deck, heading for the armoury. Behind him a Royal Marine drummer began to beat out the call for 'Action Stations'.

As the sound of the drum beat echoed through every deck, seamen dropped whatever they were doing and ran to their allotted battle stations. Gun ports sited along the black-painted bands on each side of the ship like tenement windows were hooked open. For a while the sea-going sounds of creaking spars and timbers were lost amidst the cries and shouts of gun-crews, each toiling for the honour of being first to report their cannon ready for action.

By the time Kernow returned to the deck with a boarding-party of ten Royal Marines, the *Sans Pareil* was fully ready for any action that might take place. A pinnace for the boarding-party, manned by canvas-jacketed sailors, was suspended over the ship's side. As the marines took their places in the centre of the boat, the *Sans Pareil* drew level with the junk and a warning shot rang out, fired across the bows of the Chinese vessel. At the same time a shout went up for the pinnace to be lowered into the water.

The sailors on board the man-o'-war were anxious not to miss any of the forthcoming action. The boat was lowered so swiftly it crashed into the water with an impact that rattled Kernow's teeth. The *Sans Pareil* was still under way. Had it not been for the swift reaction of the pinnace's crew the boat would have been dragged beneath the water by the speed of the larger vessel.

The crew swore loudly at the careless boat handlers on board the *Sans Pareil*, but the man-o'-war had already forged ahead, heeling over in a tight turn to cut across the path of the Imperial junk.

Minutes after the warning shot, the junk's sail was lowered and the high-sided vessel slowed to the speed of the sluggish current.

There seemed to be some dissension among the Chinese crew. When the pinnace had covered no more than half the distance to the junk, the large lop-sided sail was raised once more and the vessel began to forge ahead. At the same time there was a puff of smoke from the small cannon on the junk's deck and a round shot fell harmlessly in the sea, well to one side of the pinnace.

The shot did nothing to deter the young Royal Marine officer and Kernow called on the crew of the pinnace to pull harder towards the Chinese craft. The sailors responded with every ounce of strength they could muster.

The captain of the *Sans Pareil* had seen the incident and his action was swift and effective. A thunderous and accurate broadside was fired from the man-o'-war, momentarily hiding the warship from view behind a cloud of pungent gunpowder smoke.

The junk seemed to stagger drunkenly in the water as falling shot churned up the water around the Chinese vessel.

There were as many misses as hits, but when

the junk emerged from the spray it had gaping holes in the timber hull and pieces of splintered wood bobbed in the wake of the clumsy vessel.

The crew of the pinnace had rested on their oars when the crash of the man-o'-war's salvo rolled over them. As they began pulling towards the junk once more, Kernow called, "Wait! The *Sans Pareil*'s coming about. I think she's going to fire again."

The young second lieutenant was right. The captain of the British man-o'-war was bringing his ship around in a tight turn. No sooner was the manoeuvre completed than the guns on the starboard side of the ship thundered into action with no less effect than before.

This time the *Sans Pareil*'s cannon brought down the stricken vessel's mast and sail. The junk wallowed lopsidedly in a slight swell, its broken mast hanging over the side, a long red and gold Imperial pennant trailing forlornly in the water.

The junk's list increased as the sailors watched and it was apparent it had been holed beneath the water line by shot from the *Sans Pareil*.

"Pull!" Kernow shouted excitedly. "I don't want the junk to sink before we get to it."

The pinnace's coxswain repeated the order, adding a few colourful expletives to add emphasis to the young Royal Marine officer's words.

The junk was listing badly now, but the side of the vessel was still far higher out of the water than the *Sans Pareil*'s pinnace. Leading his boarding party of Royal Marines, a sword

45

in his right hand, Kernow found it impossible to climb to the slanting deck of the wallowing vessel until two of the sailors in the pinnace literally pushed him on board.

For a few moments he stood alone on the deck of the Chinese craft. He was prepared to fight for his life, but there was nothing to be feared from the junk's crew. Two grey-clad seamen lay dead on the deck, killed by the devastating broadsides of the *Sans Pareil*. No one else was to be seen.

Suddenly the junk began pitching and bucking alarmingly, caught in the wake of the man-o'-war. The *Sans Pareil* had come about once more and was passing no more than three ship's lengths away. Only now did Kernow become aware of a sound that sent a chill of horror through him. From somewhere below the deck someone was screaming — and it was the scream of a woman.

Behind the young officer a Royal Marine scrambled to the junk from the pinnace. He was quickly followed by another — but Kernow hardly noticed. A young girl wearing a tight, blood-spattered blue satin dress had stumbled from a hatchway to the open deck. When she saw Kernow and the marines standing before her she screamed anew and tried to return the way she had come, but other blue-clad girls were clambering from the hold, making return impossible.

By the time the last of the marines succeeded in boarding the junk there were seven blue-clad girls standing on the deck, many of them weeping. There were also eleven men, two of them eunuchs, their bright silk clothes looking out of place among the drab grey uniforms worn by the junk's crew.

"Do any of you speak English?"

Kernow asked the question more in hope than expectation. The blank stares of the men and women provided an unspoken reply. In the silence he heard a sound from the hold beneath him. It sounded like the whimpering of an animal, but he could not be certain.

"Two of you come with me," he said to the marines. "The rest of you stay here and guard these."

Kernow clattered down the ladder to the hold, the marines behind him. At the bottom of the ladder he was forced to halt, his sword raised defensively until his eyes became accustomed to the gloom.

There was a movement in a corner of the hold and a woman's voice said in uncertain but defiant English, "You come kill us? Then you kill this girl, She-she, number one. Maybe you stop her hurt."

Kernow could see now despite the poor light in the passenger hold. A girl dressed in a similar fashion to those who had escaped from the hold was kneeling on the wooden deck, supporting the head of another, slightly built girl on her lap. Behind her was a gaping hole in the side of the hold through which he could see an expanse of muddy-green water. There were others in the hold. Bodies. One was that of a young girl, also dressed in blue. The remainder were men dressed in silk, like the two mustered on the upper deck.

"Is she badly hurt?" Kernow leaned over the girl held in the other's arms.

"Hurt bad. You no touch." The girl's arms closed defensively about her friend.

"We have a surgeon on board the *Sans Pareil* . . . "

Seeing the girl did not understand him, Kernow said in frustration, "It doesn't matter. We'll have you out of here and off the junk as quickly as we can."

He turned to the marines who had accompanied him to the hold. Pointing to the girl who had spoken, he said, "Get her up on deck. I'll carry the wounded one. We'll send them back to the *Sans Pareil* in the pinnace. We'd better take the other women too. Go in the boat with them and tell Captain Hamlyn the junk is sinking. We'll need to take everyone off. It will probably be quicker if he lowers another boat to help out."

At first Kau-lin protested when Kernow tried to take the badly wounded and unconscious She-she from her, but the gentle manner in which he lifted She-she succeeded where brute force would have failed.

Kernow picked up the wounded girl, surprised by how little she weighed. The movement brought a gasp of pain from her. As he climbed the ladder, leaning against the junk's acute list, she opened her eyes momentarily. They were dark eyes, almost black, and they were filled with a pain that made him wince in sympathy for her. In the daylight he could see her more clearly.

She was young, even younger than himself. She was also slim, beautiful — and bloody.

Ten minutes later the nine surviving blue dress girls were being rowed back to the man-o'-war in the pinnace while the marines carried out a thorough search of the vessel which was settling ever lower in the water.

Kernow and his marines found a great many official-looking documents on the junk. When another boat arrived they took the documents to the *Sans Pareil* with them.

By the time Kernow stepped on board the man-o'-war water was washing gently over the junk's upper deck. The vessel's all-wood construction made it doubtful whether it would ever sink completely, but it would have been both uncomfortable and dangerous for the blue dress girls and the junk's crew to have remained on board.

★ ★ ★

On the *Sans Pareil* Second Lieutenant Kernow Keats found he was required to defend his decision to take off the junk's passengers and crew.

Captain Hamlyn sent for him and when Kernow entered the captain's cabin he found the commanding officer seated behind a huge, polished desk. The naval officer's eyebrows were locked together in a frown and his greeting was anything but friendly.

"Mister Keats, what the devil do you mean by sending those Chinese girls to my ship?"

"I couldn't leave them on a sinking boat, sir. They're . . . women."

"Chinese women, Mister Keats." The tone of Captain Hamlyn's voice suggested they were talking of two different species. "You've made life damned difficult for me. What's more, Chief Steward Lu tells me the women belong to the household of the Chief Customs Officer of Canton. They're concubines. Why, they even have eunuchs with them! Perhaps you can suggest what I should do with them now?"

"Take them back to Hong Kong?" Kernow made the suggestion hesitantly, not certain whether he was expected to reply. "The wounded girl will probably need to go to hospital there anyway."

"At least we're agreed on *that*! The surgeon says he has no facilities on board to treat the Chinese girl — and I have no intention of having my ship's routine disrupted because of a handful of foreign women."

Captain Hamlyn stood up and began pacing the room. The captain of the *Sans Pareil* was a bachelor. Rumour had it that he actually disliked women. He had been heard to state that they had destroyed the career prospects of more good fighting men than had the enemy.

Suddenly the man-o'-war's captain came to a halt in front of Kernow. "My orders from Admiral Seymour are to maintain a blockade here, Mister Keats. To intercept Imperial shipping attempting to force a passage through the Bogue. Those are my *orders*. Now do you see the predicament you've placed me in?"

Kernow nodded, but he was determined to defend his actions. "I'm sorry I've put you in an awkward spot, sir, but I boarded a vessel that was sinking as a result of our action. I found a number of women — albeit *Chinese* women — on board. I had no alternative but to bring them off. I'm quite sure you, or any other Englishman, would have done the same."

"Perhaps, Mister Keats — or perhaps not."

Apparently unwilling to pursue this line of argument, Captain Hamlyn said, "You have presented me with the problem, Mister Keats. I am therefore looking to you to provide a solution. You will take the pinnace and convey these 'ladies' you have so nobly rescued to Hong Kong."

Kernow was taken aback. Taking command of such a small boat presented no problems. Hong Kong was no more than a few hours' sailing time away. But carrying nine young Chinese women as passengers, one of them badly wounded, was a different matter.

"Begging your pardon, sir, what do I do with the women when I get there?"

"I leave that entirely to your initiative, Mister Keats. The wounded girl will need to go to the mission hospital. If you talk nicely to Doctor Jefferies, the principal, the missionaries might accommodate the remainder."

Captain Hamlyn allowed himself the rare luxury of a smug smile. "You possess a chivalrous nature, Mister Keats. I have no doubt you'll think of something."

6

THE blue dress girls belonging to Li Hung remained on board the *Sans Pareil* overnight. Anchored off-shore, the man-o'-war was out of range of the guns of the Bogue, but a sharp look-out was kept against any surprise attack that might be launched against the ship from the mainland, or downriver from Canton.

An even more stringent watch was kept outside the ship's sick bay, where the nine Chinese girls were billeted. The blue dress girls were used to entertaining *Fan Quis* and their dark eyes were bold as they lingered on men far younger and more attractive than the merchants they had known in the house of the Canton *Hoppo*.

Such was Captain Hamlyn's concern for the mayhem the presence of girls on his ship was capable of creating, he ordered a strong guard to be mounted on the sick bay. It was composed of Royal Marines, officered by a Royal Navy lieutenant, and was changed every hour of the night. In addition, the officer-of-the-watch had orders to visit the guard at least once every hour and enter the visit in the ship's log-book.

Kernow visited the girls, saying he wanted to be certain the wounded Chinese girl would be capable of making the voyage to Hong Kong by open boat the following morning.

He was accompanied by the officer-of-the-watch, and the ship's surgeon. The surgeon thought it would make very little difference whether She-she travelled or not, declaring pessimistically she was probably going to die anyway. Whenever she regained consciousness she was in great pain and all he was able to do was keep her opiated.

He voiced this opinion in front of Kau-lin and the Chinese girl rounded on him angrily. "She-she not die! I take good care of her. Maybe find Chinese doctor Hong Kong. He make her number one good again."

"She'll die whether or not someone sticks a few pins in her," said the ship's doctor, with heavy sarcasm, referring to the use by Chinese doctors of acupuncture. "Her only hope is that Doctor Jefferies at the Mission hospital will spot something that has eluded me."

Kernow looked down at She-she. The opiate given to her by the ship's surgeon had sent her into a deep sleep. Her long black hair was lying loose on the pillow, accentuating the pallor and tight-drawn lines of her face.

He remembered the dark eyes that had opened briefly when he carried her from the hold of the sinking junk. He hoped he might see them again, this time free from pain.

It seemed a vain hope at this moment. She had lost a lot of blood. Nevertheless, she was a lovely-looking girl, so slim as to appear fragile, and with a childlike appeal. It would be a tragic loss if she were to die.

"Don't worry," he said to Kau-lin, with more

confidence than he felt. "I'll get her safely to Hong Kong and there'll be someone there to make her well."

Glaring at the ship's surgeon who had sniffed scornfully at Kernow's attempt to comfort her, Kau-lin returned her attention to the lieutenant and said, "You good man. Take She-she Hong Kong quick. No get better here."

With this judgement on the talents of the *Sans Pareil*'s surgeon, Kau-lin turned her back on the three men and made a great show of tucking the bed-clothes about her sleeping friend.

★ ★ ★

Despite the forebodings of the *Sans Pareil*'s commanding officer, dawn arrived on the Pearl River estuary without any dire calamity having befallen his ship.

As men awoke to face a new day in the cramped quarters of the man-o'-war, Second Lieutenant Kernow Keats was subjected to a great deal of good-natured banter from the other young officers who occupied the gun-room quarters. All secretly envied him the mission for which he had been detailed.

Kernow's orders were to take four marines with him as an escort for the nine young women he would be delivering to Hong Kong. Once there he needed to ensure they were suitably accommodated and provided for before returning to the *Sans Pareil*.

During the voyage to Hong Kong he would be in sole command of the pinnace. True, it carried

54

no more than a twelve-man crew, but the boat mounted a twelve-pound howitzer and flew the ensign of the Royal Navy. It could be loosely classified as a fighting vessel. Furthermore, there would be no censorious senior officer peering over his shoulder during the voyage.

Although the task had been given to Kernow as a 'punishment' for bringing the Chinese women on board, there was not a young officer on board the ship who would not gladly have taken his place.

Kernow was aware of the problems he would face when he reached Hong Kong with the Chinese girls, but before that he intended enjoying the five-hour voyage to the harbour as commander of the *Sans Pareil*'s pinnace. It was an opportunity that occurred all too seldom for young naval or Royal Marine officers.

Kernow and his 'cargo' were given a noisy send-off by the ship's company of the man-o'-war. The men clung to the rigging and waved from open gun-ports. When the ribald calls threatened to get out of hand Captain Hamlyn sent his officers among them with the threat of public floggings.

In the pinnace, Kernow gave the order to raise the sail. Within minutes the *Sans Pareil*, tugging impatiently at her anchor rope, was left behind. Second Lieutenant Kernow Keats was taking Li Hung's blue dress girls to Hong Kong and an uncertain future.

When a steady course had been maintained for some time and the man-o'-war no more than a dot on the horizon, Kernow made his way from the stern of the pinnace to where She-she occupied a stretcher placed just in front of the mast. Kau-lin sat beside her, holding her friend's hand. She-she had been opiated on board the *Sans Pareil*, but the effect of the drug was wearing off.

"Is she all right?"

Kernow put the question to Kau-lin but he smiled at She-she as he talked. Her expressive dark eyes were open today and he was very much aware of them staring up at him.

"Her name She-she. I Kau-lin. You speak name. She-she say hurt too much."

Kernow's face expressed his sympathy. "I'm very sorry about that. Tell She-she I'll get to Hong Kong as quickly as I can. There'll be a good missionary doctor there to take care of her."

The young Royal Marine smiled down at She-she once more, but she seemed not to be reassured. Her eyes opened so wide she appeared almost occidental for a moment or two.

At that moment the coxswain of the pinnace called to Kernow from the stern, "There's a junk dead ahead, sir. Some way off yet, but coming up fast. It seems to have a couple of banks of oars, like that pirate ship we chased off Formosa a couple of weeks back."

Kernow straightened up immediately and looked ahead. These waters were notorious for pirate activity and there were rumours that the Imperial Chinese authorities had recently broken up one of the large rebel triads — a Chinese secret society that had

56

been terrorising the countryside around Canton for many months. The members who had been captured were immediately executed, but a great many escaped to swell the ranks of the pirates in the Canton river area.

The junk was a couple of miles away, but the oars could be clearly seen, propelling the Chinese craft through the water like the legs of some giant, menacing spider.

"Pass me the boat's telescope, coxswain."

Taking the heavy brass telescope without removing his gaze from the approaching vessel, Kernow thought quickly. It was not only pirate junks that were powered by banks of oars. Imperial war junks were often operated in the same way, especially in coastal waters.

He could see the junk clearly through the telescope now. It had no Imperial pennant flying at the mast head, but there was at least one cannon on the upper deck. It might be an Imperial war junk, but Kernow suspected the coxswain's deduction to be correct. If so, there was good reason for concern.

Pirate vessels were common around the China coasts and were destroyed whenever they were encountered by Royal Navy vessels. Because of this they usually stayed well clear of any vessel flying an ensign. But Kernow and his crew were sailing in an open pinnace. They were small enough for pirates on a well-armed junk to try to wreak revenge.

"Alter course to starboard, coxswain. We'll go as close to shore as we can. It'll give the junk less room to manoeuvre if it does turn out to be unfriendly."

The boat's passengers heard the urgency in Kernow's voice. Realising that something was wrong, some of them stood up in an attempt to see what was happening.

"You . . . the girls. Get down in the boat. *Right* down."

In an aside to the coxswain, he said, "If it is a pirate boat they'll probably not risk taking us on without a very good reason, but the girls could prove reason enough. Get down, I say!"

Kernow's words were not understood, but his gestures were clear enough. The blue dress girls moved to obey him swiftly, used to following the command of anyone in authority.

"What's happening?" She-she saw the movement all about her and put the question anxiously to Kau-lin who now crouched beside the stretcher.

"I don't know. I think it's another boat. Perhaps an Imperial war junk."

Her words caused an immediate stir among the cowering blue dress girls.

"Shouldn't we show ourselves to them?" The suggestion came from one of the youngest.

"Why?" Kau-lin rounded on the speaker. "An Imperial war junk wouldn't turn around and carry us to Foochow. We'd be taken to Li Hung at Canton — and he doesn't want us there right now. We're an embarrassment to him."

"He wouldn't send us away," said another of the girls, confidently.

Conversation ceased as the coxswain signalled

for the girls to crouch still lower in the boat. The unidentified junk had altered course in response to the pinnace's change of direction. It would appear that someone on board the junk was determined to intercept the small British vessel.

"Check your muskets," Kernow gave the order to his marines. If the crew of the menacing junk tried to board the pinnace he was determined his marines and the sailors from the *Sans Pareil* would give a good account of themselves.

Kernow's main fear was that the other, larger vessel would deliberately run down the pinnace. The naval vessel was stoutly built, but it would prove no match for the heavily timbered junk in a collision.

Not until the very last moment did the junk alter course, passing no more than ten boat's lengths from the pinnace. Kernow was convinced now it was a pirate vessel. It had altered course to allow the Chinese on board to inspect the small naval vessel.

Nevertheless, the other craft passed by without any show of aggression, but just when Kernow was beginning to breathe more easily the wash from the junk hit the pinnace, causing the smaller boat to bounce alarmingly for a few moments. As a result one of the blue dress girls — the one who had suggested earlier they should show themselves — was thrown off balance. Instead of remaining in the bottom of the boat, she struggled to her feet and clung to the mast to steady herself.

A number of the Chinese pirates were hanging

over the stern of the junk, gesticulating derisively at the British sailors. When they caught sight of the blue dress girl a great yell went up.

Hearing the sound, Kernow knew they were in trouble. His fears were confirmed when the junk began to execute a wide, ragged-oared turn.

There was only a light breeze blowing. The pinnace could not outsail the junk and the use of oars would not greatly increase their speed. It was doubtful too whether the pinnace could win a race to the uncertain sanctuary of the shore.

"Coxswain, have your men bring the howitzer aft — and hurry! What shot are we carrying for it?"

The howitzer was heavy and as a weapon it was not particularly accurate, but fired from the stern of the pinnace it might prove sufficient to beat off an attack by the pirate vessel.

"We're carrying half-a-dozen canister shot, sir. Is that the sort of thing you want."

"It's exactly what I want. Is there someone in the crew who's expert in firing the thing?"

"I'm as good as anyone, sir — but if them pirates keep up their speed they'll run us down before I can get the gun loaded."

In spite of the coxswain's pessimism and the speed of the pirate junk, the first shot from the howitzer was got off when the junk was still many lengths astern of the pinnace. However, the shot fell short and to one side of the pursuing junk.

The second shot had a good line, but this time it dropped behind the pirate vessel. At the same time there was a puff of smoke from

60

a cannon in the bows of the junk. Fortunately it was fired wildly and the round shot dropped harmlessly into the sea, far from the pinnace.

"We can't afford to miss again, coxswain. Another minute or two and they'll run us down."

Kernow spoke in near desperation. The junk was overhauling the pinnace at an alarming rate. He would need to order avoiding action very soon, but this was likely to bring only a brief respite.

"We won't miss again, sir. I've got their range now. Watch this . . . "

The coxswain fired off a third shot. Once again the pinnace shook with the force of the explosion. At the same time a shot from the junk's cannon hummed low overhead to splash in the sea, close enough to send spray over the occupants of the pinnace. It was the best shot so far from the Chinese and one of the blue dress girls screamed in fear.

Suddenly there was an explosion from the direction of the pirate junk and a plume of smoke rose from its deck. The oars on both sides faltered momentarily and Kernow thought they had scored a vital hit, but the oarsmen recovered quickly. The shot had not affected the junk's progress, although it appeared to have silenced the cannon.

"I thought I had their range. Now let's see what this one will do," the coxswain muttered as he fired yet again.

The shell from the howitzer landed squarely upon the junk once again, but with far more effect than before. The explosion was more muffled and the smoke marginally later in rising. However, when it came it rose not only from the deck, but billowed from the ports housing the oars on either side of the junk.

A number of oars were actually blown clear of the pirate vessel and strewn around it in the water. The few oars that continued to thresh the water were hopelessly unsynchronised and soon became entangled with each other, causing the junk to slew around in the water, presenting its beam to the pinnace.

As a great cheer rose from the sailors on board the pinnace, Kernow ordered his marines to commence firing upon the pirates who could be seen staggering about the upper deck.

"That was a fine shot, coxswain. It must have dropped through a hatchway to the rowing decks."

"I can't ever remember making a better one, sir, nor one that was more needed, but don't ask me to try it again. I reckon we had a lucky escape there, and no mistake."

"Nonsense, coxswain. We taught those pirates that it doesn't pay to attack a vessel of the Royal Navy, whatever it's size. I'll see that your remarkable gunnery skill is brought to the attention of Captain Hamlyn when we return to the *Sans Pareil*. Well done indeed."

Pleased with Kernow's praise, the coxswain ordered the return of the howitzer to its position in the bows before resuming his place at the helm.

The blue dress girls realised it was now safe to

sit up but they rose from the bottom of the boat uncertainly, as though expecting to be ordered to crouch down once more.

One of the sailors pointed to the junk drifting aimlessly astern of the pinnace, smoke still seeping from the oar-decks. The blue dress girls immediately recognised the pirate vessel for what it was and set up an excited clamour.

Making his way among them, Kernow looked down at She-she. Still flushed with the excitement of his first successful engagement with an enemy whilst in command, the young marine officer felt a twinge of disappointment when he saw a momentary expression of fear cross the girl's face at sight of him.

Kau-lin did not share her friend's apparent aversion to *Fan Qui* men, especially not a smooth-shaven young *Fan Qui* officer. She smiled at Kernow when he looked in her direction.

"Tell your friend the excitement's over now. We'll have her in Hong Kong before long," said Kernow, returning the smile.

"Kau-lin take care She-she." Kau-lin pointed to where the pirate junk was now far behind the pinnace. "You shoot them good, eh?"

Kernow's smile spread. "That's right, we shoot them good." He glanced down at She-she once more then returned to where the coxswain was steering the pinnace farther out into the estuary once more.

Watching Kernow chatting to the coxswain of the pinnace, Kau-lin turned her head and saw She-she was watching him too.

"The young *Fan Qui* officer likes you, She-she. Why are you so frightened of him? He's not hairy, like Trader Courtice."

She-she started guiltily, as though caught out doing something wrong. She looked away from the young Marine second lieutenant. "He's a *Fan Qui*. His eyes are cold. Like the sky."

"The sky in summer is more blue than in winter, She-she. I don't think the *Fan Qui* officer is cold. He is a brave man. A good man too. His name is Lieutenant Keats, I heard the men say. He has twice saved our lives. He could have left us on Li Hung's junk when it was sinking. It would have been better for him. These sailors say the number one man on the *Fan Qui* ship was angry with Lieutenant Keats for saving us. The number one man did not want us on his ship. He has punished Lieutenant Keats by making him bring us to Hong Kong. Now he has saved our lives again. The pirates are our people, yet they would have treated us far worse than any *Fan Qui*. It would have been better to be dead than taken by them. We should all be grateful to Lieutenant Keats. I am. I will show him if I get the chance."

She-she knew the form Kau-lin's gratitude would take and should have been shocked, but she was feeling too tired — and confused. In spite of her remarks to Kau-lin she did not find the young officer unattractive. He was not like the bearded and hairy Trader Courtice.

She-she was also in pain. The effects of the opiate had quite gone now and every small wave encountered by the pinnace sent pain stabbing

64

through her wounded side.

"What is to happen to us when we reach Hong Kong?"

"Lieutenant Keats says he will take us to the 'Shang Ti people', those they call missionaries."

One of the listening blue dress girls gave a gasp of horror. "It's said the Shang Ti people suck the spirit from the Chinese and offer it as a sacrifice to their Gods."

"Who is better for us, a missionary who takes our spirit or Li Hung who lets men use our bodies?" retorted Kau-lin. "You're repeating gossip passed on by fools. Anyway, I like the Fan Qui officer and so does She-she. He can have my spirit if he wants it — or my body if he would rather."

7

ENTERING Hong Kong's busy harbour, the pinnace threaded its way through an armada of trading vessels from which flew the flags of a dozen nations. Around the larger vessels lighters clung like leeches, three and four deep.

Shoals of sampans, propelled by a single oar over the stern, plied between ships and both shores. In spite of the current hostilities between the government of China and the Western nations, Hong Kong was rapidly becoming one of the most important trading centres in the world.

Kernow directed the coxswain to the foreshore on the Wanchai side of the growing town of Victoria. He knew from earlier visits to the colony that this was the most convenient spot on the waterfront for the mission hospital.

Once the pinnace had been pulled half out of the water, Kernow left the blue dress girls in the care of the marines and sailors from the *Sans Pareil* while he set off to locate the mission doctor.

When Kernow returned he was accompanied by Doctor Hugh Jefferies, Hannah, the doctor's wife, and a number of coolies. They discovered an inquisitive crowd had gathered about the boat and its attractive cargo. Most were Chinese, but there was also a fair sprinkling of Europeans, some dressed in Chinese clothes. These were men who had come to Hong Kong as seamen, or employees of a trading company, and had chosen to remain and cast off Western ways, when their contracts had ended. They now occupied a twilight world that embraced both east and west, although they were fully accepted by neither society.

Some of those gathered about the boat were carrying on an increasingly animated conversation with the pinnace's passengers, but they parted to allow Kernow and the missionaries through.

Much of the excitement had been caused by the revelation that the girls belonged to the *Hoppo* of Canton, but their account of the battle with the river pirates was also being loudly repeated to newcomers joining the crowd.

The merchants in the crowd were most concerned over the actions of a Royal Navy man-o'-war in sinking a vessel belonging to the *Hoppo*. It marked a further deterioration in relations between China and Britain.

A desultory and uncertain state of hostility had existed between the two nations for some time, but the traders had never taken it too seriously. Those engaged in commerce between the two countries hoped it would prove to be mere posturing, a prelude to a new trade treaty between the two countries. It had often been so in the past.

The *Sans Pareil*, by sinking the *Hoppo*'s junk, had dealt their hopes a serious blow. The Chinese authorities would undoubtedly take action to avenge the sinking.

The Chinese in the crowd had mixed feelings about the situation. Many were resentful of a European presence in their country, and highly critical of the arrogance shown by Britain's diplomats, confident in the support of their vastly superior navy. Other Chinese were merchants, dependent for their living on the very lucrative trade centred upon Hong Kong. Any disruption of commerce was to be avoided at all costs.

Kernow faced a barrage of questions, levelled at him by the Europeans among the crowd. Most were a demand to know what was happening upriver, in the Canton area. Only a few proffered congratulations to the young Royal Marine officer on his victory over the pirate junk. It was these Kernow chose to answer.

"It was my coxswain who saved the day by his splendid shooting. He's the one to tell you about the battle — but will you first clear a way through from my boat? There's a badly wounded girl on board who needs to be taken to the hospital."

As the crowd cleared a narrow path from the water's edge, She-she was lifted in the stretcher from the boat by the mission's coolies and carried ashore. Everyone was eager to catch a glimpse of her and it seemed to She-she that she was caught in some dreadful nightmare, submerged beneath a sea of faces, some leering, some grinning, many mouthing words she could not hear.

The truth was that the rigours of the eventful voyage were beginning to take a heavy toll upon the wounded girl. The opiate she had been given by the *Sans Pareil*'s surgeon had not been effective for as long as was intended. In great pain for the final part of the voyage she was now close to delirium.

The difficulties the coolies were having in carrying the stretcher through the inquisitive crowd added to her torment in these final minutes of the long journey. When he became aware of the problem, Kernow came to their aid. With harsh words and occasional physical force he succeeded in clearing a way for She-she's stretcher, helped by a shrill-voiced Kau-lin. Without seeking permission from anyone, she had left the pinnace to accompany her wounded friend. No one attempted to stop her.

Meanwhile, still on board the small open boat, the remaining blue dress girls were less certain of what was expected of them. Unused to acting upon their own initiative, they huddled in the centre of the boat, waiting for someone to tell them what to do.

They were rescued by Hannah Jefferies, wife of the mission doctor. Hannah was a missionary of the China Inland Mission who had spent many years in the country before meeting and marrying her husband. Smiling reassuringly at the blue dress girls, she spoke in their own language. "You girls will come with me. I'll take you somewhere a little quieter than this and find you something to eat."

As the blue dress girls filed from the pinnace, more than one well-known Hong Kong trader stepped back into the anonymity of the crowd, nervous of being recognised by these new and unexpected arrivals in the colony.

When the crowd had been left behind and only a few curious children were still following them, one of the girls asked Hannah, "Where are you taking us?"

"To the mission."

The gasps of dismay and fearful exchanged glances did not escape the missionary. She smiled. Missionaries in China were fully aware of the wild rumours that circulated about their activities.

"Don't worry. If you're ever fortunate enough to find God you'll realise He *gives* to you, not takes. You need remain at the mission no longer than you wish. No one's going to force you to stay against your will and you'll be given every assistance to continue your journey to wherever you wish to go."

Her words brought some reassurance to the blue dress girls. Most were from simple backgrounds, brought up in villages where superstition loomed large in community life. Hannah Jefferies open manner coupled with her impressive command of their language had reassured them.

★ ★ ★

His assigned task successfully concluded, Kernow told the coxswain of the pinnace to secure the boat and take his crew to the new naval depot, recently established nearby on the waterfront. The four Royal Marines would go with them. After spending the night ashore they would all return upriver to the *Sans Pareil* the following day.

Leaving the coxswain to carry out his orders, Kernow set off for the naval headquarters building. It was his duty to make a report on his skirmish with the river pirates. He also had some despatches to deliver, entrusted to him by the captain of the *Sans Pareil*.

A Lieutenant Baker was duty officer at the Royal Navy headquarters building. Baker was one of a very small band of naval officers to be granted a commission after serving for many years as a rating on the lower decks of Her Majesty's men-o'-war. Old enough to be Kernow's grandfather, Baker recognised the elation felt by a young man who has carried out a successful action as commanding officer of a ship's boat.

When Kernow had given his verbal report, Baker said, "You've had a very exciting couple of days, Mister Keats."

Kernow grinned at the older man. "It's what I joined the Royal Marines for, sir."

"Quite. All the same, you handled the situation with the pirate junk very well. Very well indeed. You stay here for a while, lad. I'm going to have a word about you with the flag-lieutenant."

The flag-lieutenant was the admiral's *aide-de-camp*, and for Kernow to be brought to his attention was tantamount to a commendation. When he tried to thank the elderly officer,

Kernow was told to take a seat and await the duty officer's return.

Kernow could not sit still after the excitement of the day. When the duty officer had gone, he stood up and paced about the room, until he was attracted to the window by the sounds from outside.

The headquarters overlooked the busy harbour foreshore. As sampans and lighters plied to and from the ships anchored in the harbour, long lines of coolies trotted between beached boats and a newly built warehouse. Each was burdened beneath an incredible load. It would have brought strong protests from the well-meaning European ladies of Hong Kong had the loads been carried upon the backs of donkeys.

Engrossed in the scene outside, Kernow did not hear the duty officer return to the office. When he spoke, Kernow started in surprise.

"This is your day for glory, Mister Keats. The admiral himself was in the office when I spoke to the flag-lieutenant about you. He was very impressed when I described your brush with the river pirates. He wants to meet you."

"The admiral wants to meet me?" Kernow repeated, uncertainly.

"That's what I said — and you'd best be quick about it. Sir Michael Seymour is a very busy man, these days."

The offices in the headquarters building opened off an open corridor that was more in the nature of a balcony, fashioned to take advantage of any welcome breeze blowing in off the hill-enclosed harbour.

Straightening his tunic and white webbing belt hastily, Kernow walked along the corridor in the wake of the duty officer. He was far more nervous about meeting Admiral Sir Michael Seymour, the naval commander-in-chief, than he had been of doing battle with the Chinese river pirates.

But this was to be no formal interview. Admiral Seymour was seated on the edge of his flag-lieutenant's huge wooden desk, sipping from a glass of cold, China tea.

Bringing his feet together noisily in a stiff posture of attention, Kernow snapped off a smart salute. It would have met with the full approval of the drill instructor on board H.M.S. *Excellent*, the Royal Marines' training ship at Portsmouth.

"At ease, Mister Keats. Lieutenant Baker tells me you had an encounter with Chinese pirates today. Left them badly mauled, I believe. Tell me about it."

Kernow related the details of the pinnace's skirmish with the pirate junk, once again calling attention to the skilful part played by the coxswain-gunner from the *Sans Pareil*.

The admiral listened intently to Kernow's account. When it ended he rose to his feet and punched the fist of one hand into the palm of the other.

"Well done, Keats. Well done indeed! What wouldn't I give to be involved in an incident like that once again? It reminds me of when I was a young midshipman at Navarino . . . "

The flag-lieutenant and duty officer braced

themselves for one of the admiral's notoriously long and detailed stories, but he caught a glimpse of their exchange of glances and held himself in check.

"I'll see that a commendation is awarded to the coxswain through his commanding officer." Halting before the young Royal Marine, Sir Michael Seymour looked thoughtfully at Kernow. "But what am I going to do with you, Mister Keats? How old are you now, and how long is it since you left the training ship?"

"I'll be eighteen in a few months' time, sir — and I left H.M.S. *Excellent* close to two years ago."

"What of your family, Mister Keats? Where are they?"

"My mother is dead, sir. My father and two older sisters live in the family home, in Cornwall." After a slight hesitation, Kernow added, "My father was a captain of Royal Marines, sir. He left the corps when he lost a leg in the China wars in eighteen-forty-two."

"Ah! Then you have the service in your blood, Mister Keats. Your father will be proud of you when he learns of your actions today . . . and with just cause."

Admiral Sir Michael Seymour looked at Kernow speculatively. He saw an eager young Royal Marine officer, tall, smooth-shaven, with blue eyes and fair hair, characteristics that were accentuated by a tropical sun-tan. Kernow looked very fit.

The admiral thought this young man a fine example of the junior officers being recruited by both the Royal Navy and Royal Marines. They had boundless enthusiasm. Given experience they were all capable of becoming first-class admirals and generals, men able to shoulder the heavy responsibility of defending their country's ideals. To them would fall the task of extending the great empire conquered by their predecessors.

"Do you have any aptitude for learning foreign languages, Mister Keats?"

Kernow's quick blink hid his surprise at the unexpected question. It seemed totally unconnected with anything that had gone before. The two naval officers in the room seemed equally bemused.

"I speak good French, and passable Italian, sir. I've also picked up one or two Chinese phrases since I arrived on the station."

"Excellent!" The admiral cast a triumphant glance at the two naval lieutenants. "You're just the sort of young man I've been looking for. I'd like you to join my staff as a Chinese interpreter."

Kernow could not disguise his astonishment and dismay. "But . . . I don't understand sufficient Chinese to be an interpreter."

"You will. I was speaking to Hannah Jefferies the other day. She was telling me she intends commencing some pretty intensive Chinese classes for three or four new missionaries who've recently arrived in Hong Kong. She thought it a splendid idea when I suggested sending one of my staff along to join them. I've thought for a long time now that I need an Englishman as an interpreter. Trouble with these damned Chinese is one can never be sure which side they're on. Not to mention the money they make by 'forgetting' to tell me many of the things I ought to know when I'm involved in negotiations with Chinese officials. I've been looking out for a bright young man to fill the post. I think you fit the bill."

"But what about the *Sans Pareil*, and the pinnace . . . my kit?"

It was a series of foolish questions, as Kernow realised the moment he had uttered them. His kit would be safe on the *Sans Pareil* until the man-o'-war returned to Hong Kong harbour, and the loss of a young second lieutenant of Marines would hardly bring the ship's routine to a halt.

The admiral dismissed the questions with a brief wave of his hand. "The coxswain of your pinnace sounds as though he's quite capable of taking the boat back upriver to the *Sans Pareil*. He'll carry a letter from my flag-lieutenant informing the captain of your appointment to my staff. Arrangements will be made to send your kit to you. Does that meet with your approval, Mister Keats?"

Determined to raise no more foolish objections, Kernow nodded his head. "Of course, sir. Thank you."

"Good, then it's settled. My flag-lieutenant will allocate quarters to you. By the way, when did you say you'll be eighteen?"

"The fourteenth of August, sir."

"You will be promoted to substantive

76

lieutenant on that day, Mister Keats, as a reward for your actions today. It should give a useful boost to your career, but I will expect you to work hard for me in return. Good day to you, Mister Keats."

8

KERNOW'S first day at the mission school was a difficult one. Not a deeply religious young man, he felt uncomfortable during fervently spoken prayers which preceded morning and afternoon lessons, and which enclosed the midday meal like a thick-bread sandwich.

The mission school was in the same building as the hospital and situated with a view of the foreshore of the growing town of Victoria. Through the open windows Kernow could hear the clamour of the waterfront as he worked. As he began struggling with the complexities of the Chinese language he would have given a great deal to be out there, surrounded by familiar sounds and smells, and people who lived their lives motivated by mere earthly ambitions.

Kernow's language-course companions did little to ease his sense of isolation. There were four of them. Most prominent was Esme Pilkington. A large, loud-voiced, energetic woman in her mid-forties, her accent told the world she came from a 'good' family background. Her 'Allelujahs' during the prayers drowned the responses of her companions and she attacked her language studies with the same whole-hearted enthusiasm she applied to everything else.

Two of the remaining three students were

equally dedicated, although they were content to be dominated by the ebullient personality of Miss Pilkington.

Nancy Calvin, her husband Ronald and son Arthur were from the city of Birmingham, in the industrial Midlands of England. Husband and wife were quietly devout Christians who relied upon faith to solve every one of life's problems for them. They had hitherto done very little on their own initiative. However, such was their joy at being committed Christians, they wished the whole world to share their experience. They never doubted for one moment that the Chinese nation would be as delighted as themselves to learn about Jesus Christ and would rejoice with them in love of Him.

Kernow believed their eventual disillusionment would prove painful beyond belief. His unspoken opinion was that the Mission Society was irresponsible in sending such people to China. Unimpeachable in their love of God and total belief in His greatness, they were woefully lacking in worldliness.

Arthur Calvin, a nervous young man of twenty-four, did not share the unshakeable faith of his parents. In fact, he seemed to believe in nothing at all with any degree of conviction. This lack of faith extended to his own person. His manner was one of permanent apology.

By the time the day was ended, Kernow was entertaining doubts about his own ability to survive the language course.

Lessons ended at four o'clock in the afternoon,

as the day had begun, with a prayer. Afterwards, each pupil left the mission classroom clutching a book in which would be recorded their progress in the weeks and months ahead. Within its covers were a number of words for them to memorise in preparation for the following day's lessons. As the words were concerned solely with prayer and faith, Kernow could not foresee their application to war and the needs of the armed services. But he had been given his orders by the admiral — and this was only his first day. He would not allow his doubts to show so quickly.

Kernow did not know the others well enough to want to remain in their company after lessons were over. They had insufficient knowledge of the Chinese language as yet for it to be common ground between them. He left the classroom alone. As he walked along the corridor that linked school and hospital with the main entrance, he saw Doctor Jefferies talking to a Chinese medical orderly.

The sight of the tall, hook-nosed doctor reminded Kernow of the errand that had brought him to Hong Kong. When the doctor inclined his head in acknowledgement, Kernow paused to speak.

"Good afternoon, Doctor Jefferies. How is the wounded Chinese girl?"

"Young She-she? Much better now I've removed a sliver of wood from her body. It was pressing against a kidney and causing her great pain. How your ship's surgeon came to overlook it I don't know."

Kernow grimaced. "Surgeon Fox's reputation

rests heavily on the speed with which he can amputate a shattered limb at the height of a battle. I've heard no one mention any other skills."

Doctor Jefferies snorted derisively. "Such so-called 'skills' can be learned at the butcher's block. I have long questioned the capabilities of surgeons employed by the army and navy, especially those who serve in Her Majesty's men-o'-war. Unfortunately, their shortcomings pass unnoticed in the heat of battle and the fog of gunsmoke."

Aware he had stumbled upon a subject about which the mission doctor felt very strongly, Kernow attempted to change the conversation quickly. "Will you be releasing the Chinese girl soon?"

"Not just yet. We've a way to go before she's quite ready to face the world again." Hugh Jefferies scrutinised Kernow's face before adding, "She-she is a very pretty young thing. Come along with me and see her progress for yourself."

"I'm not at all sure I'll aid her recovery. She seems to find me frightening."

Doctor Jefferies smiled. "It's nothing personal, I can assure you. The Chinese race lacks the variety of eye and hair colouring that we Europeans take for granted. Consequently it takes some of them a while to become used to blue eyes and fair hair, especially those brought up in the more remote villages, but it comes with time."

As he spoke, the mission doctor was leading

Kernow along the corridor to the hospital wing of the mission building.

She-she and Kau-lin were in a two-bedded room at the rear of the hospital. Much to Kernow's delight, She-she was propped up in bed, looking far healthier than she had during the voyage to Hong Kong. Kau-lin was seated on the edge of her friend's bed. Between the two girls was a board drilled with a number of shallow holes, each containing a coloured bead. It appeared to Kernow to be a type of complicated game.

Doctor Jefferies greeted the two girls in their own language and was rewarded with smiles from each of them.

Kernow had only that day learned the Chinese phrase for 'Good day', but his use of the words drew blank stares from both girls.

"I'm afraid you are speaking the Chinese of the Mandarins," explained the doctor. "These are simple Hakkas who are more used to speaking in Cantonese. They *do* understand the Chinese of their superiors, but I'm afraid you have not quite mastered the necessary tonal differences needed to make it recognisable to them."

"I can see that learning Chinese is going to be a great deal more difficult than I anticipated," said Kernow, sheepishly.

She-she said something to the mission doctor and when he nodded his head she shyly looked in Kernow's direction and said haltingly in English, "Good day, Lieutenant Keats."

Kernow's expression of astonishment caused

both girls to clap their hands in delight and for a moment the faintest of smiles softened the stern lines of Doctor Jefferies' face.

"It seems my wife has been busy here too, Mister Keats — and apparently with greater effect than in the mission classroom. You are honoured. She-she must have asked especially for your name in order that she might greet you in the correct fashion."

Sensing just the faintest hint of disapproval in the mission doctor's manner, Kernow made no attempt to pursue a near-impossible conversation with She-she, much as he enjoyed simply looking at her. Instead, he addressed the doctor.

"I'm very happy to see She-she looking so well. There was a time on the voyage when I wasn't at all sure she was going to survive."

"Had she remained on the *Sans Pareil* I believe she would be dead now," said Doctor Jefferies, bluntly. "But we won't pursue that line of thought. I'll tell She-she you're delighted to see her recovering so well."

As the mission doctor passed on a message that was a great deal longer than the few words he had suggested, She-she's gaze remained fixed on Kernow's face. There was still uncertainty in her expression, but she seemed to have conquered her fear of him and a childlike curiosity occasionally came to the fore to bring life to her dark brown eyes.

When she replied to the doctor, Kernow noticed how soft and gentle her voice was. When she ended, a trace of a smile lingered around her mouth.

"She-she is grateful to you for your concern, Mister Keats. She also wishes me to thank you for bringing her safely to Hong Kong and says she is no longer frightened of you."

The doctor fingered his short grey beard, "What she actually said is that she no longer looks upon you as being a frightening hairy foreign devil. Regrettably, this is the way the Chinese see us. It makes it extremely difficult to spread the word of God when you're looked upon as belonging to the other side."

"So that's why she seemed so terrified every time I came close to her!" Kernow hesitated. "Will you ask her if there's anything she needs?"

The missionary doctor's disapproving expression returned again and Kernow hastened to give him an explanation, "I led the boarding party that took the junk on which she was travelling to Foochow. That was when she received her wound. I feel in some way responsible for her . . . for all the girls."

The explanation seemed to satisfy Doctor Jefferies and he turned to She-she once more. This time he spoke to her only briefly.

She-she's reply was even briefer and quite unmistakable. It made Kernow wonder how the doctor had phrased the offer.

There was no time to ask for an explanation. The doctor said he had other patients to see. Kernow hardly had time to smile a farewell to the girls before he was ushered from the room.

Outside, in the corridor, Kernow asked, "Where are the other girls?"

"Occupying a hospital ward I built to house

the casualties we expected the last time we almost had a war with the Chinese. The girls can be kept apart from the other patients while they are in there. Unfortunately, I believe it to be a necessary precaution. I am given to understand that the morals of the Canton *Hoppo*'s blue dress girls are more than a little suspect. It's rumoured among my porters that they were kept by the *Hoppo* especially to entertain those merchants from whom he extorted large customs dues. No doubt such ministrations made their payments somewhat less painful."

"You mean all those girls — Kau-lin and She-she too, are . . . prostitutes?"

"I wouldn't go as far as to say *that*, Mister Keats, but many Chinese customs leave a great deal to be desired. There can be no doubt many of the girls have an over-familiar manner when speaking to men. Europeans in particular."

"If this is so, how do you explain She-she's great fear of European men?" Kernow found himself inexplicably indignant at the doctor's suggestion.

"I offer no explanations, Mister Keats. I was merely passing on the rumours circulating among my porters, together with the evidence of my own observations. I admit that She-she does not behave as do the others — but there is a most disturbing boldness in the manner of her friend."

The thought of Kau-lin made Kernow smile. There was as much cheekiness as boldness in her manner. But his thoughts quickly returned to the quieter She-she and the way she had cringed from him on occasions during the voyage. There was no familiarity with *Fan Qui* men in her attitude. He resolutely refused to accept the rumours repeated by Doctor Jefferies. Neither did he attempt to analyse the reason why he felt so inclined to leap to her defence.

9

DURING the course of that summer Kernow needed to work very hard to keep up with his fellow students. The missionaries had a burning hunger inside them to learn Chinese. It was a hunger fuelled by an eagerness to go forth and spread the word of their God to the unenlightened millions who were starved of Christianity in the vastness of the land that was China.

Esme Pilkington quickly forged ahead in her mastery of the Chinese language — and of her fellow missionaries. Her loud and booming voice was quite capable of cowing any mere mortal. Fearing neither man nor woman, she gave her love solely and completely to the God she had come to China to serve. It was difficult to hold a debate with the highly opinionated Esme. The world in which she lived was either white or it was black, Christian or heathen. There were no shades of grey. In spite of such bigotry, Kernow found himself respecting the bluff missionary, and she seemed to like him.

The Calvin family were very different. Husband and wife were undoubtedly dedicated Christians, but only Nancy Calvin possessed any real zeal for missionary work. A small, busy woman, she wore thick-lensed spectacles and her expression carried a permanent air of disapproval for the world about her.

Ronald Calvin, her husband, was also small, and decidedly weedy. Kernow gained the impression he was a reluctant missionary. It was generally accepted by all who met them that the path for the whole family had been decided for them by Nancy, and neither father nor son had ever been heard to disagree with anything she decided.

Nevertheless, Nancy Calvin's own commitment could not prevent her son from falling behind in his studies. He apologised constantly for his many mistakes and lack of learning ability, but it was evident to everyone at the mission that he lacked the will of his fellow students to learn the new and difficult language.

Six years older than Kernow, Arthur Calvin had unfortunately inherited his mother's poor eyesight and his father's hesitant manner. Yet neither parent had been able to pass on their own strong religious beliefs.

Possibly as a result of his own inadequacies, or merely because they were more of an age, Arthur Calvin sought out Kernow's company in the mission classroom. Whenever possible he would join Kernow outside too, asking if he might accompany him on a walk about the bustling town streets, or along the foreshore to look at the ships in the harbour.

One day, when the book was closed on the day's lessons, and prayers had been said, Ronald and Nancy Calvin hurried away to collect the mail which had arrived from England earlier that day. Nancy's youngest sister had been expecting her first child when the family left for China.

The missionary hoped the mail might bring her news of the event.

The others were in less of a hurry to leave and Kernow was adding some notes to his book when Hannah Jefferies spoke to him. "The girls you brought to Hong Kong will be boarding a ship bound for Foochow in a few minutes. I thought you might wish to go to the government jetty and say farewell to them."

The news took Kernow by surprise. "Are She-she and Kau-lin leaving Hong Kong too?"

She-she had made a good recovery and Kernow frequently met her and Kau-lin about the mission, where they were busy learning English with one of the other missionaries. He had last seen both girls only two days before. Neither had intimated they would soon be leaving Hong Kong.

Hannah Jefferies raised an eyebrow at Kernow's evident concern. "She-she and Kau-lin will remain in the mission for the time being, at least. I have high hopes that both girls will one day become Christians."

"Can I come to the jetty with you?" The unexpected request came from Arthur Calvin. He felt the need to justify his presumptuousness and added, "We've been having Chinese lessons for months now, yet I've never stood among the Chinese and listened to them talking together. If I did it might help me understand the language a little better."

Hannah Jefferies was about to suggest Arthur should first seek the consent of Nancy Calvin. She checked herself in time. Arthur was not a child but a young man, some years older than the young Royal Marine lieutenant standing before her. If he were to be of any value to himself or the missionary movement it was time he showed some independent thought.

"I'm not at all certain that being among a crowd down at the jetty will help your understanding of the Chinese language, Arthur. There are so many dialects spoken in Hong Kong you'll end up totally confused. But I'll be there to point out what you should be listening for."

"I'll come along too." Esme Pilkington was not in the habit of waiting for an invitation to do something she wanted to. "Those girls are an interesting bunch. I've spoken to them in Chinese once or twice. I only wish I'd found more time to get to know them properly while they were here."

"Then we'll all go, Kau-lin and She-she too. It will be the farthest She-she has walked since she left the hospital, but there'll be plenty of us on hand to help her if the need arises."

* * *

Arthur Calvin had met none of the blue dress girls before. Their chatter as they all made their way to the government jetty left him more tongue-tied than ever. He tried to stay close to his fellow pupils but both Kernow and Esme Pilkington were walking with She-she and Kau-lin. Between them they managed to maintain a fairly successful conversation and Arthur too was

90

forced to reply to an occasional question.

It proved to be a noisy farewell. The crew of a man-o'-war anchored just off the jetty added their own ribald comments to the calls of the departing blue dress girls. Some of the remarks made by the sailors went far beyond what Hannah Jefferies deemed to be proper. Once the junk taking the blue dress girls on their voyage cast off from the jetty, she led the others away as quickly as possible.

On the way back to the mission, Kernow and Arthur, walking with She-she and Kau-lin, fell behind Hannah Jefferies and the voluble Esme Pilkington.

The two Chinese girls no longer wore the blue dresses that signified their place in the *Hoppo*'s household. Instead they were dressed in drab brown cotton tunic and trousers. Kernow found their new garb even more fetching than the bright silk dresses of their departing companions.

Looking over her shoulder, Hannah Jefferies frowned when she saw the four young people laughing together. She had learned a great deal about the life led by the blue dress girls in the *Hoppo*'s Canton home.

Hannah had few doubts about She-she. The girl had been in the *Hoppo*'s house for no more than a few days before being packed off to Foochow. She believed the Lord had seen fit to save her from a life of sin — although she had been called upon to pay a price for that salvation.

The missionary was less confident about Kau-lin's morals. The girl was bright and vivacious.

Most men, Chinese and European, found her attractive, a fact of which Kau-lin was fully aware. Yet Hannah Jefferies was convinced there was good in the girl. Great good. The devotion she had shown to her wounded friend throughout She-she's long recovery was quite exceptional.

Nevertheless, Hannah would have dropped back to join the others had she not noticed that Arthur Calvin was involved in animated conversation with Kau-lin. He was talking with an eagerness she had not seen him display since his arrival in Hong Kong. It could be that talking to the two girls would give him the incentive to learn the Chinese language that religion had so far failed to provide.

She would have preferred it to have been mission work that had provided the key but, in the words of the poet and hymn-writer William Cowper, 'God moves in a mysterious way, His wonders to perform.' Anything that motivated Arthur Calvin would ultimately serve the Lord's purpose. Hannah hoped his companions too might eventually provide her with a convert — possibly two.

She continued to walk in company with her fellow missionary, her comforting thoughts providing a buffer against the loud voice of Esme Pilkington.

Hannah might have felt less reassured had she been close enough to listen to the conversation between Kau-lin and Arthur.

Kau-lin had enough experience of men to recognise the painful shyness of Arthur Calvin.

She set about tackling the problem in her usual straightforward manner. Moving to his side whilst Kernow and She-she were talking together, she asked him, "You a missionary?"

"N . . . no . . . " Arthur stuttered in his eagerness to reply to this girl who had singled him out to make conversation. "I . . . my mother and father are." He needed to repeat the reply twice before Kau-lin comprehended his garbled words. But she still looked puzzled.

"You have no wife?"

"No."

Arthur kept his reply simple, desperate not to frighten her away by the difficulty of making conversation with him.

"Why no wife?"

At a loss about how to reply to such a blunt question, Arthur said lamely, "I've never found the right girl."

In truth, his mother had allowed him no opportunity to find a *wrong* girl — or any other girl.

"Some *Shang Ti* men . . . " Kau-lin used the Chinese word for 'God' " . . . never take wives. You all same them?"

Arthur shook his head vigorously. "No, they're Catholics. They're not the same."

"Not same? Not Christians?"

"Yes, they're Christians." The puzzled expression had returned to Kau-lin's face and Arthur wished fervently he had concentrated more on his Chinese lessons. "It's just . . . they don't worship the same as us."

"Have different God?"

93

"No."

Lacking the command of Kau-lin's language, Arthur did not know how to reply, yet he desperately wanted her to continue to talk to him. "We all have the same God . . . but ask Mrs Jefferies, she'll be able to explain it to you better than I can."

Still puzzled, Kau-lin nodded acceptance of his reply. "I ask." Unexpectedly, she added, "My brother a Christian."

Her statement startled Arthur. He had learned enough about missionary work to realise that a Christian Chinese was still a very rare phenomenon. This was despite all the work carried out in China by missionaries of a dozen denominations. "Does Mrs Jefferies know about your brother?"

"I tell her, but she say he a Taiping. Not same Christian. Perhaps he like Catholic."

"Did I hear you say your brother is a Taiping?"

Much to Arthur's disappointment, Kernow turned back to rejoin them.

"Yes, very important man. General."

Kernow's interest quickened immediately. Although he was on a language course with missionaries, he was still a Royal Marine officer. The Taiping rebels were of great interest to all military men.

Many years before, a Chinese named Hung Hsiu-ch'uan had suffered an illness during the course of which he had visions of rising to Heaven and being welcomed as part of the family of God. Later, enjoying a brief sojourn in Canton with the American Protestant missionary, Issachar Roberts, Hung received a limited instruction in Christianity.

Inspired by the writings of the New Testament, Hung became convinced that during his illness he had been carried up to Heaven. He also arrived at the conclusion that he was the younger brother of Jesus Christ and had been sent to earth to rid China of those who refused to accept God's will — especially the Manchus who ruled the country.

Among his own people — the Hakkas, to which tribe both Kau-lin and She-she belonged — he gained immediate and impressive support. Hung imposed the strictest discipline upon his followers including the segregation of men and women, even husbands and wives, yet his support grew to mammoth proportions. It seemed not to matter that the segregation rule did not apply to the Taiping leaders, each of whom acquired huge harems.

In 1851, with Hung now calling himself 'The Heavenly King', the Taipings rose in rebellion and swept all before them. Conquering almost half of China, the armies of 'The Heavenly King' advanced to the very gates of the Chinese capital, Peking, before being checked.

The momentum of the first all-conquering uprising had faltered in the six years that had passed since 1851, but the 'Heavenly King' and his followers still occupied a sizeable territory. It was centred upon the important valley of the Yangtze-kiang, China's greatest river. The walled city of Nanking, on the

Yangtze, had become the capital of Hung Hsiu-ch'uan's Heavenly Kingdom.

Many senior and junior officers of the British army and navy, exasperated by the procrastination and corruption of Imperial China, felt that the British government should have backed the Taiping rebellion, thereby ensuring its success.

A number of missionaries took the same view. Hung's version of Christian religion left much to be desired, but it was a beginning. It held far more promise than the implacable hostility of Imperial policy.

"Where is your brother now?"

"Nanking, with *T'ien Wang* — the Heavenly King."

"Do you hear from him sometimes?"

"No," Kau-lin admitted reluctantly. She liked the importance the young English officer attached to the fact that she had a brother who was a Taiping general. It was something she had learned to say nothing about while she was a blue dress girl in the Canton *Hoppo*'s household. "But my cousin here, in Hong Kong. He tell me about brother."

"You have a cousin here in Hong Kong? One who is in touch with the Taiping rebels?"

"Yes. He Christian too. Work with Reverend Legge."

"At the London Missionary Society?"

Kau-lin shrugged, "Only know with Reverend Legge."

Arthur's expression was becoming increasingly downcast. Kernow knew the reason. Arthur had been talking to Kau-lin when he had broken in on the conversation. Forming new relationships was not easy for the missionaries' son. Kernow had no wish to stand in his way.

"We must talk some more about your brother — and your cousin sometime," he said to Kau-lin. "I hope one day to meet up with the Taiping. Quite apart from their religion, they've earned a reputation as excellent fighting men."

"Not only Taiping men who fight," corrected Kau-lin. "The *T'ien Wang* says women are all same men, good fighters too. He has women's army. Fight beside men."

"I'm even more impressed! A man who can form and control an army of men *and* women must be very special indeed. We'll talk about this some more, Kau-lin."

10

A FEW days after the other blue dress girls set sail for Foochow, Hannah Jefferies arrived for the morning lessons accompanied by She-she and Kau-lin.

"I think most of you have already met," the missionary addressed her small class. "You will be pleased to know the girls are joining us for future lessons. Their English has improved so much I thought we would all benefit by their presence. You have all done exceptionally well with your Chinese studies, but now we need to study the Cantonese dialect in more detail. I am hoping the girls will be able to help me out, and at the same time further their own knowledge of English."

Kernow was as delighted as Arthur Calvin at the thought of having the two Chinese girls join their class. Witnessing the smile with which Kau-lin greeted Arthur, Nancy Calvin did not share the general enthusiasm. However, amidst the loud and exuberant welcome given to the girls by Esme Pilkington, only Ronald Calvin recognised the narrowing of his wife's lips as a measure of her disapproval.

It quickly became apparent that both She-she and Kau-lin were bright girls and they were quick to learn. Far from slowing down the lessons, they put everyone on their mettle. Arthur, in particular, tried valiantly to make up for his lethargy in earlier weeks. Unfortunately, he had dropped so far behind the others his efforts were largely in vain.

Lessons ended early that afternoon. There was to be a memorial service in Hong Kong Cathedral for the wife of a missionary who had died on board ship during the voyage between Shanghai and Hong Kong the previous week. Nancy and Ronald Calvin had met the woman two years before, when she was on leave in England. They particularly wanted to attend the service, but Arthur declined to go with them.

"I don't feel particularly well. I'd like to carry on with my Chinese studies quietly," he said to his mother when she tried to insist that he accompany her and his father to the service. "I'm only just beginning to realise how far I've fallen behind everyone else. I'd like to try to catch up."

"I help you," said Kau-lin, who had been unashamedly listening in to the conversation. "Me and She-she. We good teachers, you see."

Before Nancy Calvin could voice her objections, Esme Pilkington's voice boomed out, "What a splendid idea! I'll join you. I was not acquainted with Sister Margaret. I am quite sure I can best serve her memory, and the cause of the Lord, by using the time to speed the day when I am carrying on her good work."

"I might as well continue working too. I can't have word getting back to my admiral that I took time off when others were studying."

Kernow realised how disappointed Arthur was that he was not going to have the Chinese girls — Kau-lin in particular — to himself, but with Esme in the classroom he would probably welcome the support of another man.

"Very well." Hannah Jefferies spoke to Esme. "When you've had enough of studying perhaps you'll see that She-she and Kau-lin get back to the house safely."

"Our house? You mean the mission house?" The sharp question came from Nancy Calvin.

The mission house was the home of the Jefferies, but the Calvins and Esme Pilkington were also living in it. They would remain there until they were sufficiently fluent in the Chinese language to be allocated mission stations of their own.

"That's right. I've given She-she and Kau-lin the room we had fitted out for any convalescent brothers or sisters who might pass through Hong Kong. It will be much more convenient than having them remain in the mission hospital now that She-she is almost fully recovered. But come along, if we don't hurry we'll be late. We don't want to incur the wrath of the bishop."

When the others had gone it was not Esme Pilkington who took charge of the remaining class-members, but Kau-lin. Indicating Esme and Kernow with a wave of her hand, she said, "She-she teach you. Arthur need good teacher. I take care him."

Arthur's face turned a bright pink at Kau-lin's words but the embarrassment hid his secret pleasure as she took his arm and led him to a corner of the room, away from the others. Arthur was immediately set to work reciting the

Chinese vocabulary he had written in his book, and Kau-lin firmly corrected the many mistakes he made in pronunciation.

She-she's methods were less direct, but nonetheless effective. She allowed Esme and Kernow to go over the lessons taught by Hannah Jefferies, and answered questions as they were raised.

The weather had become very hot and humid and it was particularly oppressive that afternoon. After no more than an hour's work, Esme announced that she needed to go outside for a drink of water and some air.

After her departure, Kernow and She-she worked steadily on. Whenever Kernow glanced across the room he saw Arthur and Kau-lin sitting with their heads close together, looking at pictures in one of the books that belonged to the mission, with Arthur trying to describe, in Chinese, what he saw.

"Those two get on very well. Kau-lin's good for Arthur. I don't think he's known many girls."

"You not all same man as Arthur. You know many girls?"

"Not many. I've spent too much time on board a ship, or learning to fight."

She-she shook her head. "Fighting not good, but you Hong Kong long time now. Must know Chinese girls?"

"You and Kau-lin are the only ones."

She-she scrutinised Kernow's face as though trying to ascertain whether he was telling the truth. When she was satisfied, she said, "You

101

think Chinese girls as pretty as *Fan Qui* girls?"

"I think *you* are much prettier . . . " Kernow hesitated. He wanted to say more, but he paused as he remembered what Hannah Jefferies had said about the blue dress girls. "How about you, She-she? Have you met many men — European men?"

Something in his voice made She-she look up at him quickly. She wondered how much he knew of her place in Li Hung's household. She would rather he knew nothing at all. It had been a time of shame.

When she replied it was in an even quieter voice than usual. "Sometimes they would come to the house of Li Hung and I would see them."

The memory of Trader Courtice returned suddenly to haunt her and she shuddered suddenly.

"Are you all right, She-she?" There was concern for her in Kernow's voice.

She nodded, trying hard to blot out the mental picture of a large, hairy *Fan Qui* lying spreadeagled on the floor of her room, his carp-like eyes staring up . . .

"You first *Fan Qui* I see without hair hiding face."

"What did you do in the *Hoppo*'s house?"

"What you mean, what I do?" She-she's voice rose sharply. She knew very well what Kernow meant, but she did not know how to reply to his question. If he learned the truth he might lose all respect for her. She suddenly realised how unhappy this would make her.

102

Kau-lin had taken an interest when she heard the line of Kernow's questioning. Now she came to the aid of her friend. "No good you ask She-she what girls do in house of *Hoppo*. She only just come from her home when we have to leave. No time anyone tell her what do. You want know? I tell. *Hoppo* very important man. Many *Fan Qui* come his house pay him plenty money. When they come we serve them tea, sing songs, sometimes. One girl, gone Foochow now, sing very well."

The glib explanation rolled off Kau-lin's tongue easily. Much of it was true. The girls *would* sometimes sing and one of the girls actually played a musical instrument.

"Wasn't there some scandal involving one of the traders? I seem to remember one of them died in the *Hoppo*'s house . . . "

"Not in house. Found dead outside. He too fat. Drink too much rice wine." Glancing quickly at She-she, Kau-lin saw she had paled alarmingly. "You take us home now. Too hot here. Where you live? You have house near to mission house?"

Kau-lin was still chattering when they walked outside the classroom and met Esme returning. Kernow had thought the missionary would be disappointed not to be working for most of the evening, but Esme seemed relieved. She was a large, overweight woman and was finding the intense heat of a Hong Kong summer well-nigh unbearable.

At the mission house, Kernow declined an offer to go inside and have a drink before returning to the wardroom of the naval barracks, where he had his quarters. Although he was on a language course during the day he was required to fulfil various duties inside the barracks during the evening. He did not want to have to make excuses for returning later than expected. It was his birthday in a few weeks' time. He was due to be promoted to full lieutenant's rank on that day and wanted nothing to interfere with the promotion.

She-she knew nothing of this. She thought he had refused to come inside the mission house because she had said something to upset him. She suspected he might have known a great deal more than he had admitted about the duties of a blue dress girl in the household of Li Hung.

She would have walked inside with her unhappy thoughts had not Kernow reached out and grasped her arm, bringing her to a halt.

"Are you all right, She-she?"

"I all right. Why you ask?"

"I thought I might have upset you by talking about the *Hoppo*, and Canton. Made you homesick, or perhaps set you wishing you'd gone to Foochow with the other girls."

"Other girls no matter to me. Kau-lin my friend. She matters."

When Kernow released the grip on her arm, she walked up the pathway to the house. Before reaching the door, she paused and turned around.

"You maybe wish I go Foochow with other blue dress girls?"

"No, She-she, I'm glad you stayed behind. In fact, I would have been very unhappy had you gone with the others."

She-she's gloom dropped away immediately and she was her usual happy self when she entered the mission house.

In her room, Esme Pilkington pulled back the curtain to allow any breeze to enter through the window, should one unexpectedly spring up. She witnessed the brief exchange between She-she and Kernow. Although she could not hear the conversation, she knew that whatever Kernow had said made the Chinese girl suddenly very happy.

Esme Pilkington's large build, loud voice and positive manner had always frightened off potential suitors. For the same reasons she had never made any close friends. Consequently, no one was aware that at heart she was a romantic.

She watched as Kernow hesitated outside the house until She-she passed from his view. Esme smiled sadly. They would have made a wonderful young couple had they met in another place, under different circumstances.

As it was, Kernow Keats was a young Royal Marine. An officer. He was bound by a great many service regulations — and very many more social conventions. There could be no permanent place in his life for a Chinese girl. Especially one who was reputed to have been used by the *Hoppo* of Canton to satisfy the lusts of European merchants.

Fanning herself as she moved away from the

window to go downstairs and join the others, Esme Pilkington hoped Kernow would let Sheshe down with as much gentleness as possible. Commonsense told her she could pray for no more.

11

NANCY and Ronald Calvin were late returning to the mission house that evening. When the memorial service ended there had been an unexpected invitation to a reception at the home of the Bishop of Victoria. The Calvins might have stayed even later had not Nancy been concerned for Arthur's well-being.

When husband and wife walked in to the lounge of the mission house it appeared to Nancy at first glance that her concern had been well founded — although it was no longer associated with his health. Arthur and Kau-lin were alone in the room. Their heads close together, they were both giggling as though sharing some secret.

Had Nancy cared to ask for an explanation, she would have learned there was an innocent reason for their merriment. Busily engaged in his Chinese studies, Arthur had pronounced a Chinese verb in a manner which gave it a new and decidedly vulgar meaning. Esme and She-she had been with them until only minutes before when Esme retired to her room suffering from heat exhaustion. She-she had gone with her because she was concerned for the missionary.

Nancy Calvin was in no mood to seek reasonable explanations. The room in which the reception had been held was hot and humid.

107

Her clothes had become glued to her body by perspiration and her head felt as though it were encased in an over-worked kettle-drum. She erupted in an outburst of totally unreasonable anger.

"What do you think you're doing? You told me you didn't feel well enough to come to the memorial service and I've been worrying myself sick about you for hours. I've hurried back here and what do I find? You as fit as a fiddle and alone in the house with this . . . this Chinese hussy!"

"Kau-lin is not a hussy. We've been working hard on my Chinese language and we're not alone. She-she has just gone upstairs to help Esme to her room. She's feeling the heat."

In a desperate bid to cool his mother's anger, Arthur continued, "We have some tea here, would you like some?"

"No, I would not — and you'll need to do better than suggesting that other Chinese girl is a suitable chaperone. They're both as bad as each other. You go up to your room, this instant."

Arthur looked at his mother with an expression of hot-eyed humiliation on his face. "If you don't like seeing me talking to my friends and sharing a joke — an *innocent* joke — then *you* go to your room and you won't have to watch me."

Nancy's jaw dropped in astonishment momentarily, then she erupted in anger. "How *dare* you speak to me in such a manner? I've been married to your father for almost thirty years and he's never spoken to me like that. I'll certainly not

108

accept it from you . . . "

"What's going on in here? I'm in my room nursing a dreadful headache and suddenly there's bedlam down here. What on earth do you think you're up to?"

Esme Pilkington, her heavily built body hidden inside a voluminous flannel nightdress and with a scalloped nightcap hiding her hair, boomed a broadside at the angry Nancy Calvin as she sailed majestically into the lounge.

Taking advantage of the diversion, Kau-lin retired from the room, taking with her She-she who had entered the room behind the missionary.

In the lounge, the argument between mother and son raged on with Esme attempting loud-voiced mediation and Ronald Calvin maintaining a silent neutrality.

The argument continued until Doctor Jefferies returned to his house and intervened. Before the medical missionary had fully grasped the cause of the noisy altercation, Arthur turned on his heel and made his way to his room, ignoring his mother's demand that he return and explain his actions.

★ ★ ★

The next morning Hannah Jefferies did her sensible best to placate the still ruffled Nancy Calvin. She explained that the hot and humid summers in this part of the world invariably affected the tempers of newcomers. July and August had become known among the colonists as the 'suicide months'. She added they might with equal justification be referred to as the 'murder' months. It was a time of year when tempers were strained to breaking point. Once this was understood, said Hannah, it was easier to control irrational outbursts such as that which had disturbed the tranquillity of the mission house the previous evening.

Nancy heard Hannah out with polite reservation. Suicide months or murder months made no difference to her. She had never before had such an argument with her son. It was the fault of that brazen girl from the household of the Canton *Hoppo*. She should never have been allowed to take up residence in the Mission house. Nancy Calvin had come to China to save souls, not to barter them for her son's moral well-being.

It was Hannah's intention to explain away the argument to Arthur in the same manner as she had to his mother, but the youngest Calvin did not put in an appearance for breakfast. Instead, he dressed in his room and went straight from there to the mission school, speaking to no one.

That day the Europeans had the classroom to themselves. Hannah had tactfully suggested to She-she and Kau-lin that they remain at the mission house that day and give Nancy Calvin's temper time to cool.

Kernow was aware of the tension within the Calvin family, but when he asked Esme what had happened, she said only, "It's the heat, dear boy. It's getting to all of us, but it affects some more than others."

110

Arthur looked very pale and was perspiring heavily. The heat was worse than ever. No one was surprised when, halfway through the morning, he said to Hannah Jefferies, "I don't feel terribly well. I think I'll go back to the house and lie down for a while."

"Of course. Stay in the shade and try to drink as much as you can. It's very important."

"I'll come with you." Nancy stood up.

"No, you won't. I'm quite capable of getting back to the house and putting myself to bed, thank you."

With this curt refusal, Arthur turned his back on his mother and left the classroom. After a moment's indecision, a tight-mouthed Nancy sat down again and resumed her lessons. The Chinese girls were at the house and she believed she knew why Arthur had gone back there, but she could say nothing without causing a scene in the classroom.

When lunch time came, Nancy declared that she and her husband were returning to the mission house to check on the well-being of their son.

"I might as well come with you," said Kernow. "It's far too hot to eat anything."

Little was said by the members of the small party as it made its way to the house, but Kernow did not mind. There was so much of interest all about them. They passed by houses where children and women sat on the doorsteps, each scooping a mixture of fish and rice at great speed from a bowl held up to his or her chin. The smell of cooking drifted through open doorways behind the Chinese, frequently accompanied by the sound of high-pitched and fast-talking voices.

Once, as they passed along a narrow alleyway, they were forced to flatten themselves against a wall as a grinning coolie trotted by with a sagging bamboo pole over one shoulder. At either end of the pole was suspended a huge cage, stuffed to near-suffocation with a variety of complaining chickens.

Nancy wrinkled her nose at the smells, screwed up her eyes in apparent pain at the noise and made room for the chicken-bearing coolie with a bad grace.

Watching her, Kernow wondered how much thought she had put into the decision for the family to take up missionary work. He did not doubt she had faith enough for the task. He was equally convinced she lacked the patience needed to work among the Chinese. There was also an absence of a genuine and essential affection for them. It was something she would need to acquire if she were to succeed in her task.

His awareness of Nancy Calvin's shortcomings led Kernow to analyse his own feelings for the Chinese. He accepted that their fatalistic approach to life, coupled with a penchant for prevarication, made dealing with them frustrating. They also tended to say what they thought the European to whom they were talking wanted to hear. Either that or they would agree with whatever he was saying, finding it easier than expressing the truth.

In spite of such minor irritating traits, Kernow had developed a genuine liking for them as a people. He was content to spend time on the foreshore, surrounded by noisy hard-working coolies. Walking through the street markets at night, surrounded by the sounds and smells of a hundred eating shops, he felt at ease. Safe even. Then there was She-she . . .

It was easy to feel affectionate towards any girl as dainty and attractive as She-she. Yet even taking this into account he knew there was something special about his feelings for her. Something that went far deeper than casual affection for a pretty girl.

He was unable to share his thoughts with any of the other officers who resided in the naval barracks wardroom where he was quartered. The official attitude among service officers was that the Chinese were 'natives'. As such they were tolerated, perhaps smiled upon occasionally, but one did not express affection for a native girl. Had Kernow intimated that he was attracted to a Chinese girl he would have been transferred immediately. Sent to a man-o'-war heading for some far-distant port with all chances of promotion gone.

The trio had been walking in silence for some time when Nancy suddenly said, to nobody in particular, "I do hope Arthur is in his room in the shade, and not lying out in the sun roasting his body. Unless I'm there to tell him, he seems to think there is something to be gained by burning his skin to the colour of an Indian."

"You must allow Arthur some independence,

Mrs Calvin. He's sensible enough to think things out for himself."

"You *would* say that, Mister Keats, but I need no advice on how to bring up my own son from someone not yet of age. Your mother may have allowed you to join the army — or marines, whatever it is — at an age when you should still have been at school. That doesn't mean it's all right for everyone. Certainly not for Arthur."

"My mother died when I was quite small. I've never known what it is to have someone care for me in such a way. Perhaps that's why I'm particularly concerned to see a rift growing between yourself and Arthur."

Somewhat mollified, Nancy said, "I'm sorry to learn about your mother, young man, and I have no doubt you mean well, but I know Arthur better than anyone else does. I know what he needs."

Despite her apparent assurance, Nancy thought about what Kernow had said to her. Perhaps this young man was right and Arthur had finally found the maturity he had been lacking for so long. If so, she wondered how much of it was due to Kernow. If Arthur was finally achieving manhood she would need to treat him with a little less parental authority and begin taking his views into account. Perhaps a conciliatory approach *was* the answer.

Her good intentions vanished in an uncontrollable explosion of anger the moment she stepped inside the mission house garden. Arthur was not tucked up in his bed. Neither was he relaxing in the sun on the balcony outside his room. Her son lay back in a cushioned cane chair in the garden, enjoying the shade of a large, flowering tree. Kneeling on the ground beside him, Kau-lin mopped his brow with a damp cloth.

Had she been a more worldly woman, Nancy Calvin would have recognised the emotion she felt at seeing Kau-lin tending Arthur in such a way. It was sheer unadulterated jealousy. But she did not pause to analyse anything.

Hurrying across the grass she reached Kau-lin and Arthur before either realised they were no longer alone. Snatching the cloth from Kau-lin's hand, Nancy threw it from her and vented her anger upon her son. "So this is why you pretended to be ill, is it? Scheming away from your studies in order to be with this . . . this *hussy*!"

As Kau-lin beat a strategic retreat, Arthur protested, "That isn't true, Mother. Kau-lin saw me return from the school and said I looked ill. She suggested I come out here in the garden, in the shade. Kau-lin and She-she have both been very kind to me."

"I don't doubt it!" Nancy Calvin was deeply angry. "From what I hear these two girls have far more experience at being kind to men than any nice girl should have."

Arthur felt unwell and it would not help to lose his own temper. He tried again. "She-she and Kau-lin have taken turns to keep me cool with a fan. Now She-she's gone to make a cup of tea. They've made me feel far better than I did when I left the mission school."

115

"I'm sure they have," agreed Nancy, her voice heavy with sarcasm. "And what would they have done for you next, I wonder?"

Arthur was painfully embarrassed to have been spoken to in such a manner in front of Kau-lin but his head ached far too much to have a prolonged argument with his mother. Rising from his chair he walked wearily towards the house.

Nancy would have pursued him, but Kernow interceded on Arthur's behalf. He assured Nancy that all Chinese girls were brought up to tend to men. If they thought Arthur was not well it would have been natural for them to do everything within their power to make him comfortable.

"I would expect you to side with Arthur — and to make excuses for those . . . *trollops!* After all, it was you who brought them here. You who've encouraged Arthur to behave in a manner he would never have dreamed of back home in England."

"This *isn't* England, Mrs Calvin, and Arthur is no longer the small boy you've sheltered from the world for much of his life. He's a *man*. Old enough to meet girls, to fight in a war — or to go his own way if he wishes. But I didn't come here to have an argument with you. I came to see how Arthur was. I've done that. When I've made certain both girls are all right, I'll go."

At Nancy's side, her husband said hesitantly, "You know, there's sense in what Mister Keats says, dear . . . "

Before he could explain further, his wife

116

rounded on him. "Oh, so you *do* have a voice? I didn't hear you using it when your son needed setting straight about his behaviour. Well, I've tried talking him, now it's your turn. Go on! What are you waiting for?"

Kernow waited a few moments for Ronald Calvin to speak, but the unhappy man said nothing. He stood looking at the ground at his feet. After fixing him with a scornful look, Nancy snorted derisively and walked away.

Kernow hurried to the room shared by Kau-lin and She-she, believing they would be upset as a result of Nancy's outburst. He need not have been concerned about them. When he raised a hand to knock at the door he could hear them giggling inside the room.

She-she answered his knock. When he declined her invitation to enter their room, she said, "Why you not come in? You have a mother here too?"

Her words brought on another fit of giggling and Kernow hurriedly changed his mind about entering the room. If Nancy heard such hilarity at her expense her fury would be uncontrollable. Stepping inside, he closed the door behind him, "Mrs Calvin isn't used to Hong Kong. The heat is getting to her. It's getting to everyone."

Kau-lin only partially agreed. "Yes, Hong Kong too hot — but Mrs Calvin hot inside, no matter where she live. She call me 'hussy'. What is hussy?"

Kernow tried to think of a diplomatic way to phrase his reply. "A hussy is . . . well, a girl who is too friendly with men. But you mustn't take

117

too much notice of her. She's trying too hard to protect Arthur, that's all."

"Why? Arthur is a man now. She must let him go."

"That's what I told her. Arthur did too. He said you'd both been very kind to him."

"Arthur said that to mother? He speak for us against her?"

"He did." Kernow grinned. "You're making a man of him, Kau-lin."

She nodded gravely. "I make man of him, but mother don't want him man. She want small boy, say 'Do this, Arthur', 'Do that, Arthur'. He do. I make man — she make trouble."

"I shouldn't worry too much about it. I think Mrs Jefferies is on your side. She knows what Nancy Calvin is like."

"You on our side too, Lieutenant Keats? You not think me and Kau-lin . . . 'hussy'?"

"No, She-she, I don't think you're hussies. I think you've put some excitement and interest into what might easily have been a very dull language course, but I'd better go now. It's my birthday next week and the admiral has promised to promote me on that day. Instead of being a number two lieutenant, I'll be a number one lieutenant. I can't afford to have Mrs Jefferies complain about me spending too much time in the room of two very beautiful young Chinese girls."

Kau-lin seemed amused. "Why *Fan Qui* men all frightened of women? I think maybe because a woman and not a man number one in your country. I think I like come your country. Tell all men, 'You do as Kau-lin tell you, or I shout at you, like Mrs Calvin'."

Her comments, made in a fair imitation of Nancy Calvin's voice, brought on another fit of giggling.

"I must go now."

As Kernow opened the door to leave, She-she asked, "What day your birthday?"

"Wednesday — *Lai-pa'ai saam*."

"How old you?"

"I'll be eighteen."

"You work that day? Come to mission school?"

"Yes, why do you ask?"

"Thought maybe you stay with men from ships. Drink too much. No matter, you go now. Next week you be number one lieutenant. Very important man."

★ ★ ★

When Nancy Calvin had the garden to herself she walked among the flowering trees and shrubs until she arrived at a small garden arbour, hidden from the view of the house by a hanging wall of flowers. From here she could see out across the busy Hong Kong anchorage to the mainland peninsular of Kowloon, with its backdrop of nine irregularly shaped dark hills.

It was hotter than ever and she felt like panting. Yet even heavier than the air was the desperately unhappy feeling inside her. It was quite unlike the contrition she usually felt after an outburst of her ill-controlled temper. Today there was something more. Kernow Keats had pointed out that Arthur was no longer a boy who could be ordered to do her bidding. She knew in her heart he was ready to go his own way, yet today she had driven a wedge between them, widening a rift that might never be fully bridged again.

As she stood there thinking about her son, tears suddenly welled up in Nancy's eyes. Dropping to her knees, she began to pray. She asked for guidance from the only One whose help she had ever asked.

12

THERE were no other Royal Marine officers in the naval barracks and Kernow had formed no close friendships among the naval officers sharing the wardroom. Nevertheless, a small party had been arranged in the wardroom to celebrate his birthday and promotion to full lieutenant's rank.

Unfortunately for Kernow, forty-eight hours before his important day, a patrolling frigate sailed into Hong Kong harbour. The frigate was one of the ships which were the eyes and ears of the British fleet in Far Eastern waters. Its commanding officer came ashore to report a huge build-up of Imperial Chinese war junks in a bay a hundred and fifty miles north of the colony.

After a hasty conference between the commander-in-chief and his senior officers, every available man-o'-war put to sea, the deficiencies in their crew numbers made up by officers and men from the barracks.

Although Kernow was not sent to sea the proposed party had to be cancelled and he awoke on his birthday in a near-empty barracks. Many of the officers had taken their Chinese servants to sea with them; among these was the servant Kernow shared with a number of midshipmen. It meant he went to the mission school still wearing the star of a second lieutenant on his collar, carrying the crowns of his new rank in his pocket.

When he reached the mission school building he found She-she waiting for him at the main entrance. Hannah Jefferies was only a short distance away in the corridor. She-she could hardly contain her excitement as she thrust a neatly wrapped package into his hands, saying, "Happy birthday, *First* Lieutenant Keats."

"Just 'Lieutenant' is good enough, She-she, and you really should be calling me Kernow by now — but what's this?" As he looked up from the package their eyes met. Whatever her present to him was, he knew it could not match the thrill that went through him in that moment.

He remained gazing at her until she said happily, "Open and see. Special for you."

The package contained a scarlet sash, of the type worn over the left shoulder by Royal Marine officers. This one was made of fine silk, its quality far superior to anything Kernow had seen worn by any of his brother officers.

"This is a wonderful present, She-she. Thank you very much indeed."

Kernow meant every word. Had Hannah Jefferies not been watching them, it would have seemed natural to him to give She-she a kiss to thank her. He wanted desperately to kiss her, but he knew instinctively that the missionary would not have approved and nothing must spoil this moment.

"It never be lost, see?" She-she, delighted with Kernow's reaction to her gift, turned the sash over. On the reverse side, where the sash ended in a tassel, were stitched the words 'First Lieutenant Kernow Keats', embroidered very neatly in gold thread.

"How did you know what to put?" Kernow was genuinely astonished.

"Doctor Jefferies show me. Write name on paper. I copy." She-she hesitated. "First time only put *Lieutenant* Kernow Keats. I say, 'No, *First* Lieutenant now?' I am right?"

"You're right, She-she. I'll be the proudest and smartest officer on parade when I wear this. Not only that, I'll be the envy of all my fellow officers."

Hannah spoke for the first time. "Happy Birthday, Kernow, but I thought you'd be proudly sporting your new badge of rank this morning. A crown, is it not?"

"That's right." Kernow fingered the stiff, high collar of his tunic where he still sported the star of a second lieutenant. He pulled the crowns of his new rank from his pocket. "I have them here. There was no one left in the barracks to stitch them on for me."

"Give me. I sew them when we finish school." She-she took the two small badges of rank from his hand before he, or anyone else, could argue.

The two girls had returned to their lessons at the school in spite of Nancy Calvin's objections. A state of wary neutrality now existed between the two Chinese girls and the Birmingham missionary. Hannah had suggested to Nancy that she substitute prayer for vituperation in her dealings with them.

123

Aware that at this stage Hannah held the key to her future as a missionary, Nancy did her best to keep the dislike she felt for Kau-lin in particular in check.

During the noon break, Hannah sought out Kernow and asked him whether he had any birthday celebrations planned in the Royal Naval Barracks for that evening.

"Not any more," he said, somewhat ruefully. "A small party had been arranged, but there's hardly an officer or man left in Hong Kong. They've all gone off to break up an Imperial war fleet that's been sighted to the north."

"Does that mean you'll need to do duty tonight?"

"No, they've spared me that, for today at least." He wondered why she was so interested in how he intended spending his birthday evening. Her next words provided an answer.

"Good! She-she and Kau-lin would like to cook a meal for you — a Chinese meal, at the house this evening. We're all invited, but it's to be a birthday treat for you."

"What a wonderful idea! I'd love to come. I wasn't looking forward to spending a depressing evening in the barracks. Now it's going to be a birthday to remember."

Something in his voice told Hannah that Kernow was a very lonely young man. The evening would be good for him. She was also aware that a lonely young man might prove to be doubly susceptible to the attentions of an attractive young woman. Lieutenant Kernow Keats would have met few girls, Chinese or

English, who were as appealing as She-she.

"It will be an occasion for all of us, especially the new missionaries. They will, quite literally, be given a taste of what they can expect when they go out among the Chinese people."

★ ★ ★

That evening Kernow arrived at the mission house resplendent in full dress uniform. His red coat was worn above smartly pressed white trousers. A new shako sat on his head and his scarlet sash was slung over his left shoulder. He also wore the insignia of a first lieutenant on his collar, stitched on by She-she.

The party was held in the mission house garden with light provided by a number of lanterns suspended from flowering trees. Colourful moths of many types and sizes fluttered around the lanterns like so many windblown flowers.

A charcoal fire burned in a corner of the garden and the cooking was shared between this and the house kitchen, with She-she and Kau-lin bustling between the two.

A number of other missionaries currently in Hong Kong put in an appearance during the evening. Among them was Kau-lin's cousin. He was undergoing instruction with the Reverend James Legge of the London Missionary Society, one of many societies represented on the island.

There was a squeak of delight from Kau-lin when she first caught sight of her cousin. After a voluble and excited welcome, she took him

125

by the hand and led him across the garden to introduce him to Kernow as 'Cousin Chang'.

A tall, serious young man, Chang had an engaging smile and an honest, open manner which immediately appealed to Kernow. He also had an extensive knowledge of the Taiping rebels and soon he and Kernow were deep in conversation.

Of all those at the party, only Arthur Calvin seemed not to be enjoying himself. Occasionally he would be asked a question by one of the guests in a bid to draw him into conversation within a group, but usually without success. After a few monosyllabic words had tripped over themselves off his tongue Arthur would retreat to the darkness of the garden once more.

Kernow introduced him to Chang and for a few minutes the shy young man seemed to gain in confidence. Unfortunately they were joined by an effusive Esme Pilkington demanding to be told *everything* about the Taiping movement and Arthur retreated once more.

It was not very long before Esme's exuberance became too much for Kernow too. She belonged to the school of thought which believed the Taiping movement offered a golden opportunity for Christianity in China. As with every cause she espoused, Esme put her point of view with great forcefulness.

Kernow looked around for Arthur, but could not see him. After a few minutes he realised that Kau-lin was also missing. It seemed that Nancy Calvin made the discovery at the same time.

She and Ronald were with a group which

126

included the Bishop of Hong Kong in its number, but her glance increasingly ranged round the garden. Her expression of pinch-faced anger left Kernow in no doubt of what was likely to happen if she did not soon catch a glimpse of her son.

At that moment the bishop spoke to Nancy and she was obliged to reply, the absence of her son put aside for a moment.

When Kernow approached the table where She-she was clearing food, she looked up and gave him a warm, welcoming smile. "Hello, First Lieutenant Keats. I thought you had forgotten me. You having happy birthday?"

"A wonderful time — but it might not last. Nancy Calvin's noticed that Arthur's nowhere to be seen. Neither is Kau-lin. Do you know where they are?"

She-she's smile vanished. "Arthur look very lonely. Kau-lin say she go make him happy."

"I think that's what his mother's afraid of . . . "

She-she appeared puzzled and Kernow said quickly, "Do you know where they've gone? I'll try to find them before Nancy does."

She-she said hesitantly, "Kau-lin take him to the room. Our room."

Kernow gasped. "Arthur let her take him there! If they're caught together in a room here the scandal will rock the missionary society. It could set them back for years."

She-she was alarmed by Kernow's reaction. "I go find them."

"Right. Tell them to get out here quickly. I'll

127

try to head off Nancy if she comes looking for Arthur."

Nancy Calvin was still talking to the bishop but her gaze had begun to wander once more and it was only a few minutes before she made an excuse to break away from the group and head towards the house.

Heading her off swiftly, Kernow tried to appear casual as he said, "Hello, Mrs Calvin. I hope you're enjoying my birthday party."

Nancy was too shrewd to be taken in by his sudden friendliness. Frostily suspicious, she said, "Have you seen Arthur?"

"No. As a matter of fact I was just asking She-she the same question. She said he was down at the bottom of the garden looking out towards the harbour the last time she saw him."

Nancy Calvin hesitated. She had intended looking for him in his room. If he was not there she would have gone to the room shared by the two Chinese hussies. But the bottom of the garden? Then she remembered the arbour and the secluded seat among the flowers . . .

Turning away, she hurried off into the darkness, leaving the lantern-lit circle around the house behind her.

Two minutes later Arthur emerged from the house looking decidedly flustered. "Where's Mother? She-she said she was searching for me."

"That's right. I told her She-she last saw you at the bottom of the garden. Here, get yourself something to eat — and pull yourself together.

I don't know what you've been doing, and I don't want to know, but you look as guilty as hell. Where's Kau-lin?"

"With She-she. They've gone to the kitchen. We weren't doing anything, you know. Not really . . ."

"I believe you, but I don't think your mother would."

"She's determined to think the worst where Kau-lin's concerned. I don't know why. Kau-lin's been kinder and more considerate to me than any girl I've ever known."

Kernow thought this was the probable reason for Nancy Calvin's intense dislike of the Chinese girl, but he said nothing. At that moment Nancy came back into the light. After giving Kernow an accusing glance, she turned her attention to Arthur. "I've been looking for you, where have you been?"

He shrugged. "Nowhere special. I got fed up with everyone talking about missions and missionaries the whole time. I thought I'd go for a walk."

"You were fed up with everyone talking about missionary work? That's the reason we're all in Hong Kong. At least, that's the reason *most* of us are here." The words were accompanied by another glance at Kernow. "What else would you expect us to be talking about?"

Not waiting for a reply to her question, Nancy asked, "Where's that Chinese girl? Was she off with you on this walk?"

"She-she and Kau-lin are in the kitchen," said Kernow. "I saw them only a few minutes ago. I think they've worked very hard putting on this party for me. I'm very grateful to them both."

"Huh!" Nancy expressed her disapproval. "They should be grateful to Hannah for giving them a roof over their heads." She flapped a hand at a moth which had passed too close to a candle flame and was now flying in frantic circles. "This *heat*! I've never known anything like it."

Fanning her face with her hand in a futile gesture, she said, "Arthur, you just stay in the light so I can see what you're up to. You hear me?"

For a moment it seemed he would argue, but he had just avoided one difficult situation. He would not tempt fate again for a while.

"I'm going up to my room. No doubt you'll want to come and check every half-hour to make sure I'm there alone."

Turning his back on his mother, Arthur said, "It's been a good party, Kernow. Thanks. Thanks for everything."

★ ★ ★

When most of the guests had left the mission gardens, Kernow saw a well-lit troop transport nosing its way to a berth in the harbour. He went to the low wall on the harbour side of the garden to watch the ship's progress. It was dark here well away from the lights of the house.

He heard no one approaching and jumped when a voice from close beside him said, "It is very pretty, yes?"

130

"Hello, She-she. Yes, it does look very pretty all lit up in the darkness." As he spoke an anchor dropped from the steamer's bow to splash into the water, the noise of the chain paying out from its steel-lined locker disturbing the night.

"You have a happy birthday?" Kernow could see She-she's face turned up to him.

"Thanks to you it's been the best birthday I can ever remember." The realisation that he was speaking the truth came as a surprise to him.

"I very happy too." She-she was standing very close to him. So close he could smell woodsmoke in her hair from where she had been cooking over the barbecue fire. Inconsequentially, he remembered being told that each strand of Chinese hair was many times thicker than European hair.

"What sort ship that one?"

"It's a troop transport, bringing in soldiers. A couple of hundred or more, I expect. I was just wondering about them. Some will have left families at home. How many will ever see them again, I wonder? Less than half, I suspect."

She-she's hand found his arm. "Must not think unhappy thoughts on birthday. Many soldiers stay Hong Kong. Find nice Chinese girl take care them. Make them very happy."

"How do you know about such things, She-she?" Her hand on his arm filled him with a childish pleasure.

"Speak to many Hong Kong girls. Girl work in mission kitchen. She live with soldier."

"Does Mrs Jefferies know about it?"

"Better she not know, I think."

131

"Yes."

She-she's hand still rested on Kernow's arm and he thought his awareness of it was probably out of all proportion to its significance to She-she.

After a long silence, Kernow said reluctantly, "We'd better get back to the house. If you're found out here with me we'll have Nancy Calvin saying you're as bad as Kau-lin."

"You think I bad girl?"

She-she's hand dropped away from his arm as she looked up into his face in the darkness.

A pulse in the side of Kernow's neck seemed to be beating loudly enough to be heard by She-she as he said, "I think you're the most wonderful girl I've ever met."

"Then no matter to me what Mrs Calvin say. No matter what anyone say."

When Kernow kissed her, she felt so soft and light in his arms that he was afraid to squeeze her to him for fear she might break.

Suddenly she was leaning against him, shaking.

"What is it, She-she? Are you all right?"

"What you do?" She had suddenly remembered the stories she had heard about the *Fan Qui*, sucking the soul from any Chinese who fell into their clutches.

Kernow had heard the same absurd stories and he hugged her reassuringly. "It's all right, She-she. That was a kiss. It took nothing from you."

He hugged her again, tighter this time.

"Indeed, I *gave* you something. Part of my heart. The heart of a *Fan Qui*. It will always be yours, and there's nobody will ever be able to take it away from you."

133

13

LESS than a week after the birthday party put on for him by She-she and Kau-lin, Kernow found himself a guest at a very different function. He attended a party at the United States consulate in Hong Kong.

Due to the absence of so many more senior officers, off serving with the fleet, Kernow was invited to more of the colony's many social functions than was usual. Most he was able to decline, pleading the need to study. However, this particular invitation had reached him via the admiral's office. It was one he could not refuse.

Kernow did not feel at ease at such large receptions. As he dressed in the small room he occupied in the naval barracks he doubted whether this one would be different to any of the others he had been unable to avoid.

The United States consulate was situated in a new and impressive house, some distance from the British naval headquarters. He realised it was a very large party indeed when he saw the assortment of transport queuing outside the lofty doorway to disgorge the cream of Hong Kong society. There were carriages; locally made pony traps; saddle-horses and rickshaws. There were even a few sedan chairs in evidence. Few arrived, as did Kernow, on foot.

The reception took the course he had

anticipated. At first a number of guests spoke to him, believing that a junior officer attending such a party must belong to a very influential family. Once they had established the truth, they drifted away once more, in search of someone of greater importance.

As the evening progressed, Kernow gradually edged his way towards the door. He was almost there when he reached the sanctuary offered by a huge indoor plant that erupted from a stone tub placed on an eight-foot-high pillar.

Hidden from the view of most of the other guests Kernow awaited an opportunity to slip unnoticed through the doorway and return to the naval barracks. Suddenly a voice from near at hand said, "So there *is* someone under forty living on this God-forsaken island! What are you doing hiding yourself among the shrubbery? Come on out and let me take a look at you."

The accent was American. When Kernow turned he saw a tall, blue-eyed young woman, perhaps a year older than himself, peering at him through the foliage of the hanging plant.

"I'm Sally Merrill," she introduced herself before he could say a word. "I'm here because I'm American and obliged to be here. What's your excuse? Are you rich or something?"

Kernow grinned at her. "I've been invited to the party because all the more socially acceptable officers are off with the fleet, doing battle with the Chinese. It's a story I've already repeated to at least ten other people this evening. They all quickly lost interest and left to go looking for more illustrious company. I promise not to hold it against you if you decide to do the same."

Kernow had drunk more than he was used to during the course of the evening. Had he not done so he would not have been so ready to express such views to a stranger. Not even one so seemingly unorthodox as this tall young girl.

Sally Merrill seemed taken aback, but only for a moment. Her lips parted in a wide smile and she said, "You mean you're not here hoping to further your career by collecting names to drop into the conversation in the right places? Well . . . it's nice to meet someone different from the rest, I'm sure."

"I'm here because the invitation came through my admiral's office. I dared not refuse. But I've performed my duty now. I've spent the last half-hour moving towards the door so I can slip out unnoticed."

"Not now, you can't. I've found you and I don't intend losing you for a while. Let's find another drink and go out on the terrace to get some air. It's absolutely stifling in here."

It was quieter outside on the lantern-lit terrace. They soon found a secluded table in the shadows between twin pools of light formed by two of the highly decorative paper lanterns.

Kernow studied the American girl as she cupped her hands to rescue a huge, bird-like moth that had formed a suicidal attachment to the candle inside one of the lanterns. She was too tall and too thin to qualify as a beauty by accepted standards, but she had long, attractive fair hair and an open, honest face. She also had an indefinable quality which would cause most men to look twice at her without really knowing why.

Kernow found her easy to talk to. Before long she knew more about him and his background than did his fellow officers in the naval barracks.

They had been talking together for about half-an-hour when Admiral Sir Michael Seymour came from the house accompanied by a tall man with a distinguished appearance, and a younger companion who wore the uniform of a United States captain of cavalry.

The small party stood in a doorway looking about them until the young American officer pointed in the direction of Kernow and Sally.

As the trio approached, with Seymour in the lead, Kernow stood up.

"We've been looking for you, young Kernow," said the admiral, heartily. "This is the new United States consul for Shanghai. I've just been telling him about your exploits with the pirates and he said he'd like to meet you."

The tall civilian reached out and clasped Kernow's hand firmly. "The name's Bellamy Merrill. Nice to meet you, son. I see you've already made the acquaintance of my daughter. I haven't been able to educate her to enjoy official parties. I thought I might find her outside somewhere."

Before Kernow had time to recover from the shock of learning he had spent the last half-hour monopolising the company of the United States consul's daughter, Bellamy Merrill waved a hand in the direction of the young uniformed captain. "I'd like you to meet Caleb Shumaker. He's with our consulate here in Hong Kong, as a military attaché. He's also my daughter's fiancé."

Caleb Shumaker shook hands with Kernow, maintaining considerable reserve. He resented the fact that he had found Kernow in Sally's company, yet there was a tinge of envious respect in his manner. Admiral Seymour had made much of Kernow's exploits in fighting off pirates on his way downriver in the *Sans Pareil*'s pinnace. Caleb had yet to hear a shot fired in anger.

Kernow was the first to speak. "You have my congratulations, sir. You're a lucky man."

Sally rose from the table and clasped Caleb's arm, apparently unaware she might have offended her fiancé. "There are many who'd delight in telling you that it's me who's the lucky one, Kernow. Caleb is one of America's most eligible bachelors. His father is so rich that when he went to London and took a fancy to Buckingham Palace, the home of your queen, he found the architect who'd completed the building and got him to sell him the plans. He then had a similar home built, back in Georgia."

"That's something of an exaggeration, Mister Keats," said Caleb, mollified by Sally's show of affection towards him. "Our house is on a much smaller scale."

The remainder of Kernow's evening was passed in pleasant conversation. Now he was observed on such intimate terms with Admiral Seymour and the new United States consul in

Shanghai, he found he had suddenly become a very popular figure.

He left the reception with a number of invitations to visit the homes of the United States consul's guests. The only one he intended taking up was an informal suggestion from Consul Bellamy Merrill that he join the family and Caleb Shumaker for dinner one evening, before the consul took passage to Shanghai.

Kernow little knew that fate was about to step in and prevent him from taking up this or any other invitation for a very long time.

14

THE British fleet was away from Hong Kong for ten days. During this time it sank a war fleet of almost two hundred junks.

Such were the anomalies of the situation between China and Britain that even as the junks were being destroyed, a request was received from a Provincial Chinese Viceroy asking that the British take action against a pirate base on an island a hundred miles from Hong Kong.

The request was met and the pirate base destroyed, but the Royal Navy had little opportunity to gloat over either victory.

Twenty-four hours after the men-o'-war returned to Hong Kong, a typhoon struck.

The signs had been building up as the ships entered harbour, beginning with a sudden and dramatic drop in barometric pressure. Masters of sea-going vessels began tapping the glass of their barometers with increasing frequency in the vain hope they would discover a fault in the instruments. When they dropped anchor they exchanged urgent messages with other masters, seeking reassurances that could not be given.

The sharp and exotic colours displayed in the late evening sky gave a final warning to the more experienced Far Eastern traders to prepare for the worst. A typhoon was on its way.

Each ship's captain had to make his own very difficult decision — and it needed to be made quickly. He had to decide whether to keep his ship at anchor in the harbour and risk being driven ashore, or leave and hope to ride out the fury of the storm on the high seas. It was an agonising decision and one that the captains of the men-o'-war shared with masters of the many merchantmen in the harbour.

Masters of smaller coastal trading vessels were not called upon to make such life-or-death judgements. They took their craft to typhoon shelters built along the foreshore. Here they crammed their ships together between stone breakwaters. Attached to each other and to the shore by stout chairs, everything was stowed below decks that might be blown away or torn to shreds by the frighteningly high winds they could expect.

All but a handful of the larger vessels put to sea. So too did the men-o'-war. Their crews went about their duties grave and unsmiling as the rising wind moaned through the rigging. None could be certain they would ever enter or see Hong Kong again.

Those few ships that chose to remain in harbour put out extra anchors and battened down to await what was to come. Their masters hoped the main force of the tropical storm might pass by and leave them safe.

In the naval barracks, Kernow and the other officers went around ensuring that everything capable of being blown away was either stowed safely in one of the stone-built stores, or dismantled. Few of the naval officers knew what to expect from the typhoon. Some had experienced minor hurricanes in other parts of the world, but they admitted these had been only marginally worse than a severe electrical storm at sea.

By noon the next day, the vivid colours of the sky had faded. A menacing bank of black cloud stretching from sea to sky was moving towards the land from the south. Ahead of the storm the sea was already alarmingly rough. Chinese fishermen and boatmen were enlisting the aid of friends and relatives to drag even the largest boats well away from the water's edge.

There was nothing more Kernow could do in the barracks and he was concerned for the safety of She-she. He sought and obtained permission to go to the mission and help them cope with the expected onslaught.

As Kernow hurried through the streets towards the mission house the wind howled about him. Its voice in the bamboo scaffolding surrounding the many new building projects on Hong Kong island added urgency to the activities of those taking last-minute precautions to secure belongings and property against the approaching holocaust.

Kernow turned a last corner on his way to the mission house — and was promptly blown back again. Picking himself up he went around the corner on hands and knees. When he rose to his feet he sprinted the last few yards during a momentary lull in the wind.

The mission house was closed and shuttered

and there was no response to his hammering on the door. It might have been that no one could hear him above the din of the storm. Kernow thought it more likely that everyone in the house had gone to the substantially built mission hospital building.

As he made his way along the streets once more he was surrounded by the noise of falling tiles and pursued by a variety of debris. Gathered by the wind it carved a dangerous and frenetic path through the colony.

Overtaken by basketwear, coolie hats, an occasional wooden bucket and a variety of broken bamboo scaffolding, Kernow learned to be particularly careful when he rounded corners. Once, a battered wooden shutter flew over his head, ripped from a nearby window, and all about him now was the constant noise of breaking glass.

Kernow had succeeded in rounding the last corner to the mission at the third attempt when he heard a new and terrifying sound. It sounded like the drumming of the hooves of a brigade of cavalry charging across a wooden bridge. It took him a moment or two to realise the sound was torrential rain advancing at an ominous speed across the rooftops of the town.

The time for caution had gone. Bending almost double against the strength of the wind, Kernow ran like a drunken man in a bid to reach the mission hospital before the rain caught him.

He almost made it. It would have taken him no more than fifteen paces to reach the door of the mission hospital when the deluge crashed upon him with the weight of a waterfall. Kernow was knocked to the ground. Fighting for breath, he thought he was drowning. Indeed, by the time he had fought to regain his feet he was floundering in water that swirled about his ankles and was rising rapidly.

Somehow he made it to the steps of the hospital and stumbled inside the porch. He was not even aware that his hat, secured with a leather chin strap, had been sacrificed to the Chinese Wind God.

It was more sheltered here, but he was still buffeted by wind and rain and it felt as though a giant hand was constricting his chest, trying to prevent him from breathing. Somehow in the darkness of the storm he managed to find the door handle, quietly praying the door had not been barred on the inside.

He was fortunate, the door opened — only to be snatched from his hand by the wind. It crashed inwards against the wall, the glass shattering. Fortunately it was also protected by a wooden shutter, but the sound, together with the wind that howled inside the hospital corridor, brought two Chinese hospital porters running. The combined strengths of the three men eventually succeeded in closing the door. Then the bedraggled Royal Marine officer was helped along a corridor and into a room where Doctor Jefferies was re-lighting a lamp, extinguished when Kernow had entered the building.

This was one of two storerooms, situated on the ground floor. With no windows and only one door to each room, Doctor Jefferies had decided these were the safest in the building. The whole of the hospital staff, patients and missionaries, was here. So too were She-she and Kau-lin.

Everyone in the room expressed their concern at the state of the young officer. Relieved to find She-she safe, Kernow noticed only her genuine anxiety for him. It made the terrors of the past minutes worthwhile.

"What on earth were you doing out in this . . . "

Even as Doctor Jefferies spoke the words there was a frightening crash from somewhere close at hand and the whole building shook, causing the flame in the lamp to flicker as though trembling in fear.

"I came because I thought you might need some help." It sounded foolish. Those in the storeroom were quite secure. Kernow felt like some half-drowned animal.

There was another crash and the sound of rending timbers from somewhere outside.

"We'll need all the help we can get as soon as it's possible to go outside. I don't know when that's likely to be, though. This is the worst typhoon to strike Hong Kong for very many years. It sounds as though the whole city of Victoria is being blown to pieces."

"You're lucky to be alive, young man." The comment came from Esme Pilkington. "But I admire your spirit in coming out to help us."

Kernow did not know whether he was imagining it, or if Esme's glance linked him to She-she. Right now it did not matter very

145

much. He was here and so was She-she and they were both safe.

"You'd better get out of those wet clothes." The practical suggestion came from Hannah. She called in Chinese to one of the orderlies who had brought Kernow to the room and the man hurried away.

"I've sent for some clothes for you. They will be coolie clothes and not as elegant as your uniform, but they'll be dry and you'll find them comfortable."

The Chinese orderly returned with a tunic and trousers, both made of coarse cotton, and a pair of black cotton slippers.

Kernow changed in the darkness of the corridor outside. The tunic and trousers were a good fit but the shoes were too tight for real comfort. However, it was a relief to be out of his wet clothes.

Out here in the corridor the sound of the typhoon was far worse. Kernow believed part of the roof had been brought down. This seemed to be confirmed when he found he was walking in a slowly advancing puddle of water. It was hardly likely the water outside would have risen high enough to lap over the steps. The hospital was on a slope and should have been immune from flooding.

When he re-entered the storeroom carrying his sodden uniform, She-she stood up quickly and took it from him, saying quietly, "I take these. You have them back when clean and dry."

Thanking her, Kernow told Doctor Jefferies of the water in the corridor.

"That could prove to be serious. We have a lot of equipment in the hospital that cannot be replaced. I must go and check."

"I'll come with you." Kernow's offer was echoed by Arthur and, with less enthusiasm, by Ronald Calvin.

"Arthur and Kernow can come with me. We'll bring the orderlies too. Ronald, I suggest you remain here. Take care of the women should anything untoward happen."

The Europeans and Chinese groped their way along the corridor in the wake of Doctor Jefferies. It was quite impossible to use lanterns. There was enough wind in the corridors to suggest that a window, at least, had blown in.

When they reached the stairs leading to the upper storey it became apparent that the damage was more serious than a mere window. Debris blocked the stairs and much of the passageway. Part of the roof had collapsed. Water tumbled down through the rubble and it was this that was flooding the corridor. The ground floor would have suffered far more had the rubble from the roof not blocked the stairway. It could not keep the torrential rain from pouring through, but it did block much of the wind's terrifying force.

"We can't do anything about it just yet," declared the missionary doctor, grimly. Years of hard work had been destroyed in the storm. "Let's check the ground floor ward."

Floodwater was ankle deep on the floor of the ward, but although the wind rattled the heavy wooden shutters alarmingly, they were holding. The same was true at the school end of the building. Hundreds of tiles had been torn from the roof, but the main structure was intact.

They were returning along the corridor in the direction of the store room when Kernow came to a halt.

"Listen!"

Everyone in the party stopped and after a few moments Arthur said, "I can't hear anything."

The wind had suddenly dropped and the ensuing silence was uncanny.

"We must have caught the full force of the typhoon here," said Doctor Jefferies. "We're in the calm at the eye of the storm right now. The wind will come back with renewed force in a while."

"No . . . listen again!"

Everyone fell silent. There *was* an unusual sound outside and at first everyone thought it was the low moaning of the wind in the distance. Not until it continued for some minutes and swelled in volume did they realise what they were hearing. It was the sound of human voices bewailing a tragedy of monstrous proportions.

"It's the people from the shacks behind the hospital. Their homes were far too flimsy to have stood up to the typhoon. The whole area will have been devastated!" Doctor Jefferies' voice expressed his distress. "We must help them."

"But you said the typhoon would return."

"So it will — but we can't ignore those people out there. They'll all die unless we do something to help them."

"I'll come out there with you," said Kernow. "But we'll need to be quick. I'd hate to get caught outside in that typhoon again."

Inside the storeroom refuge, Hugh Jefferies told his wife what they were about to do and lit a couple of lanterns to use should the wind outside not extinguish them immediately.

Outside the mission hospital it was as though the storm had been cut off. The air was still. Uncannily still. Kernow thought it was as though the world was holding its breath in anticipation . . .

Yet the night was not silent. The sound of water in motion was everywhere. It leaped down the side of the steep hill behind the city of Victoria in great booming torrents and surged about the feet of the would-be rescuers from the mission hospital.

There were screams and cries too, coming from the hillside. More than five thousand people not rich enough to own permanent houses had constructed hovels from anything that came to hand. These makeshift houses had been levelled by the high wind and the rain had brought thousands of tons of mud thundering down the slopes of the peak to bury the terrified inhabitants. It was as though nature had made a determined bid to reclaim what was rightfully hers.

Among the mud and buried debris were men, women and children. In some miraculous manner many had survived the cataclysm — but they could not hope for a second miracle. When the eye of the typhoon passed on they would once more be subjected to the full fury of wind and rain.

Doctor Jefferies ran amongst terrified and dazed Chinese, shouting in their own language for them to make their way to the mission hospital. The homeless people, dazed by their ordeal, were slow to obey. Meanwhile, Kernow and Arthur, with help from some of the orderlies, began to haul survivors free from the mud and rubbish of the destroyed community. It was not long before assistance arrived in the substantial form of Esme Pilkington who had been unable to remain inside while others toiled.

When Hugh Jefferies lodged a half-hearted protest against her presence in such an appalling situation, Esme dismissed it with the words, "I wasn't cut out to be a nurse, Doctor Jefferies. I'm more of a labourer and that's what I think you have need of out here."

There was need for a hundred such as Esme Pilkington, although sheer strength was not always enough. Many of those they pulled from the remnants of their homes were beyond the services of either labourer or doctor. Such traumatic discoveries had a sobering effect on the rescuers and they worked in silence, except when they needed help. A great many children were among the dead and the carnage and destruction was distressing beyond words.

They had been working for perhaps twenty minutes when Esme Pilkington suddenly straightened up. Adding more mud to her forehead with the back of a hand she asked, "Can you hear something?"

Kernow could and he knew exactly what it was. "The eye of the typhoon's passing over. Get

150

back to the mission as quickly as you can."

"There's someone here. I can't just leave her." Esme redoubled her efforts to scrape mud and stones from the body of a young woman.

"Arthur, get back to the hospital — QUICK! Take as many people as you can with you."

Without waiting to see if he was being obeyed, Kernow dropped to the mud beside Esme and dug as frantically as she in a bid to free the woman she had found. They uncovered the woman's face only to discover she was dead. At that moment the wind blew out their lantern and Kernow heard the rain coming.

Grabbing Esme's arm, he called, "Run, Esme. Run for your life!"

He ran with her, dragging her on when she would have slackened her pace, but the rain overtook them when they were still some distance from the mission. Knocked to the ground they were buffeted by wind and water as they staggered about helplessly, no longer certain of the direction in which they were going. It was sheer luck — Esme would later refer to it as God-guided luck — that brought them to the mission.

They made it to the door on hands and knees, only to find that the door itself had been half blown off its hinges, the wind playing havoc inside the building. But at least they were free of the rain here.

Kernow staggered through the door, cursing in a most un-Christian manner as he hit his shin on a piece of broken slate. Suddenly he heard She-she's voice say, "Here," and a slim hand reached out and gripped his arm. He kept his grip on Esme and hauled her after him, in spite of her protests that she wanted to go the other way.

She-she led him along the corridor, away from the storeroom, shouting above the noise of the storm, "Too many people that way. All stand. No can sit. You come me."

There were people this way too, many wailing with fright. Keeping a tight grip on Kernow, as he tripped over limbs and prostrate bodies, She-she guided him to the classroom. This room too was jammed with people, but they made their way through until She-she suddenly ducked down and spoke in Chinese. The voice of Kau-lin replied and Kernow was pulled beneath one of the tables on which they had taken their lessons.

"Is there room for me under there?" Esme's voice sounded unusually plaintive.

"Of course." The voice from beneath the table was Arthur's. "Compared with the way they're packed in at the other end of the building, there's room for a whole army under here."

Kernow was relieved to hear Arthur's voice. He had been concerned that he and Doctor Jefferies might not have made it to the safety of the mission through the deluge.

"Is Jefferies with you?"

"No, he went to the storeroom. Kau-lin met me at the door and brought me here while She-she waited for you."

"Waited for me?"

"I was afraid for you," said She-she. "You

152

very lucky one time. Maybe not two."

"I'm touched," said Kernow, and he meant it. Somehow his hand found She-she's and squeezed it. She did not attempt to take it away and for some minutes they sat with linked hands in the darkness.

"You very wet." She-she's other hand found his Chinese-style jacket. "Take off."

"It will dry in a while."

"No, take off. Wait here, I come back."

The next moment She-she had gone. Some minutes later she returned and said, "You take off?"

"I've got the jacket off but I think I'd better hang on to my trousers."

"Here, take."

She-she thrust something into his hand and he discovered curtain rings on one end.

"You've given me a curtain."

"It good. Dry."

"I wish someone would offer me something dry to put around myself. I may be built like a man-o'-war, but I don't like to feel I'm floating in water."

"Here." She-she reached across Kernow to where she judged Esme Pilkington to be. "Other curtain for you."

"Bless you, girl."

Outside, a roof from a nearby house was flung into the air. Part of it crashed against the outside of the mission, causing the building to vibrate. Some of the Chinese women and children cried out in fear.

"Do you sing, Mister Keats?"

"Me? Sing?" For a moment Kernow wondered whether the storm had caused Esme to take leave of her senses.

"I have a voice that can make itself heard above most things, Mister Keats, but I fear it will need some help if we are to drown out the sounds of a typhoon."

The next moment Esme Pilkington's voice was booming out a recognisable if not entirely musically accurate version of 'Rock of Ages'.

Kernow joined in and Arthur's more tuneful voice was soon heard. A few minutes later the tune was taken up by distant voices from the storeroom at the far end of the crowded corridor.

Alongside Kernow, She-she moved in a bid to make herself more comfortable. She made no attempt to pull away when his arm went about her and drew her in to him.

At some time during that violent night, Kernow fell asleep still holding She-she, only faintly aware that Esme's unfading voice was now stronger than the storm outside.

15

"WAKE up, Mister Keats. Wake up!"
Kernow woke with a start to discover he was still holding She-she. She was snuggled in to him asleep. It took a moment or two to realise he had not wakened of his own volition. Hannah Jefferies had a hand on his shoulder and it was clear she did not approve of what she saw.

Her disapproval was shared between Kernow and Arthur Calvin who lay in an exhausted sleep with his head resting on Kau-lin's lap.

"It's daylight. The typhoon's passed on and we're going to search the hill where the shacks stood. There's far more to be done than we can cope with. Do you think you might persuade the commanding officer at the barracks to send some of his men to help us?"

"Of course." The arm about She-she had lost its feeling. When he tried to pull it free he was awkward and woke her. She came to with the terror of the night flooding back, but when she looked up at Kernow the fear subsided.

She did not see Hannah until the missionary spoke to her. "Will you go to the hospital, She-she? A great many injured people are being brought in. Doctor Jefferies will need all the help he can get."

"I'll go too." When Esme spoke her voice was hoarse as a result of singing in competition with the typhoon. "But I need to find something more practical to wear than this curtain."

"One of the orderlies will find you a tunic," said Hannah, disapproval of Kernow and She-she still evident when she glanced in their direction. "Perhaps you will wake Mr Calvin before his mother comes in search of him. Then I think you can best help by bringing some order to the kitchen. Cook everything you can find — and make tea. Gallons of tea. It's going to be a harrowing day."

When Hannah left them, Esme drew the curtain about her upper body and struggled to her feet with many groans. The object achieved, she unexpectedly beamed at Kernow and She-she "I fear Mrs Jefferies is not of a romantic disposition. Such a pity. When I woke earlier I thought the pair of you made one of the most winsome pictures I have seen for a long time. Arthur and Kau-lin too. I'll leave you to wake them. It would embarrass dear Arthur far more were I to do it."

Kernow found he too was stiff. As he was about to rise to his feet he looked at She-she. She was quite obviously very tired and her hair was more untidy than he had ever seen it, but he thought she looked beautiful. Merely looking at her made him want to reach out and touch her. Acting on impulse he leaned forward and kissed her very lightly on the lips.

★ ★ ★

156

The Royal Naval barracks had been well secured before the typhoon struck. As a result damage had been kept to a minimum. Consequently the commanding officer was able to release a great many naval ratings to help with rescue work on the typhoon-devastated island. Kernow did not return to the mission with them.

A message awaited him at the barracks. He was to report immediately to the admiral's office. After changing into uniform he hurried away to obey the command.

The scene inside the naval headquarters was chaotic, although the building itself had suffered less damage than most others. It had a flat roof and there had been no tiles to be ripped off. However, during the typhoon a window shutter had been ripped from its hinges and the ferocious wind had smashed through the glass to wreak havoc inside.

In the midst of the chaos Admiral Seymour sat at his desk, flanked by his flag-lieutenant and a secretary, both of whom were writing at great speed. Officers far senior to Kernow arrived ahead of him to receive orders from the admiral. All departed in great haste to carry them out.

"Ah, Keats! Glad to see you're safe. I understand the area around the mission hospital suffered particularly badly from the typhoon. I've got a special task for you. One that will put your knowledge of the Chinese language to the test — how are the lessons coming along, by the way?"

Kernow was impressed. The admiral had the awesome responsibility of locating every missing ship in the Far Eastern Fleet. Yet not only had he remembered Kernow's name but had made time to ask about his progress at the mission school.

"I can make myself understood, sir."

"Good. Very good. What I have in mind will also call for a great deal of tact — something that's not always found in a young officer."

"I'll do my best not to let you down, sir."

"I'm sure you will. I have every faith in you, my boy. Have you ever sailed a *lorcha*?"

Many bastardised craft had put in an appearance about the Chinese coast since the arrival of Europeans on the scene. Each was an attempt to improve upon the sailing qualities of the vessels of East and West. The *lorcha* was a Portuguese innovation. With a European-style hull and the sails of a Chinese junk, it was a combination that seemed to work comparatively well.

"I've been on board one, sir, but I never actually sailed it."

"Then I'm afraid you'll need to learn as you go along. Nothing else of any size has survived the typhoon. I want you to go up the Canton River. Take a crew of a dozen naval ratings and try to find out what's happened to the two frigates we had up there. They were last reported somewhere in the vicinity of the Bogue forts. The chances are they were driven ashore. You'll need to question any locals you can find about the fate of their crews. Think you can do that?"

"I'll do my very best, sir."

"That's all I ask of you, Mister Keats, but spend no more time ashore than is absolutely necessary. The Chinese in that area are not renowned for their friendliness towards the British. I don't hold out a great deal of hope for our men. Any sailors who found their way ashore are likely to have been picked up and had their heads sent to the Viceroy with a complaint that they were trespassing outside the permitted areas. The same thing could happen to you and your men, remember that. Be careful, Mister Keats — and good luck."

* * *

The *lorcha* was not the easiest of craft to sail. A young midshipman who, with eleven other Royal Naval sailors, had been sent to crew the ship, commented to Kernow that: "Only the Portuguese could have put such a vessel together."

It was perhaps a little unfair. *Lorcha*s had a proven record of seaworthiness in the waters around the China coast. However, Kernow had to admit the vessel was not the most manoeuvrable of craft in the tidal estuary of the Canton river, swollen as it was in the aftermath of the typhoon.

When Kernow reached the mouth of the river guarded by the Bogue forts, he found the water thick with debris of every description. Trees, roof timbers, rubbish of all types — and bodies. There was so much floating in the swollen current that navigation was a problem.

Cautiously, Kernow took the ungainly craft close to the Chinese-manned forts, expecting every minute to hear the boom of a cannon and see a round shot splash in the water nearby.

After a while it became apparent the Chinese were far too busy repairing damage caused to their forts by the great wind and torrential rains. They did not view a small, lightly armed *lorcha* as a threat to the Chinese nation.

There was nothing to indicate the whereabouts of the two frigates. Kernow wanted to believe they had headed for the open sea as soon as the barometer began dropping. Realistically, he doubted very much whether they would both have left their patrol area, whatever the weather promised.

Had they still been in these waters when the typhoon struck it would have proved impossible to tack against the wind. With this in mind, Kernow concentrated his search on the northernmost coast of the estuary.

It was not an easy task. Wreckage and seaweed was spread for hundreds of yards inland, making it difficult to pick out any particular item. Then, after two hours of searching, one of the look-outs gave a shout.

"There's something over there that might be part of a ship's boat, sir. It's hard to be sure because there's so much weed all around it."

After peering through a telescope for some minutes, Kernow agreed it was probably the wreckage of a small boat. He ordered the *lorcha* to be run close inshore. When they were as close as they dared approach a dinghy was lowered and three men went ashore to investigate the find.

Minutes later they called back to the *lorcha* with confirmation. It was a Royal Navy boat and largely intact.

"What do we do now, sir?" asked the midshipman, uncertainly. "It could have been washed over the side from one of the frigates during the typhoon."

"I doubt it. Had it been, it would be little more than a heap of splintered wood. I'd say that boat was brought ashore by men who knew what they were doing."

Even as he was talking to the young midshipman, Kernow was deciding on his next move. "Recall the dinghy. I'll take another five men ashore with me. You and the others remain on board. There seems to be a small village about a mile inland. I'll go there and see what can be learned. Keep the *lorcha* offshore and a sharp look-out for the Chinese navy. If we're not back by dark, or if you're threatened by any Imperial junks, you're to return to Hong Kong and report to the admiral. Don't risk losing the *lorcha*. The admiral needs every vessel he has left. Is that understood?"

"Yes, sir. I'll call the dinghy back right away."

The midshipman hurried off to recall the dinghy, flushed with pleasure at the prospect of assuming command of the *lorcha*. Kernow

161

remembered his own excitement at being put in charge of a boat sent off to board the *Hoppo* of Canton's junk in this very part of the Canton river estuary, only a few months before. It seemed an age ago.

16

ON the way to the village with eight sailors from the *lorcha*, Kernow witnessed the havoc caused by the typhoon, here on the mainland. The sheer volume of rain, combined with floods pouring from the hills, had totally ruined the growing crops. The next few months would be difficult for the people hereabouts.

As Kernow and the sailors drew closer to the village the damage caused to the flimsy houses became apparent. However, Kernow thought the main centre of the typhoon had probably passed some distance away. Had this village been on Hong Kong island there would not have been a single building left standing.

The villagers were busily clearing up after the storm — but their hostility was evident. Kernow was glad he and his men were well armed. He knew this was the only reason the British sailors did not come under immediate attack. Even the children were anti-European. They ran close to the hated *Fan Qui* and spat at them, then raced back to the safety of their friends. It was significant that their actions did not bring a single word of admonishment from their elders.

Kernow asked to speak to the headman of the village. It was a request that needed to be repeated many times before an elderly, wispy-bearded man came forward and admitted that he was the village spokesman. He denied that any other *Fan Qui* had been in the area, either before or after the great storm, adding that none had been seen there since the war with Britain, twenty-five years before.

Despite the villagers' antagonism towards the *Fan Qui* and their obvious dislike of the sailors, the headman suggested they should all stay and take food with him. Kernow declared his intention of returning to the ship. If the missing sailors were not here he would need to search elsewhere for them. When the headman became more insistent Kernow grew uneasy.

"There's something very wrong here," he said to the petty officer who held the next senior rank to himself. "They make no secret of hating us, yet are desperately trying to persuade us to stay and eat with them. What does that suggest to you?"

The petty officer was a large, slow-talking West countryman, who looked all around him before he spoke. "I'd say they have more inside their sleeves than arms, sir. They can hardly have enough food for themselves after the typhoon." He looked calmly at Kernow. "Hasn't the Viceroy of this province put out a reward for the capture of an Englishman?"

"That's right. Viceroy Yeh made the proclamation some time ago. I don't think it's ever been cancelled. My bet is the headman's sent word to the local magistrate that we're here. Let's get back to the *lorcha* now — but easy does it. No panicking, or we'll have a howling mob after us. We don't have ammunition enough to

164

deal with all of them."

Kernow and the English sailors were not even halfway back to the shore across the muddy, storm-flooded fields when they saw the result of the villagers' scheming. A large body of horsemen was making for the village. Coming from the direction of the Bogue forts, the horsemen were riding hard.

"Run, men, but stay together!"

Even as Kernow called the orders, the horsemen changed direction. Now they were heading straight for the sailors who floundered through the flooded fields. Either they had seen the *Fan Qui* trying to make their escape, or someone from the village had signalled to them.

It soon became clear to Kernow that he and his men were not going to outstrip the horsemen. Suddenly the petty officer came to a halt.

"They'll be up with us before we reach the shore, sir. Leave me half-a-dozen muskets and I'll try to hold them back long enough for you and the others to get on board the *lorcha*."

"No." Kernow came to a halt and shrugged his shoulders in a gesture of resignation. "You'd be throwing your life away for nothing. We wouldn't make it either. Look!"

He pointed towards the shoreline. A strip of land just back from the water had been raised by generations of Chinese farmers in a bid to prevent high tides spilling over and inundating the crop-growing fields. Along this strip at least forty more horsemen were galloping to where the *lorcha* was turning and heading out into the estuary. The midshipman on board was carrying out Kernow's instructions. The race to reach safety had already been lost.

"Where shall we stand and fight, sir? There's a small heap of rocks over there."

"We'd be cut down within minutes. There's a time for fighting and a time for talking. Right now I think you'd better hope my Chinese is good enough to get us out of trouble. Put down your guns, men. Put them down, I say."

He needed to repeat his order because some of the men hesitated, waiting to follow the petty officer's lead.

"But, sir, we'd kill one or two before they killed us."

"You'd be no less dead, petty officer. You see that red flag, edged with gold? That's telling the world these are Tartar horsemen, the fiercest of all the Imperial Chinese soldiers. One single shot from us and we'll all be dead in no time. Put your guns down — and quickly. It's our only chance."

The horsemen were almost upon them. If the slaughter began nothing would put an end to it but the death of all the *Fan Qui*.

The sailors dropped their weapons and stood forlornly awaiting the arrival of the Tartar horsemen. The flooded fields slowed the horses, but it was only moments before the first horseman reached the unarmed men. The Tartar had a sword in his hand. As he approached he raised it high in the air then lowered it again, seemingly uncertain of what to do next.

This was exactly what Kernow had been hoping would happen. Stepping forward with his right hand held up, palm forward, he said in Chinese, "We come in peace to search for men who were lost in the typhoon."

The Tartar soldier raised his sword once more — and lowered it yet again. Other horsemen splashed to a halt, surrounding Kernow and the sailors.

After long moments of uncertainty one of the mounted Tartars pushed his way through the group. Perhaps two years older than Kernow, he was swarthy-skinned and wore a uniform the colours of the banner carried by one of his men. The Tartar looked down at Kernow for some minutes before speaking.

"I am Shalonga, captain of my father's army. Are you so contemptuous of the Chinese that you launch an invasion with only eight men?"

Kernow tried to hide the relief he felt. This was hardly an opening gambit from a man who intended slaughtering them.

"We are few because we come in peace, on a mission of mercy. I seek sailors from two ships believed to have been lost in the typhoon."

"Many ships were lost. Many lives on land too. Why are these men so special?"

Kernow knew it would be no use lying to the bannerman captain. "They belong to the English Navy. My admiral ordered me to look for them."

"Why here? Why choose this village?"

"We found a ship's boat on the shore. I think the villagers know something of the sailors, but they would not tell me."

Shalonga looked thoughtful for a few moments. Then he said, "We will go to the village and speak to the headman."

Kernow was more heartened than ever by their conversation. Had the Tartar officer intended killing them, he and his men would all be dead by now.

No attempt was made to secure the British sailors. Indeed, no restraint was necessary. They were entirely at the mercy of the Tartars.

On the way to the village, the Tartar officer rode alongside Kernow. He seemed in a talkative mood. "Where have you and your men come from?"

"From Hong Kong."

"You suffered much from the typhoon there?"

"It was very bad. Thousands were killed and there has been much damage."

"It was not so bad here, and at Canton it was no more than a summer storm. But typhoons are sent as a lesson to us all, *Fan Qui*. Our war machines are as nothing compared to the weapons of the Gods."

Kernow thought it was a strange way for a fierce Tartar soldier to be talking, but he made no comment. A few minutes later Shalonga kneed the horse he was riding and took his place at the head of his horsemen.

By the time the Tartars and their prisoners had reached the village the whole population had turned out to meet them — and now they were openly hostile. It was not only the children who spat at the *Fan Qui*. The women did too, and many of the men aimed blows at the sailors, using fists and sticks.

An order from Shalonga put an end to the one-sided attack. He gave a clipped command to his men and they beat back the villagers using the flat edge of their swords. The blows struck by the horsemen were far harder than those aimed at the prisoners. Kernow realised there was little love lost between the Tartar horsemen and the Cantonese villagers.

As though reading his thoughts, Shalonga reined his horse in beside Kernow once more. "If we were Taiping rebels and you were captured Tartars they would behave in the same way. Such people as these are always on the side of the victor, even though he might be last week's enemy."

Wondering what sort of officer this was, Kernow said, "You have a low opinion of your people."

"They are not *my* people, Englishman — and they would be the first to say I am not one of them. I am a Tartar. A Manchu. We took the throne of China more than two hundred years ago — much as the Normans once took the throne of England. But you accepted your conquerors and became one with them. The Chinese, in particular the Cantonese, have never forgiven us."

Shalonga's words astounded Kernow. "You have a remarkable knowledge of Western ideas — and of English history."

"Not English but French. My father is a great general, a war lord who rules on the borders of the country some call Annam, others the land of the Viet. We call it Vietnam. He has won many battles there, conquered much land — and acquired many women. Among them was a Frenchwoman, kidnapped from a trader. She became my father's favourite concubine. As a small child I would spend many happy hours talking with her."

"Did you learn to speak French?"

"I did even though it was forbidden. You too speak French?"

"It's my favourite language." Kernow responded in French and Shalonga beamed with delight.

"We will talk some more of this, Englishman."

It seemed Shalonga was about to ride off and Kernow asked quickly, "What do you intend doing with us?"

"Who knows? If I enjoy talking to you I might keep you here. Find you a few women, perhaps, and come to speak to you sometimes."

Kernow had a feeling the Tartar captain's reply was not entirely made in jest and he said hastily, "My ship will go back to Hong Kong and report our capture by you. My admiral will take action."

"So? You are on our land. China and your country are in dispute. His Imperial Majesty could protest that this is an act of aggression. He might justifiably order your heads be cut off."

"He could, but it would be a barbaric act. I came looking for missing sailors."

"The truth is often put to one side when diplomacy dictates it should be so, Englishman. Fortunately for you I believe you tell the truth.

Ah, here is the village headman."

The headman's low bow drew only a perfunctory nod of the head from the Tartar officer and he snapped, "It is possible some *Fan Qui* sailors were driven ashore by the great storm. Do you know anything of them?"

"I do. We captured them. Rounded them up like goats and handed them over to the *Tao-tai*'s men. There is a Viceroy's reward for the capture of *Fan Quis*. May I humbly remind you it was my message that led to the capture of these enemies of the Emperor too?"

"Send for the *Tao-tai* to come here."

The village headman paled. The *Tao-tai* was the district magistrate, a very important official in the rural communities of China. "I would not dare to *demand* that such an esteemed official come to my humble village."

"I would — and I do. Tell him Shalonga of the Red Banner would speak with him."

The name appeared to mean something to the headman and he bowed himself out of the presence of the Tartar bannerman.

As the headman departed, one of the villagers edged closer to the sailors. In his hand he held a heavy bamboo pole and there was little doubt of his intentions.

"Keep away, or I will turn the pole upon you." Kernow spoke in the Cantonese dialect. The man lowered the pole and backed away.

Shalonga turned and saw with some amusement that the problem was in hand.

"You wear the uniform of a soldier, Englishman, yet you speak the language of the Chinese as though you were a missionary. You also use the dialect of the Cantonese as though you were a Hakka. Did your father have Chinese concubines, perhaps?"

"No, he too was a soldier-sailor, like myself. Although he fought the Chinese twenty years ago I doubt if he had any concubines, Chinese or any other nationality. But you are right. I am learning Chinese from a missionary in Hong Kong. At the same time a Hakka girl is teaching me the dialect of the Cantonese."

Shalonga smiled. "I have seen some of your missionary women, Englishman. I think I would find learning from a Hakka girl more enjoyable. Come, we will find someone to cook food for your men and mine while we wait for the *Tao-tai* to come and explain his actions to me."

As he followed the Tartar officer, Kernow wondered when She-she would hear news of his capture and how she would take it.

17

THE district magistrate did not put in an appearance until the late evening, by which time Shalonga's patience was wearing thin. Nevertheless, he took pains not to allow his displeasure to show while he was conversing with Kernow. It did not surface until the magistrate finally arrived, and stepped gingerly from his carrying-chair to the mud of the village street. Dressed in expensive silken robes and wearing the hat and insignia of a Mandarin of the eighth grade, the *Tao-tai* carried the weight and the airs of a pampered Chinese official.

When the village headman hurried to the soldiers' camp to tell Shalonga the magistrate had arrived, the Tartar captain waved him away and continued his conversation with Kernow. He kept the magistrate waiting for more than an hour in the village street, by which time the local dignitary was furious.

When Shalonga finally announced his readiness to speak to the *Tao-tai* he kept Kernow with him. The presence of an unfettered and apparently unhumiliated *Fan Qui* in the company of the Tartar captain came as a great shock to the magistrate. When he recovered himself, he presented a shallow bow to the bannerman and announced himself.

"I am Ho-kin, His Imperial Majesty's

173

magistrate for this district. You wished to speak with me?"

Barely acknowledging the greeting, the Tartar soldier replied, "I am Shalonga, captain of the Red Banner regiment, sent by Imperial orders to serve the emperor and put down the rebellion of the Taipings. I *commanded* your presence. *Fan Qui* sailors, driven ashore by the typhoon, were given into your keeping. Where are they?"

The *Tao-tai* had already realised that his tardiness in obeying the summons of this apparently junior officer had perhaps been a grave error. Shalonga wore a golden sash about his waist which signified a close relationship with the family of China's Imperial rulers. It far outweighed his own very junior Mandarin rank. However, he was taken aback by the presence of Kernow and puzzled by Shalonga's interest in the fate of a few *Fan Qui* seamen.

"I have them in cages, exhibited for all to see."

"Why?"

The district magistrate was more than ever puzzled by such a question. "The *Fan Qui* are enemies of our people. They landed in an area that is forbidden to them and were captured. They will be kept on public view and then executed."

"They were driven ashore by a typhoon that brought destruction to Chinese and *Fan Qui* alike. You will bring them to me, here."

"They came to attack the people of the Middle Kingdom. This I know. One of their number has made a full confession."

"I would speak with the man who made such a confession. Where is he now?"

The *Tao-tai* dropped his gaze. "Unfortunately, he died only hours after signing his confession — but I have witnesses."

"Witnesses to a confession extracted under torture! How many more of the *Fan Qui* sailors have died in your hands?"

"Only three."

"Four *Fan Quis* dead and only a single confession?" Anger was mixed with Shalonga's mockery. "All your 'confession' will achieve is to bring the armies of the English to avenge their sailors. Who will be waiting to fight them and drive them back to the sea? You?"

The *Tao-tai* inclined his head once more. "I regret, I am a mere magistrate, not a soldier of his Imperial Majesty."

"You are a fool! Do you think the Emperor will thank you for bringing *Fan Qui* ships to sink our junks? *Fan Qui* soldiers to take our cities?"

"Surely with your brave Tartar bannermen to fight them off, we need have no fear of the puny *Fan Qui* armies?"

"You do not fight the wars, *Tao-tai*, neither do you usurp the powers of the Emperor by dictating policy. I and my soldiers are here to drive the Taiping rebels from lands that *Tao-tais* like yourself should have held against their depredations. You will order the immediate release of the *Fan Qui* sailors."

This was more than the district magistrate would accept, even from a man who wore a sash of the Imperial colours. "The *Fan Quis* were arrested in a forbidden area. The Viceroy himself has decreed that any foreigner found outside the Canton factories area must be arrested and put to death."

"Viceroy Yeh is a man who has washed his hands in the blood of a hundred thousand of his own people. His attitude towards the *Fan Quis* will as surely bring about the deaths of a hundred thousand more. You will order the release of the *Fan Qui* sailors, or I will send you to Hong Kong with this English Officer. He will carry with him a full report of how you deal with men driven by storms to the shores of your district. I will write it myself."

"You wouldn't dare. The Viceroy . . ."

"My father is General Tingamao. He will be in the province before the new moon. With him are fifty thousand bannermen, most of them Tartar horsemen. Such an army brings its own laws. Even a Viceroy would dare not dispute them. Viceroy Yeh will not raise so much as a finger to help you."

Tao-tai Ho-kin knew Shalonga spoke the truth. He accepted defeat with as much grace as he could muster. "I am sorry, Your Excellency. I was not told I had been summoned by the son of the great war lord Tingamao. I will go and arrange for the release of the *Fan Qui* sailors immediately."

"You will stay here and answer to me should anything go wrong. Issue your orders for the release of the sailors. Half my men will go with your messenger to bring the *Fan Quis* back here."

When the cringing magistrate had bowed himself from the presence of Shalonga, Kernow tried to thank the Tartar bannerman for his actions. He was waved to silence.

"What I told the *Tao-tai* was the truth. You are a *Fan Qui*. What would your people do if news reached them that the sailors who survived the typhoon were executed on his orders?"

"They would come upriver, destroy the Bogue forts yet again, and raze to the ground every village and town for miles around."

Shalonga nodded. "It is as I said — and more. In the event of such an attack I and my bannermen would be forced to take part in the battle. Until my father's army arrives we are not enough to defeat you. The only winners would be the Taiping rebels we have come here to fight."

Yet again Kernow found himself impressed with the sound forward-thinking of this Tartar officer. He wished that some of the officers in the Royal Marines and Royal Navy who were contemptuous of the Chinese character might have an opportunity to meet Shalonga. Unfortunately, the only time they were likely to meet would be in battle. At such a time neither side could be expected to appreciate the finer qualities of the other.

★ ★ ★

There were eight survivors from the Royal Navy frigate *Fury*. Thirteen had miraculously made their way to the Chinese shore when the

177

frigate capsized and sank, but five had died as a result of the beatings they had taken from the villagers and the torture inflicted upon them by the *Tao-tai* and his men.

Incensed by their weak condition and the stories they told of the brutal treatment they had received, Kernow protested to Shalonga.

Surprisingly, the Tartar officer shrugged off the complaints, saying, "They were treated no differently to a Chinese who is taken prisoner by a *Tao-tai*."

"Is that supposed to make it all right? It's *barbaric* — and you have the nerve to call us 'barbarians' and 'foreign devils'?"

"In China we would consider it bad manners to enter another's home, uninvited, and proceed to criticise the way he runs his household. I do not say that all we do is right, nevertheless it is our way."

"This is true, and you have saved the lives of these eight men — and the lives of myself and the sailors I brought ashore. I am sorry, Shalonga, you deserve my gratitude, not my censure. I *am* grateful, but I'd like to be in a position to deal with that *Tao-tai*."

"You would like to take him to Hong Kong with you? It would not be impossible to arrange."

Kernow opened and closed his mouth twice without uttering a sound, before saying reluctantly, "The admiral wouldn't thank me for handing him the problem of dealing with a Chinese magistrate. Besides, you'll have enough explaining to do as things stand now. It wouldn't

178

do to have to tell the Viceroy you've sent his *Tao-tai* to Hong Kong to face trial for torturing *Fan Qui* prisoners."

"I have no fear of Viceroy Yeh. More of a problem to me is how to return you to your own people in Hong Kong. I fear there is not a junk left afloat in the whole area. I will need to send to Canton. In the meantime, we will enjoy each other's company, Englishman. By the time we part I may be speaking French once more and you will be more familiar with the language of the Mandarins."

18

THE day after Kernow's capture by Shalonga, Hannah Jefferies called She-she to her office in the typhoon-battered mission hospital.

All lessons had been suspended and She-she and Kau-lin were helping Esme Pilkington in the very busy hospital kitchen. Since the destruction of the shacks on the slopes behind the mission, the kitchen had been kept fully occupied providing food for the survivors. They were also brewing tea continuously for the sailors and troops who had been sent in by the island authorities. The servicemen had spent all the daylight hours and much of the night searching through the debris for survivors from the worst typhoon the colony had suffered in living memory.

She-she was happy to be working at something she felt was useful. It also warded off her guilt that in the midst of such horror and devastation, she had somehow found a new and very special relationship with Kernow. It gave her a warm feeling deep inside whenever she thought about the night hours spent with his arm about her.

She had not felt this way about any man before and would never have believed it could happen with a *Fan Qui*! But Kernow was like none of the *Fan Quis* she had ever seen.

180

He was not hairy but smooth-skinned, like a Chinese . . .

Entering the office, She-she smiled at Hannah and an expression akin to pain crossed the missionary's face.

"Please sit down, She-she." Hannah motioned the Chinese girl to a chair. "I have something to say to you."

Disturbed by the missionary's manner, some of the happiness left She-she. As she perched on the edge of the chair she asked, "I do something to upset you? I make you unhappy? I sorry . . . "

"No, She-she, I don't think you've done anything wrong at all. I trust you — although I must tell you that I was disturbed by what I saw when I found you the morning after the typhoon. I felt you and Mister Keats were far too friendly. It's him I have brought you here to talk about."

"We do nothing wrong! I like him very much, but we do nothing wrong!" She-she was genuinely upset that something that meant so much to her should be misjudged by anyone — especially this missionary woman who had been so kind to her.

Hannah stood up and walked around the desk to She-she. Crouching before her, she took her hand. "I believe you, She-she. I really do. I don't doubt that you and Mister Keats are genuinely fond of each other. Unfortunately, it makes what I have to tell you even harder."

Squeezing She-she's hand tightly, she said, "Mister Keats was sent up the Canton River yesterday morning, to search for sailors feared lost in the typhoon."

She-she's eyes opened wide. "Something happen to him? He die?"

"I don't believe he's dead, She-she, but he went ashore and was seen to be taken prisoner by Chinese soldiers. I'm very sorry to be the one to tell you about this, my dear, but I wanted you to hear it from me and not from some complete stranger."

For many minutes She-she looked down at her lap, saying nothing. When she looked up again there was nothing in her expression to show the numb despair she felt inside as she said, "If he taken by soldiers, better he dead. Viceroy Yeh hates *Fan Qui*. Says all should have heads cut off."

Despite her fierce determination to be brave, tears welled up into She-she's eyes. As they spilled over and began to roll down her cheeks, Hannah said sympathetically, "You'd better return to the house for a while. I'll go and tell the others."

"No. Better I work, then no time to think. I go now."

In the kitchen Kau-lin was speaking to Esme when She-she came through the doorway. One look at her friend and she stopped in mid-sentence.

As Esme turned to follow her glance, Kau-lin hurried across the kitchen. "What's the matter? Is Mrs Jefferies cross with you about something?"

"No, she's not cross. She wanted to tell me

about First Lieutenant Kernow. He sailed to the Canton River to search for sailors lost in the typhoon. He's been taken prisoner by Viceroy Yeh's soldiers."

Kau-lin's face expressed the dismay she felt on behalf of her friend. Suddenly She-she let out a wail of anguish that caused every head in the kitchen to turn in her direction. Hurriedly drying her hands on the apron she wore, Esme advanced across the kitchen and held out her arms.

Gathering She-she to her, she said, "You poor child. I am *so* sorry. I know how much you think of him — and he of you. He is such a nice boy. Perhaps they'll let him go when they learn he meant them no harm."

"Viceroy Yeh never let go of a *Fan Qui*. I never see First Lieutenant Kernow again."

Suddenly, She-she pushed Esme from her. Turning away from the two women, she said, "We work now. Plenty work."

★ ★ ★

Late that same evening Kau-lin's cousin Chang came to the mission hospital. He had received a letter from Kau-lin's brother, the Taiping rebel commander. Writing from Nanking, the rebel capital, General Peng Yu-cheng disclosed that news of his sister's arrival in Hong Kong had reached him. He suggested both she and Chang should come to Nanking.

Because Peng Yu-cheng was a general and he and Kau-lin were distantly related to the Taiping leader, she would be welcome in the city. As Chang was a full cousin to Hung Hsiu-ch'uan — the *T'ien Wang* or 'Heavenly King', leader of the Taiping rebels — he was assured of high office. All Hung Hsiu-ch'uan's close relatives received privileges in keeping with their blood ties with the man who claimed to share divinity with Jesus Christ.

The conversation took place in the hospital kitchen, when the last large meal of the day had been cooked and distributed. Many of the Chinese helpers had left, but Esme was present during the discussions and as Chang spoke excellent English, she was not excluded from them.

As Kau-lin considered the proposal, Esme said, "It's a wonderful opportunity, Kau-lin. A chance to do something with your life. To *be* someone. After all, what is there for you here? What will you do if you stay in Hong Kong?"

"Mrs Jefferies wants me to become a Christian."

"The Taipings *are* Christians," said Chang. "I know they are not accepted by any of the missionaries as being *true* Christians, but they are eager to learn more. Your own brother says as much in his letter."

"What a golden opportunity!" enthused Esme. "On the ship travelling to China I heard military men talking about the Taipings. They declared they have the ability to conquer all China. Think of what would happen if they set out with pure Christian ideals. With God on their side they could not fail. It would be a true crusade, and victory would bring four hundred million souls to Jesus. How truly wonderful to be part of such a glorious army! An apostle for Christ in China!"

"You could be part of that army, Miss Pilkington." Chang had watched the enraptured Esme and now a more calculating expression replaced his initial astonishment. "The *T'ien Wang* — Cousin Hung — would welcome you. He too has a vision of a Christian China. Come with us to the Taipings, Miss Pilkington."

Reality momentarily took the place of fervour. "It isn't possible, Chang. I would need permission from Mrs Jefferies and from the Mission authorities. Even if it were given, which is extremely doubtful, how would I travel to Nanking?"

"Permission for what, Miss Pilkington? To go out and take Christianity to China? You already have it. This is why you are here in my country. Besides, what would have happened if all the great evangelists had sought permission for every step they took in going out and spreading the Word of God? There would have been no Saint Paul, no disciples . . . and who would have given permission to Our Lord? No, Miss Pilkington, despite all that others may say, I believe Cousin Hung was sent to earth as part of a divine plan to help my people. Take up the challenge with him and you will gain more converts than a whole army of missionaries could gather in a thousand years."

Chang's reasoning refuelled Esme's fervour.

"You're right, of course. I know you are. But without Hannah Jefferies' approval I'll never obtain the consul's permission to travel in China, and without it how will I get to Nanking?"

"I'll take you there, Miss Pilkington. You and Kau-lin." His glance shifted to She-she, and remained on her for longer than was polite. "You are Kau-lin's friend, why don't you come too?"

Kau-lin rounded upon Chang. "I haven't said I'll go yet. Anyway, why are you so keen to go to Nanking? I thought you were settled here as Minister Legge's number one convert. Mrs Jefferies told me you would one day be the mission's very first Chinese Protestant minister. Why should you want to join up with the Taipings?"

"For the reasons I have given to Miss Pilkington. I'm convinced that with the backing of the European nations Cousin Hung can convert the whole of China to Christianity."

"He might also become Emperor of China if he wins this war — this crusade. Do you expect to gain something in this world, or will you be content to wait for your reward in the next?"

"Cousin Hung has already suggested I might care to become one of his ministers. He needs men around him he can trust, just as our Lord needed his disciples. There is nothing to say I cannot serve Cousin Hung and God at the same time."

Chang returned his attention to She-she. "You

186

have said nothing in answer to my suggestion. What do you think?"

"I've said nothing because there was nothing for me to say. This is a discussion about your family and your family's religion. I have no place in either."

She-she's thoughts were still with the missing Kernow. She could find no enthusiasm for Chang's idea.

"I'll make a place for you. If we all go to Nanking, to the Taipings, will you come with us? You will be happy there, I am sure. Cousin Hung has great respect for women."

She-she knew very little about the Taipings. Until her arrival in Hong Kong she had thought them to be just another army of rebels, of which there were perhaps half-a-dozen in every Chinese province. The thought of a rebellious group being powerful enough to topple the throne of China was hard to believe. That she might hold a favoured position within such a group seemed equally far-fetched.

But there was nothing to keep her here now Kernow had gone. In fact, she would be relieved to get away from the memories that Hong Kong held for her.

"I will go if Kau-lin does, but I agree with Miss Pilkington. Without official authorisation it will be difficult to travel through China."

"We will travel by boat along the Yangtze river. But first we need to find a way to get to Shanghai. From there it will be a simple matter."

She-she thought that Chang was being unduly

optimistic about the whole idea. However, it was nothing she needed to concern herself with immediately. Before it became 'a simple matter' they needed to reach Shanghai — and that great city was a thousand miles away.

19

THE news that Kernow had been taken captive by the Chinese army horrified everyone at the mission hospital and all in the colony who knew him. Sally Merrill was among those who were particularly upset. The news came as she and her father set sail for Shanghai where he was to take up the post of United States consul. Her father could offer no glimmer of hope for Kernow's survival. The fate of Europeans who fell into Chinese hands at such times as these was well known. Consul Merrill doubted whether Kernow had lived for more than a few hours after his capture.

Even Nancy Calvin spent an extra five minutes on her knees at bedtime that evening. She prayed he might be spared the suffering that had befallen so many others who had ventured into China to help others and by so doing had found martyrdom.

Kernow's loss hit Arthur Calvin particularly hard. He had looked upon Kernow as his friend — and Arthur had never found it easy to make friends. Because he knew that She-she also grieved for Kernow, he spent more time than usual with the two Chinese girls. This did not please his mother and arguments between the two became commonplace.

One morning, when he felt he could take no more, Arthur decided to absent himself from

189

lessons at the mission hospital school. Leaving the house soon after the others had gone, he made his way aimlessly through Wanchai. A sleazy, Chinese-occupied area it extended along the waterfront to the east of the capital Victoria.

Wanchai was an area studiously avoided by the missionaries. This was where the merchant seamen and off-duty soldiers and sailors found their pleasures.

Hong Kong was one of the busiest trading ports in the world and the Chinese were astute businessmen. Once they discovered how off-duty *Fan Quis* enjoyed spending their money, they set out to satisfy their needs. Vice of all descriptions flourished here.

Wanchai had as many seedy beerhouses and brothels as any port in the world. Enough to cater for the sailors of the many ships anchored in the harbour — and they were enjoying a busy time.

The typhoon had raged across the South China Sea before devastating Hong Kong. Many of the vessels reaching harbour had been fortunate to survive. After such an experience, their crews came ashore with a single purpose: to celebrate being alive.

At midday Arthur was casually watching a cargo of livestock from the Chinese mainland being unloaded on the narrow beach when a boat from one of the merchantmen was run ashore nearby.

Half-a-dozen seamen, on their first visit to the colony, jumped ashore and looked about them with an air of eager expectancy. One of them spotted Arthur and called, "Hey, mate! Where can a bloke find a cold drink around here?"

"A cold drink *and* a hot woman," corrected one of the other seamen, prompting howls of agreement.

"I'm not sure," said Arthur, embarrassed as much by being singled out for their attention as by the question. "But I can find out for you."

Turning to one of the Chinese coolies who was driving a squealing pig up the beach by the simple but painful expediency of gripping the pig's tail and twisting it cruelly, Arthur repeated the seaman's question in Chinese.

The coolie gave directions to the 'best drinking house in Wanchai'. He guaranteed it to have 'clean women' and added that it was owned by a cousin who had spent many years as a sailor and whose sole aim in life was to bring happiness to the *Fan Qui*.

Arthur passed on this information and the sailors went on their noisy way, with the exception of the man who had made the enquiry about a beerhouse.

"You speak their lingo well."

"Not as well as some," replied Arthur, honestly.

"You come from Birmingham too, same as me, I think?"

"That's right." Arthur had recognised the distinctive accent when the man first spoke to him.

"What you doing here? You're not from one of the ships?"

"No. My parents are missionaries."

"You're kidding!" The seaman looked at Arthur in disbelief. He could see immediately that Arthur was not 'kidding' and added, "I didn't even know there were any missionaries out here. Come and have a drink with us. You can tell us all about Hong Kong."

Normally, Arthur would not have dreamed of joining a crowd of seamen in a beerhouse, but he had been wandering the streets of Wanchai for some hours. He was thirsty and hungry and felt desperately lonely.

"All right."

On the way to the beerhouse Arthur learned that his companion's name was Bill, and that he and his shipmates had not seen England for more than a year. They had also lost two fellow crewmen overboard when the edge of the typhoon struck the ship, a couple of hundred miles off the China coast.

Not all the sailors were pleased to have Arthur join them. However, when he spoke to the owner of the beerhouse in Chinese and succeeded in almost halving the price asked for their drinks, he was accepted as a useful member of the party.

Arthur had rarely tasted strong drink and before long his head was swimming. Fortunately, he did not particularly like the taste of either the gin, brandy or ale being swilled down by the seamen and so drank far less than any of them.

Soon after their arrival in the beerhouse they had been joined at their table by a number of Chinese girls. Each was drinking a highly coloured but innocuous 'lady's drink' on which they received commission. This was an area where all Arthur's persuasion failed to win a price reduction, although his knowledge of their language earned the praise of the girls.

At some time in the afternoon, the seamen announced they were going upstairs *en masse* with their young hostesses. Arthur was invited to go with them. When he asked what they intended doing they set up a howl of derision. Arthur felt a sudden urgent need to get outside in the air, away from tobacco smoke, alcohol fumes and more foul language than he had ever heard before.

Stumbling through the doorway of the beerhouse he weaved his way towards the mission house. He tried to walk in a straight line, but his gait was stiff-legged and jerky and he was convinced that everyone was stopping to look at him.

It was with a feeling of great relief that he eventually tripped through the doorway of the mission house. He had made it!

The stairs presented a more serious problem than had the streets outside. At his first attempt he missed his footing and fell down three stairs. He was trying again when Kau-lin and She-she, attracted by the noise, came from the kitchen and found him.

Kau-lin was filled with concern for him, "Arthur! Where you been? Your mother came back at noon. She said you didn't go to school this morning. What matter? You ill?"

"No, I'm . . . fine. Fine . . ."

He accompanied his words with a dismissive flap of his hand that would have unbalanced him once more had Kau-lin not been at hand to support him.

Suddenly Kau-lin turned to She-she who stood at the foot of the stairs watching in some concern. Wrinkling her nose she said to She-she, "He's not ill. He's been *drinking*!"

Both girls looked at each other in disbelief, then they began to laugh.

"What's funny? What you laughing at? You're laughing at me, Kau-lin. I don't like you laughing at me."

"Come, Arthur. Not laugh. Help you upstairs."

"His mother will be home soon. I don't think she will find it funny," She-she warned.

Kau-lin had managed to ease Arthur up two more stairs. Now she paused. "His mother must not see him like this." She hesitated for a moment, then said, "We'll put him in our room for a while."

"Is that wise?"

"Look at him. He needs help. He needs *friends*. You stay here in case anyone comes in while I'm upstairs. I'll be down as soon as I've settled him."

Settling Arthur was not as simple as Kau-lin would have liked. When he lay down he complained that the room was moving about him. Then he said he felt sick. Fortunately, he was not ill, but then he began apologising to Kau-lin for being such a nuisance to her. He came close to tears, and this she found hardest of all.

When Kau-lin eventually persuaded him to lie down on the bed and remain down, his mumbled apologies became quieter and less intelligible. When they ceased altogether she tiptoed across the room to the door. Arthur was asleep.

As Kau-lin came downstairs the missionaries returned from the school. Nancy's first thought was of her son.

"Have either of you girls seen Arthur?"

"Yes, came home this afternoon. Went out again. Said not feel like going school." Not looking at She-she, Kau-lin added, "I think he miss friend, Lieutenant Keats."

"That's no excuse for not attending school. I'll have something to say to him when he returns."

Hannah Jefferies was less concerned than his mother. "I think Kau-lin is probably right. Arthur's worked really quite hard recently. I'm certainly not going to get upset because he takes a day off once in a while."

Before Nancy could argue with her, Hannah said, "You haven't forgotten we're all attending a talk given by the Shanghai superintendent of missions tonight? We don't want to be late, Nancy."

Turning her attention to She-she and Kau-lin, she said, "I'd like you two girls to come too. I've told the superintendent a great deal about you both and he's expressed a wish to meet you."

Kau-lin grimaced, as though in pain. "She-she

195

will go. I would like to, but I have a very bad headache. I think it might be the weather. I hope there is not another typhoon on the way."

"We'll all say amen to that, dear. The superintendent will be very disappointed, but if you don't feel well then perhaps you ought to go and lie down. The weather has become terribly heavy again."

★ ★ ★

Kau-lin allowed Arthur to sleep until all the others had left for the mission superintendent's talk. It was almost dark outside and the house was quiet. She thought it an ideal time to wake him. She would tidy him and take him to his own room before the others returned.

Waking Arthur from his drunken stupor did not prove to be as easy as she had expected. He did not want to wake. But eventually, with the aid of a sponge and cold water, Kau-lin got through to him.

"That better," she said when he was sitting on the edge of the bed, his feet on the floor. "You have some tea now?"

"I don't know what I want — unless it's to die."

"Must not say that. No good to talk of dying. Why you like this? Why you go drinking? Who with?"

"Oh, shut up, Kau-lin," Arthur groaned. "You sound just the way I know my mother will when she catches up with me. Where is she now, by the way — and what's the time?"

"Time you went your own room while mother can't see. She go talk missionary man. All go. I stay, get you back your room before big trouble."

"Thank you, Kau-lin. I appreciate it . . . " He had trouble with the word 'appreciate' " . . . but there's going to be trouble whatever you do. I've decided I'm not going to the mission school again. I've had enough."

"You right. She make *big* trouble. Why you feel this way, Arthur? Who you drink with today?"

"I met some sailors, in Wanchai. They took me drinking."

"Ai-yah! You drink with sailors? Big surprise you come back at all. Where sailors now? Go back ship?"

"No."

Kau-lin was curious about Arthur's obvious embarrassment. "Where sailors go? Why you leave them, come back here?"

"They . . . they went off with some women. Wanchai women."

"Wanchai women very bad, but sailors like bad women. Why you not go with them? You no like Chinese women?"

"I . . . I like you, Kau-lin. It . . . I . . . I don't think I could have come back here and faced you if I'd gone off with one of those women. Besides . . . I wouldn't have known what to do. They'd probably have laughed at me . . . like you did when I was trying to climb the stairs."

It was a very honest baring of his soul and it had not come easy for Arthur. Kau-lin recognised it for what it was and she was deeply touched.

"You very gentle man, Arthur. I like you very much too — but I no good for you. Be plenty trouble."

"I don't care about that. You're the first girl who I've ever really liked. The first one who's ever said she liked me. It doesn't matter what anyone else says."

"It does, Arthur. One day you know that. But good for now, maybe."

Kau-lin reached up and laid the palm of her hand against his cheek. "I like you, Arthur. You like me. I teach you about women. You not be afraid again . . . "

* * *

When Nancy Calvin returned from the talk given by the Shanghai superintendent of missionaries she went immediately to Arthur's room. Her intention was to leave him in no doubt what she thought about his absence from school that day.

When she entered the room it was in darkness. At first she thought he had still not returned but when she lit a candle she saw him lying in bed, asleep. There was a look of contentment on his face that took her back to the days when he had been a child, entirely dependent upon her and content with his lot.

She stood looking at him for a long time before blowing out the candle and leaving the room as quietly as she could.

20

"HAD I known how things were going to turn out I would never have brought you to Hong Kong. You've changed, Arthur. You've changed enough to break a loving mother's heart."

Arthur had just told his mother he would no longer be attending Chinese lessons or religious instruction at the Hong Kong mission. Her reaction was more or less what he had expected.

The decision to announce the news at the breakfast table was deliberate. The presence of Hannah Jefferies ensured that his mother would need to hold her anger in check.

"I've not changed, Mother." Arthur spoke quietly but firmly, successfully hiding the turmoil he always felt when he opposed his mother. "It's you who refuses to accept that I've grown up. I'm no longer a small boy. I'm a man now."

"I'll believe that when you behave like one," snapped Nancy. "How are you going to live, have you thought about that? You'll get no money from me, and Mrs Jefferies won't have you living here. This is a mission house, not a poor house. I had hoped you would take advantage of your Christian upbringing and serve God as a missionary. Instead, you seem set upon throwing everything away and wasting your life. I just don't know what people will think, I'm sure."

"It's all right, Nancy." Hannah spoke soothingly in an attempt to head off yet another argument. "Arthur is right. He is a young man now. He must choose his own path in life. Like yourself, I hope he will choose the way of the Lord. But we *are* a Christian community here. Until Arthur decides what he wants to do, he must regard this as his home."

"Thank you, Mrs Jefferies. I hope to find some sort of work as soon as I can. Until I do I'll be happy to help about the house and garden."

Ignoring Nancy's snort of derision, Hannah stood up. "Good. Now that's settled we can all begin the business of the day. The superintendent of missions from Shanghai was telling me last night that they urgently need help there. He was asking me how well your Chinese lessons were coming along . . . ."

★ ★ ★

"You really want find work?" Kau-lin put the question to Arthur as she helped the two mission servants clear the breakfast table. She-she had gone to the kitchen.

"What I really want to do is be able to spend more time with you."

Arthur seemed to be everywhere that Kau-lin went. She felt that if she stopped moving for even a moment he would reach out a hand to touch her.

She stopped what she was doing and turned

to face him. "You say you stop taking lessons because of me?"

"No . . . well, not exactly. I'd had enough of being told what to do all the time. After last night . . . I want to be with you."

"You must work. Be own man."

"But if I leave the house to go to work I'll never see you."

"You see me. All same last night, you see me. Find work, maybe find house too. Be very important man."

Arthur had to admit that if by working he could have his own house, the prospect had infinite possibilities. Kau-lin might even consider coming to live with him.

"How do I go about finding work? Where do I start? I can't even think of anything I might be able to do."

Kau-lin realised that although Arthur had taken the first step towards independence, it was likely to prove a long road. He would need to lean heavily upon others for a very long time yet. Perhaps, like his father, he would always need to have someone else make his decisions for him.

"You speak Chinese not bad. Go see Cousin Chang. Everyone Hong Kong good friend Chang."

"All right." Arthur was once more almost within touching distance, but he came no closer. "Can we . . . ? Will I see you when I come back?"

"I stay this place. Here all time."

"All right. I . . . I'll go and see Chang."

Arthur left the room as though expecting, perhaps hoping, he might be called back by Kau-lin.

★ ★ ★

Chang was working on a translation of various Chinese letters for the Reverend Legge, but he assured Arthur it was work that could be put down or taken up at any time. He listened patiently to Arthur's rambling explanation of why he wanted work, before asking, "What can you do?"

"I'm good at figures, I write well — and I have a fair knowledge of Chinese."

"Ah! Then I might be able to help. A merchant, Pi Wang, has just begun trading in Hong Kong. He was telling me only the other day that he needs someone to help him trade with the British. Come, we will speak with him."

Pi Wang was an ancient Chinese with a thin, straggly beard. He looked as though he should have retired from all forms of work many years before. His appearance was deceptive. The Chinese trader was a very shrewd businessman and unexpectedly decisive. Within an hour of meeting Arthur, the two were travelling out to a mooring in the harbour. They were on their way to negotiate with the master of a merchantman for the purchase of a portion of his cargo.

After Arthur had read the ship's manifest and translated details of the cargo for his new employer, Pi Wang made offers for a great many items. Most were accepted and, on the way back to the island, Pi Wang expressed himself highly satisfied with his new assistant.

Arthur enjoyed his first day at work, but neither his mother nor Hannah Jefferies shared his enthusiasm. Nancy thought it was beneath her son's dignity to be employed by a Chinese trader. Hannah's reservations had a moral foundation.

"Pi Wang is a notorious opium trader," she explained. "When he was a younger man the Chinese governor of Kwantung Province put a price on his head for smuggling opium up the river."

"But trade in opium is legal," said Arthur. "All the European traders deal in it. For many it's their main merchandise."

"It may be legal," admitted Hannah, "that doesn't make it morally right. The mission societies have been campaigning against its sale for many years. It's a wicked trade."

"Of course it is," agreed Nancy, immediately. "Tomorrow you'll tell this Chinese man you can no longer work for him."

"No, I won't. I'll work for him for as long as it suits me. I'll decide what I'm going to do about helping him buy opium when the occasion arises."

Arthur did not have long to wait. An opium ship arrived in the harbour the following day. He and Pi Wang were among the first of the merchants to go on board. With Arthur acting as interpreter the aged Chinese merchant offered a good price for the whole cargo and the ship's master was happy to agree to a sale. If Arthur felt any qualms about his part in the deal, he said nothing.

★ ★ ★

When Arthur was paid for his first week's work he spent most of the money immediately, buying a jade bracelet for Kau-lin. It was not as expensive as the one She-she sometimes wore, and which had been a present from Li Hung, the Canton *Hoppo*. Nevertheless, it was dainty and pretty and he felt very pleased with his acquisition.

He needed to wait for another three days before the right opportunity came along to present it to her. Another missionary had arrived in Hong Kong en route for a well-earned leave in London and was giving a talk about her work. This time the missionary was from Ning Po, a city about a hundred miles south of Shanghai.

The Calvins had gone to the talk with Hannah and Hugh Jefferies. Esme was still in the mission house but she was in her room trying to teach the art of embroidery to She-she.

Kau-lin went about the house lighting lanterns and Arthur helped her.

When they reached the corridor outside his room, he asked Kau-lin to wait for a few minutes and disappeared inside. Moments later he returned and without a word held out the bracelet to her.

She took it from him. Then, looking up at

him in bewilderment, she asked, "Where you get this?"

"I bought it. It's a present."

"For *me*?"

"Of course." After a few moments' hesitation, he added, "It's the first present I've ever bought for a girl." .

Kau-lin circled her wrist with the bracelet and fastened the clasp. "It beautiful! I go show She-she."

She took no more than half-a-dozen paces before looking back. What she saw made her stop and turn around.

"I show She-she later. In our room." Taking Arthur's hand she said, "You want love me now?"

Not trusting his voice, Arthur could only nod his head.

"Tonight we go your room. I never been in here." Holding his hand, Kau-lin led him through the open doorway into his bedroom.

★ ★ ★

The missionary from Ning Po had just travelled from a city in which cholera had been rife for much of the summer — but she had not left the disease behind her. She had not been feeling particularly well since transferring from the ship bringing her from her mission station and no more than ten minutes through her talk she collapsed.

There was a suggestion that someone else might wish to give a talk in her place, but by the time the missionary had been carried from the hall no one felt like sitting through an impromptu talk. Doctor Jefferies accompanied the sick woman to his hospital and Hannah returned to the mission house with Nancy and Ronald.

There were no lights on in Arthur's room but Nancy could not find him in either the sitting room or the kitchen. Surely he would not have left the house at this time of night? Puzzled, she made her way to his room, thinking that he too might be ill.

Nancy's angry shrieks were heard throughout the house and brought everyone hurrying to Arthur's room. By the time the others arrived the screams had become an almost incoherent torrent of abuse. It was not necessary for her to explain her anger. The scene that met the eyes of the others was self-explanatory.

Kau-lin was shrugging a dress over her head. Arthur, his clothes strewn about the floor, sat up in bed. He held a sheet up to his chin and there was a frightened, glazed look in his eyes.

★ ★ ★

The debate in the mission house lasted well into the early hours of the morning. It involved everyone who lived in the house, including the unfortunate Doctor Jefferies. He had walked into his home at the height of the heated discussion after spending an exhausting couple of hours in a vain attempt to revive the Shanghai missionary.

Nancy Calvin insisted that Kau-lin must leave the house immediately. She accused the Chinese girl of being the chief culprit in the sorry affair. Nancy pointed out that a girl with Kau-lin's background could not be trusted around men — any men!

In this instance, Hannah agreed with her. Even taking into account her instinct for Christian forgiveness, it would be impossible for Arthur and Kau-lin to remain beneath the same roof. She tentatively suggested that he might find somewhere else to stay in view of the fact he had now found employment elsewhere, but Nancy would have none of it. Arthur had been led astray. He needed to be brought under a mother's influence once more. She would terminate his employment and bring him back under her protection.

Only Esme Pilkington took Kau-lin's part. Arthur was some eight or nine years Kau-lin's senior. If blame had to be apportioned for what had happened, then much of it had to be accepted by Arthur. He could not spend the whole of his life evading responsibility for all that happened to him.

Esme's declaration almost brought a physical response from Nancy, but by three o'clock in the morning a solution was found that was acceptable to all five missionaries.

Shanghai had made a formal request for helpers at their understaffed station. The missionary superintendent himself was returning there that very afternoon. Esme would go as a volunteer missionary. Kau-lin and She-she would accompany her as helpers.

Once the decision had been reached the two Chinese girls were called to the room and the proposition put to them. For the one it would be a last chance to mend her ways and take up a Christian life-style. She-she would go too because she insisted upon remaining with her friend.

Hannah was sorry to see the younger Chinese girl leaving the Hong Kong mission. She had high hopes for She-she's future within the Christian community. It was to be hoped that in their new surroundings she might prove a guiding influence on her friend.

No one deemed it necessary to call on Arthur to voice an opinion. No one even considered doing so. The unfortunate matter had been decided in a satisfactory manner by everyone who mattered. Nancy Calvin was once more making the decisions for her son.

★ ★ ★

As the anchor was raised on the steamship taking them to Shanghai, She-she said, "I am surprised Arthur did not come to say goodbye to you. He's not even at the jetty to wave."

"I spoke to him earlier today." Kau-lin did not say where, or how.

"Did he ask you to stay?"

"Yes, but I said that it would be no good for either of us while his mother was still in Hong Kong. I said if he wanted me he should leave her and come to Shanghai too."

"Wouldn't he come?"

"He could not make up his mind. Arthur is not yet a man. He is still his mother's boy. I told him so."

"You shouldn't have done that, Kau-lin. He is very fond of you."

"Perhaps." She fingered the jade bracelet. "But he is frightened of his mother more."

★ ★ ★

Through the high window of his room, Arthur could see the steamer on which Kau-lin was sailing. He imagined her as he had so often seen her — excited and filled with the joy of living. He also remembered the scorn in her voice as she told him he was a boy and not a man. It had hurt him far more than any of the abuse or criticism hurled at him by his mother. The pain had not yet subsided.

In the harbour the steamship sounded a farewell blast on its steam-whistle and Arthur knew that Kau-lin was about to depart from his life forever.

Awkwardly, he kicked the chair from beneath his feet. His last thought was that he could not even do this properly. Suddenly the chair fell sideways, the rope attached to a lantern hook in the ceiling snapped tight about his neck and slowly Arthur Calvin's brief unhappy life choked away.

21

KERNOW was returned to Hong Kong exactly a month after his capture. He and the sixteen sailors with him were passengers on a trading junk requisitioned by Shalonga. They arrived in the colony just in time.

A small fleet of men-o'-war had been assembled by Admiral Sir Michael Seymour. It was his intention they should sail up the Canton river carrying men of the 59th Regiment who were currently garrisoning Hong Kong. After destroying the Bogue forts en route, they would demand the surrender of Canton. Once it was in their possession they would hold the city until a satisfactory reply had been received about the fate of the missing men.

The arrival of Kernow brought this plan to a halt and caused a great stir in the colony. It also provoked considerable anger. Two of the sailors had not recovered from the treatment they had received at the hands of the *Tao-tai*. They had to be carried to the Royal Naval barracks, but were overjoyed to be back among their own people.

When news of their return reached Admiral Seymour, he sent for Kernow to report to him immediately.

Kernow was impatient to hurry to the mission to see She-she once more, but the admiral's summons had to be obeyed. Upon his arrival at headquarters he was shown to the conference room where all the senior army and naval officers on the island had been hurriedly assembled.

After shaking him warmly by the hand and congratulating him upon his safe return, the admiral called upon him to tell the assembled officers the story of his four weeks in the hands of the Chinese.

His story was received in a respectful silence, but there was an outburst of anger when Kernow spoke of the ordeal of the survivors of the frigate at the hands of the local Chinese magistrate.

When his story came to an end there was an eruption of talk among the senior officers.

Holding up a hand for silence, Admiral Seymour said, "I think we must all agree that Mister Keats has performed his duties admirably. Not only did he return without losing a single man from his own crew, but his actions resulted in the release of eight men who would otherwise most certainly have been put to death. The fate of their unfortunate companions must be condemned in the strongest possible terms. It was a series of barbaric acts against men who had just survived a shipwreck."

There was another upsurge of anger among the assembled officers and a red-faced army colonel said to the admiral, "Lieutenant Keats did damned well, Sir Michael, but the behaviour of this Chinese magistrate was inhuman. I trust we're still going upriver to teach him and those like him a lesson they won't forget?"

The admiral saw Kernow's puzzlement and explained, "I intend to carry out an attack on

Canton city, Mister Keats. Colonel Talland and the 59th are waiting to embark on the few ships I have available."

Sir Michael had lost more ships as a result of the typhoon than his great idol Admiral Lord Nelson had ever lost in an engagement with the enemy. Of those that remained to him more than half had severe damage that would take months to repair. Putting a fleet together had not been easy.

"My men are so eager to get at the Chinese they'll accept being towed upriver in open boats to Canton. When we're done the Chinese will think twice before murdering English prisoners again."

"With all due respect, Sir Michael and Colonel Talland, I believe it would be a grave mistake to attack Canton at this time."

For a young lieutenant to advise senior officers against a planned action bordered on the insolent. Kernow was painfully aware of this, but he believed he would be failing in his duty if he remained silent.

The explosion of indignation from the officers in the room made Kernow wince, but he kept his gaze steady as he looked at the admiral.

"Perhaps you would care to explain yourself, Mister Keats?"

"The father of Shalonga, the Tartar officer who saved my life, is General Tingamao, war lord of a great expanse of land along the borders with Vietnam. He has been ordered to march against the Taiping rebels. The army is already in Kwangtung province. An advance party arrived at Canton shortly before I left. They are actually encamped outside the city walls at this very moment."

"A few more Chinese soldiers, no doubt weary after a long march, won't deter my men, Sir Michael," the red-faced colonel boasted. "We'll deal with them first and then tackle Canton."

"We're not talking of a few soldiers, sir — and they're not your usual ill-trained bannermen. General Tingamao is an exceptionally powerful war lord. He has an army of fifty thousand men with him, most of them Tartar and Mongol horsemen. All are seasoned fighters."

Colonel Talland's face became a deeper red than before and Admiral Seymour said to him, "Your strength is less than five hundred, I believe, Colonel?"

The colonel tightened his lips, but said nothing in reply.

"You say this war lord has fifty thousand men? How did you arrive at this figure, Mister Keats?"

"It was given to me by Shalonga."

One of the senior officers uttered a derisive snort, but Admiral Seymour ignored the sound. Speaking quietly and evenly to Kernow, he asked, "You believe him?"

"Yes, I do," Kernow replied without hesitation. "When the figure was mentioned Shalonga wasn't trying to impress me. He gave it as a reason why neither the *Tao-tai*, nor Viceroy Yeh would risk upsetting him. The troops won't be remaining in the province for long. They're on their way northwards to fight the Taiping rebels but they'll certainly be around for a week or two. As I said, I've seen the advance guard, sir. They were well armed and well mounted. I'd be proud to lead such troops."

"Thank you, Mister Keats, I'm obliged to you. Colonel Talland, do you have any questions?"

The colonel shook his head, resignedly. "If what Keats says is true it puts a somewhat different complexion on the situation."

"It does indeed. Even your gallant regiment can't be expected to face odds of a hundred-to-one, Colonel. No, gentlemen, I think an assault on Canton must be held in abeyance until we are reinforced by regiments from India. By then this war lord and his army should have moved on and we'll be able to give the Chinese a drubbing they'll remember. In the meantime I'll make quite certain the governor conveys the British government's outrage to the Chinese authorities in Peking. To emphasise the strength of our feelings I'll send the fleet up the Canton river to reduce the Bogue forts, yet again. I think that will be all for today, gentlemen. I'll be calling another meeting for next week unless something develops in the meantime. Mister Keats, will you remain behind, please?"

As the officers filed out, Admiral Seymour spoke to Colonel Talland. "I think Mister Keats deserves your thanks, Colonel. Without his information your regiment would have suffered grievously. As it is, I'm confident you'll one day see 'Canton' listed among the 59th's battle honours."

Colonel Talland inclined his head in the young

Royal Marine officer's direction in response to the admiral's words. However, Kernow was left with the impression that, far from being grateful, the red-faced colonel resented the fact that his regiment had been prevented from tasting action before the walls of Canton.

When the only occupants of the room were Admiral Seymour, his secretary and Kernow, Sir Michael looked after the departing colonel and shook his head. "Sadly, we are all hounds of war, Mister Keats. Panting after the enemy in pursuit of honour and promotion. I fear army men are the worst of all."

Dropping to a chair, the admiral leaned back and stretched his legs out before him. "My faith in you was well placed, Mister Keats. Had it not been for your information, Colonel Talland and his regiment would have got a bloody nose, I would have been replaced as commander-in-chief, and British prestige would have suffered a severe blow. I'd say that's a remarkable achievement for a young officer. Wouldn't you, Charles?"

The question was addressed to his secretary who smiled. "I'd say we all owe him a great deal, Sir Michael — as indeed do the rescued seamen from the frigate."

"That's so. Your knowledge of the Chinese language has stood us all in good stead, Mister Keats."

"I was fortunate to meet up with Shalonga, sir."

"Indeed! He would seem to be a quite remarkable man. Nevertheless, not every young officer would have used the opportunity to such good advantage. I think the best thing I can do is to use your talents on my personal staff right away. Charles, you're always complaining of being overworked. How would you like to have Mister Keats as an assistant, aide-de-camp, or whatever you care to call him? He could take on special responsibilities for all interpreting. He'd be useful to you, I'm quite sure. He'd also be available whenever I needed him. The Provisional Royal Marines Battalion will be joining us from Calcutta very soon, plus two more battalions straight from England. It will make their commanding officers happy to know I have a Royal Marine on my staff."

"I'm deeply honoured, sir, but would it be possible to continue with my Chinese lessons, if only on a part-time basis, perhaps? Shalonga and I could converse well enough, but I realised my shortcomings. The greater knowledge I have of their language, the more 'face' I'll be able to command in my dealings with them. It's important not so much for me, but for you and for Britain, sir."

"Very well, Mister Keats — but I think we'll drop the 'Mister' if you're coming to work in my office. Your first name's Kernow, I believe?"

He nodded and the admiral continued, "I know all about Chinese 'face', Kernow. I agree with your reasoning, but you'll need to continue Chinese language studies in your own time. The language course at the mission came to an abrupt end while you were away. Some young fellow committed suicide up at Hannah

216

Jefferies' house. You probably knew the lad. It was over some pretty young Chinese thing, or so I believe. Anyway, the upshot is that the lessons have been cancelled. All the spare missionaries are being shipped out of Hong Kong as fast as boats can be found for 'em. Damned inconsiderate, of course, but I suppose we can't expect missionaries to behave like sailors — or marines."

22

HANNAH JEFFERIES was delighted to see Kernow safe and well. Yet even as she was giving him a hug of welcome she silently thanked God that She-she had gone to Shanghai with Esme and Kau-lin. The suicide of Arthur Calvin had rocked the Hong Kong missionary community. Hugh and Hannah Jefferies' mission station would not survive another such scandal.

The visit by this young Royal Marine officer to the house so late in the evening on the very day of his dramatic return to the colony was an indication of the strength of his feeling for She-she.

Hannah would have been even more concerned had she known how thoughts of She-she had occupied Kernow's thoughts during the long days and nights spent as a 'guest' of Shalonga.

Kernow's first words to Hannah were of the shock he felt at the news of Arthur's tragic suicide. He asked if he might express his sympathy to Nancy and Ronald Calvin. Hannah replied with the news that both had left to return to England only the previous day.

She realised this too was a blessing. The suicide of her only son had released a well of bitterness from some deep, dark recess in Nancy Calvin's soul. Such was the virulence of her language that Hannah realised the Birmingham woman was no longer suitable for missionary work. Certainly not among the Chinese, whom Nancy blamed for her son's death.

The chief target of her bitter anger was the absent Kau-lin. Kernow had been instrumental in bringing the Chinese girl to Hong Kong. It would have made no difference that he was merely carrying out orders. His safe return to the colony would have provoked an angry and distressing scene.

"Poor Arthur," Kernow said. "I feel guilty about his tragic death. Had I been here he might have confided in me. I could at least have helped him talk things through. He must have been a very unhappy man to do something like that."

"Sadly. Arthur was never allowed to be any sort of a man, Kernow. I cannot condone the morals displayed by Kau-lin while she was in this house, but she probably came closer to helping Arthur find manhood than anyone else. I fear that Nancy's greatest strength, and her greatest weakness, was the hold she had over her son. While she lived he would never have found fulfilment. Nancy loved him, I have no doubt of that, but it was a possessive love that has eventually destroyed them both. Now Arthur is no more and Nancy is on her way home, her life and vocation in ruins. I pray she will find consolation in God and in her husband, but I fear that at the moment she is convinced both have failed her."

"You speak of Kau-lin as though she is no longer in the mission." Kernow tried hard to hide the deep anxiety he felt. "Where is she

219

— and what of She-she?"

"They are both with Esme, in Shanghai. We ... I felt it would be better if Arthur and Kau-lin were parted. They were found together in Arthur's room, you know. She had to be sent away. It was all most distressing. A sin against the Lord, although certainly not one deserving the punishment Arthur inflicted upon himself."

"She-she?" Kernow was dismayed to learn she was no longer in Hong Kong. He had been certain she would wait for his return.

"She chose to go with Kau-lin." Hannah paused, wondering whether to say what was on her mind. When she did, her words were prompted not by expediency, but by true caring.

"She believes you dead, Kernow. It would be kinder if she continued in that belief. Not only kinder, but sensible. I know you are very fond of She-she and I was aware that she returned your affection. However, nothing good could possibly come of it. You are an officer with a promising career ahead of you. An involvement with She-she would put an end to your prospects. Oh, yes, you could take her as your mistress. I don't doubt she would be perfectly willing to come to you on such terms — but would you be happy with such an arrangement? You have seldom joined in our worship at the mission, but I believe you've had a Christian upbringing. Would your conscience allow you to take She-she as a mistress? I don't think so. By sending her to Shanghai with Esme I have given her an opportunity to find the Lord — and left you free to pursue your career. Leave it so, I beg you. Accept the situation as being in the best interest of both of you, Kernow."

"Is it written anywhere in the Bible that a Christian may not love a Chinese girl, Mrs Jefferies?"

"You're too young to know what love is, Kernow. Oh, you *think* you know, but love comes gradually, believe me. It is born out of respect and understanding. Contrary to the popular belief of the young, it is not something that falls from the sky armed with the right to chase away all other senses."

"Perhaps love, like religion, comes in many guises, Mrs Jefferies."

Hannah's expression contained a great deal of sympathy as she looked at Kernow. "I am saying only what a mother would tell you. Please think about what I have said."

"I realise you mean well, Mrs Jefferies, but I *do* intend seeing She-she again. I wish I could tell you what I'll do then, but I don't yet know the answer to that myself. Goodbye, and thank you for your kindness in the past."

"Kernow!" Hannah called after him as he walked away from the mission door.

When he turned, she said, "I might one day regret telling you this, but Chang, Kau-lin's cousin, will be travelling to Shanghai some time soon. He might take a message for you."

She had not changed her mind about the dangers of a liaison between Kernow and She-she, but if Kernow sent a message to Shanghai it would defer any rasher action. No doubt Chang would tell the girls of his safe return anyway. Acting on the spur of the moment She-she might return to Hong Kong without thinking of the consequences. Hannah intended speaking to Chang before he left Hong Kong. He was a sensible young man. He would realise the dangers of a relationship between the two young people. Hannah believed he too would do his best to bring it to an end.

★ ★ ★

Chang was leaving Hong Kong the next day, booked on a steamer sailing from the colony, but he was taking a roundabout route to Shanghai. He intended calling at the island of Formosa first. It would be many months before he reached Shanghai.

When Kernow was shown to Chang's room he found it crowded with European and Chinese friends, gathered to make their farewells. Kernow's arrival wearing full uniform caused a stir. For some minutes there was an uncomfortable silence until it was broken by Chang.

"Lieutenant Keats! I heard today of your blessed escape from the clutches of Viceroy Yeh's men. Very few Christians have been as fortunate. Everyone was very worried about you. My cousin Kau-lin, and Esme too. They are both very fond of you. But how kind of you to come and bid me farewell."

As the two men shook hands the others in the room relaxed and began talking once more. These were Churchmen and missionaries, their

222

talk solely of their calling, their hopes, and their despairs.

It was a world in which Kernow was an outsider. After half-an-hour of small talk, and two cups of tea, he excused himself.

As he had anticipated, Chang accompanied him to the front door of the mission. Along the way, Kernow said, "I wish you well in Shanghai. I believe you are hoping for ordination there?"

"The future of every one of us is in the safe hands of Our Lord, Mister Keats. I will do whatever He dictates."

"No doubt you'll be meeting Kau-lin and She-she? Please pass on the news of my safe return."

"Of course. They will surely be overjoyed to learn of your safe return." Chang said nothing of the roundabout route he was taking to Shanghai, or when he expected to arrive there.

Kernow fingered the silk sash he wore as he spoke once more. "Will you tell She-she in particular that I was very disappointed not to have found her here in Hong Kong upon my return? Tell her also, if you will, that her present was a constant reminder of her during my weeks in China. The Tartar army commander to whom I owe my life says I have her to thank for speaking Cantonese like a Hakka. Tell her . . . tell her we *will* meet again, I make this promise to her."

Chang bowed his head in acknowledgement of Kernow's words, but when the door closed

223

behind the young soldier, he remained deep in thought for many minutes.

For the duration of his thoughts the expression on Chang's face would have startled his Christian mentor.

23

ALTHOUGH Kernow was kept busy at Admiral Seymour's headquarters, his duties as an *aide-de-camp* and interpreter were far from onerous. He was able to keep up his Chinese language studies. Yet, on the first occasion he was called upon to perform duty as an interpreter, it was not Chinese he needed to speak — but French.

For very many years the Chinese authorities had provoked Britain and France in a series of humiliating incidents. Now, far away in Europe, the traditional enemies had reached agreement on joint measures to be taken against China.

Both countries could point to recent incidents to justify taking military action. In the case of France it was the harassment of her Catholic missionaries. A French priest had been arrested by a district magistrate and summarily beheaded, his head tossed disdainfully to the feral dogs.

The British government was still seething about the seizure of the crew of a vessel, the *Arrow*, when it was flying the British flag. Lord Elgin had been sent to Hong Kong with special powers to resolve the situation.

In October, 1857, Baron Gros, a specially appointed plenipotentiary, despatched by the French government, arrived in Hong Kong. He was accompanied by a French expeditionary force and escorted by a fleet of men-o'-war.

Members of the personal staff of Baron Gros were haughty and arrogant, but Kernow soon formed a cordial association with his French counterparts. A joint plan was drawn up between the two nations on salutary action against China. Military chiefs of both countries agreed that Canton would be a convenient target.

Most of those with business interests in the Far East were loud in their acclamation of such action. It was not before time. The Chinese had to be taught the elementary rules of Western civilisation — whether or not they felt the need for *Fan Qui* influence upon their ancient way of life.

There had been some apprehension about General Tingamao and his army. If he was still in the vicinity of Canton he had enough men to turn an Allied victory into defeat. Fortunately, intelligence reports reaching Hong Kong from mainland China suggested that he and his fifty thousand Tartar and Mongol troops had passed through the province in their pursuit of the Taipings. They were now many miles away, heading northwards to do battle with the Taiping rebels who held the lower reaches of the Yangtze River basin.

By December all was ready. Kernow boarded the flagship in Hong Kong harbour with Admiral Sir Michael Seymour. Wasting no time in weighing anchor, the ships carrying the British and French plenipotentiaries set off for the Canton river escorted by the combined French and English navies.

The Bogue forts had already been reduced

to rubble by a naval bombardment. Now the combined navies were bound for Honam Island, a river island close to the walled city of Canton.

When the destination was reached, the island was quickly overrun. The Allies had virtual control of the river and the British and French warships anchored bow to stern in a long and menacing line in front of Canton.

Now began a dangerous war of nerves. Training their guns on the city, the powerful warships threatened its million occupants with sudden and violent death.

Despite the menace posed by the European forces, for ten days the only action was a series of minor skirmishes against small bands of Chinese bannermen. Then, on Christmas Day Lord Elgin issued an ultimatum to Viceroy Yeh and the Canton city authorities. They must surrender the city within forty-eight hours, or it would be stormed by the armies of Britain and France.

The deadline arrived — and passed. From the occupants of the city there was a defiant silence.

Admiral Sir Michael Seymour wanted to begin a bombardment immediately, but, at Lord Elgin's request, the barrage was delayed. The plenipotentiary minister wanted to give the Chinese: 'An hour or two longer to ponder on their folly.'

The extension of the ultimatum proved futile. At 6 a.m. on 28 December signal flags were hoisted to the yard-arm on the Admiral's ship. Five minutes later they were lowered, and the bombardment of Canton commenced. Within a matter of hours the great wall of Canton city was breached. An assault on the main objective of the Allies was immediately launched.

Admiral Seymour, Charles Cavendish, his senior *aide-de-camp*, and Kernow watched in nervous silence as troops, sailors and Royal Marines formed up and marched towards the breached wall.

The fighting was fierce, but mercifully brief. By the end of the day British and French forces had taken the northern, strategically important sector of the city. To all intents and purposes Canton had fallen. The cost to the British and French had been only fifteen dead, with a further one hundred and thirteen wounded.

Sir Michael Seymour called for a halt in the fighting. He felt confident that a formal surrender from Viceroy Yeh would be forthcoming when he realised his city was in the hands of the *Fan Qui* armies.

The British Commander-in-chief waited in vain. Urged by Lord Elgin to have patience, he waited for a full week for the formal surrender of the city. Then his patience ran out.

Calling his various commanders together, Seymour issued an order for Viceroy Yeh's arrest. Kernow was present at the briefing and when the admiral had issued his orders, he turned to his junior *aide-de-camp*.

"This is your chance to see a little action, Kernow. Go into the city with the search parties. Question whoever you wish — but find Yeh and bring him back here."

Leading a company of about a hundred Royal Marines, Kernow plunged into the maze of streets inside the walled city. His was one of many companies entering the city through various gates, each striking for the heart of Canton.

On the river-bank, Kernow had spoken at length to some of the refugees who had fled from the city. As a result of what they had told him, he and his company made for a large house owned by the lieutenant general of the Tartar garrison.

Occasionally asking directions from curious but non-belligerent residents, Kernow soon arrived at the lieutenant general's house. Sending some of his men around both sides and to the rear of the spacious, detached building, Kernow entered without pausing to announce his presence.

In a passageway inside the house he was met by a distinguished, elderly Chinese man dressed in silken robes. The man bowed politely in greeting and said, "Welcome. May I ask what it is you seek?"

"We're looking for Viceroy Yeh." Kernow's reply was curt and pared of traditional Chinese etiquette. "I have reason to believe he is hiding in this house."

"You need search no further, *Fan Qui*. I am Yeh Ming-che'en, His Imperial Majesty's Viceroy for the province of Kwangtung."

Kernow smiled at the elderly Chinese. "A

worthy try, sir. However, unless I am mistaken you are in fact the lieutenant general in charge of the Canton garrison. I apologise for the manner in which I and my men have entered your house, but you must lay the blame upon Viceroy Yeh . . . ''

At that moment there was a shout from the rear of the house. Brushing past the disconsolate lieutenant general, Kernow hurried through the house until he emerged in a very attractive garden.

He was in time to see a portly Chinese, dressed in ill-fitting servant's clothing, being helped down from the high garden wall by some of Kernow's marines.

A sergeant said to Kernow, "We've just caught this man trying to make his escape over the wall, sir."

One look at the portly man's immaculately manicured hands confirmed Kernow's suspicions.

"Thank you, sergeant. The honour of capturing his Excellency Viceroy Yeh has fallen to you and your men. I can't help feeling that *true* justice might have been better served had you shot him down, but you have done very well. Very well indeed."

24

"**Y**OU seem to have found your way around Canton well enough, Kernow. Interesting city, is it?" Admiral Seymour, Charles Cavendish and Kernow were in the admiral's cabin on board the flagship. It was nightfall and the senior *aide-de-camp* had just produced drinks for the three of them.

"Fascinating, sir. It has a very long history. It's supposed to be the place where the Gods brought rice to mankind. I'd like to spend more time in the place."

Admiral Seymour and Charles Cavendish exchanged glances and the admiral said, "I think we can arrange that for you, young man. It's been suggested that the French and ourselves put a joint force of police into the town to keep order. A hundred Royal Marines and thirty Frenchmen is the figure agreed upon. It would obviously be a very great help if one of the British members of the force spoke both Chinese *and* French. That would seem to make you the ideal choice. I can't place you in command, of course. That will have to be given to a major, but you will be his adjutant. How does that appeal to you?"

It appealed to Kernow greatly, although his enthusiasm was dampened somewhat the next day when he met the man who was to be his commanding officer.

Major Thaddeus Kelly was a man whose reputation had made him a legendary figure in the Royal Marines. He had led men in action in the Lebanon and in Egypt, seen action in many other parts of the world, and had been rewarded for extreme bravery in an action up the Songibesar River in Borneo when a pirate stronghold was wiped out in a fierce battle.

But Major Kelly's reputation had been made many years before. His prowess as a fighting marine had not brought him promotion to the high rank he felt he justly deserved. He laid the blame for this at the door of men of 'good' family. Such men were able to use money and influence to gain promotion that should have gone to *fighting* men, like himself.

Major Kelly was now approaching retirement age. In recent years he had been drinking far too much and the alcohol served to fuel his smouldering resentment. There had been a time when fellow officers would have hidden his shortcomings from the outside world, but he had few loyal colleagues now. Most of those who remembered Kelly as a man of action had left the service. Newer officers saw only a man who drank too much, shouted too often, and whose judgement was frequently flawed.

This was the man who had been given command of the 'police' force brought in to maintain law and order in the walled city of Canton.

Kelly took an instant dislike to Kernow when the younger man arrived at the house that was to be their headquarters inside the city. It was late evening and Major Kelly was enjoying his customary drinking session.

"So you're to be my adjutant, are you, sonny? Well, this isn't a staff posting. You'll find things different with me. You can forget about sending men off to do your fighting while you stand on board the flagship wearing a fancy silk sash and holding a drink in your hand. You'll be leading your men from the front. We're here to keep these Chinese in order. If it means running a few of them through with a fancy sword, I'll expect you to set an example, you understand me?"

Kernow nodded. He and Major Kelly would have many differences of opinion about the way to carry out their duties in the Chinese city, but the almost empty brandy bottle standing on the table gave its own warning. This was not the time to discuss anything.

"Good. Now put your things in your room and get out on patrol. I want the Chinese to know we're here. They can expect to see us every time they turn around. What's more, they'll move out of our path when they meet up with us in the street. That's the only way to gain the respect of these people. They were defeated in battle and we mustn't let them forget it. Well, what are you waiting for? You've got your orders. Go out and get on with the job."

Kernow's first interview with his new commanding officer set the pattern for the days that followed. Kernow maintained a permanent night patrol, although this did not mean he was excused duties during the day. He was expected to help with administrative duties and receive

233

complaints and delegations from the officials of the Chinese city.

Late at night a few days later, Kernow and a patrol of a dozen men were making their way towards the main city gate. Suddenly they heard a commotion coming from a house not far from the building where the marines were housed.

Hurrying in that direction, Kernow was in time to see a Royal Marine in the midst of a crowd of Chinese. He appeared to be fighting for his life. Kernow and his patrol ran to the rescue. Snatching the marine, they beat back the angry crowd.

"What's this all about?" Kernow demanded in Chinese, speaking to a man who seemed angrier than any of the others.

The Chinese jabbed a finger in the direction of the marine, who was dusting himself down in a manner that suggested he had been drinking that evening. "Your soldier attack my wife. Knock her to the ground and rape her in front of my children."

"Do you have any witnesses to this?"

"*I* am a witness. So are my friends. They hear what is happening but are frightened to go near my home. They come and find me. I get home but . . . I am too late."

For a moment it seemed the angry and distraught Chinese would set upon the marine once more, but Kernow stepped between them. "If this is true the man will be severely dealt with."

Turning to the marine, Kernow said, "This

man has accused you of attacking his wife. What do you have to say?"

The marine looked at him scornfully. "I didn't attack anyone. She wanted me to do it."

"Have you been drinking?"

"What if I have? There's nothing wrong with that, is there?"

"What's your name?"

"Marine Halliday. I'm Major Kelly's batman."

Kernow did not allow his surprise to show. Speaking to the Royal Marine sergeant who was second-in-command of his small patrol, he said, "Keep him here while I go off and speak to the woman involved."

The angry Chinese man took Kernow inside the house and one look at the woman was sufficient to see the truth of the matter. The woman sat on the floor in the corner of the room, her back against the wall. She was crying. She also had a bloody nose, one eye was almost hidden by swelling flesh and her dress was torn from chest to waist.

She was surrounded by other women, all talking agitatedly among themselves. When Kernow entered the room they drew back from the woman to allow him through to her. She looked up and saw him and immediately began screaming.

Kernow had seen enough. Backing out of the room, he left the house, promising that the marine would be dealt with as he deserved.

In the street once more, Kernow had difficulty controlling his anger. "Sergeant, take this man back to headquarters and keep him under guard.

He's to be charged with rape."

Kernow was required to deal with one further incident during the first half of the night's patrol. It involved a trio of French sailors attached to the 'police' force who had been looting from a shop. Kernow made them return their booty and then sent them back to their own headquarters under escort. He doubted whether they would suffer any penalty. They and their officers seemed to take it for granted they had the right to confiscate anything that took their fancy.

Shortly before midnight, Kernow returned with his patrol to their headquarters for a meal break. As he entered the building he met the sergeant leaving in company with the two men who had acted as escort to Marine Halliday.

"What have you done with Halliday? I hope you left him under lock and key."

"No, sir. Major Kelly came in and told us to release him. Said he had some work for Halliday to do for him."

"Did you tell Major Kelly why Halliday had been arrested?"

"Yes, sir. He said the Chinese were lucky we hadn't turned the marines loose in Canton to rape *all* their bloody women."

"Where is Major Kelly now?"

"He went to his quarters, sir. Halliday went with him."

When Kernow knocked at the door of Major Kelly's quarters it was Halliday who opened it. Brushing him to one side, Kernow entered the room.

Major Kelly was stripped to the waist. Leaning over a bowl, he was swilling water over his head. Reaching blindly for a towel, he called, "Who's that, Halliday? Tell them to go away. I'll see them in the morning."

"You'll see me now, Major. I demand to know why you've released this man. I arrested him for raping a Chinese woman."

"You demand! You! Godammit, Keats, who do you think you are? Coming into my quarters *demanding*!"

Major Kelly was rubbing his face vigorously with the towel, but his cheeks owed their high colour to anger and not his ablutions.

"This man was sent here under escort. It's my intention to have him charged."

"Do I need to remind you that *I* am in command here, Mister Keats? I'll decide who's going to be charged and who isn't. I say that Halliday can't be spared right now. When he can, *I'll* be the one to say whether or not he'll face a court martial. And don't think you can go running to the admiral to complain about me. He sailed back to Hong Kong today. You'd better go now — before I put you on report for not being out on the streets carrying out the duties I've set out for you."

Kernow left Major Kelly's quarters fuming at the commanding officer's disregard for the very law and order he was in Canton to uphold. The smirk on the face of Marine Halliday as he let Kernow out of the quarters did not help his temper. He determined that the marine would not escape the justice he so patently deserved.

★ ★ ★

The next day a deputation of Canton city officials came to the small police force's headquarters to complain about the actions of Marine Halliday and the looting of the city by the French sailors.

They left with the wrath of Major Kelly ringing in their ears. He declared they should consider themselves lucky the whole town hadn't been burned down around their ears. It most certainly would have been had *he* been in command of the operation.

"Good, that's got rid of them. I doubt if we'll have any more complaints from them." Major Kelly opened a desk drawer and lifted out a bottle of brandy. "If we do we'll need to organise a few search parties, looking for hidden weapons in the houses of the officials."

"I thought we were here to keep order, sir. That's hardly the way to set about it."

"It's *my* way, Mister Keats. If I need an opinion from you I'll ask for it. Until then I'll be obliged if you carry out your duties with a little more efficiency, or I'll be forced to make a complaint to the admiral about you. All this talk of complaints reminds me . . . it's been reported that some of these so-called river pirates have been raiding houses down by the river. You can take a patrol along there tonight. See if you can catch some of them. That should make your Chinese friends happy."

"How many men shall I take?" The river pirates operated in large numbers and were

238

notorious for their ruthlessness.

"A sergeant and six."

It was a dangerously small number as Major Kelly must have realised, but when Kernow protested, he was told it was all the men who were available.

"You know how few men we have to spare, Mister Keats. After all, it's you who has been telling me about the breakdown of law and order on the streets of Canton. Off you go now, I'm a busy man. I expect to have a report on my desk in the morning that you have eliminated the threat of river pirates from the area."

25

"IF I was you, sir, I wouldn't try to argue with the major." The sergeant of marines spoke confidentially to Kernow as they led their tiny patrol along the river-bank in the darkness. "I've served with him a long time. He was a good soldier once. The best. But I've watched him go down over the years. He's bitter about not being given more promotion. I'm not saying he hasn't deserved it, but the answer to them sort of problems can't be poured out of a bottle."

"It's not *his* problems I'm worried about tonight, sergeant, it's ours. These Chinese pirates travel in strength, and they don't give up easy. I'd be happier if we had twenty-five or thirty more men."

"Never mind, sir. Just think yourself lucky you're taking marines and not soldiers."

Kernow allowed himself a wry smile in the darkness. There wasn't a good marine alive who didn't consider himself the equal of four or five regular army men — and Kernow did not doubt these were good marines.

"There are some huts a little way along the river-bank, sir. Shall we go 'round 'em?" The voice belonged to the marine Kernow had sent ahead in the hope he might prevent the remainder of the small platoon walking into trouble.

"No, I'll go into the largest of them and have a chat with whoever's inside. The remainder of you wait for me outside — and keep a good look-out. Our lives may depend on it."

The occupants of the hut chosen by Kernow had already gone to bed and his intrusion terrified them. However, Kernow soon succeeded in soothing their fears and he persuaded them to talk to him.

He sat across a candle-lit table from the head of the house while the man's wife and a great many children peered at him over the edge of their bunks, bedclothes drawn up as far as their dark eyes.

"I haven't come to harm you," explained Kernow. "I and my men are here to try to protect you from the river pirates. Have you had any trouble with them?"

"We have always had trouble from them," declared the fisherman, still not certain Kernow was telling him the truth about the purpose of his visit.

"Have they raided this area recently?"

"Twice in the past month," admitted the man. "It was not so bad the first time. They attacked the house of the *Hoppo*, but Li Hung had a hundred bannermen to protect him. They beat off the pirates, killing eleven of them. Then the *Hoppo* left and the second attack was on our village. The pirates carried off some of our women and killed two fishermen. They'll return again as soon as they learn there are no bannermen guarding the *Hoppo*'s house now."

Talk of the *Hoppo*'s house aroused Kernow's

interest immediately. This was where She-she and Kau-lin had lived. The key to their past lives lay here.

"Where is the house — and why has the *Hoppo* left? He has nothing to fear from our armies."

"He is an official in the Imperial service. Many chose to leave when they learned your ships were coming upriver from Hong Kong. But you will find his secretary still at the house. It is just along the river from here. The large house with a walled garden."

"Thank you." Kernow stood up and smiled at the faces staring at him from all sides of the room. "I am sorry for disturbing you and your family, but you may sleep more peacefully knowing we are near at hand."

The Chinese man bowed Kernow from his house, but just before closing the door called into the darkness after him: "We have taken precautions against the pirates that you might find useful. There are bells strung on ropes and tied to stakes in the water at each possible landing place. Any boat coming close to land in the darkness will strike one of these. They are not loud, but an alert man will hear."

"I'll remember."

"What was that all about, sir?" The sergeant's voice carried the respect of one who had difficulty with his own language for a man who had mastered at least two others.

"He was telling me there's been a pirate raid on the house of the Chief Customs official. The local fishermen are expecting another. I think

242

we'll make our way there."

On the way to the *Hoppo*'s house Kernow told the sergeant and his men about the bell warning system laid out by the fishermen. "They'll do nothing to stop anyone coming in, but it should give us sufficient warning to have a surprise waiting for anyone who tries to land."

Kernow felt he had sufficient justification for going to the Canton *Hoppo*'s house now, but he would have found an excuse for going there anyway. He wanted to learn all he could about She-she.

The moon was playing hide-and-seek among some high clouds when they reached the *Hoppo*'s house, but there was sufficient light for Kernow to see. It was a very impressive building with long gardens that extended for hundreds of yards to the riverbank. It would be a natural target for any river pirates bold enough to mount an attack on the home of a high Imperial official.

There was a stout gate to the grounds and it was guarded by a watchman who was reluctant to allow Kernow and his men inside. He was eventually persuaded to open the gate, but not until he had sent a sleepy-eyed young lad from the gatehouse to warn Secretary Po that he had *Fan Qui* visitors.

Once inside, Kernow sent the sergeant and five men to the river-bank, to keep watch there until he sent for them, keeping only one man with him as a personal escort. Through the grille-bars of the gate he could see a light in one of the rooms and someone moving around inside. By the time he reached the front door the man was dressed and waiting for him.

"Welcome to the house of Excellency Li Hung, His Imperial Majesty's *Hoppo* of Canton. I regret His Excellency is not at home to receive you."

Secretary Po's English was good, but he spoke slowly and precisely, as though he was unused to conversing in the language.

"My apologies for the lateness of the hour," Kernow replied in Chinese. "We are carrying out patrols to deter river pirates. As this house has already been attacked and is likely to be a target again I thought I should come to speak to you."

"That is most thoughtful of you. I must compliment you on your command of our language. It is most refreshing to find one of your people who has taken the time to learn it so well."

Secretary Po was almost gushingly polite, yet Kernow had an uncomfortable feeling that this man liked Europeans no more than did the captured Viceroy Yeh.

"Please, you will come inside and take some tea with me?"

"Thank you. My men will remain close to the river while I am in the house."

"Ah, yes, the pirates. It is possible they will attack the house again, but very unlikely they will be able to force an entrance. You will observe, every window has bars outside and heavy shutters within. There are also small

244

holes through which a gun might be fired at them. If you look more closely you will see the doors are fitted with much iron. It would need a cannon to break them down."

"You are very wise to take such precautions. No doubt Li Hung has a great deal to protect. Has he taken his family away with him?"

"I alone am left, with the servants. A *Hoppo* can fulfil few duties when there is war. I trust he may soon be able to return."

"The wish of my government is for more trade, not less . . . "

At that moment both men heard a commotion in the garden. It was coming from somewhere in the direction of the river.

Kernow said quickly, "Go inside the house and secure the doors. I'll find out what's happening."

He was halfway to the river when he met one of the marines hurrying towards the house.

"We've caught someone landing in the garden, sir. Them bells you told us about started tinkling and the next minute a sampan came in to the bank."

"Is it pirates?"

"I don't think so, but the sergeant caught 'em. It seems to be a man and a girl, that's all."

Kernow relaxed. "They're probably only fishing. But tell the sergeant to bring them up to the house. If they've come in off the river they might have seen or heard something."

Kernow reassured Secretary Po that all was well and as the two men stood in the doorway a man accompanied by a girl was escorted to the house.

As the two passed through the light slicing from a window, Kernow received a shock. For a moment he thought this girl was She-she. When she reached the door he realised she was at least a year or two younger, but the likeness was uncanny.

The man bowed low to Secretary Po, but the *Hoppo*'s cousin was less than polite in his response. "What do you mean by trespassing in the gardens of the *Hoppo*'s home? Does your foolish head mean so little to you that you put it at risk in such a manner?"

"I am not trespassing, Excellency. I came here to beg to speak to the *Hoppo*, out of concern for my daughter."

"The *Hoppo* is not here. I am his secretary. But what is this nonsense? What would Li Hung have to do with a Hakka girl?"

"She is one of his concubines. The chief eunuch of his household came to my village and chose her. I was given the post of head boat man on my part of the river because of this."

"Your daughter, what is her name?" Kernow put the question to the man, although he believed he already knew the answer.

The man was startled to hear a *Fan Qui* speaking his own language and he looked at Secretary Po, not replying until Po inclined his head.

"Her name is She-she. Li Hung's chief eunuch took her from my home to bring her here. I missed seeing her leave because I was busy in the

246

Hoppo's service. I wept bitter tears because of it — but her sister was there. She will tell you I speak the truth. When we heard of the war here, at Canton . . . " There was a sidelong glance at Kernow once more. "I had to come. I gave her to Li Hung, but I am still her father."

"You are a fool! Li Hung has the choice of every daughter in the Province. Why should he choose a Hakka? Yes, I remember She-she, but she was not a concubine. She was a blue dress girl. A servant kept by Li Hung to entertain his guests. She is no longer here. I doubt if she is even alive. She was sent to Foochow with the other blue dress girls but the junk carrying them was sunk by a *Fan Qui* ship. Some of the girls were saved, but no one knows how many. Go home, old man. Be happy that you have the honour to be in the *Hoppo*'s employ. Go and work hard for the benefits he has given to you."

As Secretary Po turned away, She-she's father let out an uninhibited wail of anguish and staggered away into the darkness, pursued by his young daughter.

"Wait!" Leaving the startled secretary behind, Kernow set off after the grief-stricken man, guided by the noise he made as he blundered through the shrubbery.

They were well away from the lights of the house by the time Kernow caught up with father and daughter. It was doubtful whether the man even knew he was being followed until Kernow reached out and caught him by the arm.

"Wait. She-she is not dead. She's all right."

The man was still wailing so loudly it was doubtful whether he heard Kernow — but the girl did.

Taking her father's other arm she pulled him roughly to a halt. "Father, listen to the *Fan Qui*. He says She-she is not dead. She-she is alive."

The young girl's shrill voice broke through her father's grief. "How would a *Fan Qui* know about She-she?"

"I know because I took her to Hong Kong after the *Hoppo*'s junk was sunk. She spent some time there and then went on to Shanghai. She is there now."

There was a long silence before She-she's father spoke again in a hoarse whisper. "This is true? You do not lie?"

"Why should I want to lie? She is well. The missionary doctor and his wife at Hong Kong thought very highly of her. I have spoken to her very many times. You see this sash I wear? She-she made it for me, for my birthday. She is well and happy and will be very much happier when I meet her again and tell her I have spoken to you."

"You will do this? You will tell her I came here out of concern for her?"

"Of course."

She-she's father was silent for a long time, then he reached out and gripped Kernow's arms. "I do not understand why she is not a concubine. I was told . . . but it does not matter now, she is alive and well. This is enough. Tell her I wanted to see her before she left our home but there was an accident on the river. Two men died. I had to search for them."

"I will tell her."

"One more thing, *Fan Qui*. Do not tell her I know she is not a concubine of the *Hoppo* Li Hung. That would make her very unhappy."

"I will say nothing that might make She-she unhappy, I promise you. But you need feel no shame for her. She did not spend enough time in the *Hoppo*'s house to learn what went on here. Her friend has told me so."

"I will return home with Hau-ming now, *Fan Qui*. I thank you. I have done all I came to do. She-she's mother will be happy to know her daughter is well. She was very worried when she heard about the war."

"Why not stay here for the night and travel on in the morning?"

"It is better to travel at night on the river. There are many pirates, and Hau-ming will soon be as beautiful as her sister."

"That is true. When I saw her in the light of the window I thought I saw She-she. You are fortunate indeed to have such daughters."

Kernow saw the whiteness of Hau-ming's teeth in the darkness as she smiled at him.

"I thank you, *Fan Qui*. If it is within your power, I beg you to take care of She-she. For the sake of a father, as you will also one day surely be."

"I will take care of her always. This I promise you."

She-she's father walked away in the darkness, heading for the river. Kernow thought the girl had gone too, but suddenly she stood before

249

him again and pressed something into his hand. "Please, you will give this to She-she?"

"What is it?" It felt like a polished stone pendant, on a thin leather cord.

"It is mine. She-she always admired it. Give it to her and she will know you tell the truth about meeting her father and her sister."

The girl was gone again in an instant, but suddenly her voice came back softly to Kernow. "Tell She-she also that I am glad she has found the sort of man we used to talk about. You may be a *Fan Qui*, but I would rather have you than some fat old *Hoppo*."

26

THE morning after Kernow's meeting with She-she's father and sister, the Royal Navy removed the immediate threat of a pirate attack on the riverside communities. A steam-gunboat on routine patrol discovered two pirate junks sheltering in a creek only a couple of miles downriver from Canton city. After a brief and one-sided exchange of fire, one junk exploded in a spectacular manner when a shell landed in its store of gunpowder. Minutes later both Chinese vessels were destroyed.

Many pirates were killed in the battle but half-a-dozen were brought captive to Canton and Kernow questioned them about their activities. He learned that the presence of the British and French fleets had frightened most pirates from the area. They had moved their operations farther along the coast. Pickings were leaner there, but the risk of death or capture, which amounted to the same thing, was reduced accordingly.

The pirates of the two junks found by the gunboat had chosen to remain and take their chances against the allied navies. It was one of these ships that had raided the *Hoppo*'s house and the fishermen's homes along the river bank.

After the pirates had been questioned, Major Kelly ordered that they be handed over to the magistrate of Canton. It was tantamount to a sentence of death upon each of the men, but even Kernow could not find it in his heart to protest on this occasion at his commanding officer's action. River pirates were ruthless and savage outlaws and these were no exception. Sailors from the gunboat had gone on board the surviving junk before it foundered and had found the bodies of two young captive women. Their throats had apparently been slit when the British gunboat opened fire.

Kernow's questioning of the pirates occurred at a time when he would normally have been sleeping. He was desperately tired after his long night duty and decided to return to bed to snatch a couple of hours sleep before returning to duty that night.

His rest did not last for very long. He was awakened by an urgent hammering at his door. As he fought his way to wakefulness, a voice called: "Lieutenant Keats! Lieutenant Keats. Wake up. We've trouble, sir. Big trouble!"

The room was in darkness. Still half asleep, Kernow knocked over a small table on his way to the doorway. Pulling the door open he saw a young Royal Marine outside in a state of nervous excitement.

"What is it? What's happening?"

"We've a riot on our hands in the street around the corner, sir. A marine's been killed. Major Kelly's gone there and taken some men with him, but the duty sergeant told me to come and fetch you."

Even as the marine was explaining the nature

of the emergency, Kernow was pulling on his clothes. Moments later, still buckling on his sword belt, he and the young marine left the building at the run. On the way they gathered up a dozen armed marines coming in off another street patrol.

The sounds of an angry crowd reached them as they approached the street where only a few days before Kernow had arrested Major Kelly's batman.

When they turned the corner they saw a seething mass of Chinese. Most were crammed into a small area halfway along the street surrounding Major Kelly and perhaps another dozen Royal Marines. Conspicuous by their red coats, the marines had a house wall to their rear and a crowd of some two or three hundred Chinese about them, hemming them in.

With the patrol were two Chinese men, apparently prisoners. All the marines had bayonets affixed to their rifles and only by making free use of these were they successfully holding the hostile crowd at bay.

"Fix bayonets and form a line across the road," Kernow snapped the order to his men. He knew he needed to rescue Major Kelly and his men before the sheer weight of the Chinese pushing forward overwhelmed them. Kelly and his men might kill a few of the rioters, but it would earn them only a brief respite.

Standing at the centre of his thin line of men Kernow said, "When I give the order those men on my left will fire over the heads of the crowd and reload as quickly as possible. Then we'll advance and clear the road."

The crowd was shouting for the head of Major Kelly as Kernow and his party advanced. He quickly realised that a diversion was urgently needed.

"Ready? Fire!"

The shots rang out above the noise of the crowd and every head turned towards the newly arrived marines. Suddenly, those at the rear of the crowd, who had been ready to sacrifice the lives of those in front of them for the opportunity to take a *Fan Qui* head, were less certain. Now they ran the risk of being among the first to be killed the situation had changed dramatically.

"Advance! Slowly now. We'll get closer and then take aim at the crowd. That should make them start moving."

Kernow and his dozen men moved slowly towards the crowd and there was a barely perceptible movement away from them. Kernow saw it and knew he could end this riot without further trouble. But fate, in the form of Major Kelly, decreed otherwise.

The Chinese closest to the major and his marines had heard the volley of shots, but the mass of the crowd was between them and whatever was going off elsewhere in the street. Their confrontation was still with the *Fan Qui* marines trapped in their midst. The newcomers posed no threat to them.

One of the Chinese who had been particularly vociferous continued to hurl abuse at Kelly and his men. Had the major remained calm, all would have been well. But the arrival of

254

Kernow and marine reinforcements had changed the extremely dangerous situation he was in. The major suddenly let out a shout and lunged at his tormentor.

Instead of trying to escape, the Chinese grabbed Major Kelly and pulled the Royal Marine officer towards him. The crowd closed in about them in an instant. There was a flurry of arms, the flash of a steel sword and suddenly the scarlet figure disappeared from view.

As the major's patrol bayoneted its way towards their commanding officer, Kernow's line of marines came to a halt. At his command they fired a volley into the crowd that left seven men sprawled in the street.

Moments later the crowd broke and fled when the line of Royal Marines charged them with bayonets fixed, but it was too late to save Major Kelly. He lay in a rapidly spreading pool of blood where he had fallen, his jugular vein severed by the first sword stroke that had been struck.

There were other casualties. Seventeen Chinese men died in the rioting and two Royal Marines were wounded. Another marine lay dead in a nearby doorway. The dead man was Marine Halliday, Major Kelly's batman, and it transpired that he had been the cause of the riot.

The story came out when Kernow questioned the two Chinese men held by the party of marines who had been with Major Kelly.

Halliday had not learned from his earlier encounter with the Chinese. After another drunken spree, he and two companions made their way to the house where the woman he had raped lived. When they tried to force their way in the woman's husband attacked Halliday with a meat cleaver, urged on by a gathering crowd of friends.

Suddenly far more sober than they had any right to be, Halliday's two friends fought their way through the Chinese and fled to the headquarters of the Royal Marines police. Here they gasped out the information that Halliday was being attacked by a rioting mob.

The duty sergeant advised Major Kelly to call in at least half a company of his men before taking any action, but Kelly had been drinking heavily. He boasted to the sergeant that with no more than half a company of Royal Marines he could take Peking, if the opportunity arose. It needed no more than a dozen men to put down a riot.

Major Kelly paid for his drunken bravado with his life. The next day he was given a funeral that was all he would have wished. Every marine from the fleet anchored off Canton paraded for the ceremony. The senior chaplain's eulogy dwelled on the hero he had been, rather than the drunken, embittered officer he had become.

The parade of Royal Marines was meant as a show of strength to deter any future rioters and it was indeed impressive, but Kernow doubted whether the British 'police' force in Canton would have any more trouble.

Shortly before the funeral he had called a meeting with the Cantonese authorities. Between them they had thrashed out an agreement whereby the Chinese authorities would continue to administer the city, but with the aid of the British and French 'police' — and the commanding officer of the joint force would be the ultimate authority in any dispute.

It was a satisfactory solution and one Kernow believed Admiral Sir Michael Seymour would find acceptable. Nevertheless, waiting outside his cabin on board the flagship, upon the admiral's return upriver, Kernow wondered whether he might not have greatly exceeded his authority. Such an arrangement should not have been made without consulting the commander-in-chief first.

He need not have worried. Lord Elgin was in the cabin with the admiral and it seemed he and his advisers had already decided to adopt a very similar form of 'government' for the city. The only difference they had in mind was that the British and French would leave a small, diplomatic mission in the city to assist the authorities in the administration of Canton. There would also be Royal Marines Light Infantry encamped outside the town to back up any unpopular measures the mission might feel were necessary.

"Will I be remaining with the force policing Canton, Sir Michael?"

Kernow asked the question hopefully. Despite his experience during the recent riot he liked the people of the city. He felt he could make a worthwhile contribution to the maintenance of law and order here. He also secretly hoped that despite his age and lowly rank he might be given an opportunity to retain command of the British 'police' force.

But it was Lord Elgin who dashed Kernow's hopes.

"The new commanding officer of the force in Canton has already been appointed, Lieutenant Keats. He will be assisted by two of the men from my mission who are fluent in Chinese. However, Sir Michael and I are very impressed with your conduct in this unfortunate matter. You kept a cool head and forged a most important link with the city authorities. I think your qualities might prove of use to us in the weeks ahead."

It was fulsome praise from the British minister, but Kernow was no clearer about what lay ahead for him. It was left to Admiral Seymour to explain what Lord Elgin had in mind.

"You're returning to duties as my aide, Kernow — and you'd better brush up on your *Imperial* Chinese. Lord Elgin intends to be received by the Chinese government in Peking. Meanwhile we're all going to Shanghai while the details are worked out. Who knows, you might be the first Royal Marine to meet His Imperial Majesty, the Emperor of China."

Book Two

1

THE steamer carrying Esme Pilkington, She-she and Kau-lin took five days to make the voyage from Hong Kong to Shanghai. Among the other passengers was an alert and sun-tanned American adventurer who was not slow to strike up an acquaintance with the Englishwoman and her two companions.

Erin Veasey was a man who, in another time and another place, might have been a privateering captain paying allegiance to Queen Elizabeth I of England. Master of a sailing barque, he had been trading arms in the Manila Islands when a typhoon, similar to the one which struck Hong Kong, had driven his boat ashore on a remote island.

Unlike many men of his type, Veasey had his vessel adequately insured. Obtaining the insurance money had taken him longer than he would have liked, but he was now on his way to pick up a new trading vessel at Shanghai. This one was a steamer, less reliant upon the vagaries of the weather.

All this he told Esme after introducing himself to the members of the small party as they strolled on deck, the first day out from Hong Kong.

"Doesn't it bother you to sell the means by which unsophisticated natives can kill one another, Mister Veasey?" As was her way, Esme openly expressed the disapproval she felt at his way of life.

"No, ma'am, I have to admit it does not. I look at it this way. My guns kill far fewer men than the opium sold by your British traders, and they cause a sight less misery to their families. Most of the guns are used for hunting, preventing a great many children from starving. Besides, from what I've seen of the native people in these parts, they don't get to fighting with each other until someone puts the idea in their heads. If you'll pardon me being so downright blunt, ma'am, they've had a darn sight more to fight about since we started trying to stuff religion into their heads than they ever had before."

"Mr Veasey!" Esme bristled with indignation. "We bring the word of the Lord to heathen people — and the word of the Lord is 'Peace'."

"I wouldn't dream of suggesting you were anything but well intentioned, ma'am, but it seems to me things don't always work out the way you want. You take the Taipings now. They have a claim on Christianity and you might expect that christian countries would be eager to give them support. Yet, as far as I can see, there's no Christian religion holding out its arms to welcome *them* to the fold."

"The Taipings have a somewhat distorted view of Christianity, Mr Veasey. However, I accept your point. Nevertheless, attitudes can change. They certainly will if I have my way. I would like to see Christian missionaries flocking to the Taipings and showing them the right way of worshipping Our Lord."

"You're not thinking of taking a mission to them yourself, ma'am?"

"And why not? I certainly won't be able to do anything to help unless I go among them. I have no fear for myself. I believe they have considerable respect for women."

Erin Veasey inclined his head. "I believe they do."

"Besides, Kau-lin has a brother among them. He's a general, no less."

Erin Veasey's interest quickened noticeably. "Is that so? What's the name of this brother of yours, Kau-lin?"

"Peng Yu-cheng."

"You're a sister of Peng?" Erin's expression showed both surprise and interest. "You do him less than justice by calling him a general. Peng is a 'commandant', the highest rank in the Taiping army. Not only that, he's one of the best leaders they have. A man of sound common sense, and that's a rare quality in any soldier."

"You know Peng?" Kau-lin displayed a childish delight.

"We've met," Erin said gruffly.

"So you sell arms to the Taipings too?" Esme spoke accusingly.

"I have in the past, ma'am." The American refused to go on the defensive. "If you've an interest in the future of the Taipings you'll realise that *someone* has to get arms to them. If the Imperial army ever takes Nanking the Yangtze will be so choked with Taiping bodies you won't get a ship upriver for months and you'll find it's a waste of time preaching the gospel to dead men."

Esme shivered. "I hardly think such a graphic description is necessary, Mr Veasey."

"China's no place for the squeamish, Mrs Pilkington."

"I was thinking only of the girls," Esme lied. "And it's Miss, not Mrs. Although I prefer Esme to either Miss, Mrs or Ma'am."

"Then I'd be obliged if you called me Erin. I apologise if I've said anything to offend the girls or you. All three of you are far too attractive to be upset by an American sea captain who has spent so long at sea he's forgotten how to behave around women."

"You haven't forgotten the art of flattery, Mr Veasey — Erin, but I'm given to understand that's a national trait."

Esme found the American amusing. He might also prove very useful in the future. The thought of a mission to the Taipings had lost none of its appeal for her. She was convinced Erin Veasey was on his way to pick up a ship with the intention of trading with the rebels. It was almost as though the Lord had ordained that their paths should cross in such a way . . .

★ ★ ★

Erin Veasey and Kau-lin spent much time in each other's company during the five days of the voyage. Closeted together in the confines of such a small vessel it was inevitable that tongues should wag. The wife of a British consulate official at Shanghai, travelling on the steamer, thought it her duty to speak to Esme about the relationship.

The diplomat's wife left Esme's cabin considerably ruffled. Esme had said very forcefully there was nothing immoral in the 'friendship' that had developed between the American sailor and the Chinese girl. She suggested that perhaps 'evil was in the eye of the beholder' and not in the situation itself.

Esme really did believe the friendship between the two was purely platonic. Had she not, she would have felt it her duty to intervene, even though she entertained hopes of enlisting Erin's help to fulfil her ambition of carrying the *true* gospel to the Taiping.

Unfortunately, Eliza Goodge, the head of the mission in Shanghai where the new arrivals were to stay, did not share Esme's interpretation of the relationship between the American sea captain and Kau-lin.

The diplomat's wife who had been Esme's fellow passenger on the ship was a woman of some influence within the small, isolated British community at Shanghai.

Immediately upon landing she voiced her disapproval to Eliza. There was support for her suspicion of Kau-lin's morals. In a mail bag on board the steamer was a carefully worded letter from Hannah Jefferies to her counterpart in Shanghai. The letter gave the background of the two Chinese girls. Armed with this, Eliza left Esme in no doubts about her feelings.

"I really don't know what Hannah was

thinking of to send us two girls — two *Chinese* girls, of doubtful morals. The situation should properly have been dealt with in Hong Kong. We have enough problems of our own in Shanghai. For years we've lived in fear of the Chinese, with a city of a million inhabitants at our back. Now we have refugees flooding to the area from the Yangtze river valley, driven out of their homes by the fighting between Imperial and Taiping soldiers. We have a desperate problem trying to keep the Chinese out of the settlement — and that's another thing. Where do these two girls expect to live? It is forbidden by law for any Chinese to live in the British settlement. I'll need to find somewhere for them to stay in the city, or with a Chinese family in the suburbs. That will not only cost a great deal of money, but it means it will be impossible to maintain any control over them whatsoever . . . "

"If the two girls can't stay here, then neither shall I," declared Esme firmly. "Perhaps you'll be good enough to find accommodation for all three of us together? As for the cost . . . I have certain private funds. They may be small, but they will suffice, I think."

It was Esme at her most positive and Eliza Goodge was taken aback. "That will not be necessary. I will find somewhere suitable for them. In the French Concession, perhaps. They are not so particular about such matters. I know of a mixed family there who might be pleased to have a little extra income."

"What exactly do you mean by 'a mixed family'?"

"He is a Scot, married to a Chinese girl. Nevertheless, I feel he has sound Christian principles. Yes, I think that will be an acceptable solution."

"Splendid! I'm quite sure we'll all be very comfortable there. When can we speak to this Scotsman and find out if he's willing to take us in?"

"Mrs Pilkington, I have already said such accommodation is not for you. You'll have a room here, in the mission. I'm sure you'll be very comfortable and you'll have God's work to keep you busy. I don't doubt you mean well by your devotion to these two young girls, but you are a missionary. You have a station in life to uphold and the well-being of your fellow missionaries to consider. This is not a mission headquarters, nor yet a training school. Here in Shanghai we are in the front line of the evangelical movement and there are very few of us to carry out our work. We struggle very hard to maintain a precarious finger-hold in the vastness that is China. But it's a wonderful challenge, Mrs Pilkington. A *glorious* challenge."

"It's *Miss* Pilkington, not Mrs, and I am more than ready to meet any challenge that China has to offer. However, I have no doubt that I'll meet it just as well from a shared house in the French Concession, if that's the only way to remain with She-she and Kau-lin."

2

THE Shanghai missionary community was scandalised by Esme Pilkington's decision to make her home in the French Concession, sharing the house of a mixed family with two Chinese girls. They pointed out that the two girls were not even committed Christians. Furthermore, it was by no means certain that Colin Strachan was *legally* married to Nan, his Chinese wife. Besides, Esme was a single woman. A missionary woman.

They tried to involve the British consul in the matter. It was suggested he should warn her that unless she moved into the English settlement with her fellow missionaries she would be asked to leave the foreign settlement altogether. Wisely, the consul declined to interfere. He deplored Esme's decision to leave the British settlement and live in such a fashion, but it was a domestic affair. One for the missionaries to solve for themselves. Perhaps they should ask the Bishop of Victoria to intervene on his next visit from Hong Kong?

Not every missionary was against having Chinese girls living among them. She-she and Kau-lin were both pretty girls and some suggested there was a very good chance of converting them to Christianity. Nevertheless, whatever private thoughts were entertained about such an arrangement, in public the

268

official missionary line was maintained.

In fact, the order excluding Chinese from residing in the foreign settlements had been made by the Chinese government. It was an attempt to prevent its own people from being 'corrupted' by the *Fan Qui*. The missionary *Fan Qui* in particular.

Esme did not mind her ostracism by the British community. She threw herself into the work for which she had come to China and proved she was a determined and resourceful woman.

Most days Esme went out on her own. She did not feel in the least threatened, whether she preached among the Chinese multitudes inside the Shanghai city walls, or stood surrounded by thousands of refugees outside.

She seemed to take on a new life amidst the not always wholesome aromas that rose from the narrow back streets of the city. The worker-bee hum that rose from Shanghai to assail European ears seemed only to charge her with renewed energy.

Before long Esme was conducting regular services for the close friends of the Strachan family, in their small home. She got on extremely well with Nan and with Colin Strachan too, and admired their loyalty and love for one another. Each had sacrificed a rightful place among their own people in order to live a life together. Despite their many problems it was a relaxed and warm household. Esme particularly enjoyed the late evenings when she helped Nan to bathe the small children and put them to bed.

One evening, watching the large missionary woman handling the small children with unusual gentleness, She-she said to Kau-lin, "Esme would have made a wonderful wife and mother had she been able to find a man to understand her ways."

"He would have needed to be a strong man to be ruler in his own house with Esme for a wife."

She-she shook her head. "You are wrong. Esme would give her all — yes, life itself for someone she loved."

"Perhaps."

"Nan and her husband have both given much, yet they are very happy."

"Yes, they are happy in their own way. It would not suit everyone."

"What do you mean?" She-she challenged her friend.

Kau-lin knew that whenever She-she looked at Nan and Colin Strachan she was thinking of what might have been had Lieutenant Keats come back from his rescue mission on the Canton River.

"Strachan is a different man to your lieutenant."

"How is he different?"

"Nan was telling me about him. Strachan knew no mother or father. He was sent to sea when a young boy. Always shouted at and bullied, nothing he did was right. Then he met Nan. She was a flower-boat girl. She too had nothing. No one. Suddenly two half-people became one person and they went away and lived together. When she expected their first baby they were married. Now she sews and washes to make money for them all. Sometimes, when things are very bad, she becomes a flower-girl again for just one time — but Strachan knows nothing of this. He too works very hard helping to make houses, tables, gardens — anything that needs doing. Nothing matters to him if it keeps his children fed. It is the same with Nan."

Kau-lin paused and looked pityingly at She-she. "Such a life as this would not have made Lieutenant Keats happy. He was a special soldier. A number one man. He had too much to think of risking it for a blue dress girl, I think."

Before She-she turned away, Kau-lin saw the tears that had started to her eyes.

"It doesn't matter any more. Kernow is dead."

"I am sorry, She-she. You liked him very much, didn't you?"

"Very much."

Kau-lin put an arm about her friend's shoulders. "You will find someone else. When the American, Erin Veasey, comes back to see me perhaps he will have a friend . . . "

★ ★ ★

Esme and the two girls remained in the French Concession for almost a year. During this time the refugee situation deteriorated to the point where it threatened to overwhelm the European way of life in all the areas allocated to them.

The only change was that the refugees no longer fled from the Taiping rebels. Imperial troops had begun pushing the rebels back towards their captured capital of Nanking. Now the populace was running from their own 'liberating army'. Most had learned to live with the Taiping rebels. They now discovered they would certainly die at the hands of their own ill-disciplined troops.

The refugees brought with them little in the way of belongings. Life was the only precious commodity they possessed. Yet even in this they carried the seeds of self-destruction. Cholera had stalked them on the long road to safety and it finally caught up with them at Shanghai.

Only now was the barrier broken down between the errant missionary and her friends, and the mission community. There was an urgent need for anyone who could converse in both English and Chinese to work in the makeshift hospitals that sprang up outside the city walls of Shanghai as the disease spread and wreaked a terrible toll.

Not until the colder weather returned did the epidemic ease its fatal grip on Shanghai. It was now that Kau-lin's cousin Chang arrived in Shanghai from Formosa.

His arrival reopened the debate on whether 'respectable' Chinese should be allowed to lodge in the British settlement. At the height of the cholera epidemic no one in the British community had cared where Kau-lin and She-she slept. Exhausted from days and nights spent tending the sick, they had frequently slept in the hospital in the British settlement, resuming work the moment they awoke.

Now the emergency was coming to an end the colonial diehards reasserted their authority. She-she and Kau-lin were told they must no longer spend nights in the settlement. They ceased work at the hospital and returned to the house of Colin Strachan. Esme, disgusted with the narrow-minded attitude of her countrymen and women, went with them once more.

Chang too left the British settlement, but it had never been his intention to remain here. He did not move in with the Strachan family. Instead, he disappeared into the straggling suburbs of Shanghai, occupied with business that had little to do with the life he had led for the past few years.

This was not the Chang the three women had known in Hong Kong. Gone were the smart clothes and pious manner. Chang spent much of his time dressed as a coolie. By so doing he could pass unnoticed among the hordes of refugees, by day and by night.

Early one evening, Chang came to the Strachan house and stayed to have a meal here. When everyone had eaten, he suggested that the two girls and Esme might like to walk with him along the ramparts of the city wall, as was customary for thousands of city dwellers.

It was evident from Chang's manner that he had something of importance to say but he kept it to himself until they reached the shade of a small watchtower. Here he stopped to point out the view across the roofs of Shanghai. The sun was low and its fading rays cast light and shadow on the rooftops that made the city appear like some great ocean of waves. It was an apt simile. Like the sea, there was a vast turmoil of life beneath the surface of what was visible to the naked eye.

Such was the view expressed by Esme, and the others agreed with her. Chang added that there was a hint of poetry in her words, something that was very close to the hearts of the Chinese.

"Poetry is an ancient Chinese art form," agreed Kau-lin. "But you haven't brought us up here to watch the sunset on the roofs of Shanghai and talk of poetry, Cousin Chang."

"No," he confessed. "I am about to take a step that will change my life. I have received a letter from cousin Hung himself, the 'Heavenly King' of the Taipings. He says he has had a vision. In the vision he scores a great victory over the Imperial army and ascends to the throne of China, surrounded by the whole of his family. Hung has had many such visions in the past. Almost all have come to pass. He says this one will be fulfilled too — but not before his family have gathered round him. He wants me to go to Nanking and promises me high office when I arrive there."

"Do you believe all this, Chang?" The question was asked by She-she who had watched with interest the fervour that gripped Kau-lin's cousin while he was talking. This was not the modest, hard-working and humble man who had created such an impression among the missionaries of Hong Kong.

"I do. It was Cousin Hung's visions that opened the way for a Christian rebellion that has gathered millions of followers. I am convinced he will one day oust the Manchu usurpers from the throne of China. He is obeying God's will."

"Have you not spoken to the tens of thousands of people who crowd outside the walls of Shanghai and spill into the fields and villages for miles around the *Fan Qui* settlements? They have fled from their homes because the Taiping are being driven from the lands they conquered. Soon Nanking will be the only city left to them. Is this how your cousin is going to overthrow the Manchu Emperor of all China?" She-she was scornful.

"The Imperial armies are having some successes now, it is true, yet even as we speak other Taiping armies are rushing to the aid of their brothers. When they arrive they will fall upon the Imperial armies and destroy them."

"All this boasting of fighting and destroying is hardly Christian talk! Does your cousin say this in his letter, Chang, or are you expressing your own views?" The passion in Chang's voice alarmed Esme.

"I am talking only of what must be. You have read the scriptures. You know that the Lord's wrath is greatest when he fights the Devil. Hung is fighting the Devil on behalf of the Lord."

"What will you do in Nanking?" She-she put the question to Chang.

"Anything that is required of me. Hung needs his family about him. We can be trusted with high office as he can trust no one else. I have also been a Christian catechist in Hong Kong. Hung needs those who have studied the Bible. He and his followers are Christians, but they have strayed from many Christian principles. I will try to persuade Cousin Hung to make changes that will be more acceptable to the Europeans. Support from the nations of the West is essential if he is to defeat the armies of the Manchu emperor — and he *will* succeed. Think of it, Miss Pilkington. The prospect of helping to lay the foundations of a Christian China is breathtaking. There has not been such an opportunity since the disciples of Jesus went out to spread His Word!"

"Will you take me with you?" Chang's vision of a Christian China engulfed Esme and she pleaded to become a part of it.

"Your mission authorities will not approve of you going to Nanking."

"They don't approve of me anyway — but I do not seek earthly justification for what I do. Take me with you, Chang. You'll find me a powerful helper when it comes to carrying out the Lord's work."

"I do not doubt Cousin Hung will give you all the honour due to a Christian missionary. I will be happy to have you accompany me."

Chang turned his attention to Kau-lin. "Cousin Hung also honours you with a mention. The single women, like the men, are formed into regiments. He says he can offer you command of one of these regiments."

"Me?" Kau-lin was sceptical. "I know nothing of fighting."

"You will not be expected to fight. Women fought in the early days of the Taiping movement, it is true, but things have changed. There are now other duties for the women to perform."

"What are these 'other duties'? No matter, I expect I could fight as well as any man if I had to. I will go."

"What of you, She-she? Will you come to Nanking with us?"

"Go . . . stay. What difference does it make? Here in Shanghai I do not belong among our own people because I am a Hakka, and they are not. The *Fan Qui* will not have me living among them. Even if I became a Christian I would not be the same as them. Maybe I will be a good Taiping Christian — maybe not. I don't know. I am not a cousin of this 'Heavenly King'."

"Of course you will come, She-she." Kau-lin was indignant that she had even considered refusing Chang's offer. "If I am to become an important woman in Nanking I will need a good friend to help me."

"Yes, you must come with us to Nanking, She-she. You too will find great honours there."

"What sort of honours?"

"You must wait and see. We will speak again when we reach the city of Cousin Hung."

"It's all very well being fired up with enthusiasm," said Esme. "But how are we to get to Nanking? By all accounts there are Imperial junks by the score on the River Yangtze between there and Shanghai."

"It has been arranged. We will take passage with an American *Fan Qui*. He has made the voyage many times. He will get us there safely."

"Are you talking of Erin Veasey?"

Chang was startled by Kau-lin's question. "How do you know of this man? Who has spoken his name?"

Kau-lin smiled. "He was on the ship that brought us from Hong Kong. Twice he has been here to speak to me. Yes, Erin Veasey will take us to Nanking safely, I do not doubt that. But I do not think he will be in a great hurry to get there."

3

ESME, She-she, Kau-lin and Chang boarded Erin Veasey's ship the *Trade Wind* in the dead of night. Rowed out to the vessel in a small boat crewed by four members of Erin's all-European crew, She-she sat huddled in the stern with the others, shivering even though she wore a padded jacket as protection against cold such as she had never experienced in Hong Kong. As the water lapped against the bow of the small craft, She-she wondered what she had let herself in for. She alone of the four passengers was travelling to Nanking without a purpose. But life itself had little purpose now. She wondered what would have happened to her had Kernow not been sent to search for missing *Fan Qui* sailors after the typhoon . . .

Such thoughts were foolish, she knew, but She-she had found herself thinking of Kernow often in recent weeks. Too often for her own peace of mind. Suddenly the dark form of the ship they were to board loomed up and whispered orders were passed in the darkness to the passengers.

The *Trade Wind* was a small screw-driven steamship. Standing off the land, well away from the anchorage used by vessels of the Royal Navy, the ship showed no lights. As soon as the passengers were on board, and while the boat that had brought them from shore was still being hoisted from the water, the vessel got underway.

In the darkness She-she clattered awkwardly down a wooden ladder fitted with steel reinforced rungs. Below decks she entered a world where she was immediately aware of the monotonous beat of the ship's engine, hissing steam pipes and a pervading smell of coal dust. All would remain with her for the whole of the voyage they were to make, battling against the flow of the Yangtze-Kiang. The journey would take two weeks, and yet they would journey only a fraction of the length of the great river. The Yangtze rose almost four thousand miles away in the heights of Tibet, wandering through the very heart of China on its long journey to the sea.

She-she and the others were led to a large and spacious cabin. Lanterns swung from hooks in the low deck-head, sending shadows chasing each other in a silent game of tag about the creaking bulkheads. All light was kept securely inside the cabin by brass deadlights secured over glass port-holes.

"The cap'n will be down to see you soon, ma'am," said their seaman escort, addressing Esme as the natural leader of the party. Indicating a sideboard with bottles secured in half-depth wells, the seaman added, "Cap'n Veasey said you're to feel free to help yourself to something to drink if you've a mind."

"We don't drink alcohol, thank you, young man, so you can stop ogling She-she and go off and find us a cup of tea."

280

Erin Veasey and the tea arrived in the cabin at the same time. The warmth of the young American sea-captain's welcome for Kau-lin was missed by Esme but it brought a smile of understanding from She-she and a deep frown to the face of Chang.

"Well, I must say it's good to see you ladies looking so well. Nice to see you too, Chang. I think your cousin's going to be pleased to see you, especially when we deliver what we're taking to Nanking along with you!"

"How long is the voyage likely to take?"

"About twelve to fourteen days. Maybe a little longer. It depends on what we meet along the way, and how many times we run aground."

"Run aground? But we'll be travelling through government held territory. What happens if they capture us?" Chang expressed his alarm.

"They won't. I've got more guns on board the *Trade Wind* than a British warship. Imperial war junks won't come within half a mile of us and there's not a fort worth a damn between here and Nanking. But I can't stay down here talking to you, much as I'd like to. I'm needed up on deck. I'll have you all shown to your cabins. You ladies are accommodated here, in the stern of the ship. Your cabin is up in the bow, Chang. I'm sorry I can't keep you all back here, but I'm not in the business of carrying passengers. I've had to fit you in best I can."

Erin Veasey gave Kau-lin another warm smile, but his words were for them all. "We'll have lunch together here tomorrow. Now I must go back up top. We're still too close to Shanghai

281

for my liking. Your steward's name is Thomas — and you need have no fears for the chastity of your two girls with him, Miss Pilkington. Thomas was castrated by Moors when he was captured in North Africa, many years ago. They couldn't do away with his memories, but that's about all he's got left."

Erin Veasey returned to the upper deck smiling at the expression on Esme's face. The missionary was left with the feeling that she really should be more shocked and indignant than she was at the manner in which the very personal affliction of the unfortunate steward had been disclosed. Instead, she felt a sneaking admiration for the happy-go-lucky attitude of the American adventurer who captained the *Trade Wind*.

★ ★ ★

The following morning She-she was awakened from sleep by the sound of chain rattling from a locker and splashing into the water. The vessel was dropping anchor in a small cove fringed by bamboo and rushes.

The vessel remained at anchor for only an hour. During this time its true name was painted out and the *Trade Wind* became the *Enchantress*. When the ship got under way once more the Hong Kong-registered vessel was also flying a new flag. Instead of the Union Jack of Britain, the stars and stripes now fluttered from the flagstaff at the rear of the vessel.

When Esme commented on this, Erin Veasey

shrugged. "It's only a small deception, Ma'am. I'm American, as are most of my crew, and the ship was purchased with United States money. Besides, nobody who's likely to object is going to get close enough to check on the ship's credentials."

The river traffic was quite heavy, but no vessels of the Imperial navy were encountered until they were no more than twelve hours steaming time from Nanking.

Erin pointed the war junks out to Kau-lin as they stood together on the deck under a sky that threatened snow. The captain and the Chinese girl were on such familiar terms that even Esme had commented upon it. She-she hoped the missionary had not heard the quiet footsteps that passed from one cabin to another in the dead of night.

The junks were anchored in a long, loose line that stretched from bank to bank, across the wide Yangtze river.

"How will you pass them?" Kau-lin looked up at Erin in concern. "There are too many of them for one boat to fight."

"Don't you believe it, Kau-lin. None of the Imperial sailors would fight us if they were given an option. We'll need to deal with no more than two at the most. They'll be the two we pass between, but a couple of shots should be enough to send their gunners scuttling for cover."

Chang secretly seethed to see the sister of one of the 'Heavenly King's' generals having such a close liaison with a *Fan Qui*. But Chang and

283

the Taiping movement needed the services of Erin Veasey and his ship. He was so important that even Kau-lin could be sacrificed for such a cause, if need be.

"Should the women not be sent below if there's going to be fighting?"

"The chances are we'll not have a shot fired at us. But stay close to the hatch, just in case."

Erin Veasey shouted an order to one of his crew and men were called from below decks. The crew of the *Trade Wind* took their places at the eight guns that had been placed in position on the upper deck soon after Shanghai had been left behind. The time had come for them to prove they deserved to receive three times as much pay as sailors who crewed vessels which went about their lawful business on the oceans of the world.

Incredible though it seemed, the crews on board the Imperial war junks were not aware of the presence of the steamer until it was almost upon them. By the time the sound of frantic warning gongs boomed out across the water, the steamer was less than a quarter of a mile away. Slicing through the water, the steamer drew on every ounce of power the heavily perspiring stokers could produce.

The *Trade Wind* was almost alongside one of the junks before the first shot was fired by the Chinese gunners. It missed, the gunpowder in the ancient cannon being touched off before the gun was properly aimed.

The gunners on board the disguised *Trade Wind* carried out their task with an almost

284

contemptuous calm efficiency. Three guns on either side of the ship's deck were fired in quick succession. Loaded with grapeshot they cut down every man standing on the upper decks of the war junks. Long before more Chinese sailors dared show their faces to man the antiquated marine cannon, the steamship had passed between them to safety.

She-she looked back, expecting to see the war junks weighing anchor and setting off in pursuit to seek revenge. Nothing happened. The only movement among the fleet was that caused by the wake of the *Trade Wind* as the steamship rapidly passed beyond range of the Chinese guns.

Seeing the sailors of the Imperial navy cut down in such numbers distressed She-she. Unlike Chang she could not share the jubilation of the Americans who had manned the *Trade Wind*'s guns, although Kau-lin too was caught up in their excitement.

"You don't like seeing your countrymen die, She-she? I regret it was necessary. If we hadn't shown them our fire-power they'd have thrown everything they have at us. If they'd dared to come after us we'd have had a hell of a fight on our hands."

"It makes me unhappy to see anyone die, no matter whether they Chinese, American or English."

"Yet Kau-lin told me you loved an English Royal Marine, a man who was trained to kill others."

The mention of Kernow made She-she's eyes

suddenly burn and she was angry with Kau-lin for having spoken of her relationship with Kernow to this man. Defensively, she said, "Kau-lin should have said nothing of this to anyone."

"I'm sorry." Erin Veasey moved away, as though about to leave her. Instead, he suddenly turned back. "She told me he was killed when he went up the Canton River to search for sailors lost after the big typhoon last year. Is that right?"

She-she nodded, not wanting to talk about Kernow, but the American persisted.

"You know, I may be wrong about this, but on one of my trips to Hong Kong I heard someone talking about that. It seems the Royal Marine officer wasn't killed after all. He returned to Hong Kong and managed to bring some of the missing sailors with him. Why don't you ask Chang about it? From all accounts it caused quite a stir in Hong Kong. This marine officer was a big hero. Chang must have heard about it."

4

CHANG was below decks with Esme, saying a prayer for the souls of the sailors killed on the Imperial war junks in the brief, one-sided battle. Unceremoniously interrupting their prayers, She-she tackled him about Kernow.

Apparently unconcerned at not passing on news of the young lieutenant's survival, Chang shrugged off She-she's anger.

"Why should anything that happens to a *Fan Qui* matter to a Hakka girl? Anyway, it all happened a long time ago. Yes, Lieutenant Keats returned safely to Hong Kong. He even came to see me, to ask about you."

"And you never told me of this? How *dare* you! How dare you decide what I should or should not know?" She-she went pale with fury. As she stood facing Chang with fists clenched, Esme feared she might pounce on him and strike him.

Moving between them, she said, "You should have mentioned something about it, Chang. After all, we were all together at the mission school and became good friends."

"Friendship between a Chinese girl and a *Fan Qui* man is not possible. Even if it were, no one would believe it. When the man returns home the girl becomes a *Fan Qui* cast-off, scorned by her own people. You deserve better than this, She-she."

She-she was on the point of retorting that there was more scorn attached to being a blue dress girl in the house of Li Hung. She stopped herself in time. The less said about the life she and Kau-lin had shared at Canton, the better it would be for both of them.

When Kau-lin hurried from the upper deck to find her friend, Chang addressed her. "Perhaps you would like to know what happened to one of *your* 'friends' at the mission? The son of the two missionaries named Calvin. I believe they did their best to keep it quiet, so you might not have heard in Shanghai."

"Do you mean Arthur? What did he do, run away from his mother and get married?" Kau-lin tried to imagine Arthur defying his mother in such a way and the thought made her smile.

"No, he did not marry, but he certainly escaped from his mother. He put a rope about his neck and killed himself. It happened on the very day you left Hong Kong for Shanghai."

Kau-lin's face contorted with horror and anguish at being told the news of Arthur's suicide in such a callous manner. Suddenly she turned and fled in the direction of her cabin, causing Chang's eyes to narrow. He wondered what Arthur had meant to her. It was a good thing he had brought both the girls away from Shanghai when he did. A scandal involving cousin Kau-lin could have tainted them all and might have damaged his chance of a senior post in the Taiping capital. It would have touched upon She-she too — and he had plans for her . . .

"That was a cruel way of breaking such news, Chang. You disappoint me."

Esme was more than disappointed. She was dismayed to have witnessed a facet of Chang's nature she had not seen before.

"Why? Neither *Fan Qui* man could ever have meant anything to Kau-lin or She-she. Cousin Hung is most strict about such things. Among the Taipings for many years it was forbidden for women to mix with the men. He has relaxed the rule for married men and women, but immorality between single men and girls is punishable by death. It is best Kau-lin and She-she should understand this now. Women have full equality among the Taiping — but they are also subject to the same laws and punishments."

In Kau-lin's cabin, She-she did her best to comfort her weeping friend. "Don't upset yourself so much, Kau-lin. I'm sure the death of poor Arthur had nothing at all to do with you."

"It did, She-she, I know it. Arthur killed himself because I went away. I thought I had helped him become a man, but I only gave him someone new to lean on. When I left he was unable to stand by himself."

"Shh! You must not blame yourself."

Even while she was comforting Kau-lin, She-she's own heart was singing. Kernow was alive and he had asked for her on his return to Hong Kong. One day she would see him again. She knew it as certainly as she was aware that Chang was someone she could not trust. Life had taken on meaning for her once more.

The new arrivals to the Taiping capital received gruesome confirmation of Chang's warning the next morning. The heads of about a hundred men and ten women were displayed for view on poles above the city gates. All had broken one of the many laws imposed by the 'Heavenly King' upon his people. The heads were intended to serve as a warning of the fate awaiting those who flouted the will of the Taiping ruler.

The Taiping authorities were no different from the Imperial Chinese in exhibiting the heads of those they executed, but it was something She-she had never grown used to. She shuddered as she and the others passed beneath the high archway and entered the walled city of Nanking.

The discovery by the Taiping customs officer that the *Trade Wind* was carrying a relative of the *T'ien Wang* had caused great excitement. A messenger was sent into the city and it was not long before an escort of a hundred men came at the trot to take Chang and the others with them inside the great walls of Nanking.

She-she was greatly impressed by the high walls that stretched for almost as far as the eye could see. She expected the city to match up to this first view, but she was sadly disappointed.

Although the walls extended for more than twenty miles, only a small area within them was built up. There were many fields and open spaces inside the city's perimeter — and extensive, depressing areas of ruined buildings.

The houses left standing were meaner than those She-she had seen in Hong Kong and most required urgent maintenance. Even the palaces of the most influential of the Taiping hierarchy were less than impressive. All except the palace of the *T'ien Wang* were still under construction.

The newcomers were escorted to the *T'ien Wang*'s palace. Upon arrival they were met at the entrance by two girls dressed in yellow silk dresses. The captain in charge of the escort explained that the *T'ien Wang* employed only girls in his palace. He gave as a reason for this the fact that the Heavenly King felt safer surrounded by women who were less inclined to intrigue than eunuchs.

The smirk that accompanied this explanation made it clear that the officer might have given them other reasons for the arrangement.

Only Chang was allowed inside the Taiping ruler's palace. Esme, Kau-lin and She-she were taken on to a large house where they were welcomed by a woman of no more than thirty, who carried an air of authority Esme had never before encountered in a Chinese woman.

Introducing herself as General Su-san, the woman informed them she was in charge of one of the five regiments of women attached to the army of the *T'ien Wang*. In answer to a question from Kau-lin she said the women had gone into battle against the Imperial army on a number of occasions, especially in the early days of the movement. Now, they were mainly used on noncombatant duties, although they remained trained for warfare, should they be needed.

"Do you know whether any plans have been made for us? Will I be allowed to preach to the people of Nanking?"

The question came from Esme. She was bitterly disappointed at not being accommodated in the palace of the 'Heavenly King'. She was eager to meet the man who claimed to have been sent to earth to rid China of the 'Devils' who taught a false religion. A man who claimed heaven for his rightful home, and Jesus Christ as his elder brother, would have to be a remarkable being. The claims were preposterous, of course, yet Hung and his followers had achieved phenomenal success against those he sought to oust.

"Such decisions will be made personally by the *T'ien Wang*. There will be great honours for Chang, and for you too." She nodded in Kau-lin's direction. "You are a cousin on your mother's side to Chang, and he belongs to the *T'ien Wang*'s earthly family. You are also the sister of commandant Peng Yu-cheng. For the others . . . who knows? You are good friends of Kau-lin and have travelled to Nanking to be with her. The *T'ien Wang* rewards loyalty, and he can be very generous."

"You hold a very high position in the Taiping army. Are you related to Hung . . . to the *T'ien Wang*?"

Su-san smiled. "No, Kau-lin. My husband was leader of a rebel band in Kiangsi province.

292

He went to parley with the Viceroy under a flag of truce and was treacherously murdered. I took over the leadership of the rebels and won many victories against the Imperial soldiers. When the *T'ien Wang* brought the Taiping army through Kiangsi, I took my rebels over to him and he made me general of a women's regiment. We have seen good days and fought many notable battles, but I fear the best days are over."

"Why do you say that?" Esme spoke with a new respect for this young woman.

"There have been many internal dissents. Much Taiping blood has been shed by other Taiping factions. The *T'ien Wang* is our leader and his visions have given us the paths we must travel, but a holy man is rarely a general. At this time we have need of a soldier. A *brilliant* soldier — yet one who has no ambition to take the Taiping throne. Perhaps the great God who guides the *T'ien Wang* will send us one soon. I hope so because the Imperial army is slowly tightening a noose about Nanking. We must break out before it chokes us."

5

THE *T'ien Wang*, Heavenly King of the Taiping people, was convinced God had at last sent him the man to rejuvenate the Heavenly rebellion. During the course of the next ten days, Chang rose at breathless speed through the ranks of the Taiping hierarchy. Promotion came to him on a daily basis, his new rank promulgated each morning in edicts sent out from the palace of the *T'ien Wang*.

On the tenth day, he was given the title of 'Prince' and entrusted with the task of dictating the future course of the war against the armies of Imperial China.

"It will not endear him to the leaders of the armies," commented Su-san, when she gave the news to Esme and the two Hakka girls. "Many have fought for the Taiping cause since the beginning of the rebellion, only to be rewarded with suspicion and accusations of plotting against the *T'ien Wang*. Whenever there's a lull in the fighting half the generals suffer demotion."

Su-san had been out in the cold and as she spoke she struggled free of her heavy, padded clothing. "Chang has never heard a shot fired in battle, yet he has been given the power to tell experienced generals how they must conduct the war. They will not like it."

"There must be a reason why Cousin Hung

— the *T'ien Wang* — has appointed Chang and not one of the generals who has been with him for so long."

"There is a very good reason," agreed Su-san. "The *T'ien Wang* no longer trusts his generals. Soon after we came to Nanking they fell out among themselves and fought private battles, slaughtering families and followers too. For weeks people feared to walk the streets. Men, women and children would be stopped and asked to which faction they belonged. A moment's hesitation before answering was enough to set the executioner's sword singing. During those bloody months the *T'ien Wang* lost some of his finest generals, and many of his closest advisers. Men he had trusted since the beginning of the rebellion."

She-she shuddered. "Why did the *T'ien Wang* allow this to happen?"

"Had he tried to put a stop to it they would all have turned upon him. Anyway, he was more concerned with visions of heaven and the affairs of his own palace than with what was happening to the Taiping cause. He still is."

"You seem to have a very low regard for the *T'ien Wang*, Su-san. What would happen to you if he knew how you felt?" The question came from Kau-lin.

"I would be executed. But your own brother is also not happy with the Taiping leadership. When he was last in Nanking he made no secret of his belief that the *T'ien Wang*'s two older brothers have far too much influence in Taiping affairs. Neither is very clever. Many good soldiers and officials have died as a result of their petty quarrels."

"Do you know my brother well, Su-san?"

"Better than anyone else in Nanking. It was I who advised him to move his family out of the city and to take his army higher up the Yangtze valley. He is now garrisoned at Wuhu. He will return only if Chang is able to take full control of things here."

"I hope it is soon." Kau-lin stood up and began pacing the room. "I'm tired of sitting around here. I had expected Hung — the *T'ien Wang* — to send for me before this. I thought he might give me something useful to do. Is there any way we can go to find my brother? He will be pleased to see me, I am certain."

"I'm fed up with being cooped up here with nothing to do all day too," declared Esme. "I came to Nanking to meet Hung Hsiu-ch'uan. To discuss his ideas on religion and see what could be done to guide the Taiping people to true Christianity. It might help to improve his image with the nations of Europe. Unless he sends for us soon I'm going out on the streets to start preaching. At least I'll feel then that my journey here hasn't been an entire waste of time."

"That would not be wise," said Su-san, genuinely alarmed. "Only the *T'ien Wang* can decide what the people should hear about religious matters."

"When it comes to teaching the word of God there is a higher authority than Hung Hsiu-ch'uan, whatever he decides to call himself

— and I am the Lord's servant, no one else's."

★ ★ ★

As the venue for her first sermon to the people of Nanking, Esme chose the spot where the edicts of the *T'ien Wang* were posted on the wall each day. It ensured she had a ready-made audience.

Her arrival took the city officials by surprise. They had not been informed she would be speaking to the people, but at first they could not believe she would dare to preach in such a manner without the authority of someone very high in the Taiping government.

People gathered around Esme in hordes. Many of them had never seen a European woman before and they marvelled at her size. She dwarfed most of the men about her. Her voice too had a power that few men could equal. The content of her sermon hardly seemed important — until it was realised she spoke of matters over which the *T'ien Wang* claimed sole jurisdiction.

Esme had been speaking for two hours when the crowd suddenly scattered at the arrival of Taiping soldiers. She was placed under arrest by a guard force ordered to the scene by a minor court official who had listened to Esme with some alarm.

The guard commander was in a quandary about what to do with the missionary woman. No Taiping had ever arrested a *Fan Qui* — and this one had come upriver with the newly created Prince Chang, a man of rapidly increasing power and influence.

It was agreed that Chang himself should be the man to make a decision on her. Unfortunately he was out of Nanking for a couple of days, meeting with the commanders of the army of the north, many miles from the city.

Requests for guidance on what to do with the *Fan Qui* missionary were passed to increasingly higher authority, until a palace official, prostrate on the ground before the *T'ien Wang*, craved guidance from the Heavenly King on the dilemma facing a lowly guard commander.

The request found Hung Hsiu-ch'uan in quixotic mood. That morning one of his favourite wives had given birth to a boy child. God was smiling on the world today. He ordered Esme brought before him.

She arrived weighed down with chains that clanked on the marble floors of the Heavenly palace and brought an expression of pain to the face of the Taiping ruler.

"Have them struck off immediately," were the first words Esme heard uttered by the being who claimed kinship with the Saviour of the world.

A few minutes later she shook herself free of the last chain and as it dropped to the floor she was ordered to prostrate herself before the *T'ien Wang* who had sent for her.

Esme was not at all overawed in the presence of the Heavenly King. Furthermore, she was considerably disgruntled at being dragged through the streets of Nanking weighed down with shackles.

Her anger showed clearly on her face and Hung said quickly, "We will pray together. May I ask you to kneel while we seek His blessing on our talk together?"

Esme realised it was a clever face-saving ruse on the part of the man who sat on the throne before her, but she was also aware that prevarication on her part might throw away the opportunity for which she had waited so long: the chance to talk face-to-face with the man who could introduce true Christianity to millions, who would otherwise die faithless.

When she dropped to her knees and clasped her hands before her a sigh of satisfaction went up from the palace officials. They had been apprehensive about this large woman. She had managed to cow those who had taken her into custody. Now honour and protocol had been satisfied. All would be well.

Hung murmured a brief prayer, in which he called upon God to give His blessings to their talk together. It was a prayer with which no churchman could have found fault. Then the Taiping leader called for Esme to be seated in a chair that was brought and placed on a wide step, two treads below the level of the throne.

"You have come from Shanghai, travelling with my earthly cousin, the Prince Chang? I trust you had a comfortable voyage?"

"I would have endured any discomfort rather than miss an opportunity to come to Nanking and preach to the Taiping people."

"Ah yes, your preaching. This is why you were arrested. You will understand it is necessary for me to make orders restricting such activities? There are few in the Taiping ranks who understand Christianity but many who would influence others for their own mischievous ends. We must not have them preaching falsehoods to the people."

A more critical missionary might have taken the opportunity of such an opening to comment upon Hung's own interpretation of the Christian religion. It did not even occur to Esme. She could think only that the man who sat on the throne was like no man she had met before. Something about him suggested to her that he had been touched by an experience such as few men — perhaps no man — had known.

"I teach only what is written in the Bible. If that influences people it is God's doing, not mine."

"Your motives are admirable, Miss Pilkington, as are those of your colleagues. I am always delighted to welcome missionaries to my city, but the Taipings are simple people. They can put a wrong interpretation on the simplest statement of fact. You are not Chinese, Miss Pilkington, and although your knowledge of our language is excellent, it is not perfect. One wrong word is capable of causing a great deal of misunderstanding."

"Yes. Yes, I can see that. I'm sorry . . . "

"Please, you must not apologise for serving God, my father. It pleases me, as it pleases Him. It pleases me so much that I wish you

300

to stay here, in my palace, as a member of my household. Your main duty will be to teach the Bible to my wives, to my concubines and to those who serve me. All are women. I allow no man to enter my palace. It has been difficult until now to find someone to take on such a delicate task. You will, of course, submit to me all you intend saying to them and, should there be differences of opinion, you will bow to my wishes. Is this understood?"

Had any other man told Esme Pilkington she must bow to his wishes, whatever the subject, she would have turned the full force of her considerable wrath upon him. But she had already concluded that Hung Hsiu-ch'uan, the *T'ien Wang* and leader of the Taiping rebellion, was no ordinary man. Like many men and women before her, Esme had fallen completely under his spell.

"I understand. It will be a great honour to be a part of your household."

"Good! I will send for someone to show you to your new quarters. We must find servants for you too — and you will need a title. Something to command respect from those you teach. From my ministers too. What shall it be? I know, you will be Commandant Messenger of the Heavenly Word. You will rank with my generals and have equal authority. You will, of course, be required to kneel when you enter my presence, but you will be kneeling not to me but to God, my Heavenly Father. I welcome you to my household, Miss Pilkington. We will speak again soon."

6

SHE-SHE and Kau-lin greeted the news of Esme's appointment to the household of the *T'ien Wang* with incredulity. It was brought to them by Su-san to whom had gone the task of packing Esme's few belongings and conveying them to the palace.

"They'll not get along." Kau-lin shook her head incredulously. "Esme is such a positive woman. She will never agree with the *T'ien Wang*'s views."

"My sister is a captain of the palace guard. She told me the *T'ien Wang* and Esme spoke together for a long time. She said Esme seems so besotted with him, she would probably have accepted had he suggested she become one of his concubines."

The thought of Esme becoming a concubine set all three girls giggling. They had not lost their smiles when Prince Chang came to the house a few hours later. He arrived riding a small Tartar pony, direct from his visit to the generals. As befitted his new exalted status, he was escorted to the house by a company of Taiping soldiers.

Su-san bowed low when he walked into the house, but Kau-lin walked around him, admiring his fine yellow and red silk clothes. "My, you have done well for yourself, Cousin Chang. What would the missionaries in Hong Kong think if they could see you now?"

"It might be better if you called me 'Prince' Chang when speaking to me in the company of others." He frowned at Kau-lin in annoyance. She should know better.

"Has the *T'ien Wang* sent you to tell me he wishes to make me the Princess Kau-lin? Is this why you have come to visit us? But I doubt if he even knows the sister of Commandant Peng Yu-cheng is here in Nanking."

"He knows. I myself have told him."

"Then why doesn't he send me to my brother? Does he wish him to forget he has a sister? Or perhaps my brother Peng will soon be returning to Nanking?"

"I cannot look into the mind of the *T'ien Wang*, but it is well known he fears all generals who are popular with their soldiers. Peng is one of the best liked, and most successful. It is better for him to remain in Wuhu for a while, keeping the Imperial army busy."

"Then I will go to Wuhu to find him. Will you arrange a permit for me?"

"I may be able to do better than that. If I am to conduct a successful war against the armies of the Manchu emperor, I must speak with all the *T'ien Wang*'s commanders. Since most are reluctant to come to Nanking, I must go to them. You can come to Wuhu with me."

"That will be difficult, Your Excellency."

Custom decreed that Su-san should bow her head when she spoke to a prince of the Heavenly Kingdom, but her voice carried authority. "The *T'ien Wang* has set out the strictest rules for

303

women. They are not permitted to accompany men on the march, whatever the rank of the men."

For a few moments it seemed Chang might be angry, then he said, "That is so. I have read the *T'ien Wang*'s order myself. However, it *is* permitted for women to go with the army if they travel as a women's regiment and maintain the strictest discipline. Is your regiment capable of sharing escort duties with a regiment of men?"

Su-san had difficulty keeping her enthusiasm in check. "I commanded an active duty regiment before women were assigned to other work. Most of the officers and many of the women who were with me then are still serving with my regiment."

"Then you will become an active service regiment once more. I will call in another women's regiment to perform your duties in Nanking. Have a list made of the older women. They can transfer to the replacement regiment and explain their duties to the new women. You had better take on Kau-lin as a lieutenant — no, a captain. It will be a temporary rank only, to satisfy the decrees of the *T'ien Wang*."

"What of me? I have no intention of staying behind in Nanking." She-she was alarmed at the thought of being left behind, deserted by everyone she knew.

"I will take you into my regiment too. You can be a lieutenant in Kau-lin's company . . . ."

"No!" Chang's voice carried the weight of his recently acquired authority, but he had not yet grown accustomed to his status. When he saw the startled expressions on the faces of Kau-lin and She-she, he shrugged apologetically. "I wish to speak to She-she alone, if you please."

Now it was Su-san's turn to appear startled. For a moment it seemed she was about to recall some edict of the *T'ien Wang* forbidding such a discussion between a man and a woman. Before she could speak, Kau-lin took her by the arm.

"Come." Giving She-she a warm smile, she led Su-san from the room.

Left alone with Chang, She-she had an uncomfortable feeling that she knew the subject Chang was about to broach. She wished it could be avoided . . . but he had already begun speaking.

"It is a long time since we first met in Hong Kong, She-she. Much has happened since then. Indeed, we have travelled far from the Hakka villages of our childhood. We have seen strange things and learned much about Christianity and many other matters. Now another new page is about to be written. The *T'ien Wang* has honoured me beyond my wildest expectations. He has conferred the title of 'Prince' upon me. You heard Su-san. When she spoke she addressed me as 'Your Excellency'. It will not end here. Next to the *T'ien Wang*'s two brothers I am his closest relative. There will be more honours for me."

"You have done very well indeed, Chang . . . Your Excellency."

He waved away her words. "There is no need for you to address me in such a fashion. Not when we are alone. Indeed, if you agree to

305

what I have to say, it will never be necessary again."

She-she lowered her gaze to the ground. This was the moment she had been dreading. It was as she had feared.

"I wish you to become my wife, She-she. It will bring honour upon you and your family. You will be my foremost wife, accorded the full honours of a princess. You will live in a palace that is to be built for me beside the palaces of the two brothers."

"Foremost wife? You have others?"

"Not yet, but the *T'ien Wang* has decreed that a man of my rank should have six wives."

"He tells you how many wives you must have!" She-she found his words difficult to believe. "Does he also tell you how many children each wife must bear for you?"

"If the *T'ien Wang* considered it to be of importance he would issue an edict on the subject. But you have not answered my question. I am offering to make you my number one wife."

Chang was making She-she an offer such as few girls would ever know. True, the Taiping movement was a rebel one. Yet it was the most successful rebellion China had experienced for hundreds of years. It was not incapable of overthrowing the Manchu dynasty and taking over the government of the country.

If this happened, the wife of Chang would become one of the most important women in the land. She-she, daughter of a Hakka fisherman, was being offered the opportunity to become that woman. It was a breathtaking prospect — but She-she did not like Chang. She did not trust him. Nor could she forgive him for keeping news of Kernow's safe return a secret from her — and she realised that the Englishman would always stand between them.

"I . . . I don't know what to say. Your offer comes as a great surprise to me."

"Why? I have never tried to hide my admiration for you." Chang looked at her suspiciously. "Does your uncertainty have anything to do with the *Fan Qui* officer?"

"I have told you your proposal has taken me by surprise. That is the truth. I had no idea you were considering taking me for a wife."

"When we first met I had no thought of taking anyone for a wife. Things have changed very much since then. But you still have not given me an answer."

"You do me a great honour, Chang, yet I must think about this. I am not certain I will be able to cope with the responsibility of being married to such an important man. Becoming a princess."

"When will you give me an answer?"

"Allow me to go to Wuhu with Kau-lin. I will think along the way and give you my reply when we return to Nanking."

Chang was annoyed. "It should not be a difficult decision to take. Nevertheless I will wait for a month. I can give you no longer. The *T'ien Wang* has ordered me to choose my six wives before his birthday. That is less than three months away. If you delay too long I will need to take someone else for number one wife."

7

KAU-LIN and Su-san thought She-she crazy not to have accepted Chang's offer of marriage immediately.

"He is handsome, clever, young — and will make you a princess!" pointed out Su-san. "You will never receive such an offer again. Never."

"Probably not," agreed She-she. "But I don't like Chang very much. What does it matter whether I'm called princess, empress — or frog or toad for that matter — if I am unhappy?"

"A frog or a toad will spend its life in the mud of a pond with others who will never be anything but frogs or toads. You have been given the chance to make something of yourself. You will soon be beyond marriageable age. Which is better, to be alone and unhappy in a hut, or in a palace, surrounded by servants and with fine clothes to wear? I wish Prince Chang had asked *me*. But I cannot stay here trying to change the mind of someone who has apparently lost her reason. I have work to do. A regiment to prepare. Why I should agree to take a lieutenant who can't see the opportunity of a lifetime when it's thrust at her, I don't know!"

When Su-san had left the house, still shaking her head, Kau-lin said to She-she, "What's your real reason for not accepting Cousin Chang? Has it anything to do with your Lieutenant Kernow?"

308

When She-she made no reply, Kau-lin said sharply, "You must put Hong Kong and all that happened there behind you, She-she. It is gone. Part of the past."

"Kernow is alive. Your *Fan Qui* said so and Chang admits he has spoken of me to him."

"So? Kernow is in Hong Kong. Chang is here. Face reality, She-she. You will never see Kernow again. I am not telling you to forget him. I would never say such a thing. Remember the times you and Kernow spent together as happy times. Something to dream about when you are old and surrounded by grandchildren. But don't throw your life away waiting for a dream to return. Your life is here with the Taipings. Take all you can, while you can. That is how I look upon the time I have spent with the American *Fan Qui*. I like him, I like being with him, I like what we do together. But if I never see him again I will be content with my memories. Be sensible, She-she, I beg you. I only wish someone would give *me* an opportunity to become the number one wife of a prince — any prince!"

★ ★ ★

While all was being made ready for Prince Chang's journey to Wuhu, an event occurred which caused great excitement in Nanking. In late November word went about the city that five *Fan Qui* warships were on their way upriver. They were expected to pass by the Taiping-held city sometime that day.

Kau-lin and She-she were among those who

309

rushed to the high city walls overlooking the river. The warships were a splendid sight. Three were large vessels, bristling with guns. The other two were smaller, but these were also very well armed.

Seeing the flag they flew made She-she think of Hong Kong and of Kernow. She would have liked to wave, purely as a symbolic gesture. In view of the events that followed, it was as well she did not.

It was as well, too, that she did not know Kernow was on board one of the vessels.

He was accompanying Admiral Sir Michael Seymour and Lord Elgin. The British minister had just concluded a treaty with the Imperial Chinese authorities at Tientsin. It had yet to be ratified by Peking, but this was believed to be no more than a formality.

Under the terms of the treaty, Britain, together with other European nations, would be granted much wider freedom of trade, including access to the Yangtze River. One of the Chinese negotiators, more crafty than his fellows, had suggested that while a reply was awaited from Peking, the British peer might care to take a cruise up the great Chinese river. It would be an opportunity to view the prospects for trade for himself.

Much of the middle reaches of the river was in Taiping hands. The sudden appearance of heavily armed warships was likely to lead to trouble between the rebels and the British. It was a prospect that greatly appealed to the Imperial Chinese authorities. When Lord Elgin accepted the invitation they were delighted.

Lord Elgin was used to negotiating with the Chinese. He was under no illusions about the dangers of undertaking such a voyage. Nevertheless, it was an opportunity too good to be missed. He would take along a naval surveyor to map the great river. A full report would also be made to the British government on the strength and disposition of the Taiping rebels. In an attempt to safeguard the expedition, Elgin had sent a note to the rebel authorities in Nanking, informing them that he would be passing along the river with his small but deadly fleet.

One of the British gunboats headed the convoy of British warships. Flying a white flag of truce it passed through the blockading fleet of Imperial junks, sailing well within range of the Taiping shore batteries.

One by one the batteries fell behind until there was only one remaining. As the gunboat came level with this final defence, the Taiping gunners inexplicably opened fire, scoring a number of hits upon the vessel.

The British ships retaliated promptly. One by one, as they passed the battery, the men-o'-war returned the fire and She-she saw more than one hit strike home in the fort containing the Taiping guns.

Finally all the British warships passed out of range of the battered fort. However, instead of continuing upriver they dropped anchor.

She-she did not share the exaltation of the Taiping residents of Nanking who had little love for the *Fan Qui*. She felt a strong sense of disquiet. It was her strong belief that the British would not allow the matter to end in such an indecisive fashion, especially when it might be construed by some as a Taiping victory.

She-she was right. At dawn the following morning the British ships steamed back to the scene of the previous day's action. This time they operated as a fleet and their gunfire was devastating. Not only did they destroy the gun battery that had fired on them, but the other batteries too.

The Taiping casualties were heavy and when the British warships sailed away, the junks of the Imperial navy took advantage of the situation. No longer threatened by the Taiping batteries they sailed in close to the shore and pounded the suburbs of Nanking, their shells falling among the crowded houses that huddled against the city wall. The Taipings had paid a high price for the over-enthusiasm of one of their gunners.

★ ★ ★

Prince Chang and his two escorting regiments left Nanking in a blaze of coloured uniforms to the accompaniment of drums, gongs and voices, all providing a great cacophony of sound. There were more than five thousand soldiers in his small army, half of them women. Marching ten abreast the men's regiment marched ahead of Prince Chang and his retainers, with women soldiers forming the rearguard.

Each regiment carried the flags of its

sergeants, lieutenants, captains and colonel. They fluttered above the marching men and women giving a carnival atmosphere to the mile-long parade. At intervals among the ranks of the marching army rode the officers, men and women, mounted on wiry little Manchu ponies.

Two hundred Taiping cavalrymen rode ahead of the main body. Their duty was to prevent a surprise attack by roving Imperial units. The lands through which they would travel were in the hands of the Taiping rebels, but their hold was a tenuous one. Possession was claimed by those on the spot.

The mounted vanguard also appraised villagers along the route of the approach of Prince Chang. The villagers were expected to prepare food for the whole army and, if necessary, provide accommodation for the prince and his senior officers.

The distance between Nanking and Wuhu was no more than eighty miles and the journey was expected to take the army five days. For the first part of the journey it was necessary to keep away from the river where the junks of the Imperial navy were gathered in considerable force. Farther upstream the danger fell away. The great river split into a number of channels for some miles. The channels with the deepest water were narrow and ran close to the southern bank, which was occupied by Taiping rebels. The Imperial navy would not run the gauntlet of the rebels' ancient but frequently accurate cannons.

Twice along the route the Taiping column came under attack from the Imperial army. The first incident was little more than a skirmish. A barrier had been thrown up across the road, manned by no more than three hundred Imperial bannermen. It was a foolhardy attempt to delay Taiping progress and the bannermen paid for such impudence with their lives. Those who survived the initial onslaught of the Taiping cavalrymen were rounded up by infantrymen and promptly beheaded.

She-she was horrified at the summary execution of the Imperial soldiers, apparently without any reference to senior officers. She begged Su-san to ask Chang to spare their lives, but Su-san refused to intervene.

"Once I might have done so," she explained. "But when we lost a battle against the Emperor's soldiers at Wuchang, the women of the Taiping regiments were so badly treated they would have welcomed instant execution. Since then we have given no quarter to soldiers of the Imperial army."

Not all the Imperial soldiers died stoically. She-she rode to the rear of the column, hoping to escape their screams and hysterical pleas for mercy. Had she not done so the executed bannermen might have been swiftly avenged.

The attention of the Taiping soldiers, men and women, was focused upon watching the enemy die. They were not guarding against a surprise attack as they should have been. A belt of trees hid a valley that extended inland at right angles to the line of march. She-she was riding towards the trees when she glimpsed a splash of colour among them.

Such colour was out of keeping with its surroundings. Reining in her pony, she stared into the shadows cast by the trees. At first the only movement seemed to be that of the undergrowth beneath the trees. Suddenly She-she realised it was not undergrowth, but the movement of men. *Thousands* of men, carrying green banners that merged with the trees. The barrier had been a diversion. The dead bannermen had been deliberately sacrificed in an attempt to lull the Taiping soldiers into a false sense of victory.

She-she wheeled her pony and galloped back to the column, crying out for the Taipings to turn and face the new and far more dangerous threat of the soldiers advancing through the trees.

She was only just in time. As Su-san spurred her horse through the ranks of confused women warriors, the bannermen broke free of the trees.

Now, for the first time, She-she experienced all the horrors of a pitched battle involving thousands of men and women — and it was a close-fought engagement.

When the Imperial bannermen realised they were faced by a regiment of women, they howled their delight. Victory was assuredly theirs. Once it had been secured they would enjoy the women before their bodies became separated from their heads. It would be a victory that would be told and retold around countless campfires for generations to come — and it would lose nothing in the telling. Those who were here today would be hailed as heroes, envied by their sons and grandsons. Or so they believed.

Disillusionment was not long in coming to the bannerman warriors of the Chinese Emperor. The first shock came when the women of Su-san's regiment failed to break formation and flee before the charging bannermen. Only a few of them were armed with modern weapons, but their muskets were discharged with devastating effect. Then pikes and swords were brought into play to bring the charge of the bannermen to a shocked and bloody halt.

Before they had recovered from the shock of such unexpected and stiff resistance, Su-san called on the women to counterattack.

The response was instantaneous. Shrieking shrill defiance, the women counter-attacked with pike and sword, musket and bayonet.

Their sheer ferocity threw the bannermen into astonished disarray. Even before the regiment of Taiping men ran to the aid of their sisters, the bannermen were in confused retreat.

The retreat quickly became a rout and She-she found herself caught up in the pursuit.

Kau-lin was in the forefront of the women, her sword rising and falling among the fleeing bannermen. She-she rode beside her, caught up in an orgy of killing. It did not cease when they had overtaken the bannermen. She looked back to see the slaughter being completed by the men of their fellow regiment.

Suddenly, She-she began shaking uncontrollably. In a sudden fit of revulsion she threw her sword away, into the seething mass of men and women locked in furious battle all around her.

She-she felt her stomach rise to meet her gullet and with the battle still raging all about her she was sick. Sick as she had never been before. Her revulsion at the bloodshed she was witnessing did not come to an end until Su-san was carried into view nearby.

The commander of the women's regiment had been seriously wounded by a pike that had passed through her chest and come out immediately beneath her right shoulder.

8

THE men of the Taiping regiment were jubilant at their victory over the Imperial bannermen. The celebrations of the women were more muted due to the serious wound sustained by their popular commanding officer.

In addition to Su-san, another twenty-seven women had received serious wounds and thirty-five had been killed. In view of the numbers involved in the fighting the casualties were light, but it was a close-knit regiment and many of their number had been together for a long time.

The wounds were also likely to prove fatal because there were no doctors with the party. It was still being debated whether they should carry the wounded women with them to Wuhu, or return them to Nanking, when the sound of a ship's engine reached them. Minutes later three of the British naval vessels came into view from behind one of the many tree islands that dotted the river.

A white flag waved vigorously at the water's edge brought the ships to a churning halt. As they edged in close to the shore a shouted conversation was carried on between Prince Chang and the officers and diplomats who crowded the deck of H.M.S. *Furious*.

In reply to a question from the commanding

officer of the *Furious*, Chang requested the services of a doctor for his wounded.

"How were they hurt?" The question came from Lord Elgin, who stood at the rails, flanked by some members of his large staff.

"We were attacked by Chinese bannermen."

"Then we are unable to help you. We have agreed to remain neutral in your war with the Emperor."

"Most of our wounded are women. Unless you help they will die."

The information caused a stir upon the warship. The bulk of the women's regiment had been sent to make a camp well back from the river, among some trees. Although Kau-lin and She-she were with Chang, they were dressed in padded coats and hats that made them as shapeless as their long-haired male counterparts.

After some discussion on board the warship, the captain said, "I'm edging in to the bank. My doctor will come ashore. Do not try to board the ship without permission or you will be shot."

Chang had not held his exalted title for long, but it was long enough for him to resent being given orders. She-she saw his lips narrow, but all he said was, "Thank you. You are very kind."

The doctor was a young man with an athletic build. He jumped from the boat to the bank when there was still eight feet of water between them.

It took him only a few minutes to ascertain that Chang had not exaggerated the condition of the wounded women.

Calling to the titled diplomat on board the *Furious*, he said, "He was telling the truth, my Lord. Some of the women are so badly wounded I can do little here. *Cruizer* has more facilities than *Furious* for dealing with casualties."

Tactfully, he did not point out that this was because the *Furious* was over-crowded with Lord Elgin and the staff he had brought along for the river voyage.

"*Cruizer* should be along in an hour or two. If you care to go on, I'll have the wounded taken on board and conveyed to Nanking. It's the least we can do, my Lord, for humanitarian reasons."

He spoke hurriedly, aware of the disapproving frown on the face of Lord Elgin and more than one of his entourage. "Most of the women will surely die if any attempt is made to move them overland."

There was another flurry of conversation during the course of which as many heads were shaken disapprovingly as were nodded.

Eventually, Lord Elgin asked, "Is this your considered professional opinion, Doctor Latham?"

"It is, my Lord."

"Very well, you may remain with the women until *Cruizer* comes up. If the surgeon on board agrees with you the women may be conveyed to Nanking. We will anchor there and try to persuade the Taipings to prepare for your arrival. Waste no time on the way. My invitation to go to Peking is probably awaiting me at Shanghai."

Once again there was considerable shaking

of heads among the diplomatic staff on board the warship, but Lord Elgin had made his decision. Moments later the *Furious* steamed off, a heightening wave curling back from the upright bow as the ship gathered speed.

* * *

It was four hours before H.M.S. *Cruizer* reached the spot where the doctor waited. The warship had suffered a delay caused by running aground on a mud bank. The ship had a slightly deeper draught than the *Furious* and the captain grumbled about having to manoeuvre his vessel alongside the bank where a plumb-line showed the depth to be exactly the same as the water drawn by the warship.

However, the ship did not run aground on this occasion and the women were carried on board with great gentleness by the sailors. Although battle-hardened fighting men, they were distressed to see such wounds as the women had.

On shore, Chang said to Kau-lin, "It needs someone with them who speaks English. You had better go."

"No!" She-she said quickly. "The only reason we're here at all is because Kau-lin wants to meet up with her brother. Anyway, she'll be more use to you than I will. I've seen enough fighting today to know I was never meant to be a soldier."

"Are you sure that's the reason you want to return to Nanking? It's not because you wish to put off making a decision about marrying me?"

"I have told you, today has given me enough soldiering to last a lifetime."

It was partly true. She-she was putting off nothing. She had already made up her mind that she would not marry Chang. But this was not the time to tell him.

"Then I will approve your decision. I am not in favour of women pretending to be men and fighting as soldiers. We will speak again when I return to Nanking. Now I will write an authorisation for you to take the wounded women to Nanking. It will allow the doctor and as many men as he needs to enter the city."

★ ★ ★

There was a senior naval surgeon on board H.M.S. *Cruizer*. Even as the wounded women boarded the vessel he was having one of the mess-decks usually occupied by sailors converted into a hospital to accommodate them.

For two hours She-she was kept busy following the doctors around, interpreting their questions into Chinese for the women, then repeating the answers in English.

Two of the women needed to have limbs amputated, operations that She-she helped with, although the sight of so much blood caused her stomach to churn.

Shortly before dusk, the engines of the warship slowed and there was a bump as another vessel came alongside. When the engines picked up speed once more, a sailor came to the mess-deck hospital and began to light a number of lanterns. However, it was still fairly dark when She-she became aware of a figure standing nearby.

She was comforting one of the women whose arm had recently been amputated and did not look up until a voice said quietly, "My prayers have been answered at last, She-she. I was beginning to despair that we would ever meet again."

She-she gasped. As she swung around disbelief changed to uninhibited delight.

Standing before her, the crimson sash she had made for him slung over one shoulder, was Kernow!

Had Kernow and She-she not been standing in the shadows, his career prospects might have come to an abrupt end right there and then. As the long months fell away She-she began shaking, but when he held out his arms to her she came to him.

The embrace halted her trembling, but it lasted for moments only. The sudden screaming of one of the girls as she was operated on reminded them where they were and they drew apart.

"I thought you were dead for such a long time," said She-she. She searched her mind for something to say that would tell him how she felt at being with him once more, but the words would not come. Not here.

"Didn't Chang tell you I was alive?"

"Not until we were on our way to the Taipings. I was very unhappy."

"I have more news for you. I've met your

323

father — and one of your sisters too."

She-she's exclamation of delight was so loud that the surgeon turned around to look in their direction.

"How is he? And which sister?"

"Who's that. A marine? What are you doing here, sir?"

Surreptitiously placing in her hand the pendant given to him by Hau-ming, Kernow said to She-she, "The one who wore this. We'll talk later."

Replying to the surgeon he said, "I've been sent by the admiral to act as an official interpreter."

"Why? The girl's doing very well — and she's a damned sight more attractive."

"I agree, sir, but those are my orders from the admiral."

"Very well, but make yourself useful, sir. If you help to hold this young lady down we'll get our task done a lot more quickly. Now where did I put that saw . . . Attendant, get some more lanterns in here. Immediately!"

9

THE voyage downriver to Nanking took the British warship *Cruizer* a mere twenty-four hours. It was far too brief a period for Kernow and She-she but they managed to spend much of the time together.

It was accepted by the two surgeons that She-she would stay awake with her fellow Chinese women. Some of them were very badly hurt and needed almost constant attention. Kernow was allowed to remain with her because he too spoke Chinese and could understand their needs. He was also available to warn off any inquisitive sailor.

For many of the dark hours She-she and Kernow sat across a small table from each other in a shadowy corner of the dimly lit improvised hospital. Occasionally their hands touched but Kernow ached to hold her as he had all too briefly in the past.

During the night they managed to narrow the yawning gap of the past year. There were tears from She-she when he spoke of her father's concern for her, and smiles at the sauciness of her young sister.

Not until the Chinese dawn outshone the light from the lanterns did the conversation move on to the present and their futures.

"What will you do now, She-she?"

"Remain at Nanking. What else can I do?"

"Come to Shanghai. It won't be easy, but I'll persuade Lord Elgin to allow you to continue your journey downriver."

"What would I do in Shanghai, Kernow? Will you be there too?"

Reluctantly, he admitted he would not. "My base is still Hong Kong — but I doubt if I'll be spending much time there either. Events are moving fast in China, She-she. The most far-reaching changes your country has ever known are happening around us. The great ports are to be opened up to trade. But if you come to Shanghai I'm sure I can arrange for you to stay at one of the missions."

She-she shook her head sadly. "It cannot be. At Shanghai I would be made to live within the walled city, or in the French Concession where you would be noticed coming and going. We would neither of us be happy about that."

"Well, Hong Kong then. I'll find a place for us there."

She-she shook her head unhappily. "Kernow! What would I do in Hong Kong? I could live with you while you were there, perhaps. Although if the missionaries found out they would have you sent elsewhere, never to return. And what would I do while you were away, perhaps for many years? I would always be tormented with the thought that you might never return to me — and I would never know!"

"I would always come back to you, She-she. That I promise you."

She-she moved quickly to seal his lips with a

slim finger. "No promises. You are a very clever officer. One day you will be a great man."

She reached out and fingered the silk sash he wore. "Whenever I hear your name I will wonder whether you still wear this and if you remember She-she, who made it for you . . . "

Her voice almost gave her away, but at that moment Su-san called out. She-she left the table and hurried to where the Taiping soldier-woman lay gasping with pain.

There was a mixture of opium and water on a table nearby. She-she poured some for the wounded woman and carried it to her. She was struggling to prop Su-san up and put the opiate to her lips when Kernow came to her aid.

He was as gentle as was possible in the cramped conditions, but he could not prevent Su-san crying out in pain as she almost writhed from his grasp.

"It's all right. Let She-she give you a drink and try not to struggle."

Kernow thought he detected a trace of blood on her lips, but he said, "You're going to be all right. You'll be back in Nanking sometime today being given a heroine's reception, I've no doubt."

When much of the opiate had been swallowed, Kernow eased her back gently on the narrow cot. When she had stopped gasping for breath she looked at him for some minutes from tired eyes before her gaze shifted to She-she.

Kernow had spoken in Chinese. When Su-san spoke to She-she it was in a breathless Hakka version of Cantonese.

"Is this the *Fan Qui* you have told me about? The one you thought had died on the Canton river?"

She-she nodded.

"He is gentle, as are all the best soldiers. It would be nice making a baby with him — yet he could never make you a princess. Chang can. Make love with this one, if that is what your heart desires — but marry Chang."

Su-san's eyes closed and it seemed she had dropped off to sleep.

Kernow had understood every word she said. During his year in Canton he had met and spoken to many Hakkas, becoming fluent in their dialect.

"What did Su-san mean about you marrying Chang?"

"You understood what she said? Everything?" An embarrassed flush rose to She-she's cheeks.

"Everything. You haven't answered my question?"

Returning the remaining opiate to the table, She-she answered Kernow reluctantly. "Chang has asked me to marry him. To become his number one wife."

Kernow looked at her in alarm. "You've refused him, of course?"

"He is a prince now. Should I throw away the chance to become a princess?"

"It isn't what you want, She-she, and becoming a Taiping princess isn't as grand as it sounds. Your experience with the Canton *Hoppo* should have taught you about such things. Your father spoke of the hopes and expectations you

328

had when you left your home. Don't make a second even worse mistake."

As She-she's colour rose, Kernow said earnestly, "You know more about the Taipings than I, She-she, but looked at from the outside I'd say the movement is doomed. The Imperial army grows stronger while the Taipings are tearing themselves apart with their internal squabbling. Their best generals are leading separate private armies all over China, refusing to return to Nanking for orders, for fear of being caught up in the intrigues of the court and forfeiting their heads. You've seen it from the inside. You must know what I'm saying is the truth."

"What your *Fan Qui* says is so, She-she." Su-san was not yet asleep although she opened her eyes with some difficulty. "I will fight to the death for the *T'ien Wang* and our people, yet in my heart I know we will lose the last battle."

"Shh! You must rest."

"I have plenty of time for rest. If you will not become a princess you should listen to the advice of your *Fan Qui*. He talks much sense."

"Have you forgotten that it is you who have urged me to accept Chang? You told me how you would seize an opportunity to become a princess."

"I have advised you so because it is what I would do. I see now this is not the way for you. Chang is not a prince among men. Oh, he is not a bad man, but he will not save the Taipings. I saw fear on his face when the bannermen attacked. Our people — especially the *T'ien Wang* — need a brave leader."

"There!" Kernow spoke triumphantly. He had not expected support from such a quarter. "I'll speak to Lord Elgin today. Perhaps instead of stopping at Nanking we'll go on to Shanghai. You can all seek asylum there."

Su-san shook her head. The movement caused her to wince. "I will find asylum nowhere. Years ago, in a surprise raid on a Manchu camp, I killed a son of the Imperial family. An order was issued by Emperor Hsian Feng that I was to be executed wherever I was found — no matter what the circumstances. So, you see, the fate of the *T'ien Wang* and of the Taipings is my fate too. She-she can accompany you if she wishes — although if she does so it will go hard with the missionary woman. It will be thought she came here as a spy for the *Fan Qui*. Chang would sacrifice her to ensure no suspicion falls upon him for bringing She-she to Nanking."

"Neither Chang nor the *T'ien Wang* would dare harm an English missionary. It would be all the excuse the British government needs to take on the Taipings in a war."

"You are talking of the logic of earthly beings. The *T'ien Wang* is of heaven. His decisions are not always understood by mortal men and women."

"Is it possible for me to speak to Esme? I might be able to persuade her to return to Shanghai with She-she. That would be all right. They arrived together."

She-she shook her head. "The only men allowed in the *T'ien Wang*'s palace are the

330

most senior Taiping officials, and then only as far as the audience room. Besides, if you did see Esme it would solve none of the problems of which we spoke in the night. There is no place for me in Shanghai. Esme would tell you so herself."

"Listen to me, *Fan Qui*." Su-san's voice was growing weaker now. The opiate was beginning to take effect. "My sister is a captain in the palace guard. She will come to see me when she hears I am wounded. I will ask her to speak to the missionary. Arrange a meeting with you — outside the palace. Meanwhile you two should make the most of the time that remains to you here. There will be no chance for you to talk when we reach Nanking. Go now, I must sleep."

Sounds from other parts of the warship told Kernow that the day was beginning for the ship's crew. A boatswain's whistle; the bullying shouts of a petty officer rousing his men from sleep; the grumbling of sleepy sailors and the clatter of wooden buckets on the upper deck as men employed on punishment duties washed down the decks.

"If I can I'll speak to Esme in Nanking, She-she, but it might not be possible to see you again before you leave the ship. I know there are many obstacles in our way. It's likely there'll be times when we'll both despair of things working out for us. But I have one question I need you to answer honestly, right now. It's the key to the future for both of us. Don't think of all the reasons it might not happen, just answer yes or no. If it can be achieved would you *want* us to be together — for always?"

From She-she's expression it was apparent that she was about to raise another argument, but Kernow cut it off before it began.

"Yes or no?"

She-she took a deep breath. "I want us to be together more than I have ever wanted anything in my life. But . . . "

"No buts. You've said all I want to hear. It's what I want more than anything else too, She-she. Now you're going to need to have faith in me. Great faith, because it won't happen right away. But I promise you that one day we *will* be together. Believe me . . . "

They could hear the sound of voices from along the corridor beyond the door of the make-shift hospital.

Kernow looked about him with an expression of near-desperation. Drawing her into a curtained-off area, he kissed her briefly but passionately.

"I love you, She-she."

"I love you too, Kernow." As they heard the door to the ship's hospital opening, she added breathlessly, "I will become a Christian so that if we do not meet in this world we will meet again in your heaven. I will wait for you, I promise."

10

DURING the voyage of the British warships on the Yangtze river not one, but two letters were received by Lord Elgin from the Taiping authorities. Both contained apologies for the incident in which the ships were fired on by the batteries at Nanking.

The first was from the Taiping military commander. The second was from the *T'ien Wang* himself. His apology was accompanied by an invitation for Lord Elgin to pay him a visit. Both apology and invitation were almost overlooked in an extremely long and rambling dissertation. In this the Taiping leader pointed out the Christian aims of his movement. He also described at length how he, as the younger brother of Jesus Christ, had descended from heaven to bring the message of God to the unenlightened people of China.

The contents of the letter were hardly likely to persuade a peer of the British realm to meet with the writer. Lord Elgin dismissed the invitation. However, he agreed to send some of his staff on a visit to Nanking to meet with the 'Heavenly King'. Included among Elgin's delegation to the Taiping capital was Kernow.

Upon the ship's arrival at Nanking, he had to stand by helplessly as the women left the ship. Only She-she was walking. The remainder were carried off in bamboo litters.

She-she paused on the quayside, her eyes seeking and finding Kernow. She raised a hand to shoulder height and waited until she received an acknowledgement. Then she turned and was gone.

When Kernow told Lord Elgin about Esme Pilkington, the British plenipotentiary was aghast at the thought of a lone British woman living in the palace of the Taiping revolutionary leader.

"After reading the translation of this 'Heavenly King's' letter I'm convinced the man is insane," declared Lord Elgin. "Do all you can to persuade this missionary woman to leave Nanking immediately. Carry her back to the ship over your shoulder if you think you can get away with it."

Kernow smiled at the thought of heaving the substantial bulk of the missionary over his shoulder and abducting her from Nanking. "She's a strong-minded woman, my Lord, but I'll do all I can, I assure you."

Kernow meant it. He wanted Esme to leave the city. He was equally determined that, when she did, the missionary would be accompanied by She-she.

The visit by the delegation to the walled city got off to a bad start — and things did not improve. Snow had fallen during the night and the wind howling down from the surrounding hills was bitterly cold. Horses were brought to the dockside for the use of the British delegation, but they seemed to be riding for miles before the only gate open to the visitors was reached.

Nanking was frequently besieged by the Imperial army and the mighty Yangtze river was securely under the control of their war junks. Because of this the city gates closest to the river had been walled up. Others were closed and locked, for reasons known only to the Taiping authorities.

At the gate there was an inevitable delay while the details of the party were entered in the gateman's official ledger. Not until the man had counted and re-counted them three times did he allow them to pass through the gateway to a city which had been in existence for longer than two thousand years.

When Kernow entered Nanking his first impression was as disappointing as She-she's had been. The many cultivated fields contained within the city walls meant there was no sense of being in a great metropolis. Neither were there crowds of people, or any bustle in the streets when the party reached the built-up area. It was as though they had entered a town where there was no longer a sense of joy in living.

Questioning their guide, Kernow soon realised the reason for this. All trade within the walls of the city had been banned by order of the *T'ien Wang*. Anyone who wished to buy or sell anything needed to go outside the city walls and conduct business in the suburbs.

Trade, it seemed, was brisk in the many markets that sprang up outside Nanking, but it was transitory. Beyond the protection of the city walls a man, his family and his goods were at the mercy of wandering units of the Imperial army. The Imperial navy also made a habit of bombarding the suburbs, sometimes creating a bloody diversion by landing a raiding party. In addition, there was the constant threat of river pirates, while roving brigands with no loyalty to either side were forever on the look-out for easy pickings.

The delegation from the small British fleet expected to be taken straight to the palace of the *T'ien Wang*. Instead, they were led to a dilapidated hall where one of the middle rank of officials had his home. Here they were kept waiting until late afternoon.

Eventually, a polite and unruffled Taiping official came to the hall. It was to be regretted, he said, but the *T'ien Wang* was unable to see them that day. The noble Taiping army had won a notable victory against government troops in the north. He and his palace officials were giving thanks in prayer. If the honoured guests would make themselves comfortable for the night the official was optimistic the *T'ien Wang* would speak to them in the morning.

The senior member of the British party was Maxwell Brooks. A young, red-haired Scot, Brooks lacked the patience of a skilled diplomat. Furthermore he had nothing but scorn for the longhaired Taipings who were in rebellion against China's lawful government. They were a rabble. He regretted that Lord Elgin had acknowledged their existence, even on such a level as this.

"We came here to see the *T'ien Wang* — *today*. If he won't see us then I demand that we be taken back to the ship immediately."

"Wait!" Kernow was alarmed. He had other things to do before they left Nanking. "Let's talk about this before we do anything hasty."

Kernow was a junior officer. Although seconded to the staff of Lord Elgin he had spent little time on the warship carrying the British minister's staff. He and Maxwell Brooks barely knew each other. Brooks' angry expression showed that he resented Kernow's interruption.

"There's nothing to talk about. By slighting us they are insulting Lord Elgin. We'll leave immediately."

"You can do what you think is best," declared Kernow firmly. "I've been ordered by Lord Elgin to make contact with a British missionary — a woman who is living in the *T'ien Wang*'s palace. I intend seeing her before I leave."

Maxwell Brooks hesitated. He knew better than to countermand a direct order given by the British plenipotentiary. However, he had stated his intention in the hearing of others. He could not allow a junior Royal Marine officer to overrule him. He arrived at a compromise.

"If you feel it's your duty to remain here then you must do so, but it will be placed upon record that you do so against my recommendation. The remainder of us will return to the ship."

The hitherto unruffled Taiping official lost some of his dignity when Kernow explained the intentions of the diplomatic party.

"It is the *T'ien Wang*'s wish you should all stay. It is not good to incur his wrath."

"It is the order of the Lord Elgin that

337

his emissaries return onboard the warships by nightfall today. I risk his wrath by remaining here to speak with the woman missionary who serves the *T'ien Wang* in his palace. You will arrange a meeting. Perhaps it may satisfy your leader, and mine."

Kernow was concerned that the official did not have sufficient authority to arrange a meeting with Esme. He became more hopeful when an escort arrived to take the diplomats back to the river and did not insist that he go with them.

He was less certain when darkness fell and he was left in the high-roofed hall without even a light for company.

Just when he was beginning to think he had been forgotten, there came the unmistakable sound of a door being opened at the far end of the hall, although no light was produced.

Then the low voice of the official who had attended the delegation from Lord Elgin called softly, "Lieutenant Keats?"

"I'm here," Kernow replied cautiously. He was concerned that the Taipings might have planned something unpleasant for him because the remainder of the delegation had not obeyed the wishes of the *T'ien Wang*.

The official moved towards him in the darkened hall and Kernow sensed the man was not alone. Fearing a trick, he backed towards the wall.

"Who is it? Who have you brought with you?"

"You wished to see the missionary woman. I have brought her, but I have been unable to obtain the express permission of the *T'ien Wang*. I will be in great trouble if I am found out. You must talk in the darkness."

Kernow was aware that in the darkness there could be others listening too. Perhaps this was a ploy to learn what was said between Esme and himself. He would need to be careful.

He was still hesitating when there was a movement towards him. It was someone much lighter on their feet than Esme. He tensed in readiness to ward off an attack, when a voice called softly, "Kernow?"

It was She-she.

The next moment he was holding her and she was clinging tightly to him. But only for a moment.

As she pulled away from him, he reached for her hand and gripped it tightly as heavier footsteps came closer. A voice that Kernow had last heard in the mission in Hong Kong grumbled, "Lieutenant Keats? Where are you? Why the Taipings feel it necessary to play such silly games I'll never know. Where *are* you?"

"I'm here, Esme." He reached out his free hand and Esme took it in a grip that would not have shamed a man. Then she moved forward to kiss his cheek.

"It's wonderful to meet you again, dear boy. When we left Hong Kong we all feared you were dead."

"That all seems a long time ago now, Esme, but how have you and She-she met up again so quickly? I thought you were shut away in Hung's palace?"

"It was all done through the influence of Su-san, the wounded girl you spoke to on your ship. Her sister is captain of the palace guard. When She-she came with a message for her, telling her of Su-san's wounds, she was allowed to visit me. She was still with me when word came that you wanted to speak to me. What's it all about?"

Dropping his voice so that any unseen listener would be hard put to hear, Kernow said, "I come with a message for you from Lord Elgin. He received a long, rambling letter from the *T'ien Wang*. It's alarmed him greatly. He feels that Hung's palace here in Nanking is no place for a British woman and would like you to leave. He offers you a passage with us to return to Shanghai. I agree with him, Esme. I think you should leave Nanking — and I want you to bring She-she with you."

There was a considerable pause before Esme said, "Is it *me* you're concerned for or She-she?"

"Both of you, and that's the truth. Lord Elgin has agreed a treaty with the Imperial Chinese authorities that is meant to bring about freer trade between our two countries. The Taipings in the Yangtze basin stand in the way of trade here. You saw what happened when our ships passed upriver. Sooner or later Britain will move in to help the Imperial Chinese forces in the war against Hung and his armies. When this happens our country, mine and yours, will be at war with the Taipings. You'll find yourself in an impossible position."

"I didn't come to China for an easy life. I could have had that in England had I cared to stay there. I came to bring God to the people of this country."

"And how much success have you had with the Taipings?"

"You can't put success on a set of scales, Kernow. I am sowing the seeds of Christianity among these people. I may not be here to reap the crop, but I hope to be able to remove many of the weeds that might otherwise choke the infant plants."

"Presuming the *T'ien Wang* is the gardener, is he going to be happy to have you decide how he should manage his garden?"

The immediate silence said far more than Esme's next words. "I wish I could be certain of that. I only know I have to try."

"Your life will certainly be at risk if you stay here, Esme."

"My life on this earth doesn't matter to me. I came here to serve God. I shall remain in Nanking for as long as I feel there is purpose in my staying."

Very much aware of She-she's hand held within his, Kernow tried again to make Esme change her mind, but she was implacable and he eventually had to concede that the missionary was not going to leave Nanking.

"I was hoping for more from you, Esme. Much more. But do you promise you'll return to Shanghai if you feel there is nothing more you can do here?"

"Of course! I haven't come all the way to

China to waste my time. But there is still hope. I sometimes despair of the *T'ien Wang*, but when Chang returns I hope he might use his influence on my behalf."

"I think Chang has more worldly ambitions, Esme — and it brings me to my second concern. I can't hope to persuade Lord Elgin to take She-she on board without you, but I want you somehow to arrange to have her stay with you in the palace. She'll be safer there with you than anywhere else."

"Safe from what — or from whom?"

"You know Chang wants her to marry him?"

"I do, and I think it would be a good marriage for her. For both of them."

"It's not what She-she wants, Esme, and it's not what I want. I intend marrying her as soon as I'm able. Before you say anything, we both realise the difficulties involved and that it can't happen right away, but it will, I promise you."

"You're a fool, Kernow Keats. You'll be abandoning a very promising career in the services — not that I believe there's anything particularly commendable in achieving the ability to fight better than another. I saw this situation arising when we were in Hong Kong together. So did Hannah Jefferies. She would be appalled if she could hear you now. Are you both quite certain you know what you're doing?"

"We are." The reply came in unison.

"Then I offer you the blessing of a romantic old woman. One who should know better. What can I do to help?"

"Take She-she into the palace with you. Keep

342

her away from Chang as much as you can. She wants to become a Christian. She'll be a great help to you, if you let her."

Behind Esme, the Taiping official whispered, "We must go now. To stay longer will be dangerous."

Kernow wondered whether the man understood English. So far he had spoken only Chinese, but this could have been a trick to make them speak more freely. He dismissed his suspicions. Most of what had been said between Esme and himself had been in little more than a whisper.

"Please, Esme. Do this for me. For both of us."

"How long do you expect it to be before you can have She-she with you?"

"I don't know." He squeezed She-she's hand painfully. "It may be a very long time. Will you look after her until something can be arranged?"

"Of course."

"We must go now." There was urgency in the voice of the Taiping official.

"Don't worry about me. I will wait for you, however long it is. I have promised."

She-she came to Kernow in the darkness and he held her painfully close until the voice of the Taiping official called again.

Kissing him, she said softly, "I love you, First Lieutenant Kernow Keats."

"And I love you too, She-she."

A moment later she was gone.

11

LORD ELGIN left the Far East in March 1859 on a steamer bound for London. The treaty he had negotiated with the Chinese still had to be ratified, but the delay was put down to the customary inefficiency and indecisiveness of the Imperial authorities.

Lord Elgin should have known better. Even while he was enjoying his celebratory voyage on the Yangtze river, Kiying, the aged Tartar prince who had negotiated the treaty on behalf of the Chinese, was dying by his own hand.

The Emperor had been violently displeased by the terms of the treaty. He considered that the elderly negotiator had conceded far too much to the *Fan Qui* diplomats. The thought of British warships steaming the waters of the Yangtze river, China's jugular vein, filled him and his advisors with alarm and anger.

As for allowing foreign ambassadors to reside in Peking! Such a situation was unthinkable. It would bring a breath of the West to the capital and imply that the *Fan Qui* and the Chinese were equals, undermining the assertion that the emperor was the sovereign of the world. The maps which showed great China at the centre of the world and the Western nations as mere dots in a faraway sea would need to be redrawn.

Such a treaty could bring down the whole Manchu dynasty.

Kiying was sent a silken cord by the emperor. It was a token of the sovereign's displeasure and a command that his subject take his own life by way of atonement. The Emperor would also have hurled the treaty back at the *Fan Qui* negotiators had his advisors not preached patience. The treaty needed the approval of the Emperor before it meant anything at all. Numerous excuses for not adding a seal to make it a binding document would be thought up by his courtiers. The *Fan Qui* were babies when it came to such diplomatic prevarication.

The task of ratifying the treaty on behalf of the British government was left in the hands of Frederick Bruce, Lord Elgin's brother. An able diplomat, Bruce was a sound man but did not have the negotiating skill or status of his brother. He also lacked the knack that Elgin had of surrounding himself with the right men whenever a crisis loomed.

Of more immediate concern to Kernow was the departure, at the same time as Lord Elgin, of Admiral Sir Michael Seymour. The admiral had singled Kernow out as a young man worthy of special attention and Kernow had never let him down.

Seymour's evaluation of Kernow was passed on to his successor, but Admiral Sir James Hope was a very different man to Seymour. A stern but capable sailor, he possessed entrenched and not always logical beliefs. Among these was the conviction that the Royal Navy was the only service worthy of recognition. So strongly did he hold this view that he would not deign to respond to a salute from a soldier — and he classed Royal Marines with soldiers.

Kernow's first meeting with the new commander-in-chief was not auspicious.

Parading with others of the Headquarters' staff for inspection by their new chief, Kernow was singled out for special attention. Halting before him, Admiral Hope looked Kernow up and down from head to toe, as though he had never seen a Royal Marine before.

"Who are you?"

"Lieutenant Keats, sir. I was an aide and interpreter to Sir Michael Seymour."

"Were you, be damned! Well, I'll have no soldiers on my staff."

"I'm a Royal Marine, sir."

"You can call a pig a parrot, sir, but it won't help it to fly. You're not a sailor, so you must be a soldier."

"Lieutenant Keats is an exceptional linguist, Sir James." The admiral's secretary intervened in Kernow's defence. "He's the only one on your staff who speaks fluent Chinese. He also has a proven service record. He was second-in-command of the police force we put ashore to keep order in Canton. He did a magnificent job and was commended in despatches for his bravery when the first commanding officer was killed."

"In the police at Canton? I said the lad was a soldier. Have we no naval officers who speak Chinese?"

"None, Sir James."

"Then I suppose we'll have to keep him on

346

the Headquarters' strength — but I'll have no soldier as my *aide-de-camp*. Put him in charge of something or other. It doesn't matter what it is just so long as it keeps him out of my way."

The admiral passed along the line leaving Kernow quietly fuming. Hope had spoken about him as though he considered Kernow incapable of expressing an opinion about his own future.

Kernow said as much to the admiral's secretary later that same day, but the naval officer could only shrug apologetically. "I wish there was something I could do about it, Kernow, but Sir James Hope is a law unto himself. I dread to think what will happen if war breaks out again. He's likely to have the army performing the duties of a coolie corps for a Royal Naval brigade. But enough of that. We need to find an official post for you. Something that makes full use of your talents, yet at the same time keeps you out of the way of our new commander-in-chief."

By the end of that day Lieutenant Keats, R.M., was the commanding officer of the interpreters section at the Royal Navy headquarters, Hong Kong. He had a staff of five Chinese interpreters and a suite of two tiny offices. The latter had been commandeered from a protesting sailmaker who refused to accept that his skills had declined in importance since the introduction of steam into the Royal Navy.

★ ★ ★

347

With Elgin absent from Hong Kong, Chinese prevarication became increasingly irritating. Whenever the Western ambassadors put forward a date for their entry into Peking, the Chinese countered with a new reason why it would not be possible.

Eventually, the patience of the Hon. Frederick Bruce ran out. He ordered Sir James Hope to assemble a fleet. It was his intention to steam up the Pei-ho river, gateway to Peking, and bring matters to a head.

Admiral Sir James Hope wasted no time. By June, he had gathered together a battleship, two frigates and thirteen gunboats. The French demonstrated support for the venture by contributing a frigate and a gunboat to the small fleet. The Americans had been asked to commit ships too, but they declined. They had their own problems at home with the increasing tension between North and South. However, an American warship accompanied the fleet as an observer on behalf of the American government.

On board the United States vessel was a special ambassador sent to ensure that his own country's treaty would be ratified over the sights of the British and French guns.

The Chinese had anticipated such a move against them and had been busily preparing their defences. Reports reached Hong Kong that the Chinese had amassed an army of fifty thousand troops in the vicinity of the four Taku forts which guarded the entrance to the Pei-ho river. They had also placed chains across the

348

mouth of the river and driven spikes into the river bed.

To counter this threat Admiral Sir James Hope placed his reliance upon his sailors. It was only with great reluctance that he agreed they should be supplemented by four hundred Royal Marines. Half of the marines were from a Provisional regiment newly arrived on the China station from service in India. The remainder were drawn from the ships of his fleet.

At the mouth of the Pei-ho a close examination through telescopes wielded by the officers on board the flagship revealed that the river mouth was indeed well and truly blocked. In addition to the stakes and a stout chain there were rafts linking shore to shore, joined together with heavy booms. The impression given was one of total impregnability.

The Taku forts guarding both banks of the river looked equally forbidding, and were well fortified. The long, threatening snouts of large-bore cannon protruded though gun ports, many of the weapons being pre-aimed at the line of obstacles stretching across the river.

A crowd of scruffily dressed men on the shore were taking a great interest in the Anglo-French fleet and Kernow was sent off to speak with them. His orders were to ask them to take a message to the forts. Admiral Hope demanded that an official delegation be sent to parley with himself and the ambassadors who travelled with him.

When the boat carrying Kernow was still some distance from shore the Chinese began shouting for the sailors to return to their ship. They explained they were militiamen, sent to prevent a landing by the combined English and French fleet.

"Hold off!"

Kernow passed the order to the coxswain of the boat who passed on the order to his men with some relief. The men on the shore were ragged and tough-looking — and yet Kernow thought there was something about them that was wrong. Very wrong.

From the boat, rocking gently on the water about thirty yards offshore, Kernow carried on a lengthy conversation with the Chinese. They repeated their story that they were low-ranking militiamen. Their duties were to prevent any *Fan Qui* landing, no more and no less. They had no authority to request the attendance of regular soldiers. Anyway, they assured him, there were no Imperial forces within miles of the Pei-ho river.

Kernow did not believe them. Indeed, his suspicions were growing with every passing minute. These men were dressed as poor, illiterate peasants, yet they spoke with the authority and accent of Imperial army officers.

Suddenly, Kernow caught a glimpse of a figure in the midst of the group and knew immediately that his suspicions were justified. More than this, he realised that the report of a force of fifty thousand Tartar troops in the vicinity was not idle rumour.

The man he had recognised was the young Tartar leader who had saved his life when he went ashore seeking survivors from the typhoon that had struck Hong Kong, two years before.

He was looking at Shalonga, son of Tingamao, the great war lord from the borders of Vietnam. If his father was here too then Admiral Hope and his small army were outnumbered by fifty to one. The men opposing them were battle-hardened Tartars, not the rabble of bannermen that passed for an army in many of China's provinces.

12

THE first man to meet Kernow when he stepped back on board the flagship was Colonel Lemon of the Royal Marines Light Infantry brigade. It would be his task to command any assault on the Taku forts. His questioning showed the concern he felt over an assault he believed was being contemplated without adequate reconnaissance or planning.

"What's your opinion of the mud in front of the forts? Is it firm enough to support a man in the event of a frontal attack?"

"No." Kernow had no hesitation in replying to the question. "One of the men on shore had a pony and he tried to take it across the mud to the water's edge for a drink. It sank almost to belly level. Not only that, from closer inland you can see the forts are surrounded by ditches filled with a whole forest of pointed wooden stakes. A frontal attack would be suicidal."

"That's my opinion too. Let's go and speak to the admiral, Mister Keats. Perhaps your information will make him see some sense. He won't listen to me."

Kernow might as well have saved his breath. His observations fell upon deaf ears, as did those of the colonel.

"I thank you, gentlemen, but it makes no difference. I intend sending a force ashore tomorrow to clear the obstructions to the river.

Then I'll take the forts. I'll not allow a handful of scruffy Chinese to challenge the might of the British navy. If you're nervous of mounting an attack, Colonel Lemon, you can be in charge of dismantling the river barrier. I'll put a naval commander in charge of the assault on the forts."

"I'll take my place at the head of my men, Sir James. I merely want it placed on record that I consider the conditions here totally unsuitable for a frontal attack."

The colonel had been stung beyond discretion by the admiral's words, and Kernow stepped in hurriedly. "You're not facing a Chinese rabble, Sir James. One of the men on the shore is Shalonga, son of the great war lord General Tingamao. They came here from the Vietnamese border with fifty thousand troops. Most are cavalrymen and all are seasoned fighters."

Such information could not be ignored, even by a man such as Admiral Sir James Hope. "How do you know all this, Keats? By listening to coolies? I swear half of them are being paid by the Chinese government."

When the laughter of some of the admiral's junior naval staff died down, Kernow said, "I learned of the war lord's army from Shalonga himself, when I was taken prisoner by the Chinese on the Canton river. He was the man who secured my release. He had nothing to gain by lying to me. At that time there was no threat to us from this particular army. It was on its way to fight the Taipings."

Admiral Sir James Hope had not heard the

story of Kernow's exploits on the Canton river. For a moment it seemed he might question him further. Then his arrogant confidence returned once more.

"You were probably mistaken in thinking you saw this Shalonga fellow among the rabble on the shore. One Chinaman is very like another. The attack will be mounted tomorrow, gentlemen. Be sure your men are ready by first light. We're going to teach these Chinese a lesson they won't forget in a hurry."

"May I be permitted to take part in the attack, under Colonel Lemon's command, Sir James?"

Admiral Hope beamed at Kernow. This was what he understood. A young man eager to do battle. "Of course. I only wish I was young enough to go ashore myself, but I'll bring my ships up to help you as soon as a hole's been made in that damned barrier."

★ ★ ★

Making a hole in 'that damned barrier' was not as simple as the admiral had implied. Furthermore, although Hope had told Colonel Lemon to have his marines ready for action at first light, the order for them to land was not given until mid-afternoon!

The delay was due to the great strength of the barrier on the river. Royal Marines and sailors toiled through a day that became steadily hotter before word came back that a small breach had been made. Acting on an order given

354

by Admiral Hope, the combined fleet moved forward cautiously.

During all this time the guns of the forts had remained ominously silent. Contemptuously, Admiral Hope pointed this out as a sign that the Chinese had no stomach for a full-scale battle.

Kernow thought differently, but deemed it wise to remain silent. It was his opinion that when the Chinese in the Taku forts thought the moment right they would deal the admiral a blow that would send his forces reeling.

Kernow was proved tragically right. When the fleet reached the gap in the barrier made by the sailors it was discovered this was only the first of a number of such barriers. The British and French ships were trapped, close together, in a narrow channel.

The landing party was on its way ashore by now to take the Taku forts. When the boats ran aground, the Royal Marines and sailors went over the side. As Kernow and Colonel Lemon had predicted, the whole assault party immediately found itself floundering through mud that was always knee-deep and sometimes came as high as a man's waist.

It was impossible to maintain a steady line, yet the marines and sailors, weighed down with their weapons and battle-kit, kept going until they reached the first of the massive, stake-protected ditches surrounding the nearest fort. As they were forced to a halt, the Chinese opened fire. It was a barrage such as few of the veteran Royal Marines had ever experienced.

There were far more guns in the forts than the landing party had been led to expect and they were used to devastating effect.

The short-range guns were laid on the mud flats in front of the fort, an area that provided the British sailors and marines with no cover in which to hide.

The longer range guns had been sighted and tested to range on the barrier. They now opened fire on the combined British and French fleet with such effect that two ships were sunk in the first few minutes.

Admiral Hope had promised he would be in the forefront of his fleet. He kept his word, but it made no difference to the outcome of the one-sided battle. The Admiral was wounded in the first volley from the forts and before long his ship was sinking beneath him.

As Admiral Hope was transferring to the second ship in line he was wounded once more, and yet again when his new flagship came under fire. The admiral's wounds, though painful, were not mortal. He was far better off than the men he had ordered to make a frontal attack on the Taku forts.

As the first cannonade began, supported by the ancient muskets used by the Chinese, Colonel Lemon fell at the head of his men.

Kernow, assisted by a marine, pulled the commanding officer up from the mud but it was evident to them both that he was dead.

Lemon was not the only officer to fall. In that first, bloody salvo almost a third of the Royal Navy and Royal Marine officers became casualties. Within minutes Kernow found himself in command of a company of what had begun as a hundred men but now contained less than half that number. Somehow he managed to take them across the stake-defended ditch and reach the other side — only to be faced with yet another defensive ditch, even more formidable than the first.

It was here, trapped between the two defences, that Kernow received the first of the wounds he was to suffer that day. Something hit him low down in his body. In the excitement of the moment he thought he had been struck an accidental blow by one of the marines crowding about him. When the pain persisted he looked down and saw that the red of his tunic was glistening in one particular spot. He reached down to touch it and his hand came up wet with his own blood.

There was no time to tend a wound. All around him men were screaming out in agony as they too were hit. Sudden realisation came to Kernow that all the senior officers had fallen. He, a mere lieutenant, appeared to be in command of the landing party.

It was only for a short while. Behind him, having not yet reached the first ditch, a major of marines struggled to his feet. Appalled by the number of men who had fallen, he realised that those trapped between the two ditches would soon be dead unless he recalled them.

There were no buglers left to translate an order into a call that would rise above the battle din. The major was forced to shout his command to retreat. It came in one of those sudden, inexplicable lulls that occur in every battle and every sailor and marine on the body-strewn mud flats heard the order to return to the boats.

Kernow received another wound as he took his men back across the first ditch, yet he was able to lead his men in retreat until they were halfway to the shoreline.

When a shell exploded only feet from him, he was lifted and carried through the air to land on his back in the soft mud. He lay dazed for what seemed an age until sufficient breath returned for him to make an attempt to rise to his feet.

He was unable to raise himself from the mud. Three times he tried, and three times dropped back again. He believed the retreating men about him would think him dead and leave him where he was. He tried to shout. For some reason his voice failed him too.

Then he realised he was not lying like a dead man. His arms and legs were twitching uncontrollably. Here, on a mud flat on the coast of China, he was reminded of a stag he had seen shot on Exmoor when he was a young boy. Mortally wounded, with a bullet in its brain, the animal had lain on the soft green grass for longer than an hour, trembling as though in great fear. He had watched it until tears came to his eyes and he begged a huntsman to put the animal out of its abject misery.

Lying here in the mud with open eyes, looking up at the sky, he wondered whether one of his marines would come along and do the same for him. Perhaps they had all left. If the retreat had gone to plan they would at this very moment be embarking on the boats and heading back to the fleet. He would have been left to die amidst the carnage of Admiral Hope's fiasco.

He suddenly thought of She-she, who had promised to wait for him. Would news reach her that he had died on the mud in front of the Taku forts? Or would she wait in vain for ever, wondering why he had never returned to keep his promise to her?

13

"SHE-SHE . . . She-she!"

"Shh! Quiet now. Who's this girl you keep talking about? What's she doing that you're trying so hard to tell everyone about?"

When Kernow opened his eyes he could not believe what he saw. After closing his eyes tightly for a while, he opened them again, cautiously.

She was still there — a blue-eyed woman with a ready smile, her lightly tanned face framed by blonde hair. The face was familiar, but Kernow's mind would not concentrate. It seemed to be floating at some distance from his body. He was unable to place where he had seen her before.

"It's all right, you're not dreaming, and I'm not about to disappear and become some uniformed casualty orderly or whatever you British call such men. I'm Sally Merrill, remember me? My father's the United States consul at Shanghai. You and I met in Hong Kong. You're on an American warship now. We came along to observe what happened at the Pei-ho river but got involved when things started to go badly for you. My father declared he wouldn't stand by and do nothing while Europeans were being killed."

As the memory of the disastrous attack on the Taku forts returned to him, Kernow closed his eyes, but the expression of pain on his face had nothing to do with his own wounds. He was

360

remembering others.

"We took a bad beating, didn't we?"

"Kernow, you took an almighty hammering! It was Bunker Hill all over again, only this time it was the Chinese who gave you a thrashing. My father nearly had an apoplectic fit watching you trying to reach the forts through all that mud. What on earth were you thinking about?"

"It was Admiral Hope's idea. We were just carrying out his orders."

"Isn't that typical of you British? I swear you'd jump off a cliff if someone said it was 'orders'. It wouldn't happen in America, I can tell you that. Someone would up and say, 'What the hell d'you think you're talking about? You want to do it that way then you just go ahead — but you'll be on your own'. Wasn't there anyone of you dared say that?"

"Yes, Colonel Lemon said it, although not exactly in those words. He was one of the first to die."

Kernow tried to make himself more comfortable, but he found movement difficult and his left leg hurt so much he grimaced in pain.

"You just keep still now. Our surgeon's taken enough metal out of you to sink a sampan, but he says there's still some in there."

Thoughts of British service surgeons came to mind and Kernow's eyes opened wide in fear, "Your surgeon . . . He hasn't amputated?"

"No, you're all in one piece, Lieutenant Kernow Keats. You can thank our surgeon for that. Unlike most of yours, he doesn't amputate first and wonder whether it was

361

necessary afterwards. He's the best you'll find anywhere."

A memory of lying on his back in the mud came to Kernow and he said, "How did I get on board your ship?"

"Four of your ships were sunk by the Chinese and Admiral Hope was badly hurt. Father ordered our captain to go in and bring off the wounded. As we pulled away from your ships we saw two of your marines dragging you across the mud towards the water. All your boats had either taken on survivors and pulled back or been sunk, so Father sent our boat off for you."

"I'd like to thank him . . . thank you too."

"You'll have plenty of time for that. It'll be at least five days before we reach Shanghai. Right now you ought to be sleeping. It seems I haven't given you enough opiate. Here, let me lift you a little and give you some more."

Not until Sally Merrill came to move him did he realise just how much he hurt. There was pain in his shoulder, and in his stomach, but worst of all was that in his upper left leg.

When Sally was finished with him she laid him back gently and looked down at him sympathetically, "You'll be better now but you still haven't told me about this girl you keep talking about. Whoever she is, she'll be pleased to know you're going to be all right — this time. I wouldn't fancy your chances if you tried fighting another battle as you did today."

★ ★ ★

362

Kernow slept for a full twenty-four hours. Sally was not in the cabin when he woke, but within the hour he had a surprise visitor in the shape of Admiral Sir James Hope.

The Far Eastern Commander-in-Chief limped into the cabin, liberally swathed in bandages and sporting an ugly gash on his cheek, but looking surprisingly cheerful.

"Hello, Keats. I'm glad to have found you awake at last. Every time I've looked in you've been sleeping like a baby, even though you've such a pretty nurse looking after you. I'm surprised at a young man like you not trying to take advantage of such a situation."

"She's been very kind, Sir James. I want to thank her father some time, too."

"Of course you do. I just wanted to tell you I saw you take your men practically up to the fort wall before you were called back. You did damned well, my boy. If all the others had followed you we'd have taken the fort and had a different story to tell when we returned. Never mind, can't be helped. Fortunes of war and all that. Fortunes of war."

The Admiral turned to leave the cabin, hobbling painfully. He paused in the doorway and looked back over his shoulder at Kernow. "You'll be gazetted a captain when I return to Hong Kong, young Keats. Promoted on the field of battle. Might even take you on as an *aide-de-camp*. Pity you're not a sailor though. Damned pity."

★ ★ ★

Kernow was wounded far more seriously than anyone had allowed him to know. In addition to a badly wounded leg he had been shot in the lower abdomen and had an estimated half-pound of shrapnel removed from his shoulder.

The leg was the worst of his wounds, as he realised when he was taken to hospital in the British quarter of Shanghai. He and Admiral Hope were the first British casualties to reach the international community in the wake of the defeat at the Pei-ho river. There would be many more. Eleven hundred sailors and marines had taken part in the assault on the Taku forts. Four hundred and thirty were killed or wounded. There were more casualties on the ships of the fleet, pounded unmercifully by the unassailable artillery from the forts.

A French warship from the Pei-ho, carrying her own casualties, had arrived at Shanghai almost a day before the American vessel. As a result of the news it brought, every available doctor, irrespective of nationality, gathered to cope with the influx of wounded men.

A Scots doctor was the first to examine Kernow's leg. He shook his head when he removed the dressing put on only that morning by the American surgeon.

"I don't like the look of this, laddie. There's no infection yet, but it doesn't need long for it to take hold in this climate. I think we'd better amputate the leg right away."

"Oh God, no!"

The thought of losing a leg brought Kernow out in a cold sweat. He remembered the frustrations and moments of despair suffered by his father. He had returned to Cornwall from the First Opium War with a leg amputated. "Not that! I'd rather die than lose a leg."

"What nonsense is this? What's all this talk of losing a leg?"

The American surgeon who had attended Kernow on the journey from the Pei-ho river pushed his way through the gathered doctors. He was closely followed by Sally and her father.

"There's no question of your losing a leg, Kernow. I've already told you so."

"Are you a medical man, sir?" The British surgeon gave his American counterpart a frosty look. "If you are, and have experience of this part of the world, you'll be familiar with the incidence of gangrene. It causes more deaths among wounded men than any other factor."

"You British lose men because your thinking is fifty years out of date and you're too hide-bound to accept new ideas. Amputation isn't acceptable as a *preventative*! It should be undertaken only as a last resort."

The American doctor was aware that his British counterparts were closing ranks around him. He feared they might amputate Kernow's leg now, for no other reason than to make the point that they were in command in this hospital.

"Sir," he spoke to the American consul, "is there somewhere on the American ground we can accommodate this young man? I'm convinced I can save his leg. I'd like the opportunity to prove it."

When Consul Merrill hesitated, Sally pleaded, "Please, Father. If Surgeon Gill thinks he can save the leg, we must allow him to try. We've lots of room in the consulate. You've said many times it's far too big for us."

"Very well." The consul saw the expression on the face of the senior British surgeon and added hastily, "I'll ask permission of Sir James Hope. I'm quite certain he'll raise no objection to our taking care of this young man for a few weeks longer."

Confrontation between the Americans and the British doctors was averted by the arrival of a messenger. "Excuse me, sirs. The ship bringing in the bulk of the Pei-ho casualties will be arriving in a few minutes. The admiral has sent me to ask you to meet the men as they come in. Some of them are very badly wounded. They'll require immediate attention."

"Thank you." The senior British surgeon turned back to the Americans. "I'll be keeping a close watch on this young man's progress. If I feel he's not receiving appropriate treatment I will see you never practise surgery — or medicine — in the international colony again."

When the British doctor had gone, the American grinned at Kernow ruefully. "Well, aren't you the lucky one? Unless you make a full recovery my reputation's shot among the European community here. You'll be getting nothing but the best of treatment from me, young Kernow — and have the prettiest nurse in Shanghai along with it."

366

14

AFTER the disastrous battle, the British and French fleets retired to lick their wounds while the two ambassadors pondered their next move. It was now that the Chinese authorities proffered an olive branch — albeit one that was received with considerable suspicion.

A letter from the Chinese, making no mention of the fierce battle that had just taken place, was sent to the ambassadors of Britain, France and the United States of America. The letter suggested that if the three men went to a place ten miles further up the coast they would be met and escorted to Peking to 'carry out their obligations'.

The wording of the Chinese letter was so vague that Frederick Bruce refused to acknowledge it, as did his French counterpart.

The United States special ambassador was John E. Ward, a Georgia lawyer. He had been sent to China with orders to ensure that his country obtained a treaty at least the equal of any won by the belligerent actions of the two European nations.

Ward was new to the East. He lacked his colleagues' experience of the contempt in which the Chinese held emissaries of the Western nations. Thinking to steal a march on the other two countries, he accepted the invitation.

John E. Ward arrived at the appointed spot, expecting to be greeted as befitted an ambassador representing a vigorous and powerful nation. He was disappointed. There were many Chinese on the shore, curious at the arrival of a *Fan Qui*, but no one in obvious authority, and no sign of an escort.

Just as Ward was beginning to think there had been some mistake, a minor Chinese mandarin made his way through the crowd. Behind him was a small, enclosed carrying-cart. Had Ward been more familiar with the Chinese, the conveyance itself would have given him a strong indication of what he could expect from his hosts.

Carrying-carts used for important officials and mandarins were kept newly painted. The bright blues, reds and gold were intended to reflect the status of the occupier. They were also large enough for the passenger to enjoy a degree of comfort.

The carrying-cart sent for Ambassador Ward had once been painted in a drab green, but it had not felt the touch of a paint brush for many seasons. It was small, even by Chinese standards, and the frame of the ambassador would be extremely cramped.

It was an inauspicious beginning to a journey that would take him almost a hundred miles to the near-legendary capital city of Peking.

The journey, part overland, part by canal, was one the United States ambassador would forever wish to forget. For the whole of the way he was subjected to subtle yet continuous humiliation. The accommodation along the way was of a low standard and not especially clean. Food offered to him was poorly presented and uncertain in quality. Despite such treatment, Ward reminded himself he was suffering for America. The resulting treaty would justify all the discomfort he might endure on the journey.

Ambassador Ward had been looking forward to seeing the sights of the great Chinese city. To his great disappointment he was lodged in a small house surrounded by walls so tall he could not even see over them into the next garden.

Ward was kept waiting for some days before an interpreter came to the house. With unbecoming arrogance the very junior official announced that His Imperial Highness, Emperor Hsien Feng, would give the *Fan Qui* ambassador an audience the following morning.

No time was mentioned but the ambassador was up at dawn. Carefully putting on the plumed hat and braid-bedecked uniform, he looked in the mirror and saw the reflection of a man who was attired as befitted the representative of a great nation.

By mid-afternoon the uniform had lost its crispness and even the impressive plumes had wilted in the humid heat.

John E. Ward was a patient man, but his patience with his hosts was wearing thin. He was beginning to realise why the ambassadors of Britain and France had refused to put themselves in Chinese hands for the journey to the capital.

It was early evening before the summons came. After such a long wait even the splendour of the Emperor's impressive palace with its numerous courtyards and layered pagodas could not totally dispel Ward's uncomfortable mood.

He was shown into a long room hung with silken curtains and richly coloured tapestries. At the far end, seated on a golden throne, was the man few other Europeans had seen. Richly clad in a dragon-embroidered robe that matched his throne, the slightly built Emperor wore an abstracted expression. Ward thought it was almost as though he was drugged.

Suddenly, from behind him, the interpreter called in a shrill voice, "On your knees. Kow-tow!"

Ward half turned, his surprise giving way to renewed anger. He knew about the custom of kow-towing. Every one of the Emperor's subjects was expected to throw himself to the ground when in the Imperial presence. It was a gesture of total submission to the will of the man occupying the dragon throne.

"Down!"

This time the near-hysterical order was accompanied by a blow across the ambassador's shoulders with a gold-embellished cane held in the hand of one of the courtiers.

"You will kow-tow. Now!"

Suddenly, all John E. Ward's diplomatic ambitions fell away. He was once more the man who had dominated Georgia courtrooms, and swayed political rallies with his oratory.

"Sir!" The ambassador seemed to grow in

stature as he spoke. "I bend my knee only for my God, or before a woman. I'm damned if I'll throw myself on the ground for some puffed-up popinjay!"

* * *

"Things are beginning to happen in Hong Kong. When I left news had been received from England that a General Grant had been appointed as commander-in-chief. He's coming to lead an army against the Chinese and open the way to Peking. It's rumoured that Lord Elgin will return as ambassador to take charge of the diplomatic side of things. It's said you British are committing twenty thousand troops and the French almost as many. It looks as though your government is determined on a showdown with the Chinese this time. Do you think you'll be fit enough to take part . . . not as a combat officer, of course, but on the commander-in-chief's staff?"

The news was passed to Kernow by Caleb Shumaker at a dinner attended by about a dozen guests at the house of Consul Merrill in Shanghai. The American military attaché had arrived from Hong Kong only that day and had lost no time in calling at his fiancée's home.

Caleb was based in Hong Kong, but spent as much time as his duties would permit in Shanghai. He doted on Sally. On his frequent visits to the house he would follow her around like an affectionate puppy.

Caleb was not happy that Kernow had

371

remained as a guest in the house for so long, but was far too much of a gentleman to insult a guest of the Merrill family. However, he could not help being jealous of the easy relationship that had grown up between his fiancée and the young Royal Marine officer. It had been bad enough when Kernow was confined to bed, but he was able to walk now, although he still limped badly.

"Admiral Hope came visiting when he was in Shanghai a fortnight ago. He said we could expect some action in this part of the world now the mutiny in India is finally over. I suggested I should come back to headquarters on light duties, but he insisted I wait until I'm fully fit."

Observing the young American's disappointment, Kernow had difficulty hiding his amusement. For his part, he was more comfortable in the acting consul's house than he had been at any time during his service career. He had been on the sick list now for a full six months, during which time his promotion to Captain had been confirmed. He was eager to take command of a Royal Marines company as soon as he was able, but realised he was not yet up to taking on an active duty commitment.

Meanwhile the relationship between Kernow and Sally Merrill, although close and affectionate, was one of brother and sister rather than anything else. Sally was the sort of girl Kernow would have liked to have had for a sister.

When she looked at Kernow, Sally was reminded of Houston, the brother she had adored. He had met a tragic death in a riding accident in America when she was twelve years old.

"How about you Americans? Are you going to take an active part in any war?"

Caleb Shumaker grimaced. "There's nothing I'd like more. After the way poor John Ward was treated I feel we should join in and teach the Chinese a lesson, but our war department doesn't agree. Besides, back in the United States the breach between us Southerners and them Yankees up north is widening. While there's the likelihood of trouble in our own country we'd be foolish to get mixed up in a war out here."

Both Caleb Shumaker and Consul Merrill were from the Southern States of America and for the next hour the talk around the table was of the problems facing the United States.

They were still talking around the dining table when Kernow excused himself. He made his way from the cigar smoke of the room and went outside to enjoy a few minutes in the fresh air.

He was in time to intercept a European making his way from the gate towards the house.

"Can I help you?"

"Maybe. Is this the home of the American consul?" The stranger spoke with an accent not unlike that of Sally Merrill.

"That's right. He's inside with some friends. What's your name? I'll tell him you're here."

"No." The word came quickly. "My name

373

doesn't matter and I don't want to see the consul. I've got a letter for someone I believe is staying here."

"Who's that, Caleb Shumaker? He's inside . . . "

"That's not him. The letter's for a Kernow Keats. Lieutenant Kernow Keats."

Kernow was startled. Who could possibly be sending him a letter via this unknown man? "That's me. But . . . who's it from?"

The stranger's teeth gleamed white in the darkness. "I'm sure you'll learn all you need to know from the letter, friend, although you might find the news a little out of date. I was told I'd find you in Hong Kong. It wasn't until I got there I learned you were here, in Shanghai. I'll bid you goodnight."

"Wait! At least tell me your name."

The unknown American was already walking away towards the gate of the house and his name came back to Kernow from the darkness.

"Erin Veasey."

15

IN the light cast by the lamp in his room, Kernow looked at the bold writing on the envelope of the somewhat crumpled letter he was holding. It was a hand he did not recognise.

Tearing open the envelope he turned to the signature first and gasped in surprise. It was from Esme Pilkington.

Concerned that it contained bad news about She-she, he began to read.

Dear Lieutenant Keats,

It has been almost eight months now since you asked me to take She-she into my care and protect her for as long as she remained in Nanking. I am happy to tell you I was able to bring her into the palace of the *T'ien Wang* and keep her in safety. It was easier once Chang had taken his authorised quota of wives. However, I have heard he is now collecting an assortment of concubines (so much for his Christian principles!) and I will ensure She-she keeps out of his way.

She-she is a dear girl who has proved invaluable in what painfully little progress I am able to report from here. She has been a veritable tower of strength to me during some very difficult times. Needless to say, I have grown very fond of her. For this reason and the love I know you have for She-she I must ask you to find some way to bring us both out of Nanking as quickly as possible without putting yourself in danger.

The situation in the palace has changed alarmingly. I no longer feel that by remaining here I am able to serve the best interests of the Lord. Indeed, my continued presence might even be used to propagate the very aspects of Taiping doctrine which are particularly repugnant to those of us with true Christian ideals.

Because this note is written in great haste I am unable to tell you of our problems in any detail. Indeed, as I am sending it by the hand of a senior Chinese official who has always been loyal to the Emperor, it is by no means certain it will ever reach you. I can only, as always, put my faith in God and trust that He, and She-she's brave lieutenant, will find a way to rescue us from what has become a virtual prison.

Your most humble servant,
Esme Pilkington

Esme's brief letter filled Kernow with dismay. The large, bluff missionary was not a woman to plead for help without very good reason. He wondered what could have happened. She appeared to have abandoned all the missionary ideals that had taken her to Nanking in the first place.

What alarmed him even more was the time that had elapsed since Esme had written her plea for rescue. Erin Veasey had said he had been carrying the letter for some time . . .

★ ★ ★

Only the men remained at the table when Kernow limped hurriedly into the dining room. The women had found the cloying cigar smoke too much for them.

"Does anyone here know of an American by the name of Erin Veasey?"

Consul Merrill frowned, both at the manner in which Kernow had entered the room and because of the question. But one of the guests, a wealthy American merchant, was already answering Kernow.

"I've never met the man personally, but he's earned himself something of a reputation among the seafaring community. They say he'll take a cargo anywhere, for anyone — at a price, of course. There's a strong rumour that he's been running guns to the Taipings, but nobody's been able to prove it. Haven't the rumours reached you, Consul?"

Merrill nodded. "They have, together with a great many more. What's your sudden interest in the man, Kernow?"

"I need to find him. Urgently. Does anyone know where he stays when he's in Shanghai?"

"Probably on board his ship — or among the shanties in the suburbs, beneath the wall. That's where most of the seafarers spend their time. Many of the Chinese are running very profitable businesses there, selling cheap liquor to the sailors. That's something I wanted to talk to you about, Consul. We could attract a lot of business here by building a reputable saloon . . . "

Kernow did not stay to hear the remainder of the merchant's suggestion. When he met Sally as he crossed the hallway to the door he was shrugging himself into a quilted jacket.

"Where are you going? Has Caleb said anything to upset you?"

"Nobody's said anything. I just need to go out, that's all."

"Do you want me to come with you? Get you a sedan?"

"No, Sally. I've got to begin walking on my own again. Now seems the right time to make a start. I'll tell you more about it in the morning."

As Kernow walked away in the darkness the picture of Sally and her expression of deep concern remained with him. She was fond of him, and it was comforting to have someone around who cared. But he could not confide in anyone until he knew exactly what he was going to do.

Kernow crossed the bridge leading from the American ground to the foreign settlement housing the British. He had walked a quarter of a mile and covered half the distance to the high wall of the city that towered above the sprawling suburbs. His leg was aching and he was wishing he had accepted Sally's offer to call a sedan. But he knew that while he waited for the carrying-chair to be brought to the door he would need to tell her why he was walking off into the night. The fewer people who knew what he had only half planned, the better it would be.

By the time he reached the suburbs, Kernow was limping worse than he had for a month or more. Although it was winter, the pain in the bone of his upper leg had caused him to break out in a sweat.

The Chinese were used to seeing Europeans here. He twice had to shake off the hands of wheedling men who wanted to guide him to: "Fine grog shop, plenty girls . . . "

The bars where the European seamen were drinking were not hard to find. His experience with marines had taught him that whenever they found a place to drink they also developed an overpowering urge to sing. The Shanghai suburbs proved no exception. Nevertheless, he had seldom seen men 'enjoying' themselves in such squalid surroundings.

He found Erin Veasey drinking in the third grog shop he looked inside. This one, at least, was more salubrious than the others. The dirt floor was clean and it was quieter than either of the other two.

Kernow was not aware the American sea captain had seen him but, as he reached the table, the American stretched out a hand for his drink. Without looking up, he said, "You looking for me, Mister Keats?"

"I am. You brought me a letter. I want to talk about it with you."

Without a word to the other men at the

table, or to Kernow, Erin Veasey picked up a near full bottle. With it in one hand and a half-empty glass in the other he rose from the seat. He walked to a table from which two seamen and two Chinese girls rose and disappeared through a curtained doorway at the rear of the grog shop.

"Will you have a drink with me?"

Kernow nodded and sank to the wooden bench on the far side of the table from Erin Veasey. He was greatly relieved to take the weight off his scarcely healed leg.

As the sea captain waved for another glass, he said, "You still suffering from the wounds you received when you tried to take the Pei-ho forts?"

Kernow nodded. "That's right, but I haven't come here to talk about me. The letter you brought contains some disturbing news. Are you still trading upriver to Nanking?"

The hand pouring a drink from the bottle into the glass that had been placed in front of Kernow was rock-steady. "Now what sort of question is that, Mister Keats? You know that trading with the Taipings is forbidden by both my government and yours."

"Don't play games with me, Mister Veasey. This is far too important. I need to get to Nanking. I *have* to get there."

"Just a minute now. Even if I was trading up to Nanking — and that's not an admission — even if I was, it isn't a trip for passengers. A year or two back it might have been all right. Not now."

"Then sign me on as crew to Nanking and back."

"You're mighty anxious, Mister Keats. You mind telling me what was in that letter I brought you?"

"Two friends are having some trouble in Nanking. They need to be brought out."

"More passengers . . . and from Nanking? Just who are these friends?"

"A missionary and a Chinese girl."

"You talking of Esme Pilkington and young She-she?"

Kernow was so startled he spilled the drink he was carrying to his mouth. "How do you know? Have you read my letter?"

Erin Veasey smiled. "I don't need to read anyone's letters. Since we've stopped playing games . . . I first met them, and Kau-lin, on the boat from Hong Kong to Shanghai a couple of years back. It was me who took them on to Nanking. What's happening that makes it so urgent they need to come out in a hurry?"

"I don't know." After a moment's hesitation, Kernow pulled the brief letter from his pocket and passed it across the table.

Erin Veasey's eyebrows arched a couple of times as he read. Then he passed the letter back.

"That doesn't sound like the Esme Pilkington I took to Nanking. She was full of confidence then. Was going to take orthodox Christianity to the whole of the Taiping movement."

Kernow nodded.

"I didn't like this Chang even then."

Erin Veasey took a sip from his glass and looked over the rim at Kernow. "You serious about trying to make a go of things with She-she?"

"I am."

"Does Sally Merrill or anyone else at the consulate know about this?"

"Not in any detail, but what have they got to do with anything? Will you sign me on as a crew member for your next trip to Nanking?"

Erin Veasey did not reply to Kernow's first question. Instead he said, "How soon can you be ready."

"Tonight if necessary. How soon do you sail?"

"You'll just about make it. I intend leaving on the tide before dawn. My ship's at the foreign anchorage. I'll have a boat waiting to take you out there three hours from now. I'd better rustle up a sedan-chair for you, you've some packing to do — and not a word of what you're doing to Merrill or his daughter. If you must tell them something, say you're taking a sea voyage by way of convalescence. They may not believe you, but these are unusual times. They won't question you too hard."

16

JEN-LIN, captain of the palace guard and sister of the wounded Su-san, took She-she into the royal palace of the Heavenly King through the impressive main entrance.

There was another gate to which she had a key and where they would have attracted less attention, but Jen-lin was displaying a degree of cunning. More than a thousand women lived and worked within the palace walls. Jealousies and feuds were rife. If word reached the *T'ien Wang* that his guard captain was taking girls in or out of the palace by the back door he would think the worst and Jen-lin would forfeit her head.

All the wives of the Taiping leader were virgins when they came to him. The security that surrounded them while they were in the palace ensured they would know no other man for as long as he lived. There had been doubts about the chastity of only three of his one hundred and eight wives and hundreds of concubines. All three had suffered decapitation. So too had their fathers and the men who had brought them to the attention of their Heavenly ruler.

The main gate of the palace was heavily gilded and hung on carved pillars of red and gold. Once through the gate the two women walked beneath a covered way which was supported by gilded columns. On the roof of the covered way were numerous carved dragons, each differing from the other in some small detail.

In sharp contrast to the magnificence of the Taiping leader's palace were the soldiers who guarded the building. Unkempt and dirty, they lounged in a room alongside the entrance, their uniforms worn and ragged. They sprang to their feet at the arrival of the two women. Jostling and elbowing each other for space at the door, they leered at She-she as Jen-lin took her inside the palace.

Once inside the main door She-she found herself in the audience chamber. Jen-lin told her that this was the only room in the palace to which men were admitted. It was designed to impress visitors. Gilded lanterns were hung from the ceiling by silken cords. The walls were decorated with embroidered silk panels and painted birds. Fearsome animals and exotic flowers coiled about pillars and reached out across the ceiling.

As the two women were passing through the room there came the sudden sound of drums, cymbals and gongs. Rising to a deafening crescendo, the noise went on and on, showing no sign of ceasing.

"What's that?" She-she spoke fearfully. She believed the noise to be some form of alarm, sounded because she had no right to be inside the palace.

Jen-lin smiled. "You'll soon become used to that. It's the signal to inform the household staff that the *T'ien Wang* is about to take his meal. It gives no one any excuse for not being where they should be during meal times. Come, this way."

Jen-lin led She-she through a door, across an enclosed courtyard and through a maze of passages that ended in a small suite of rooms. The door was open. Esme Pilkington could be seen inside, hunched over a low desk, writing.

When she looked up and saw She-she her face lit up in a delighted smile. Rising to her feet, she held out her arms and wrapped She-she in a warm embrace.

"She-she! You're a delight for sore eyes, my girl. I was beginning to give up all hope of having you here in the palace with me. I sometimes wondered whether I would even see you again! Every time I've seen Hung I've asked him to arrange for you to join me here, to help me with the translations he wants from me. I've been able to get no sensible reply from him."

Esme had seen the disapproving tightening of Jen-lin's lips when she failed to accord the Taiping ruler his self-styled title.

"The *T'ien Wang* has to deal with many problems on behalf of his people," said Jen-lin. "Too many of the less senior generals are afraid of making decisions. They fear to offend either of the brothers of the *T'ien Wang*, or Chang, or the more senior generals. Because of this they refer even the most petty decision to the *T'ien Wang*, knowing his word is beyond question. It was my decision to bring She-she to you, to avoid more unnecessary problems for the *T'ien Wang*."

Jen-lin remained with the other two women

for almost an hour. When she had gone, Esme said, "Jen-lin is very helpful and has a great deal of authority within the palace. But you must never forget she is fiercely loyal to Hung. Her first duty will always be to him."

★ ★ ★

Chang worked hard at his task of co-ordinating the Taiping armies. He began by visiting the many generals appointed by the *T'ien Wang*. A number of the army leaders accepted his leadership. Others had held independent commands for too long. They would take orders from no one.

When Chang returned to Nanking some weeks later he was very angry to learn that She-she had moved into the palace. Although there were many pressing matters of far more importance to the Taiping movement, he raised the subject with the *T'ien Wang* at their first meeting after his return from speaking with the generals.

Chang might as well have saved his breath. The Taiping leader's mind was filled with a scheme for having Esme translate the New Testament of the Bible. He wished her to add details of himself and the place he held in the Heavenly family. Chang remembered Esme asking for She-she's assistance and assumed he must have agreed to allow her to take up residence in the palace.

Telling Chang that one woman was of little consequence to the Taiping cause, he explained how he proposed to have the modified Bible translated into both Chinese and English. This would surely impress even the most doubting of European missionaries . . .

Unaware of Chang's frustration, She-she quickly settled down to life in the palace of the *T'ien Wang*. It was an unnatural environment. Life in the palace centred around the *T'ien Wang* and his celestial pretensions. His trances, visitations, proclamations and interminable edicts and poems were all received with an awed respect by palace wives, concubines, servants and officials. All hung on the *T'ien Wang*'s every written and spoken word with a reverence that astonished She-she and angered Esme.

"Hung is a mighty leader to his people," Esme told She-she one day. "I am also willing to believe his genius must be heavenly inspired, but if he doesn't stick to Christian principles he'll forfeit the Lord's protection. Hung has been given an opportunity to influence the world for good such as no man has known since our Lord Jesus Christ himself. It is within his power to bring millions of men and women to the true God. If he throws his chance away he'll not only lose the support of Our Lord, but will be punished for sending the souls of generations of Chinese to purgatory. The numbers will be counted in tens of millions. It will be a monstrous sin. One beyond the comprehension of mere mortals like you and I."

17

SHE-SHE never doubted the heavy responsibility shouldered by Hung Hsiu-ch'uan. The self-proclaimed deity possessed the power of life and death over millions of his Taiping followers. Nevertheless, it did not take her long to learn that the *T'ien Wang* was subject to more venal passions within the high walls of his palace, safe from public view.

The maidservant who cleaned the suite of rooms occupied by She-she and Esme was a talkative young girl. She was one of many young women who had been taken captive by the Taipings during their sweep through China. She told She-she that not a woman in the palace was safe from the amorous 'Heavenly King's' attentions. It mattered not whether she was wife, concubine or lowly servant-girl. When the mood came upon him, Hung would prowl the corridors and pavilions of the palace, making love to his women whenever and wherever he found them — and the urge manifested itself with an astonishing frequency.

The Taiping leader was also subject to passion of a more violent kind.

One day She-she was working in one of the many small gardens of the palace. It was hot inside the quarters she shared with Esme and she had brought writing paper and the Bible outside to continue her work of translating sections of the New Testament on Hung's behalf.

She heard a commotion in one of the pavilions near at hand but took little notice at first. Quarrels were often breaking out among the palace women. They had little else to occupy them during the daylight hours.

Suddenly, she was astonished to see the *T'ien Wang* come from the direction of the disturbance, followed by many of the women of his entourage. He did not observe She-she and crossed a corner of the garden farthest away from her. There was an angry expression on his face and consternation among his immediate followers.

Behind the *T'ien Wang* a single voice was raised in agonised weeping. After doing her best to ignore the sound for some minutes, She-she could eventually bear it no longer. Abandoning her work, she went in search of the wailing woman.

Inside the nearest pavilion, occupied by some of the *T'ien Wang*'s concubines, she found a pretty young girl seated on the floor of the corridor, clutching her stomach. She was obviously in great pain.

Between noisy and prolonged bouts of sobbing and wailing, the girl told She-she she was one of the *T'ien Wang*'s concubines and had long regarded herself as one of his favourites. He had come to her quarters today with the intention of making love to her.

When she broke the news to the 'Heavenly King' that she was pregnant, the Taiping ruler had flown into a rage and beaten and kicked her in a frenzied attack. The object of his fury was the child inside her and most of his kicks were aimed at her stomach.

None of the other concubines dared go to the aid of the girl who had provoked the *T'ien Wang* to such fury. After pleading unsuccessfully with them for help, She-she helped the girl to the quarters she shared with Esme.

The concubine had a miscarriage during the evening but, despite Esme's and She-she's pleas, insisted on being taken back to her own quarters that same night.

* * *

When She-she was summoned to the audience room at the *T'ien Wang*'s command a few days later she immediately thought it had something to do with the assistance she had given to the unfortunate concubine. Frightened of what the Taiping leader might have in store for her, She-she asked Esme to accompany her.

"Of course." Esme had been deeply angered by the *T'ien Wang*'s treatment of the Chinese concubine. "If he has anything to say about what you did for that unfortunate young girl, I'll tell him a thing or two about the way he treats his women. If he doesn't like it he can send me back to Shanghai. I'm beginning to think my being here has less to do with serving God than building up Hung's image."

"Don't anger him," She-she pleaded. "You are a European. He might think twice about doing anything to you; I am Chinese. No one will go to war if my head is placed on a pole outside the city gate."

The imagery conjured up by She-she's words took Esme aback. "I . . . of course I won't, She-she. But you needn't worry. I will treat any threat to you as though as it were intended for me. He'll not harm a hair of your head, I promise you that."

When the two women were escorted into the audience chamber they realised immediately that the summons had nothing to do with the unhappy concubine. There were a number of men prostrate on the floor in front of the platform on which the *T'ien Wang* sat on his golden throne. Kneeling on the top step was Chang.

"Kow-tow!" The order was given by one of the women who had brought them to the room. She-she and the escort flung themselves full-length on the floor while the *T'ien Wang* and Esme played out their charade of praying to God with Esme on her knees.

"Is this the woman?"

Hung Hsiu-ch'uan put the question to Chang after he had signalled for She-she to rise to her knees.

"She is the one. We travelled to Nanking from Shanghai together."

The Heavenly ruler nodded to Chang and then addressed She-she. "My royal cousin, Chang, commander of all my armies and most trusted of my people, wishes to take you for a wife. As you are within my household he needs to ask my permission. What do you say?"

Wishing it were possible for the floor of the audience room to open and swallow her, She-she said, "I don't want to marry him."

"Why not? Tell me, girl — and I hope for your sake it is a good reason." The *T'ien Wang* displayed something of the anger she had witnessed a few days before and She-she trembled.

"The girl has become a dedicated Christian. She wishes to continue to serve God and yourself by helping me to translate the Gospels, as instructed by you. She is indispensable to me. Without her I could not complete my work."

Esme came to She-she's rescue with an impassioned plea, the words accompanied by one of her "What's all this nonsense about?" looks.

Although neither woman could possibly be aware of the fact, Hung Hsiu-ch'uan was delighted to be able to thwart Chang, even in such a minor matter. The *T'ien Wang* and his earthly cousin had just had a serious disagreement over the role of the Taiping armies during the next few months.

The *T'ien Wang* believed the armies should combine and go on the offensive against the Imperial forces. They had reached the gates of Peking once before. He argued that if they struck boldly and determinedly the Taipings could repeat their past glories and this time occupy the Imperial capital.

He was convinced there would soon be another war between the *Fan Qui* and the Manchu rulers of China over the issue of *Fan Qui* representation in Peking. If the issue was brought to a head it would be a great coup if he were waiting at Peking to welcome the Western ambassadors to the capital. It would force the European nations to recognise the Taipings.

There was much sense in his argument. A carefully timed campaign by the Taiping armies would split the Imperial Chinese army and force it to fight on two fronts, weakening its capabilities considerably.

Chang disagreed with the reasoning of his Heavenly cousin. He had just returned to Nanking after visiting the areas occupied by the Taiping armies. The generals and their men were not equipped to mount an all-out offensive. His plan was to use what resources they possessed to break the Imperial army's stranglehold on the Yangtze river, especially in the vicinity of Nanking.

If the Taipings were to win the battle for China they needed to obtain modern weapons with which to replace the ancient muskets, swords and even spears with which most of their soldiers were equipped. For this they needed to command trade on the Yangtze river.

Chang did not have the confidence of the army's commanders yet, but if he obtained modern weapons for their men he knew they would give him the backing for his own plans.

Hung Hsiu-ch'uan had strong reservations about allowing his cousin to become too popular with the generals. Such power outside his own royal hands might prove exceedingly dangerous to the Taiping throne. The *T'ien Wang* did not want to be forced to carry out another purge similar to that of a few years before.

The *T'ien Wang* was well aware of the dangers that quickly arose when a strong man was promoted to a senior position within a revolutionary movement. He had only recently elevated Chang to his present high position, but his cousin had already gathered a following from those who attached themselves to ascending stars.

After weighing up all the issues involved, the Taiping leader had been forced for the moment to agree with Chang over the policy issue of procuring arms. However, he could afford to allow his pique to surface in other, less dangerous ways.

"I am sorry, noble cousin. She-she is too important to leave my palace at this time. She is engaged in Heavenly pursuits. A wife or concubine is a mere woman. She-she is the interpreter of God's word. That must take precedence over all else. You will find other girls — in fact, I *insist* you do so. My birthday is one month away. By then you will have taken the number of wives I have declared to be in keeping with your high office."

18

SHE-SHE'S relief at not being forced to marry Chang did not last very long. A few days later the *T'ien Wang* sent for her and Esme to come to his quarters. It was an unprecedented honour. All the way from their own quarters the two women wondered what had prompted such an invitation.

The manner in which they were received by the Taiping leader was equally puzzling. After She-she had kow-towed and Esme had shared a prayer with him, both women were ordered to sit at his feet while he spoke to them informally.

Hung's first question concerned the progress of their translation of the Gospels. When they informed him that the translation was well underway, the Taiping leader expressed his satisfaction.

"This is good. You are working well. Soon I intend giving you many of my Heavenly decrees and proclamations to translate into English. I wish to send them to missions in Shanghai and Hong Kong."

"Is this wise?" asked Esme doubtfully. "You have said many times that you are not understood by churchmen in these two places."

She had read some of the *T'ien Wang*'s proclamations. Filled with confused thoughts they were hardly likely to impress any of the

European missionaries.

"Do they not send the translations of *their* thoughts to the Chinese peoples? Are not the thoughts of the *T'ien Wang* equally important? I have been to heaven and spoken with God the father and Jesus the elder brother. I will tell them of the mission that has been given to me. I will do more. When you have translated my proclamations and decrees we will work together translating the New Testament. I will tell you where it is wrong. Your people as well as mine have a great deal to learn about my Heavenly family."

So filled with indignation was Esme that she seemed to swell before She-she's eyes, but a warning hand on her arm was sufficient to calm her, at least for the time being.

It came as a great relief to She-she when the *T'ien Wang* dismissed the two women and allowed them to leave. But all that evening she had to listen to the rumblings of her companion about the dangerous pretensions of the Taiping leader.

★ ★ ★

It was another few weeks before Hung Hsiu-ch'uan sent a messenger to the quarters of the two women. This time he wanted to speak to She-she on her own. Esme presumed that he must have forgotten to include her in the invitation, but the palace official was adamant. "No, the *T'ien Wang* said *only* She-she. Only she must go."

396

"Don't worry, Esme, it's probably a mistake. When the *T'ien Wang* sees that I'm on my own he'll surely send for you."

She-she was less certain when she was shown into the *T'ien Wang*'s quarters and he failed to comment on the absence of the missionary.

After her initial act of obeisance, She-she was ordered to sit at the leader's feet, as before. He had some more proclamations he wished her to translate. After reading a series of rambling and often unintelligible poems, he suddenly asked She-she to tell him about her family.

Uncertain of the reason for his question, She-she told him of her father, mother and younger sisters. As she spoke she realised it had been a very long time since she had last seen them. The thought made her sad.

As though reading her mind, the Taiping leader said suddenly, "I will have them sent for. I can offer your father high commands in my service. We will make him very proud of you."

She-she managed to murmur something to the effect that it would make her very happy if she could see her parents once more.

"You are content to live here in my palace?"

"Yes." The *T'ien Wang* appeared to be waiting for her to say more. After a minute or two of silence, She-she added, "The English missionary is a good woman. I enjoy working with her."

"The *Fan Qui* woman is not yet a sister of the Taiping people. She is still a missionary. Her desire is not to learn but to teach."

Still puzzled about the true reason for her summons, She-she had a strong impression that her reply had annoyed the *T'ien Wang*. After a few more polite exchanges, he told her she might go.

★ ★ ★

A week later, Hung sent for She-she once more. This time the woman guard who came to fetch She-she was uncertain whether or not the invitation included Esme and she gave way before the missionary's forcefulness and took her too.

The *T'ien Wang* did not seem pleased to see Esme, but went through the customary formalities with her. Then, addressing She-she, he came straight to the point of his summons.

"You still have no wish to become a wife to Heavenly Prince Chang?"

"None at all."

"This is good. I have decided to honour you by making you one of *my* wives."

Appearing not to notice the gasp of dismay from his intended bride, the *T'ien Wang* continued, "It had been my intention to take you as one of my concubines, but you are of good solid Hakka stock. You will make a popular wife. It is a great honour for you."

While Hung was talking it seemed to She-she that the whole room was swaying about her, but she thought quickly. "It would indeed be a great honour to be a bride of the *T'ien Wang*, but it cannot be. I am not worthy."

398

"Your humility does you credit, girl, but it is I who will decide whether you are worthy or not."

"No, your Heavenly Majesty, you do not understand. All your brides are virgins." She-she's voice trembled. "I am not."

"You are an adulteress?" Hung rose to his feet as he flung the accusation at her.

"No, but before I came here I belonged to the *Hoppo* of Canton. I was given to him by my father."

As the *T'ien Wang* continued to gaze down at her, his fury growing, Esme said, "It is no fault of hers. She should be praised. When the other girls who were with her were returned to the *Hoppo*, She-she chose a Christian way of life."

The *T'ien Wang*'s glance briefly fell upon Esme but his anger was directed at She-she.

"You will go. I do not wish to see you ever again. Go . . . GO!"

Back in their own quarters, She-she's fear came out into the open as she asked Esme, "What will the *T'ien Wang* do now? What will happen to me? He could have me executed."

"Calm yourself, my dear. You have done nothing wrong. Indeed, although selling one's daughter is one of the Chinese customs I particularly deplore, you simply obeyed the instructions of your own father. Even Hung can find nothing wrong with that. But I think the time has come for us to leave here. I'll speak to Hung and ask if we can't both return to Shanghai. I'll tell him I need to consult my Mission authorities and would like you to accompany me."

Esme's plan came to nothing. The *T'ien Wang* refused to give her an audience. What was more, she and She-she were confined to their quarters, refused permission to move freely about the palace.

For two months the only contact the two women had with the outside world was through Su-san. Although recovered from her wounds, the Taiping girl would never lead troops into action again. As a reward for her bravery in action she had been made a Chancelloress. Her duties were in the royal palace, where she took responsibility for the fittings, fabrics and decor.

Through Su-san, Esme and She-she learned of the abortive British and French attack on the Pei-ho forts that had taken place many weeks before. Su-san also smuggled a letter out of the palace for Esme, promising her she would somehow get it to Erin Veasey when he next brought a cargo upriver to Nanking.

★ ★ ★

Fortunately, perhaps, Hung Hsiu-ch'uan was occupied with military matters for many weeks after he had suggested marriage to She-she. Chang had finally persuaded the commanders of two of the Taiping armies to join forces. Together they launched an attack on the Chinese armies which had been moving steadily closer to Nanking in recent months. One of the

400

commanders was Peng Yu-chen, brother of Kau-lin.

Kau-lin had taken to warfare with a zeal that inspired those about her. She was rewarded by being promoted to deputy commander of the women's regiment formerly led by Su-san. The majority of the women's regiments had been taken off active duties, but Kau-lin persuaded her brother to keep her own regiment on his strength.

It suited Peng well. The women fought with a ferocity that was an example to his men, few of whom would retreat while the women were still engaged in battle.

With the aid of his women soldiers, Peng scored a notable victory against the Chinese army. The women launched a brief but fierce attack against a great Imperial army camp. When the regular Chinese soldiers fought back, the Taiping women retreated. It was a well-orchestrated retreat. The women stayed just far enough ahead of the Imperial troops to avoid casualties, but close enough to give the soldiers hope they would catch up with them.

The women led the Imperial army into a perfect trap, turning to join their comrades in a battle that virtually wiped out the Chinese government forces. They then returned to the Imperial army camp. After plundering it of all the stores they and their comrades could carry off, the camp was destroyed. In one brilliant stroke the Taipings had removed the main threat to Nanking.

For another month and a half Commandant

Peng led his army around the countryside eliminating the remaining camps of the Imperial army before returning to Nanking to receive the congratulations of the Heavenly King.

Peng had scored a great victory in the name of the *T'ien Wang*, but he put no trust in either the Taiping ruler or Cousin Chang. Declining an offer from the Heavenly King to have a palace built for himself inside Nanking, Peng camped outside the city walls. Here, surrounded by the tried and loyal troops of his own army, he felt safe against treachery.

19

NOW the immediate threat from the Imperial army had been removed, the Taiping ruler was able to devote his time to matters of more celestial importance. He sent for Esme to attend him in the audience chamber.

When she was shown in by a palace official, the *T'ien Wang* was seated on his throne, dressed in all the panoply of state. Esme advanced until she was standing at the bottom of the steps which rose to the throne. Hung Hsiu-ch'uan sat looking out over her head as though he could not see her.

When the silence had lasted a full four or five minutes, Esme said, "You sent for me?"

The *T'ien Wang* made a barely discernible motion of his hand and the official who had brought Esme to the chamber struck her a forceful blow in the middle of her back. "You will kow-tow to the *T'ien Wang*."

"I will do no such thing!" Esme swung round on the official with such a fierce expression on her face that the woman took a pace backwards.

"We will pray." It was a command, not a suggestion. With a far from pious scowl, the *T'ien Wang* placed his fingertips together and murmured a brief and indistinguishable prayer that was over almost before Esme had sunk to her knees.

"I have work for you to do. Much work. You will be kept very busy."

"If it is work for the Lord, I will not spare myself."

"I have written an account of my time with the Heavenly Father and the Heavenly Elder Brother. I have explained the conversations we had and the instructions given to me by the Heavenly Father, for the benefit of his children in China. I have also told of the matters I discussed with the Heavenly Elder Brother. You will find them all on a silken scroll that will be delivered to your quarters. When you have read my words you will continue work on translating the Gospels, adding to it the writings of my experiences. You will bring each chapter to me as it is completed, for my approval."

For a while, Esme looked at the man before her without speaking. She had known for many months this moment would one day come. She wished it might have occurred at a time when Hung Hsiu-ch'uan was more kindly disposed towards her.

"I will happily translate any section of the Bible for the benefit of you and your people. But the Gospels will be translated exactly as written by Matthew, Mark, Luke and John."

"They made many mistakes. Forgot much. I am the Heavenly Younger Son. You will write what I tell you. The things they have forgotten will be included."

"This I cannot do." Esme spread her hands in a gesture of despairing resignation. "I fear my usefulness as a servant of God is at an

404

end among the Taipings. I wish to return to Shanghai."

"You are employed in my court to carry out my will. You refuse to do as I tell you?"

"Until I am able to return to Shanghai I will continue to do what I came here for: to translate the true words of the Lord. I will neither add to, nor detract from, what is written in ,the Bible."

There was another hand signal from the *T'ien Wang*, this time firmer, more decisive. Suddenly Esme was seized from behind. Moments later she was being dragged from the chamber.

She did not leave quietly. At one time she struggled so violently that four women of the palace guard were sent sprawling on the floor of the audience chamber. Only sheer weight of numbers won in the end. Protesting loudly and still struggling, Esme was carried away bodily.

* * *

Su-san came to the quarters occupied by She-she later that night to tell her what had occurred.

"Where have they taken her?" She-she had been deeply concerned when her friend failed to return from the interview with the *T'ien Wang* but no one could, or would, tell her anything. She had feared the worst.

"She is locked in the room where the *T'ien Wang* keeps the women of his household who offend him. She is chained."

"What will happen to her?"

"I don't know. I've sent word to Kau-lin

405

telling her what has happened. I have suggested she try to use her influence with Heavenly Prince Chang to have her released. No good can come of this."

"Can I see Esme?"

"No. I can have messages passed to her by word of mouth through my sister, but there can be no visitors and no written notes. The guards on the door are commanded by my sister, but they cannot be trusted not to inform the *T'ien Wang* of anything that happens. Don't worry about Esme. She will come to no harm and I will let her know we are working for her release."

The next day the *T'ien Wang* sent for She-she to be brought to his private rooms. She went fearing the worst, or at least that she would be told she was to join Esme. But the Taiping leader had other plans for her.

He kept her kow-towing to him for far longer than on her previous visit to his rooms. When he eventually signalled for her to rise to her knees he seemed almost to forget her once more. Keeping his head bowed he appeared almost to be in a trance — or drugged.

When he raised his head to look at her at last, his eyes had the faraway expression of a man who sees things to which others are blinded.

"When we last met I spoke many harsh words to you. For this I have been chastised by the Heavenly Elder Brother."

The *T'ien Wang*'s reference to Jesus Christ came so naturally it was easy to realise why he was able to convince the Taipings of his divine

406

origins. She wondered what revelation he was about to make.

"He reminded me of his friendship with the woman Mary Magdalene. Although he needed to cast out seven devils from her, she was a true friend when others deserted him. She too had been known by other men. The Elder Brother knows my views on the chastity of women, but He says I must think upon his words."

She-she tried to remember what little she knew about Mary Magdalene. The *T'ien Wang*'s words puzzled her, "You mean . . . you want me as a friend?"

"I want more from you than friendship. It would be unwise for the *T'ien Wang* to be seen to take an unchaste woman for a wife, but it is my wish that you become a concubine."

"I . . . but . . . " She-she groped desperately for words. "You offer me great honour, but Jesus never took Mary Magdalene as a concubine."

"True, and it is this I find most troubling of all."

Eager to follow up on the point she had made, She-she said, "I have been reading your writings of the part you played in the New Testament. You and your father in Heaven are right to take chastity so seriously. It is at the heart of the whole Christian family — and of your own Taiping peoples. I must pray to God the Father for guidance before agreeing to something that might put at risk all you have achieved for your people. I would like to speak to the missionary woman about this."

"I am at the heart of the Taiping people. It

is I who decide what shall be done."

"This is true, your Heavenly Majesty. But you and I know the story of Mary Magdalene, your people do not. They would need to know the story before they understood why the *T'ien Wang* should wish to take an unchaste woman for a concubine."

"True. You are indeed a deep-thinking woman. I will write the story myself. You will translate it."

"I will need the help of the missionary woman." She-she made her second mention of Esme apprehensively, hoping it would not arouse the *T'ien Wang*'s anger.

"She will be released soon. A few more days should suffice to teach her to be respectful. You will go now, but we will speak again of this matter."

She-she went back to her quarters wondering how long she could effectively fob off the Taiping leader. She wondered whether Kernow had received the letter sent to him by Esme. Whether she would ever see him again. It had been more than a year since they had promised they would wait for each other. For ever if need be . . .

20

KERNOW'S abrupt departure from the home of the United States consul in Shanghai was shrouded in mystery. He told Consul Merrill only that there was something of great importance that needed to be done. The consul believed it must be something to do with the British government. A mission, perhaps, that needed Kernow's knowledge of the Chinese language. As a result, he asked no questions.

Sally was less easily satisfied. Kernow had almost finished packing the few clothes he was taking when she entered his room. She dropped in a chair and sat watching him. She said nothing, but he realised she was waiting for an explanation from him.

"Is it all right if I leave my new uniforms and most of my things here until I return?" He asked the question as much to break the awkward silence as for any other reason.

"Of course. How long will you be away?"

"I don't know. A few weeks, at least."

"Can I ask where you're going?"

"You can ask, but I'm afraid I can't tell you, Sally."

"Can't? Or won't?"

"I can't. You're the daughter of a consul. It wouldn't be fair to say."

With a sudden flash of intuition, Sally asked,

"Is it something to do with this Chinese girl you're so fond of?"

"Partly. You won't tell anyone?"

"There are a couple of reasons I can think of for such secrecy. It's either illegal or dangerous. Probably both."

When Kernow made no reply, she said, "Take care of yourself."

Suddenly, she crossed the room and hugged him. "Take very good care. If you get yourself into trouble find some way to let me know. I'll get help to you somehow."

★ ★ ★

Erin Veasey's steamer was waiting at Wusong, an anchorage not far from Shanghai. The American sea captain took Kernow to the ship in a sampan. It was dark and there was little danger of being seen, but in a heavy drizzle they sheltered inside a curved shelter woven from bamboo leaves. The sampan was propelled by a single oar wielded over the stern in the hands of a wrinkle-faced woman wearing a huge coolie hat. The hat provided her with as much shelter as an umbrella might have done. Her clothes were as black as the night and she drove the small vessel in silence and near-invisibility.

The voyage to Nanking was surprisingly uneventful. After changing the identity of the steamer, Erin hoisted the United States flag. Under cover of darkness he had no trouble evading the sole British warship patrolling the

410

mouth of the Yangtze. At this point it was some twenty miles wide.

The reasoning behind such a patrol baffled the American sea captain. Speaking to Kernow, he said, "Here you are, practically at war with the Chinese, yet you run a blockade to prevent guns and ammunition getting to the Taipings. They could win the war for you given just a bit of encouragement. Where's the sense in it all?"

"I've often wondered myself," confessed Kernow. "I once asked Admiral Seymour. He told me that when we fight against the Chinese, each side fights by certain rules. A code of war. Winners as well as losers know they're going to need to compromise eventually. The Taipings don't have such rules. They're fighting for an ideal. With them there's no meeting-place between total victory and total annihilation. If they succeed in their rebellion they'll be far more difficult to negotiate with than Imperial China."

"I doubt it. Once they got into power things would settle down and become pretty much as they were before. You can see it happening now. The Taipings have had to water down a lot of their big ideas in order to cope with the facts of everyday life."

"That isn't the impression I have from Esme's letter. She sounded pretty desperate — and Esme isn't one to panic easily."

"No doubt the inside of the *T'ien Wang*'s palace will be the last place to see any change. But you're wise to try to get her and your Chinese girl out. Last time I was at Nanking I heard rumours that the *T'ien Wang*'s behaviour gets more erratic by the day. I'd hate to be within striking distance when he finally goes over the edge." The two men were pacing the upper deck of the *Trade Wind* together. Thirty paces one way. Turn. Thirty paces the other.

As they made a turn in unison, Erin said, "Do you have any ideas yet about how you'll get them out?"

"None. I'll have to take advantage of whatever comes along."

★ ★ ★

The *Trade Wind* made good time to Nanking. The water in the Yangtze, although sluggish, was running high and there was no need for Erin to feel his way along the winding channels.

Neither was there a chain of Imperial war junks barring the way. They had been temporarily drawn off to raid the den of a river pirate. The pirate had become a little too audacious and raided the luxurious home of a magistrate. He needed to be taught a lesson.

The *Trade Wind* edged gingerly in towards the Nanking quayside. On the way it nudged wooden-hulled junks from its path when the threats of its crew and the shrill directives of those on shore failed to move them.

It was very busy around and about the quay. Many of those watching Erin's ship berth were soldiers of Peng Yu-Cheng's regiment. He was still camped outside the walls of Nanking, waiting for the arms and ammunition being brought to him by Erin.

Kernow felt no qualms at seeing so much equipment delivered to the Taipings, against the orders of the British government. It was becoming increasingly apparent that armed conflict between China and Britain was inevitable. The more Chinese Imperial troops killed by the Taipings, the fewer there would be to kill British soldiers, sailors and marines.

Kernow was surprised to see a number of Europeans mingling with the Chinese on the jetty. When he commented on this to Erin, the American spat over the side of the ship derisively.

"They've been fighting for the Taipings — and not for the money either. They belonged to the regiment of General Dun. I heard he'd been killed in action recently. Not before time. Whenever he took a town or a village he'd give his men forty-eight hours to do exactly as they liked before imposing Taiping discipline on 'em once more. Now he's gone these men have suddenly lost their stomach for the Taiping cause."

"Where have they come from?"

"Britain, America, France . . . and half-a-dozen more countries. Some are deserters from their country's army or navy. Others are adventurers who'll move on to fight somewhere else when they leave here. None has any loyalty to the country they happen to be fighting for. They hang around the waterfront trying to beg a passage from me, or from the captain of any other ship that makes its way here. I'll need to set armed guards on the gangway to keep them from sneaking on board and stowing away."

"Once we've docked I'll go ashore and have a word with them. I want to know if they've changed the system on the city gate since I was here with Lord Elgin and the fleet."

"Don't carry anything of value on you. They're incorrigible villains. They'll pick your pockets clean before you've taken three paces."

★ ★ ★

Erin Veasey had not exaggerated. When Kernow stepped ashore he was immediately surrounded by a crowd of clamouring mercenaries pleading to be taken on board and begging for food, money or tobacco. At the same time he felt hands exploring the pockets he had carefully emptied before leaving the ship.

Not until the desperate men were satisfied that he possessed neither valuables nor influence with the captain of the *Trade Wind* was he left alone. Now he was able to corner one of the less disreputable adventurers and question him about the system for passing through the gate into Nanking.

The man told Kernow he was called Bill Hawk, but it was doubtful whether this was his real name. Neither did it matter. Of more importance was the information he was able to pass on.

Kernow was dismayed to learn that the system for leaving Nanking had been tightened. "Too many of the captured women brought to the

414

city by the Taipings were escaping and going home," explained the mercenary. "All they needed to do was give their name to the man at the gate and say they were going out to the market. Once outside they just kept on walking! Now everyone who passes through the gate needs a permit. You can only get that at the magistrate's office. Anyone newly arriving at the city is escorted there and has to state his or her business before they're given one."

The news sent Kernow's hopes of rescuing She-she and Esme plummeting. There was no way he could obtain a pass for himself, let alone two more. But Kernow was talking to a very resourceful man, as Bill Hawk's next words showed.

"Mind you, *I've* got a pass. It lets me and a Chinese servant pass through the gate as many times as I care to use it. Of course, if you was to help me get a passage to Shanghai on your ship, I wouldn't need a pass, would I?"

"I can't promise to do that, but I'll pay a good price to borrow the pass for twenty-four hours."

Bill Hawk shook his head, "I don't know what you're up to, but I don't mind betting it would cost me my head if you're found out. It's a passage out of here or nothing."

It was Kernow's turn to shake his head. "Anyway, I'd need two passes. One wouldn't be enough." He had the outline of a plan in his mind.

"I could help you there too. Mate of mine was killed in a skirmish a couple of weeks back. He didn't own much worth taking, but he did have a pass. I kept it in case mine was taken from me and I needed another. Now, two passes ought to make it worth your while to smuggle me on board your ship. You can hide me away anywhere. I won't come out until you tell me to."

"Stay around, Hawk. I'll go back on board and have a word with Captain Veasey."

21

ERIN VEASEY agreed to take Bill Hawk to Shanghai — but only if Kernow came up with a foolproof plan for getting Esme and She-she out of Nanking. In the meantime, the Taiping mercenary was allowed on board and lodged in the crew quarters.

Kernow's plan was far from foolproof. In fact, it was hardly a plan at all. First he needed to smuggle a message into the palace to She-she and Esme. He hoped they could then find a means of leaving the palace, preferably in disguise. With Kernow's help they would then use the passes of Bill Hawk and his friend to leave the city.

That day Kernow used one of the passes to enter the city. Anonymously wrapped in a quilted and hooded winter coat to protect him against a strong wind and driving rain, he was relieved to note that the permit was given no more than a cursory glance. It seemed that Europeans passing through the gate had become commonplace. The official who checked the permit never bothered to look at Kernow at all.

This was the only stroke of luck he was to have in Nanking that day. When he made enquiries for Woman General Su-san, hoping to persuade her to pass on a message to She-she, he learned she was now a Chancelloress employed within the palace.

417

At the gate of the palace the guard commander refused to pass on any message. Any request to see a palace official would need to be put in writing and passed through the usual channels.

Kernow could not afford to argue with the soldier — or with anyone else. He was carrying a pass identifying him as a mercenary with the Taiping army. He would be treated as one if he got into trouble.

He remained in the city all day, leaving just before the gate was closed at sunset. During this time he tramped around the outside wall of the palace, hoping forlornly that an idea would come to him. It did not.

It was dark when Kernow boarded ship. Feeling thoroughly depressed he knocked on the door of Erin's cabin and was invited to "Come in!"

Opening the door, Kernow stepped inside — and came face-to-face with Kau-lin, dressed as a man!

Letting out a shriek of delight, Kau-lin threw herself at Kernow and hugged him with an uninhibited display of affection.

"Lieutenant Kernow!" Turning to Erin, she said accusingly, "Why you not tell me Lieutenant Kernow on your ship?"

"He's *Captain* Kernow now, and I didn't tell you because I wasn't sure he wanted anyone to know he's here. He's been in Nanking today, trying to see She-she."

"You been in palace?"

Kernow shook his head. "I couldn't get closer than the main gate. I was hoping to find Su-san, to ask her to get a message to She-she for me, but it seems she too now works in the palace."

"I get message to She-she. What you want to say?"

After a moment's hesitation, Kernow decided to trust Kau-lin and tell her why he had come to Nanking.

She listened in silence until Kernow had finished talking. Then she said, "She-she always say you come back for her one day. She only one who believed, but now you here. I hope you in time."

"In time? What do you mean? Is Chang still after her?"

"Much worse. The *T'ien Wang* wants her for a concubine. He been telling Heavenly Elder Brother about her, reminding him about friend of his name Mary. Lucky for She-she Heavenly Elder Brother take long time think about it. Esme be very happy see you too. She out of prison now, but *T'ien Wang* say she too stubborn. Put her back soon, I think."

"Esme in prison and She-she a concubine of Hung? God! What a mess. We've got to get them both out, and quickly. But how?"

Kau-lin had been speaking in English but now she lapsed into Chinese. "Su-san is still a very good friend. Her sister has a key to a small door at the back of the palace. Su-san will be able to get it without too much trouble. But we'll need passes to get them out of the city, and they can only be issued by a magistrate."

"I have passes for both of them." Kernow

explained as briefly as possible how they had come into his possession. "If we can dress them both as men She-she can be passed off as a servant. Esme has the bulk of a man. It will work if the weather is still bad, especially if we bring them out just before the gate closes. It will be dusk then and the gatekeeper will be in a hurry to shut the gate and get on home. He doesn't check very thoroughly at the best of times."

"Then it can be done. I will meet them at the back of the palace with two hooded coats. Pray hard for bad weather, that will make it much easier."

"You mustn't get mixed up in this, Kau-lin. You'll be far too well known by now. Erin's been telling me of some of your exploits. You'll be left behind so we can't have any suspicion falling on you. It would go badly for both you and your brother. It will be better if you're conspicuous somewhere else at the time they go missing. I'll meet them and bring them out."

"Can someone tell me what's going on? I heard my name mentioned then. If I'm going to be mixed up in something that sounds both illegal and dangerous, I'd at least like to know some of the risks I'm expected to take."

"I tell you everything, but later. When do you sail?"

"Tomorrow night. About this time."

"So soon?" Kau-lin took Erin's arm in a gesture of affection. "Never mind, good for She-she and Esme. They be here before you sail. Captain Kernow, you not worry about them. You wait back of palace, one hour before dark. They come."

Kau-lin still had a grip on Erin's arm and Kernow realised he was no longer wanted in the cabin. He only wished he was as confident about the next day's operation as Kau-lin seemed to be.

★ ★ ★

The weather the next day was all that Kau-lin had told Kernow to pray for. The wind was unseasonably cold and a heavy drizzle was falling.

On the jetty, Kernow hired three wiry pack ponies and a boy to mind them. He intended leaving them outside the gate to the city. Having mounts would ensure that he, She-she and Esme could return to the ship as speedily as possible. Erin had agreed to have the ship steamed-up ready to set sail. The *Trade Wind* would leave as soon as the trio was on board.

Kau-lin was waiting for Kernow outside the city gate. When he first saw her he thought something must have gone wrong, but she quickly reassured him all was well. A message had been sent in to She-she and Esme. Su-san herself would guide them to the rear gate of the palace and her sister would make certain there was no one around to prevent them leaving.

"There is one thing you should know, Captain Kernow. She-she has not been told you are here to rescue her. She knows only that someone will be waiting to guide her and Esme to a boat to take them to Shanghai. I wish you very good luck."

★ ★ ★

The area behind the palace was derelict. Many of the houses had been pulled down when the palace was built and there was still much rubble here.

Kernow felt conspicuous standing around waiting. He was thankful that rain was falling quite heavily now. Those men and women who passed by had their heads bowed against the wind and were in a hurry to reach their destinations. No one felt inclined to question the motives of a tall *Fan Qui* who had nothing better to do than stand out in the rain.

It seemed to Kernow he waited for hours for She-she and Esme. Yet it was probably less than thirty minutes. When the door to the palace eventually opened everything happened so quickly he was taken by surprise. One minute he was alone, the next there were two figures standing together uncertainly in the road outside the small gate.

Dressed as men, with hoods hiding their faces, each clutched a small bundle wrapped in silken cloth. The bundles contained all the personal possessions they had been able to bring with them.

"She-she? Esme?"

There was a gasp of disbelief from She-she and Esme's face emerged from the hood for a brief moment. Beaming she said, "Kernow, my dear boy! What are you doing here?"

"It is too dangerous for you. Why did you come? You should have sent someone else." She-she's delight at seeing him was temporarily pushed aside by her fears for his safety. Kernow took her hand, but for a brief moment only.

"It's all right, She-she, but we must go now."

The timing was perfect. Because of the rain, it was much darker than usual. So dark that Kernow feared he might have left it too late. It would be disastrous were the gate to be closed against them.

The gate was open, but when they reached it he received a shock. The colonel who had escorted him from the warship the previous year was waiting at the gate with a large escort.

Drawing the two women back into the shadows cast by the low, overhanging roof of a nearby house, Kernow said, "We must wait. I know that man. If he recognises me we're in trouble."

Waiting for the Taiping colonel to go away seemed even longer than the wait Kernow had just experienced outside the palace wall. He was worried too. If the gate closed before he could pass through with Esme and She-she, the rescue plan would fail and they would be trapped inside the city.

Just when Kernow was beginning to think he dared wait no longer there was a sudden flurry of activity and the colonel and his officers went out through the gate.

Kernow galvanised the others into immediate

action, "Come on now, quickly. Just stay behind me and say nothing."

Inside the small room beside the gate the official was clearing his table. When Kernow held out the two passes, the man said, "You're too late. The gate is closed — and don't drip rainwater on my table."

"What nonsense is this? The gate's standing wide open."

"Not for you. It has been kept open only to allow the Heavenly Prince Chang to enter."

The official's words seemed to put the final seal on Kernow's failure. Chang was the last person he wanted to meet while he was trying to take Esme and She-she out of the city. But matters had become desperate by now.

"I know all about that. The colonel told us to wait until Prince Chang entered before we left. But we have to be outside and on our way tonight."

The gatekeeper hesitated and Kernow said arrogantly, "Look, send for the colonel. He'll tell you himself — and in no uncertain terms, I've no doubt."

"I can't. He has gone out of the city to escort Heavenly Prince Chang to the *T'ien Wang*."

"Well, my mission is important too. I'll go and find him and let *him* tell you."

At that moment there was a clatter on the stone blocks beneath the archway outside and the first of the Heavenly Prince's escort cantered in through the gateway.

The gatekeeper hesitated no longer. Grumbling at those who were thoughtless enough to leave things until the very last minute and cause him extra work, he took the passes, made an entry on a piece of paper and handed the passes back. As Kernow had hoped, the man did not even glance in the direction of Esme and She-she.

Kernow hurried the two women through the gateway to the waiting ponies as the Taiping escort clattered by.

They were only just in time. As they slipped away into the darkness, Heavenly Prince Chang passed scarcely an arm's length from them, his face turned away as protection from the driving rain.

22

THE voyage downriver on the *Trade Wind* provided an opportunity for Kernow and She-she to get to know each other once more. Each had been concerned that the feelings of the other might have undergone a change.

Their fears were groundless. Two nights after the voyage began they secretly became lovers. It was then they learned their love for each other went deeper than either had dared hope.

One night, while they were still on the Yangtze river, they were called to the upper deck by Erin. They were passing an island monastery where a religious ceremony was taking place. It involved villagers from miles around on either side of the river.

Long processions of men, women and children carrying lighted torches wound down the steep hillside that linked monastery and river. The chanting of those taking part in the ceremony drifted unevenly across the water, taking its cadence from the rise and fall of the wind.

It was one of those magic moments that occur all too infrequently in life. In a bid to savour the experience for as long as possible, Kernow and She-she remained on deck long after the others had gone below, complaining of the cool wind.

Gradually the sound of chanting was left behind, although the winding torch-lit procession still snaked back and forth on the hillside.

"They are honouring their ancestors," said She-she, her cheek close to Kernow's. He stood behind her, his arms about her waist. "It is a very good thing to do."

"It's also wonderful to savour the now," he whispered. "I can't ever remember when I've been so happy, She-she."

She pressed back against him and lifted her face to his.

"I too am very happy."

They stood together for a very long time until She-she suddenly shivered.

"I'm sorry. I'm not thinking. You're cold."

"No. I am not cold. I am thinking that in a few days we will reach Shanghai. What will we do there, my Kernow?"

"Let's not worry about that until we go ashore at Shanghai. I don't want anything to spoil the few days we have left on Erin's ship."

"I am not worrying. I will be very happy with you while we are on the ship, but I want to know what you are thinking."

"Esme has told me about the problems you had in Shanghai before, and of the kindness shown to you by Colin Strachan and his Chinese wife. I'd like to speak to them and see if they will take you in again — and allow me to stay there too."

"Did you tell Esme this?" She-she swung around to face him in the darkness.

"No. I have a feeling she's turning a deliberate blind eye to what we're doing on board ship, but she couldn't condone us living together. Especially not in a place like Shanghai."

"But you will not be able to stay with me for always. One day your admiral will send for you and you will have to go and fight somewhere."

"I might. On the other hand I might leave the Marines . . ."

Turning to him swiftly, She-she reached up and touched his lips with her fingers. "You must not say that. I will not let you. You are a captain now. Esme says you must be brave man to be made a captain after a battle. One day you will be a most important officer. I will be very proud and tell my friends, 'I knew that very important man. Once I knew truly that he loved me.'"

"That's not going to change, She-she. I promise you."

"Perhaps. Perhaps not." She-she was silent for a long time before she said, "You are right, we should not talk of the future for the time we are on this ship. We will enjoy each day, each hour. Not worry about the next one."

She took hold of his hand. "Come. We will go to your cabin now. I am cold. I want you to warm me . . ."

* * *

The arrival of missionary Esme Pilkington at the Shanghai foreign settlement, fresh from the Taiping capital of Nanking, caused the biggest stir the community had known for very many years. Not only had she lived and preached in the Taiping capital, she had actually lived in the palace of the self-styled 'Heavenly King'. Had regularly conversed with the rebel leader!

428

For the first time there was someone in the community able to speak with first-hand knowledge of the absurd pretensions of Hung Hsiu-ch'uan.

The missionary authorities believed Esme would give them ammunition to support their oft-repeated claims that the Taiping leader was mentally unbalanced. Indeed, she had suffered a period of imprisonment at his hands, actually being *chained* in her cell!

At first, it seemed Esme would confirm all their worse fears of the Taiping movement. She had brought with her many of the *T'ien Wang*'s proclamations and decrees, written on silk in bold brush-strokes by the leader himself.

Scholarly missionaries pored over Hung Hsiu-ch'uan's writings, pointing scornfully to his pretensions and stated beliefs. Here was proof beyond all reasonable doubt that the Taiping leader was indeed insane.

Their case suffered a temporary setback when Esme was invited to give a talk about her experiences at the hands of the Taipings.

The talk was given in the settlement church, the building packed to capacity for the occasion.

There were many nodding heads when Esme confirmed that the 'Heavenly King's' idea of Christianity did not conform to that preached by the Western churches. However, there was a murmur of protest when she spoke scathingly of the British government. The protests grew when she criticised the missionary societies who had failed to grasp what she fervently believed to be an awesome and unique opportunity. Had

429

they offered a hand of friendship to Hung Hsiu-ch'uan it might have proved possible to guide him along Christian pathways. With courage and imagination they might have brought millions of heathen people to God.

Neither the British government, as represented by the Shanghai consular officials, nor the mission authorities, were prepared to blame themselves for missed opportunities in their dealings with the Taipings. Esme was not asked to speak publicly again. Nevertheless, some of the non-conformist missionaries privately agreed with much of what she said. Esme's words had not all fallen on deaf ears.

★ ★ ★

With the attention of the European settlement firmly focused upon Esme, Kernow was able quietly to instal She-she in the house occupied by the Strachan family in the French settlement. He moved in here too. His move meant he was ostracised by certain members of the missionary societies, but for as long as his relationship with She-she remained discreet no great degree of censure was levelled at him.

Men stationed in India and the Far East frequently took mistresses from among the native peoples. It was an accepted fact of life. As long as such women were not openly flaunted in 'decent' society, such relationships were given a metaphorical wink and a nod.

The only person to whom Kernow openly admitted the relationship was Sally Merrill.

He explained it to her when he went to the American consulate to collect his uniform and ask if he might leave some of his possessions here.

After listening to him in silence, Sally asked, "Are you quite sure of what you're doing, Kernow?"

"I've never been more certain of anything."

"It must be wonderful to feel so sure of a relationship." Sally spoke almost wistfully.

"Aren't you? I mean, aren't you certain about you and Caleb?"

"Sometimes. At other times I wish he would do something like you've just done. Suddenly arrive and whisk me off because he just couldn't bear to live without me. Instead, he'll say we must be 'sensible'. Wait until we return to the United States before getting married — because it's what our families want."

"He's thinking of your future as much as his own, Sally."

"I know that, and most of the time I realise it's the right way for both of us. But I wish he'd do something reckless once in a while — just for me."

"Caleb might do something to surprise you one day, Sally. He's a good man."

"I know he's good. I just wish he wasn't *too* damned good, that's all. Will you let me meet your She-she sometime, Kernow?"

"Of course."

"Then I wish you both all the happiness in the world. You can count on my help if it's ever needed."

431

She-she had a good friend in Nan Strachan. The Chinese woman had lived for many years with all the problems that now beset her countrywoman. She had a great many answers to the doubts She-she felt on Kernow's behalf.

"There are many difficulties for both the man and the woman when she is Chinese and he is English. It needs more love than usual if they are to be happy together."

"You and Colin have had problems?"

"Of course. That's why we're living here and not in the British settlement, even though we were married properly, in a church. Colin lost his work because he married me instead of keeping me as his mistress, as the others do."

"As Kernow is keeping me?" She-she spoke defensively. She had told Kernow she was happy being his mistress for as long as he wished, yet she was surprisingly sensitive on the subject.

"No, not like you and Kernow. He loves you and will marry you one day. You will always be happy with him. Those who know real unhappiness are mistresses who delude themselves into believing their relationship will last forever."

"I don't want him to marry me if it means he must leave the Royal Marines. He is a clever officer. Very brave. One day he will be an important man."

It was something She-she repeated to herself every day and it came out now parrot fashion.

"For some men, those who really matter,

there are more important things in their lives than work. It is especially true of those who have most to give."

Nan's youngest child came in crying, holding up a hand which had the minutest graze on the palm. Nan swung the child up in her arms and kissed the graze better before resuming her talk to She-she, over the head of the child who had now stopped crying.

"You are lucky, She-she, as I am lucky. We have both found men who would be special whatever country they came from. You will find much happiness in each other's company. There will be those who will point a finger at you and say what you do is wrong. But they will be the ones who hurt inside most when they see you laughing together and enjoying what they will probably never have."

Nan placed the baby on the ground once more and the child ran outside.

"Most couples plan for the future. Maybe they waste too much time that way. Such a way of life is not for you or me. If you wish to be happy you will not look to tomorrow. You must learn to enjoy today as though it is all you have. All you will ever have."

23

KERNOW and She-she both knew that the happiness they experienced while staying with the family of Colin and Nan Strachan could not last forever. However, they had hoped to have at least a few weeks together. Instead, they were able to snatch no more than six days and nights.

It was still early in the morning when Kernow rose from bed on the seventh day and threw open the shutters. His gasp of surprise brought She-she sitting bolt upright immediately.

"What is it?"

When he did not reply immediately she rose from the bed, slipped a loose silk gown over her shoulders and crossed the room to stand beside him.

Off the shore, tugging against the tide in the Foreign anchorage, was a vast fleet. There were warships of all sizes, steam-driven and wind-powered, and troop transports. Enough ships to carry ten thousand men with all their horses, guns and equipment.

It was a very impressive sight and She-she's eyes were wide with both wonder and alarm as she turned to Kernow. "Why are they here? What is happening?"

"I don't know for certain, but I'd say those ships are carrying the army that's going to fight its way to Peking. Admiral Hope is out there too. That's his flag flying on the large warship, closest to shore. I must go to the American consulate, She-she. That's where Admiral Hope will expect to find me. He may have already sent for me."

Try as she might, She-she could not hide the fear that suddenly gripped her. "Will you . . . come back?"

"I'll come back to you, She-she. Whatever happens, I'll come back to you."

"Then I can wait. No matter how long. I will remember this time together and stay happy just thinking of you."

It was a pretence that She-she was able to keep up even while she adjusted the silk sash that meant much to both of them, over the shoulder of his uniform. It deserted her when she waved to him as he limped away towards the British settlement and the United States consulate beyond.

When he passed from view, She-she returned to the room she had shared with Kernow for such a short time. When Nan found her she was hunched on the rumpled bed, weeping as though her heart was breaking.

★ ★ ★

Kernow did not go on to the United States consulate immediately. Early though it was, Admiral Sir James Hope was already ashore. He was at the British consulate and the whole place was the scene of great activity. There was so much coming and going that Kernow realised something important was happening and altered course to call here first.

He found the admiral in a jovial mood. When he caught sight of Kernow entering the room he broke off the conversation he was having with a naval commander and greeted the young Royal Marine warmly.

"Here you at last, Keats. I sent to the American consulate for you as soon as we came ashore in the night, but they said you weren't there. Had me worried after all I'd heard about you. I was beginning to fear you'd gone native."

Seemingly unaware of Kernow's guilty start, the admiral continued, "I see you've still got a limp, but it can't be too bad. The consul was telling me he's been kept busy piecing together details of your exploits. Gave me some story of you making your way to Nanking and bringing that missionary woman back to Shanghai! It's more than she deserves if all I've heard of her is true. It would have served her right if she'd been left there and forgotten. But it was a damned good effort on your part. In the best tradition of the Navy, and all that."

Kernow managed to hide a smile as he remembered the first time he had met with Admiral Hope and been scornfully dismissed as a 'soldier'.

"I must say, it's the sort of conduct I've come to expect from you, my boy. Pity about that limp of yours, but I've known officers on the active list with far worse. I've still got a piece of Chinese metal in me from the Pei-ho forts. The damned surgeon couldn't find it, but when we get a bit of cold weather I could tell him *exactly* where it is. Feel like cutting it out myself sometimes."

Kernow murmured a few words of sympathy, but the admiral cut him short.

"I'm glad to see you fit for duty again. There's something going on I know you wouldn't want to miss. The government back home in England has finally made a formal declaration of war with China and sent Lord Elgin out here again. He's on board my flagship. His Lordship asked after you as soon as he arrived in Hong Kong. Seems he and my predecessor talked about you at some length when they met up in London. Sir Michael even travelled down to Cornwall to congratulate your father on having such a fine son. But Lord Elgin will be able to tell you all about that. He's requested that you be included on his staff to go to Peking. That's where we're heading, my boy, to the Chinese capital. We'll both have a chance to pay back the Emperor for these wounds of ours."

The admiral had been talking to Kernow since the Royal Marine officer entered the room. Now he turned back to the somewhat disgruntled naval commander and included him in his conversation.

"His Lordship intends taking Peking, having the Imperial authorities sign the treaty, and taking himself off home again by Christmas. He's brought a soldier with him, General Sir Hope Grant — no relation, I hasten to add. We've had only sailors in our family for a hundred and fifty years. But Grant's been put in charge of the land operations. I've spoken to him a few times. Bit of a rough diamond, but by all accounts a first-class soldier — whatever *that* means. Can't see why the War Office didn't put a sailor in charge, but they never have been noted for sound common sense."

Switching his attention to Kernow once more, the admiral asked, "Can you settle up your affairs and be on board by sunset, Captain Keats? I hope to sail first thing in the morning."

"Of course, sir. I don't have a great deal to pack."

"Good. You'll see history made this trip, my boy. We're going to open up China for the rest of the world."

★ ★ ★

Kernow went to the United States consulate before returning to She-she. He had a few belongings to collect.

Sally was at home and stood in his room, leaning against a wall, as he stuffed clothing inside a small canvas kitbag.

"Have you said goodbye to your She-she yet?"

"No. I'm going to see her now."

"What will she do while you're away?"

"Stay with Strachan and his wife. They're good people, they'll look after her."

"Will you take me to meet her, Kernow?"

He looked up, startled. "Why?"

"Damn it, Kernow, there are times when I could punch you right on the nose. We're

438

friends. Where I come from friends get involved in each other's lives — because they *care*."

Kernow was about to protest but she waved him to silence. "I'm engaged to Caleb and we'll be married some day. I want to marry him, but that doesn't prevent me from being fond of you. I'd like to meet She-she because I think I could become fond of her too. I'll visit her while you're away. I'd enjoy doing that, honest."

When he hesitated, Sally said, "I know you won't have very long with her and these few hours will be very precious for both of you. I promise I won't intrude for more than just a few minutes, but please let me meet her."

"All right. She's asked about you more than once — and I'll keep you to that promise of visiting her while I'm away."

★ ★ ★

When Kernow entered the house in the company of Sally, She-she was utterly devastated. As he made his explanations and introductions with painful awkwardness, she was even more dismayed. He had come to tell her he was going away, yet had arrived in the company of this *Fan Qui* woman. It was more than her mind could take in for a moment and she was very close to tears.

Sally saw her expression and recognised it for what it was. In a moment of spontaneous affection she reached out and hugged She-she.

"I'm so glad to meet you after all this time. I nursed Kernow after he was wounded at the battle for the Pei-ho forts. He was calling your name even before he regained consciousness. Now I can see why. You're a lucky man, Captain Keats. She's lovely."

Smiling at She-she, Sally said, "Kernow and I have become like sister and brother over recent months. You mustn't worry while he's away. I'll come to visit you, and I guarantee he'll be back safely before long. He *has* to be. I want him — and you — to be guests when I marry Caleb Shumaker."

"You . . . have a man?"

She-she's relief was so patent that Sally's heart went out to her. "Yes, She-she, I have a man and he's here in China. But I promised Kernow I wouldn't take up any of the precious time you two have left to each other today. May I come and see you while he's away? Please?"

"I would like that very much."

"Good, and if you're ever in trouble, any trouble at all, you must come and find me at the American consulate. Do you promise?"

She-she nodded. She was happy to have added to her small group of friends in Shanghai — but none of them could make up for the loss of Kernow.

As Sally left the house She-she turned to Kernow and held out her arms to him. As they clung to each other she tried to clear her mind of the fear that was growing there.

Kernow was going away to war. She might never see him again.

24

LORD ELGIN was a very busy man. He spent most of the time he was in Shanghai writing and sending off very long reports. These were despatched to the British government; the British consuls in Shanghai and Hong Kong; Chinese Imperial authorities in Canton and Peking; and to his naval and army commanders-in-chief.

Yet Lord Elgin found time to greet Kernow warmly when the young Royal Marine officer was shown into his cabin on board Admiral Hope's flagship.

"Glad to have you on my staff, Keats. We've a busy time ahead of us. For the time being I intend using you as my liaison officer with the Royal Marines and army. Later I'll have need of you as an interpreter. When we get on land and head for Peking I'll be relying very heavily upon you in my dealings with the Imperial authorities and their army leaders. They're a tricky lot — but you don't need me to tell you that."

"When do we sail, my Lord?"

Kernow put the question more in hope than with any expectation of being able to spend another few hours with She-she.

"At first light. General Grant has already sailed north with an advance party of the army. They're looking for camping sites around the bay of Talienwan. It's a large bay and conveniently situated. Not too far from the Taku forts at Pei-ho, yet far enough away to prevent the Chinese from launching a surprise attack against us. It's Grant's idea. He fought in China in eighteen-forty-two and became familiar with the country then, I believe. You'll be working with him a great deal and I know you're going to like him as much as I do.

"Before we set sail, I wonder if you would translate some documents for me? They're nothing to do with our war, but were sent from Nanking by an agent we have working for us there. They purport to relate to a proposed attack on Shanghai by the Taipings. It's something I feel we should know about before we have all our troops beating a path to Peking. I'm afraid it will mean working through most of the night, but I have no doubt you'll agree with me about their importance."

* * *

When Kernow met up with the British army commander-in-chief at Talienwan he found him all that Lord Elgin had promised he would be. The army man was a stern disciplinarian and not good at expressing himself. Yet he had a quiet, honest and forthright manner that inspired confidence in those who served him. He was also a skilled musician and carried a cello with him on his campaigns, playing it whenever the opportunity presented itself. It was an eccentricity that endeared him to his

442

men, but sometimes distracted his officers.

When the two men were introduced, they found immediate common ground.

"You remind me of someone, Keats. A Royal Marine officer I met in hospital during the war of 'forty-two. Poor chap had to have a leg amputated. Come to think of it, his name was Keats too. A relative of yours, perhaps?"

"My father, sir."

"Good Lord! That makes me feel incredibly old. Is he still alive?"

"Yes, sir. He's at home in Cornwall, doing his best to behave as though he still has two good legs."

"That sounds like the man I knew then. Please send him my warmest regards when you next write to him. If you're as good a soldier as your father, I'll be very pleased to have you with me. You're to be on Lord Elgin's personal staff, I believe, but I think I have a use for you before then. Do you speak French?"

"I do, sir."

"Good. Then you can come with me to Chefoo, on the other side of the bay. General de Montauban and his French army are camped there. He seems to be spending his time thinking up excuses for not taking the field against the Chinese. Perhaps between us we can rouse him and his men off their backsides."

★ ★ ★

General Grant and Kernow managed to do more than rouse the French commander-in-chief from his lethargy. General de Montauban had an excessive share of Gallic pride. He was over-sensitive about the fact that his army was only half the size of that commanded by General Grant. Nevertheless, he was a first-class soldier and recognised the same talent in Grant. With Kernow interpreting, the two men were soon showing a mutual respect for each other.

Many of the Frenchman's problems involved obtaining horses for his cavalry and artillery. Grant was able to solve this for him. By the time Grant and Kernow left to return to the British army at Talienwan, a date had been fixed for the joint landings. Grant and de Montauban had also worked out the part the armies of each would play in the campaign to come.

★ ★ ★

The allied landings took place close to the small town of Pehtang, some six miles from the Pei-ho river and the Taku forts. Offshore, more than two hundred warships and transports prepared to land twenty thousand soldiers to do battle with the Chinese.

Two hundred men, led by Brigadier Sutton, a fiery senior army officer, formed the advance party. When the boats grounded there was still almost a mile of waist-deep mud and water to be traversed before comparatively dry land could be reached.

Swearing in a fashion that would have been heartily disapproved of by the Bible-carrying Grant, the Brigadier set an example for his advance party to follow. Stripping off trousers, socks and boots, he tied these articles of clothing to his sword, slung it over his shoulder and slipped into the water. Bellowing for his men to follow him, Brigadier Sutton led the way ashore, grey flannel shirt-tail flapping beneath a mud-stained red serge jacket. Every time he stumbled on the uneven sea bed he called down dire curses on the heads of the staff officers who had chosen such a spot for a landing.

The Brigadier, bandy-legged, ugly and very muddy, was the first man to reach dry land. When he finally hoisted himself from the ooze the men following him set up a cheer that startled a small party of Chinese Imperial cavalry waiting and watching from the shelter of a clump of low trees nearby.

Without firing a shot, the Chinese horsemen turned tail and galloped back along the causeway that led towards the Taku forts, pursued by the bullets of the leading soldiers and the fury of Brigadier Sutton. As he hopped about helplessly on one leg, the irascible Brigadier cursed them for cowards for not waiting around until he had his trousers on.

Kernow accompanied General Grant ashore with the main body of soldiers and Royal Marines, less than an hour later. There was not an enemy soldier in sight and the army settled down in the mud for an uncomfortable but undisturbed night.

The next day they moved into Pehtang, once again encountering no resistance. For the remainder of that day patrols were sent out along the causeway that led towards the Pei-ho river. They sighted small parties of Tartar horsemen, but did not engage them.

There was more excitement in Pehtang than outside that night. It began with looting by the French and was closely followed by a systematic rape of the town's women by men of the Chinese Coolie Corps, who were accompanying the army.

The coolies had been recruited in the Canton area and had little love for their northern countrymen. The provost marshal's men were out in force and many of the infantry were seconded to assist them, but their task was impossible in the darkness of a strange town. The rape of the women continued until morning.

At dawn the following day the few coolies who had been arrested by the provost marshal's men were summarily executed as a warning to their companions before the army moved off.

A few miles along the causeway the Allied armies were confronted by an area of fortifications and entrenchments. At the same time between two and three thousand Tartar horsemen emerged from behind the fortifications and attempted to carry out a flanking action on the combined British and French army.

The officer leading the horsemen was Shalonga, son of the Tartar war lord Tingamao. Kernow recognised him immediately, but it came as no surprise. He had been half expecting the Tartar officer still to be in the area.

He reported the sighting to General Grant, adding that Shalonga's father was commander of an army of fifty thousand men.

"Do you think they are in the vicinity too?" The thought of such an army was of great concern to Grant. Half his men were still on the high seas. He had kept the cavalry and much of the heavy artillery at sea until a more suitable landing place had been taken.

"I'd like to be able to say no, sir, but when I met Shalonga a few years ago, near Canton, he was acting as an advance party for his father. He might be doing the same now."

Grant thought about the situation for some minutes, chewing on his heavy, black moustache. "I can't afford to take a chance until I have the cavalry ashore. We'll return to Pehtang."

"Let me try an attack on the enemy first, sir. We'll soon see what they're made of." The speaker was a young rifleman lieutenant who had come to China fresh from England and was eager to prove himself. He had listened to the conversation between Kernow and General Grant with increasing exasperation.

"I'm sure you would, mister, but you might well find they're made of sterner stuff than you're expecting. You'll have all the action you want before too long, but I'll not throw good riflemen away unnecessarily."

When the order to retreat was given the British and French soldiers grumbled about 'officers who can't make up their mind'. But they trudged back more swiftly when the Tartar cavalry came thundering past, just beyond accurate rifle range. They put on a display of horsemanship that even the superb Indian cavalrymen of the British army would have found it difficult to emulate.

General Grant watched the Tartar cavalry's antics with grudging admiration. "They're good," he said to Kernow. "Very good — but in a few days' time they're going to learn they're not quite good enough."

25

GENERAL HOPE GRANT was a patient man, but the next few days tried his patience sorely. The artillery and cavalry had to be landed in the mud of Pehtang in far from ideal conditions. Pehtang was little more than a large village, situated in a sea of mud. It had insufficient fresh water and no food or fodder to meet the needs of an additional twenty thousand men and thousands of horses. Neither was there any to be obtained from the immediate countryside. As a result the army was forced to rely upon the stores it had brought with it.

Then, when the British army was ready to move, the French army was not. The French commander, General De Montauban, complained there had not been sufficient time for his men to unload all their stores. As if such problems were not enough for Grant, the weather chose to throw its weight behind the Chinese. It rained almost continuously while the army was at Pehtang and neither men nor horses were ever fully dry.

Not until nine days after the initial landing was the combined British and French army ready to move out along the causeway. Its first objective was the fortification straddling the route to the Taku forts.

The Tartar horsemen were waiting for the allied soldiers. As soon as the British advance

guard left Pehtang it came under attack. The
Tartars were driven off by British cavalry, but
it was only a beginning. The Chinese were
determined to make the Allied army fight for
every foot of ground that lay between them and
the Taku forts.

To make matters worse, when the British
sent out flanking parties on either side of the
advancing column of troops, the heavy cavalry
horses were hampered by thick mud. Not until
it reached firmer ground was the cavalry able
to engage the Tartar troops who were attacking
with great determination.

A series of fierce hand-to hand battles took
place. At one time three thousand Tartar
horsemen charged at the British infantry who
immediately formed their traditional squares and
fought them off until the situation was relieved
by a regiment of Sikh cavalry who succeeded in
scattering the Tartars.

During these many engagements, both minor
and major, Kernow looked out for Shalonga, but
he did not see him.

At the line of Chinese fortifications a fierce
artillery duel developed. It continued until the
position was stormed and taken by British
infantrymen. The first hurdle had been overcome
on the road to the Taku forts.

There was one more. This was the fortified
village of Tangku. It was taken only after a
fierce artillery duel during which most of the
village's defenders were killed. The tenacity of
the Chinese gunners was the subject of much
surprised comment by the allies. When they

450

occupied the village the reason the Chinese had not retreated was discovered. The gunners had been chained to their weapons.

There now began another series of written exchanges between the Chinese authorities and Lord Elgin. The Chinese wanted the army to return to Pehtang while negotiations were commenced. Elgin refused point blank to consider such unacceptable conditions.

Accompanying the first flag of truce were a number of prisoners captured by the Chinese during the fighting, returned to the British as a goodwill gesture. One was a sergeant of the Essex Regiment, another a Madras sapper. The remainder were Cantonese coolies from the Chinese Coolie Corps. They had been captured together with another soldier, a private of the Buffs.

Taken before the Imperial Chinese general, they had been ordered to kow-tow. All except the Buffs private obeyed the command. Warned of the consequences of not obeying, the private remained adamant. He would not kow-tow to a Chinese, whatever his rank.

At a signal from the Chinese general, the Buffs private was pinioned by his captors, there was the flash of an executioner's sword and the British soldier's head was separated from his body.

When the story went around the camps of the various regiments there were cries for instant revenge. It would not be long in coming. The following morning General Grant ordered a reconnoitre of the Taku forts.

Because Kernow had been to the Pei-ho before, he was sent by Grant to map out the forts, in order that the general might plan an assault.

There were four forts, two on either side of the Pei-ho river. The defences had changed little since the day Kernow had lain in the glistening mud before them, convinced he would not live to see another day. Looking at the scene now was sufficient to send a chill of sudden fear through him. Here were the same deep, water-filled ditches, the deadly crops of sharpened bamboo stakes planted thicker than barley growing in an English field. Beyond were dry ditches, ramparts of felled trees and, finally, the forts themselves.

The fort selected by Grant for his first target was the smaller of the two on the northern bank of the river. Its smooth mud and brick wall was at least fifteen feet high, bristling with guns and clearly occupied by a strong force of Imperial troops.

Taking it would not be easy, but at least the attacking forces would be advancing from the land-side and would not have knee-deep, oozing mud to slow their progress and leave them at the mercy of the fort's gunners.

During the night batteries were built for the artillery to dominate the northern fort and guns and mortars brought up. Arrangements were also made for four gunboats to inch their way as far upriver as they could travel and bombard the fort when the assault began.

When all was made ready Kernow was sent under a flag of truce to try to persuade the commander of the fort to surrender.

He advanced to the wall of the fort with a small escort and called upon the senior Chinese officer to come out and parley with him.

At first the only response was a series of derisive catcalls from the Imperial soldiers manning the walls of the fort.

Despite this, and the nervousness of his escort, Kernow persisted. Eventually an officer wearing a round hat on which was the red button of a mandarin of the first degree appeared at one of the gun embrasures.

"What is it you want? Have you come to offer me the surrender of your general and the army which has invaded our lands and offended the Emperor of the Middle Kingdom?"

Hoots of approval from the listening Chinese troops greeted the mandarin's derisive words.

"I have come with a message from General Grant to offer safe passage for you and your soldiers if you abandon this fort immediately."

"If your general wants this fort he will need to attack with all his guns and men and pay for his failure with the lives of *Fan Qui* soldiers."

The mandarin's defiant stance brought shouts of delight from his listening garrison.

"My general does not lose battles. He will take your fort as he has taken Pehtang and Tangku. His only wish is to save the lives of your men. I regret it is not your wish also. I will acquaint him with your words."

"Wait!" The call came as Kernow and his

escort wheeled their horses to return the way they had come.

He pulled his horse to a halt and turned to face the fort once more.

"Tell your general I am agreeable to a truce until the Imperial commissioners from Peking reach here. I am assured they are on their way."

"I will take him your message, but I cannot promise it will find any more favour with him than it does with me."

It seemed the Chinese mandarin in charge of the fort had no more confidence in the acceptance of his suggestion than did Kernow. When the small party was no more than a few hundred yards from the fort, the Chinese opened up a barrage with their guns that developed into a savage duel with the guns of the Royal Artillery.

Lord Elgin was at Grant's headquarters and he agreed with Kernow's assessment of the mandarin's offer. It was no more than a delaying tactic. The British and French armies would continue their advance upon Peking. But first the Taku fort had to be taken.

★ ★ ★

The attack on the first fort began at dawn the following morning. It was preceded by an artillery duel that was fiercer than the one that had taken place the previous afternoon. It continued for three hours before the infantry was ordered forward.

The artillery barrage had put many of the Chinese cannon out of action and succeeded in exploding a magazine inside the fort — but it seemed to have had little effect on the defenders manning the walls. Their heavy fire caused many casualties among the advancing men. A special target for their musketry was a party of Royal Marines who had the unenviable task of going into action carrying huge and unwieldy pontoons, intended to bridge the stake-filled ditches guarding the fort.

Kernow found the sight of so many Royal Marines falling beneath the fire of the Chinese muskets and crossbows agonising.

"Sir," he addressed General Grant when he could bear it no longer, "I request permission to go to the assistance of the Royal Marines pontoon party."

"Your loyalty to your corps is admirable, Captain Keats, but giving the Chinese one more target to shoot at will help no one. I have need of you here."

Grant resumed his watch on the slowly advancing men, turning occasionally to send a messenger racing to one or other of the commanding officers fighting their way forward.

It soon became apparent that the casualty rate for the assault was going to be very high indeed and now General Grant was running short of messengers.

Eventually, he turned to Kernow, "Captain Keats, go and tell Lieutenant Colonel Gascoigne to pull his men back until the artillery has broken more of the wall around that north gateway."

Lieutenant Colonel Gascoigne was in charge of the Royal Marines infantry who had now been joined by those of the pontoon party who survived. One of the pontoons had been hit by Chinese artillery and wrecked. The others had been abandoned as being more trouble than they were worth.

Kernow ran from the headquarters area, which was dangerously close to the fighting, to where the Royal Marines were now helping each other up the high wall of the fort.

By the time he reached the fort both the British and French flags were flying on the walls although fierce fighting was still taking place inside.

General Grant's message was no longer valid, but Kernow made for a spot where a door, some eight feet from the ground, had been smashed open. A ladder placed against the wall beneath would provide him with access.

Kernow was carrying a 'revolver', a multi-shot pistol made by Samuel Colt, given to him as a parting gift by Consul Merrill in Shanghai.

Drawing the revolver, Kernow climbed the rickety ladder and leaped through the doorway into a scene that might have been painted by an artist depicting Hades. Bodies were scattered everywhere, lying in a series of grotesque attitudes. Between their dead companions wounded men were lying, sitting, limping or weeping, nursing wounds to every conceivable part of the body. There was a lone British surgeon here too who must have entered the fort with a fighting unit.

All around the fort soldiers tussled with their enemies in deadly hand-to-hard combat.

As Kernow paused he saw a force of Chinese soldiers spill from a small bunker built into the thick mud-and-brick wall of the fort. They immediately surrounded a party of Marines who were forced to fight for their lives.

Kernow ran towards this group, firing at the Chinese as he neared them. He fired twice, downing a Chinese soldier with each shot. His next shot saved the life of Lieutenant Colonel Gascoigne. The Royal Marines' commanding officer was being threatened from behind by a Chinese with raised sword. One moment later and he would have brought it down on the Royal Marine's head, cleaving it wide open.

Other Marines had seen the predicament of their commanding officer and moments later the brief but deadly tussle was over. So was the battle for the fort. The only Chinese soldiers left were either dead or seriously wounded.

"I'm obliged to you, Captain Keats." Using his foot, Lieutenant Colonel Gascoigne turned the last Chinese Kernow had killed on to his back. It was the mandarin commanding the Chinese defenders.

Picking up the cap with the red button, the colonel looked down almost regretfully at the man who would have killed him.

"He was a very brave man, Captain. He must

have known he and his men would lose, yet he fought to the last."

Looking around him, he squared his shoulders and said, "Well, this battle at least is over. We've won. It leaves three more forts."

26

THE soldiers of Generals Grant and de Montauban were not called upon to storm the remaining three Taku forts. One by one white flags rose to the flagpoles where Imperial banners had earlier fluttered their defiance. The occupants of the forts had witnessed the defeat inflicted upon their companions by the Allied armies and had no stomach for similar slaughter.

Many of the surrendered Imperial Chinese soldiers expected to suffer execution at the hands of their conquerors. The remainder waited resignedly for imprisonment. To their astonishment, after being disarmed they were told they were free to go.

As the Chinese soldiers filed from the forts and set off westwards, the rain came down again. So hard was it that before long the causeway along which the Allied armies had advanced to the Pei-ho river was lost beneath water which swirled for as far as could be seen.

Kernow spent a miserable night sharing a table with some of his fellow officers in the guardroom of the fort he had helped conquer. His knees drawn up to his chin, he kept dry until a leak developed in the mud roof above the table. The officers were far better off than their men. Most had struggled to return along the causeway to their semi-permanent camp in the village of Tangku, only to spend a night in flooded and leaking tents.

In the sunshine of a new dawn the navy moved up to clear the entrance to the Pei-ho river of the obstacles still remaining.

"With any luck Admiral Hope's sailors should remove the last of the blockade today," Lord Elgin told him as Kernow helped to pack everything from the British plenipotentiary's headquarters which had been set up in a Tangku tax-collector's office. "When that's done we'll travel upriver to Tientsin in style, in the flagship. There's something rather majestic about arriving on a vessel, especially a warship of the British Navy."

"Will you need me with you, my Lord? The talk in the officers' mess is that the war is virtually over now we've taken the Taku forts. They're already planning a celebration when we reach Tientsin."

"They may be right, Kernow, but a celebration might prove premature. My experience is that the Chinese have a nasty habit of pulling something out of the hat when it's least expected. I think you should stay with me for a while longer — however strong the pull to return to Shanghai. I suppose it wouldn't have anything to do with that very attractive American girl who nursed you after you'd been wounded at the Taku forts last year? Never mind, you don't have to answer. Rest assured I intend remaining in China no longer than is absolutely necessary. I have a great many plans for my life — and none of them lies this side of the China Sea."

Lord Elgin's words did little to ease the nagging worry in Kernow's mind. Word had reached the Expeditionary Force only that day about the alarming movements of the Taiping army. It seemed they were advancing upon Shanghai at great speed, driving hordes of refugees before them and alarming Colonel Wolseley who had been left in charge of the garrison there. At his urgent request, General Grant had sent the Essex Regiment from his own army to reinforce Colonel Wolseley's small defence force.

Kernow would have liked to accompany them, but it would not have been possible to go without giving Grant a very good reason. Concern for the safety of a Chinese girl would not have been acceptable to the conventional commander-in-chief.

Lord Elgin's next destination was Tientsin, eighty-five miles from Peking. Ratification of an earlier treaty which had been agreed here was at the root of the current war. The significance of occupying this city would not be lost on the Chinese.

The small fleet nosed its way upriver prepared to do battle with the many small forts dotting the banks of the river Pei-ho. Landing parties put ashore along the route reported that every one of them had been hurriedly abandoned. Surprisingly, Tientsin too was surrendered without a fight, despite its recognised importance as the 'gateway to Peking'.

Lord Elgin, his French counterpart Baron Gros, and Generals Grant and de Montauban, together with their staffs, commandeered a large house belonging to Tientsin's Salt Commissioner. It was here, at the end of August, that they received three Imperial commissioners. The delegation had been despatched from Peking to sign a ceasefire treaty and then escort Elgin and Gros to Peking. Once there, it was promised, the 1858 treaty would finally receive ratification.

Although Kernow believed the fighting was over there was a nagging suspicion at the back of his mind that all was not well. It was not that he wanted it to be so. Quite the contrary. More news of the Taipings' movements had reached British headquarters at Tientsin. The rebels had broken through the lines of the Imperial forces who had been slowly closing in upon Nanking and Taiping held territory. Totally destroying one of the Imperial armies they had struck out for the coast, heading in the direction of Shanghai.

Kernow was impatient for matters to be settled here. He might then be given permission to hurry back to Shanghai and ensure that She-she was safe.

Unfortunately, for the moment he was involved with matters much closer at hand. Eventually he confided his suspicions to Lord Elgin.

After listening to Kernow thoughtfully, the plenipotentiary said, "I know exactly what you mean, Kernow. I feel uneasy myself, but unless we can prove something I will be obliged to agree to the Chinese offer. To refuse would be to risk censure at home in Britain. Do you have anything more than intuition to go on?"

"No," Kernow answered honestly. "But the Chinese commissioners are too eager to please. They seem willing to agree to almost anything in order to maintain a ceasefire and persuade you and the French ambassador to accompany them to Peking. Such a sudden about-face worries me."

"What do the other interpreters think?" There were two diplomatic interpreters with the party. One had been loaned from the governor's office in Hong Kong, the other from the consulate in Shanghai. Both had spent many years in government service in China.

"They're as puzzled as I, but they're hoping for the best. I don't think we should go along with the Chinese on hope alone. I'd like some solid proof of their good intentions."

"Follow your instincts, Kernow. I'll put off agreeing to anything for a couple of days. In the meantime find out all you can from the Chinese and their staff."

The truth came out two days later when Kernow and the other interpreters were re-examining the credentials the Imperial commissioners had brought with them from Peking. Astonishingly, it was discovered that not one of the three had been given the Emperor's authority to sign anything! Any decision reached at Tientsin would have been held to be meaningless.

At a hastily convened meeting between Kernow, the other interpreters, Lord Elgin,

General Grant, Admiral Hope, Baron Gros and General de Montauban, the matter was discussed at great length.

The French view was that it was probably an oversight on the part of the Chinese. Lord Elgin was more sceptical. "In such matters I have always found the Chinese to be absolutely meticulous. I feel there is rather more to it than a mere mistake. What's your opinion, Kernow?"

"I believe that at best it's a deliberate attempt to delay ratification of the treaty. At worst it may be an attempt to persuade you and the French ambassador to travel on to Peking with a light escort and risk being taken hostage."

While the French protested that such suggestions were absurd, Elgin turned to General Grant. "What do you suggest, General?"

Grant was not a devious man. He had no time for diplomatic ploys and intrigues. "I suggest we bring the whole matter out into the open. One thing is certain — we can't afford to stay in China for too long. It will soon be winter and we have insufficient stores to maintain a strong presence here. We'll either be starved out of China — or die where we are."

"There I think we have the answer to the Chinese tactics, gentlemen. If they keep us here for long enough they won't need to do any more fighting. Nature will do all that's necessary on their behalf. We will tackle them with this matter in the morning."

The following morning, in the presence of Lord Elgin, the diplomatic interpreters put it to the Chinese commissioners bluntly. They had no authorisation from the Imperial government. They had been wasting the time of the British and French ambassadors.

The Imperial commissioners smiled blandly. It was, of course, all a mistake. One that would quickly be cleared up. Lord Elgin and Baron Gros should remain at Tientsin. The three commissioners would return to Peking and inform the Imperial government of the unfortunate oversight.

"No, gentlemen. You return to Peking. We will follow. Once there we'll have it explained to us in person. Perhaps you will also make the necessary arrangements for quartering our army? They will be travelling with us."

With this parting shot, Lord Elgin rose from his seat, closely followed by Baron Gros. Outside, the British and French armies prepared to march still further into China.

27

GENERAL GRANT advanced cautiously upon China's capital city, intent upon securing an escape route to Tientsin and the Pei-ho river once his mission had been accomplished. Some of his troops, in particular his irregular cavalry, grumbled at the commander-in-chief's apparent excess of caution. However, the vast majority of the soldiers under his command were content for their commander to do things his way. The bible-carrying general was intent on winning battles, not gaining personal glory. He would not sacrifice the lives of his men unnecessarily.

Lord Elgin and Baron Gros travelled with the army and all along the way were bombarded with letters from Peking. The letters protested that the lack of authority invested in the previous Imperial negotiations had been 'an oversight'. New commissioners were on the way. All would be well if the two ambassadors would only return to Tientsin and await the Emperor's special emissaries . . .

When the Allied army was within a few miles of the Chinese capital, a message was received which Lord Elgin felt he could at last take seriously. A brother of the Emperor had been appointed to negotiate with Elgin and Gros. He would have all the powers of the Emperor himself. Meanwhile, arrangements were being made to accommodate the allied armies on a vast camp-site only a few miles ahead.

Calling Kernow to his tent that evening, Lord Elgin was in a jubilant mood. "I think the Imperial court has finally accepted we do not intend removing our armies from China until the treaty has been ratified, Kernow. They want me to send someone to meet their negotiators. I'd like you to go with my secretary. The two of you will be responsible for setting up a meeting with their commissioners and arranging my entry into Peking. I don't need to remind you of the importance of this mission. It will be the culmination of two very frustrating years and bring to an end the war between our country and China. Nevertheless, you will accept no slights to the Crown, neither will you be expected to suffer any personal humiliation. You negotiate for me — and I represent Her Majesty the Queen. Remember that, Kernow. I wish you good luck."

★ ★ ★

Kernow set out with a party of six diplomats and senior officers, escorted by a lieutenant and thirty cavalrymen. Behind them, Grant prepared to follow with an advance guard of some two thousand men.

Kernow and his party headed for Chang-kia-wan, a village about ten miles from the city of Peking. This was where the Chinese had suggested the French and British armies should

467

make camp while the two ambassadors entered Peking.

Before Kernow and his party had ridden very far, he began to feel uneasy. They were passing groups of Chinese soldiers who watched them with undisguised hostility which occasionally became open derision. It was hardly the attitude of a nation with whom Britain was about to sign a peace and trade treaty.

The Imperial commissioners occupied an imposing tent, surrounded by still more soldiers of the Imperial army. The Chinese officials extended a lavish welcome to the British party but Kernow's first question concerned the numbers of soldiers they had passed on the way in.

"You must not worry yourself about them," declared the oldest of the three Chinese, speaking as though the matter was one of little importance. "It is necessary for there to be Imperial soldiers in the area. Not all the people of China wish to welcome the *Fan Quis* to our land. Most of the soldiers are here merely to keep the peace. Others have been given the task of gathering food for the army which accompanies your ambassador. All will be well, you will see."

The reply was too glib. Too conciliatory. Hastily scribbling a note telling General Grant of his fears, Kernow sent off two of the troopers to carry it to the British commander-in-chief. He explained to the Chinese commissioner that it was part of a pre-arranged plan to inform the British general of the safe arrival of the negotiating party.

The remainder of the day was spent in discussion. The readiness with which the Chinese agreed to almost every proposal made by the British only served to increase Kernow's fears still more.

That night he spoke at length to Elgin's private secretary. It was agreed the diplomat would return to the advance guard of troops the following morning and acquaint Grant and Elgin personally with Kernow's fears.

The secretary set off at dawn with an escort of ten cavalrymen. On the way he passed even more Chinese troops and these had a considerable number of artillery pieces with them. Such weapons were hardly necessary to keep the local populace in order and would not assist them in the gathering of stores.

Meanwhile, Kernow and the others went to inspect the site where Grant and his army were to make camp. To Kernow's consternation, there were even more troops here than had been encountered along the route to Chang-kia-wan. They would outnumber Grant's advance guard by at least three to one. The countryside was swarming with Chinese soldiers.

"What the devil are the Chinese playing at?"

The angry question was put to Kernow by a cavalry colonel sent with the party by Grant to mark out the camping site. His task was to allocate spaces for the various regiments and army units.

"I don't know," declared Kernow. He was genuinely concerned by now. "There's only one way to find out. You stay here with the rest of the escort. I'll take one of the troopers back with me to speak to the commissioners."

★ ★ ★

While these events were unfolding, General Grant had pushed his advance guard on with uncharacteristic speed. He was no more than a couple of miles from his destination when he suddenly found himself faced with a Chinese army numerically vastly superior to his own small force.

There was a low hill nearby. Taking this as his centre, Grant immediately put his troops into a defensive position. From the top of the mound he could actually see the red uniforms of the troopers with the colonel at the place where the British and French armies should have camped. He thought it ominous that the red jackets were heavily outnumbered by the grey uniforms of the Imperial troops.

Shortly afterwards a Chinese officer rode into Grant's position, saying he had come to guide the British soldiers to their camp ground. Calmly, Grant informed the Chinese he would wait where he was until his men returned from the Chinese lines.

Suddenly, one of Grant's staff called out that the British troopers were galloping towards them through the Chinese lines.

Only four men of Kernow's escort reached the British lines: the colonel left behind by Kernow, a commissary officer and two cavalry troopers. They told how, as they awaited Kernow's

470

return, the attitude of the Chinese soldiers about them became insolent and evermore threatening. Eventually one of them seized the colonel's sword. In attempting to take it back the colonel's hand was very badly cut. Realising the lives of he and his men were in imminent danger, he called for them to gallop at full speed to the British lines.

The men had put spurs to their horses, bowling over Chinese soldiers who stood in their way. As they made their escape they were fired upon. Two of the men had been wounded and they, with the remainder of the escort, had been taken prisoner.

The incident was the signal for a general opening of hostilities. Chinese artillery and gingals opened fire and the British and French came under very heavy bombardment.

Fortunately, Grant had artillery with him and the fire was returned. At the same time he ordered a regiment from his small force to probe the Chinese lines. With them he sent one of his irregular Cavalry regiments, Probyn's Horse, to protect them from the Tartar cavalry.

Probyn's Horse had been seriously weakened by having a great many of its cavalrymen sent on detached duties. Their present strength was a mere one hundred and six men. Riding from the Chinese lines to oppose them were more than two thousand Tartar horsemen.

The odds did not deter the cavalrymen, all of whom had volunteered their services from India. With a wild yell that frightened their own infantry almost as much as it did the enemy, they drew sabres and charged the Tartars. Breaking right through their lines, they turned and repeated the charge.

The King's Dragoon Guards were sent by Grant to give support to Probyn's Horse and between them they drove the bewildered Tartars from the field.

Heartened by the success of their cavalry the British infantry, spearheaded by a Punjabi regiment and supported by artillery, drove into the Chinese lines. Reeling from the ferocity of the attack, the enemy fell back.

Before long the retreat had become a rout. The Chinese fled leaving guns and equipment on the field of battle. Advancing with his men, Grant saw for himself the numerous camps that had been set up in the area. It needed only a cursory examination of them to confirm that the Chinese had acted in bad faith throughout the whole of the negotiations. The commissioners from Peking had been bait to draw Grant and the combined armies into a trap.

The trap had backfired seriously upon the Chinese who had suffered a severe defeat within sight of their own capital city. But Grant knew they would strike back at the *Fan Qui* in some way. In the meantime he had to secure his small force until the main body of his army and that of de Montauban arrived.

Ahead was the fortified village of Chang-kia-wan. Learning that it had housed the Chinese army which had attacked his own force, Grant gave permission for it to be given over to plunder.

That night Grant's small army lay down to sleep well housed and their bellies filled with the choicest pickings of the town.

General Grant did not sleep as well as his men. He lay in a tent, gazing up at the moonlit canvas, wondering what was happening to Kernow and the remainder of the men held by the Chinese.

28

IN Shanghai the Taiping threat was of more immediate concern than the fate of the joint British and French military expedition to Peking, even for those whose hearts were with the men who might be fighting for their lives. News of the advancing rebel army dominated everyday life.

"How will everyone find room inside the city?"

She-she asked the question of Nan Strachan as they watched refugees streaming in through the gates of the walled city from the surrounding countryside. Mostly women and children, they all carried pathetically small bundles which, along with their lives, was all they had been able to save from the advancing Taiping armies.

Whichever side won the long war, Imperial Chinese or Taiping rebel, these were the losers. Once they would have been safe from harm at the hands of the Taipings, but those days had gone. The *T'ien Wang* no longer exercised the iron grip he once had on his followers. Taiping soldiers were almost as rapacious as the soldiers of the Manchu Emperor of China.

"When the magistrate decides the city can take no more people, he'll have the gates closed against them."

As Nan spoke, her gaze followed the long

line of weary, unsmiling people. It stretched as far as could be seen across the flat, featureless countryside surrounding Shanghai.

"What will happen to those left outside?"

"The same as always happens when such people flock to the cities in times of trouble. They'll fill the suburbs and hope the Taipings will be turned back before they reach Shanghai."

"I hope so too. I've had my fill of the followers of the *T'ien Wang*. I wish Kernow hadn't had to go away."

"We'll be all right, She-she. If the Taipings get this far they'll be after the city, not us. Besides, we have French and British soldiers to defend us. Colin is with the other men right now. They're busy digging trenches around the foreign settlements for our protection."

★ ★ ★

Nan's confident words seemed less reassuring when the refugee stream stopped abruptly that same night. It was a sure indication that the Taipings were very close. Soon afterwards many of the French and English soldiers were withdrawn from the settlements. To the surprise of everyone they filed inside Shanghai itself. Taking their artillery with them, they took up positions on the city walls alongside soldiers of the Imperial army.

More ominous still, other soldiers moved through the suburbs that had sprung up in the shadow of the city wall. Ejecting residents

475

and refugees alike, they set fire to the houses. Razing them to the ground would give the soldiers manning the walls a clear field of fire all around the city.

The destruction of the suburbs left the house of She-she and the Strachan family very exposed. The French were more liberally minded than either the British or the Americans, but they drew the line at having mixed-marriage families in the heart of their settlement. Colin Strachan had been obliged to house his wife and family at the very edge of the French community. However, they could draw comfort from the knowledge that they had a line of French troops, albeit a much diminished one, between themselves and the as yet unseen troops of the Taiping army.

* * *

When Colin Strachan returned home late that evening he carried a musket and wore an unaccustomed air of authority.

"They've mustered all the men from the ships in the foreign anchorage," he said. "I've been put in charge of twenty of them. We're guarding the waterfront in case the Taipings try to land by boat."

"I thought the English and French were neutral in the war between the Imperialists and the Taipings," said Nan. "Why are you fighting the Imperialists in the north and yet fighting *with* them against the Taipings here at Shanghai?"

"Bruce has explained that," said Colin Strachan. Frederick Bruce, brother of Lord Elgin, was in charge of the British community at Shanghai. "We're at war with the Chinese government at the moment, but only until we sort out a few differences. It doesn't mean we want the Taipings to take the Chinese throne. Nor do we want them to take Shanghai. It will set trade back ten years."

"Why?"

Nan's single word question left her husband groping for an answer he did not have.

"It doesn't matter," Nan shrugged. "You and I belong to neither side, my husband. Only to one another. Sit down and I will bring you food."

"I only have time for a quick meal."

"You are going out again?" Nan was genuinely dismayed. "Where?"

"We all need to stand-to tonight, in case the Taipings try to take advantage of the darkness and move in on the city."

"What of us, your family? Who will take care of us?"

"You'll be all right. There are French soldiers all around the Concession. No Taipings are going to get in to bother you while I'm away. Tomorrow I'll see if I can't get moved to the French Concession so I'm closer to home."

When Colin Strachan had gulped down his hurriedly prepared meal and left the house, She-she asked, "Do you think the Taipings will really try to take Shanghai?"

"I doubt it. Not now the English and French

have taken sides against them. They'll probably turn around and return to Nanking."

* * *

The Taipings reached Shanghai the following day. They did not attack the city. Indeed, there were only three thousand of them and they came openly towards the west gate of the city, as though they expected to be welcomed by the Shanghai inhabitants.

From their house in the settlement She-she and Nan could see the advancing Taipings and She-she caught her breath as she recognised Chang riding at the head of the troops of the *T'ien Wang*.

The Taiping party had almost reached the gate when a rain storm swept across the flat countryside and enveloped them in its grey, clammy grasp. As though it were a heaven-sent signal the guns of the soldiers on the wall of the city opened fire on the unsuspecting Taiping soldiers.

When the squall had passed on, dragging the curtain of grey behind it, three hundred Taiping warriors were left lying on the ground and the remainder were in full retreat.

The Western nationals were as jubilant as the Imperial Chinese cowering inside the walled city. The Taipings had attacked and been repulsed. Few paused to consider why the Taipings had chosen to 'attack' Shanghai with a mere three thousand men. Or why, with a huge army at their disposal, they had accepted 'defeat' without firing a shot in return.

In their mood of euphoria, a protest from Chang, delivered to the British and French consulates the following day, was ignored. In it he complained bitterly that he had been invited to Shanghai by the French and promised safe conduct. What was more, he had received information from his spies within the city that if he advanced to the gate and called upon the garrison to surrender, Shanghai would be his. The Europeans had broken their promise of neutrality. Chang demanded an explanation.

That night Colin Strachan returned to his home boasting as though he had been involved in the rout of the Taipings. He was also slightly the worse for drink. It was the first time in their married life that Nan had seen him in such a condition.

"Well, what better occasion could there be for a celebration?" he declared when Nan chided him gently for raising his voice and startling their youngest child. "We've won a great victory today. A handful of men have beaten off the Taipings. Frederick Bruce himself congratulated us. He said he'll be sending a letter to London telling them how we rallied when danger threatened. Then he opened bottles for everyone who helped in the defence of the city."

Nan doubted whether Bruce's praise meant she and her husband could now move into the British settlement and be accepted by her husband's people. She said nothing. Today at least, Colin Strachan was a man among his own people. Tomorrow would be soon enough for him to become once more 'the man who has *married* a Chinese girl'.

★ ★ ★

The Taipings had been thwarted in their plan to take Shanghai, but they were able to carry out a swift and unchallenged raid during the hours of darkness.

She-she was in a pleasantly drowsy state, hovering between wakefulness and sleep, when the door to the small Strachan home was kicked in. Before anyone was fully awake the house was filled with Taiping soldiers.

Everyone was pulled from their beds, including the children. When the baby began to scream in terror, Nan went to him. None of the Taipings attempted to stop her. Instead, the leader of the small group pointed to She-she.

As he turned away two of the Taiping soldiers grabbed her and began to drag her outside.

"Here! What d'you think you're doing? Leave her alone. She's a guest in my house."

Still befuddled from his evening's drinking session, Colin Strachan protested to the Taipings. Instead of replying, one of their number raised the axe he carried and brought it down on Colin Strachan's head.

Nan screamed as her husband dropped to the ground and lay still. Fortunately the Taiping soldier had hit him with the flat edge of the axe blade. Colin Strachan was merely knocked unconscious.

As Nan, still clutching the baby, dropped to her knees beside her husband, the men left as swiftly as they had entered. With them they took She-she.

She was on her way to Chang, commander of all the armies of the *T'ien Wang*.

29

A BLEARY-EYED British army captain listened to Colin Strachan's story in growing confusion as he repeated it for the second time.

"How many Taipings do you say?"

"I don't know. Maybe ten . . . it could have been twenty."

"And they only took this one woman? Did they take liberties with your wife?"

"No."

"Where are these Taipings now?"

"Gone."

"I don't understand . . . Look, old man. There's nothing *I* can do about this. If I've grasped your story correctly all this happened in the French Concession. They're damned touchy about any British interference in their area. I'll bring it to the attention of my commanding officer in the morning, of course, but in the meantime I suggest you report this to the duty officer in the French army camp. I think you'll find them under canvas somewhere near the Catholic Cathedral."

Colin Strachan got even shorter shrift from the French duty officer. He too had been celebrating and made no attempt to help Colin. He spoke no English, and after trying unsuccessfully to make sense of Colin's limited French, he reached the conclusion that Colin

482

was a drunken Englishman. Ordering a sergeant to throw him out of the camp, he turned his back and returned to bed.

It was the early hours of the morning when Colin woke the residents at the mission house where Esme Pilkington was staying. She came down from her room untangling cloth curlers from her hair, but when she heard what Colin had to say, all else was forgotten.

"This is shocking! We must get help right away."

"I've been trying to tell British and French officers about it but no one wants to know. A British captain said it was a French matter and the French officer thought I was drunk."

"We'll soon put them right! How long ago was She-she taken?"

"It must be three or four hours now."

Esme's spirits sank. There was no hope of pursuing and overtaking She-she's abductors, even if it were possible to learn which direction they had taken. But Colin Strachan had made such a great effort to obtain help for She-she it would be cruel to tell him it had all been to no avail.

"You've had a nasty blow on the head and must be feeling awful. It's a miracle you weren't killed. Nan must be very worried about you. Go home for a while and leave this to me. Come back and see me when you wake. I've no doubt I'll have need of your help by then."

"If you're sure, Esme . . . I have to admit my head is throbbing."

"I'm sure it is, Colin. Go home now and sleep

483

for a couple of hours, at least."

When Colin Strachan had gone, Esme made her way from the hall of the mission house to her own room. She ignored the complaints of the other residents who knew nothing of Colin's business and were aware only that they had been woken from their sleep. They grumbled that there had been enough excitement over the past few days. It was time life settled back to normality once more.

In her room Esme tried to put her thoughts in some order. She had to find some way of helping poor She-she. When an answer did not come to her immediately, Esme did what she usually did in times of dire trouble. She went down on her knees by the side of her bed and prayed.

By the time she rose to her feet there was just a hint of dawn showing at the window — and she knew what she would do. It was not going to be easy. She-she was a Hakka girl and the Hakkas were at the core of the Taiping movement. French and English consular officials would be inclined to shrug the matter off as not being of sufficient importance to provoke a major incident. There was no question of telling anyone of Kernow's love for She-she. That would only make matters worse. The reaction would be that if She-she was 'that' type of girl it was better that the Taipings should keep her.

Esme felt that Colin Strachan's experience with the French and British military would prove typical. The only sympathetic ear she could think of even remotely close to diplomatic circles was Sally Merrill's. Sally had promised Kernow she would do whatever she could to help She-she, and was genuinely fond of the Chinese girl.

Esme was so engrossed in her concern for She-she that she was not aware what time it was. Dawn came early in this part of the world. For the second time that night a household was roused from its beds to be told of the kidnapping of She-she.

After hearing an outline of the matter, a tousled-haired Consul Merrill said, "You'd better come in. I'll have the servants produce some breakfast. You can tell us all about it while we eat."

Behind him Sally, her mother and Caleb, who was staying at the consulate, had listened with growing concern.

"I'm so worried about She-she that food would choke me," said Esme. "But I could drink a cup of coffee."

Over the breakfast table, as the servants hurried about them, Esme gave the story of She-she's abduction in more detail.

She ended with the plea, "Sally, what can we do? There has to be something. We can't allow the Taipings to get away with stealing She-she from a house in the foreign concessions. We just can't."

"What do you want me to do?" As she spoke, Sally Merrill tried to chase away the last vestiges of sleep. "We've got to think of something, that's for sure."

Consul Merrill stood up abruptly, "I don't think I should listen to this conversation. Caleb, I rely upon you to see that this doesn't get out

485

of hand. Sally will be your wife one day. Don't let her get involved in anything stupid. It could affect your future. Me, I'm retiring soon anyway. Just remember, the United States has stayed clear of all these quarrels so far. I don't want us getting involved over some young Chinese or Taiping girl, whatever you like to call her — and I don't care whose 'friend' she is either, you hear me?"

Sally's mother gave Esme a smile that showed her utter confusion, then she too rose from her seat and followed her husband from the room.

When her parents had gone, Sally asked Esme, "Why do you think the Taipings took such a chance in coming into the Foreign Concession to take She-she? Because she ran away from the palace in Nanking?"

"Perhaps. Although we know Chang is with the rebels. He was leading them when they approached Shanghai on that first day. He tried to persuade She-she to marry him at Nanking — and he knew she'd stayed with the Strachans before. He would have guessed she was there again."

"Does he know anything about Kernow?"

"Oh, yes. Chang knew about him before he left Hong Kong. For a long time She-she believed Kernow had died at Canton, after the typhoon. Chang knew different, but he never told her."

Caleb listened with a great deal of interest. All this was new to him. "You mean Kernow is mixed up with a Chinese girl and you've known about this all along?"

486

He shook his head in disbelief as he added to Sally, "I always thought he was sweet on you."

"So? You've given me far more attention as a result."

"How long has he known her?"

"Since he sank the junk she was travelling in, three years ago."

"As long ago as that? He must be pretty fond of her."

"The two of them are very much in love," agreed Sally. "I promised I'd take good care of her for him. Now this has happened. He'll be devastated."

"It's not your fault," said Esme. "The only person to be blamed is Chang. Poor Colin Strachan was knocked unconscious with an axe when he tried to prevent the Taipings from taking her. It's very lucky he wasn't murdered. But the question now is, how are we to get her back?"

Caleb was a young man who ached for action. He fervently believed the United States should be militarily involved in Chinese affairs. The humiliation to which the U.S. ambassador was subjected in Peking the year before still rankled with him. In Hong Kong he attended social functions attended by English army and navy officers. All had fought the Chinese over the years. However pleasant they were to his face, he always felt they nursed a veiled contempt for the Americans. They believed his country was taking advantage of the concessions won with English and French blood.

More recently, in Shanghai, Caleb had spent

the last three days in the United States consulate while battles involving every other nation were being fought around the walls of Shanghai. He had been a reluctant spectator, sheltering beneath the flag that neither side would attack.

The flag! The answer to what he should do came to Caleb in that instant. *He* would take action. If not for the United States, then for Sally. For his own self-esteem.

"I'll go and talk to these Taipings and get the girl back."

Sally gasped in astonishment. Caleb was not given to making instant decisions. Especially rash ones, "You'd never get close to them, Caleb. After what has happened during the past few days, they'd shoot you."

"Not if I carried a United States flag with me."

"Doing that would be tantamount to involving the United States in this affair. If anything went wrong you'd be dismissed from the army."

He shrugged. "That might happen anyway. According to the latest news from the States the quarrel between the North and South is reaching boiling point. It looks as though the South will secede soon. If that happens, then I must go with the South."

"Do you speak Chinese?" The question came from Esme.

Caleb's rising sense of elation and excitement took a sudden dive.

"No."

"I do. I'll come with you."

30

THE small group of people who set out in the early morning to seek the release of She-she numbered only four. Caleb, Esme and Colin Strachan were accompanied by a Chinese servant from the United States consulate carrying a flag of truce.

Before leaving, Caleb had called in at the Strachan home to seek any additional clues to the identity of the kidnappers. When Colin Strachan heard of their plan he insisted on accompanying them. He would carry the United States flag.

Caleb protested that as the only American in the party it was he who should carry his country's flag, but Colin Strachan was adamant. The tortuous demands of Chinese 'face' meant that Caleb's status as a negotiator would be seriously undermined if he arrived in the Chinese camp holding his own flag aloft. It was important he took a standard bearer. He would actually *gain* status if that bearer were a European.

As the small party approached the huge Taiping camp a picket ran at them brandishing pikes and swords. The Taiping rebels looked so fierce, with red bandanas about their foreheads and long, flowing hair, that they terrified the Chinese servant. So certain was he that he was within seconds of being decapitated, the flag of truce shook as though in a violent wind storm.

Contrary to Caleb's belief, the Taipings were unaware that the banner carried by Colin Strachan represented a country that had taken no part in the defence of Shanghai. They saw only a *Fan Qui* in full military uniform. To them he was the enemy.

Caleb's fate hung in the balance until Esme had a brainwave. Pointing to him, she said, "This man is from the United States of America — the same as the ship which comes upriver to bring arms to Nanking. He is a friend."

The attitude of the Taiping soldiers underwent an immediate change. There were smiles and even a pat on the back for the bewildered United States military attaché.

Escorted back to the Taiping camp, they were met on the way by Kau-lin. She came galloping up on a shaggy little pony which came to a reluctant halt only inches from the leading rebel in the escort.

Throwing the rein to the man, Kau-lin leaped from the pony's back and rushed to hug Esme. "I was told a *Fan Qui* woman was coming with a flag of truce. I knew it must be you. When I saw a soldier with you I thought it must be Kernow. How is he? How is She-she?"

She had spoken in English and there was an exchange of glances among the truce party before Esme said, "She-she is the reason we're here. She was kidnapped from the Strachan home last night."

Kau-lin's expression changed to one of disbelief. "You think she was taken by us? By the Taipings?"

"We *know* she was," replied Colin Strachan. "I was knocked unconscious when I tried to stop them."

"I can't believe it! Who would have known where to find her . . . "

Kau-lin stopped in mid-sentence. She already knew the answer, as did Esme and Colin Strachan.

"Chang!"

"That's what we believe. Where is he?"

"The Heavenly Prince and his court have their own camp, close to the river. My brother's soldiers are all about him in case of a possible attack from Shanghai."

"Will we be allowed to pass through and speak to Chang?"

Speaking in Chinese, Kau-lin said, "My brother will make no attempt to stop you. He and Chang do not like each other, but it does not follow that Chang will see you. He is a very important man now, second only to the *T'ien Wang*. He will sometimes refuse to speak to anyone for days at a time."

When Esme translated for Caleb, the American said to Kau-lin, "If your brother allows us to pass through his camp I'll make sure this Chang sees me."

Kau-lin looked at Caleb thoughtfully for some time without speaking as she mulled over his words. Suddenly she said in English, "I'll tell the soldiers to bring you to my brother's tent. I'll go on ahead and speak to him."

★ ★ ★

Commandant Peng Yu-cheng was eating when the three Europeans entered the tent. His soldiers had insisted the Chinese truce-flag bearer was of too lowly a status to enter the tent of the most important general in the Taiping army. He was left outside, shaking with fear whenever a Taiping rebel passed within striking distance of him.

Commandant Peng was a squat, cheerful man who looked more like a jovial cook than a highly successful Taiping general. He spoke no English, but issued an invitation through Kau-lin for his visitors to be seated and join him in a meal.

Caleb remained standing and all three declined to eat.

Continuing his lone meal in silence, Peng eventually wiped his lips and hands on a damp cloth proffered by a young serving-boy.

"My brother eats at odd times," explained Kau-lin. "He cannot know when he will next have to go into battle."

Rising to his feet, Peng said simply, "Come," without looking at anyone in particular.

Orders had apparently been issued prior to the arrival of Caleb's party at Commandant Peng's tent. When they went outside about two hundred well-armed Taiping soldiers were waiting. They gathered about their commandant and the others as they set off for Chang's camp.

Their approach was observed and Chang's personal guard was mustered hurriedly to bar the way.

Leaving the escort behind, Peng scornfully pushed his way through Chang's guard and

492

the Heavenly Prince's personal escort fell back uncertainly to allow the others through.

Chang had been told of their approach and now he appeared at the door of the hut that had been commandeered as his quarters.

"You have visitors," said Peng, without the polite preliminaries that usually attended the meeting of two such important men. "I brought them personally to ensure they were not abused."

"We are Taipings not Manchus, Commandant Peng. We treat our visitors with courtesy."

The conversation between the two men was carried on in Chinese and Caleb became impatient. "I've come to take She-she back to Shanghai. Your men kidnapped her from the European settlement, last night."

"Kidnapped?" Chang expressed exaggerated surprise. "Why should my men kidnap a Hakka girl when there are more than enough for everyone in Nanking?"

"Don't play games with me, Chang. She-she was taken by your men from the European settlement at Shanghai. At the time she was under the protection of the United States consul. I've come here to take her back."

The use of the name by which he had been known prior to his phenomenal rise through the Taiping ranks enraged Chang, but he was alarmed by the suggestion that his men had violated American sovereignty in taking She-she. Perhaps the boundaries of the Foreign Settlements had been redrawn since he was in Shanghai. However, he was not about to confess his fears to this young American soldier.

"My men recovered a woman who had run away from the palace of the *T'ien Wang*. She will be returned to him."

"*I* ran away from the *T'ien Wang*'s palace. Will you try to send me back too?" Esme said angrily.

"You are not a Taiping woman."

"Neither is She-she."

Caleb listened with growing impatience to the exchange in a language he did not understand. Now he said, "There's been enough talking. I came here for the girl, and I'm not leaving without her. Give her to me and we'll take her back to her friends."

The Heavenly Prince looked at the United States military attaché with contemptuous amusement. "And if I refuse? What will you do then, American *Fan Qui*? Will you loose an army on us — or send another ambassador to Peking in a peasant carrying-cart to complain to the Manchu Emperor?"

Both of Chang's sarcastic questions hit Caleb on the raw, but he kept admirable control of his temper. "Neither, *Chang*. But I will ensure that neither Erin Veasey nor any other United States citizen breaks the embargo by sailing to Nanking. If you return She-she to the *T'ien Wang* you can tell him of the price he's paying for her."

Commandant Peng smiled as Kau-lin translated Caleb's words for him. Caleb had called Chang's bluff and Peng knew the American would win the day. Chang was a favourite of the *T'ien*

494

Wang but he would not maintain his position if he were responsible for cutting off the Taipings' supply of armaments. Without them the Taiping movement could not survive.

Chang also realised he had lost.

"The girl is sleeping now. When she wakes I will have her prepared for her return. It is possible she will be taken back to Shanghai tomorrow."

"Unless I have returned with her by nightfall, a brigade of United States sailors and marines will come here looking for me and you'll be at war with my country."

Chang had no alternative but to accede to Caleb's wishes. The Taiping cause would not survive a serious rift with the Americans. Nevertheless, his eyes could not disguise his anger as he said, "She will be given to you in time for you to reach Shanghai before dusk."

Kau-lin had translated the exchange for her brother. Now Peng said, "My army moves off at noon and we will travel swiftly. The girl will be released by then or you will need to rely upon your own escort to protect you from the *Fan Qui* and the Imperial army."

Chang's anger flared into the open. "You do not deliver ultimatums to the Heavenly Prince."

"At noon," retorted the Taiping commander. Turning his back on the Heavenly Prince he left the hut without another word.

The mask of aloof politeness had returned to Chang's face when he spoke to Caleb again. "There are no bad feelings between the Taipings and your country, only with France and Britain who have chosen to fight the battles of the Manchu Emperor. The girl rightfully belongs to us, but as an act of friendship she may return with you to Shanghai."

A wave of Chang's hand was a signal for them to be ushered from the hut.

Outside, Caleb asked, "Will he keep his word?" He was jubilant that the mission he had undertaken on behalf of Sally was close to success. Yet he was apprehensive that something could still go wrong. He estimated he and his companions were in the midst of an army of at least a hundred thousand armed Taiping rebels. Fortunately, the man who controlled the majority of them was well disposed towards them. However, the awesome arrogance he had displayed by coming here demanding the release of a Chinese girl he had never even met was beginning to sink in.

Kau-lin answered his question.

"Cousin Chang will keep his word, but She-she has been his prisoner for many hours. I fear what might have happened to her."

31

FROM the moment She-she was dragged from the home of the Strachans by Taiping rebels she knew that Chang must be behind her abduction. As her kidnappers hurried her away through the night she tried desperately to think of ways to escape.

While they fled through the foreign settlements a rebel maintained a grip on each arm. However, when they came to a narrow causeway that crossed a network of rice-fields one of the Taiping rebels was forced to relinquish his grip.

Seizing the opportunity, She-she managed to wrench herself free. Tumbling down a steep but low bank, she landed heavily on the ground beneath the causeway. The fields had been drained of water but the recent rains had made them muddy. Picking herself up she tried to run, but slipped and fell. Before she could take advantage of the darkness and make her escape, her captors had plunged from the bank and surrounded her.

Minutes later they were on their way once more, but this time her hands were pinioned behind her back and a rope about her waist was held fast by the man in front of her.

Gasping for breath she was hurried through the night until they reached the camp of the Taiping rebels. Muddy and dishevelled, she was thrust through the doorway of a hut that seemed to be the only permanent building within the confines of the camp.

"Kneel in the presence of the Heavenly Prince." A fist in the middle of her back sent She-she sprawling to the ground.

Raising her head, she looked up at the seated figure of the 'Heavenly Prince'. Suddenly, and without warning, she began to shake from a combination of shock and fear.

"You are as beautiful as I have always remembered She-she — but so muddy! Never mind, we will clean you up soon. It made me very sad when I learned you had escaped from Nanking. It also made the *T'ien Wang* extremely angry. No one has ever run away from his palace before. He will be very pleased to know I have recovered you. Of course, the *T'ien Wang* will not concern himself with details of the fate of such a lowly person, so I anticipate we will have many days and nights of enjoyment together."

Signalling to the guards who had been grinning at the exchange, he said, "Take her away. Have her bathed and dressed in some of the spoils that have been taken on the way from Nanking."

She-she was seized by the guards and hoisted to her feet before being bundled from the hut.

Manhandled by the rebel soldiers, She-she's ordeal was brought to an end by the shrill voice of a woman.

"Is touching a woman's body more important to you than your head? Go, before I call for the Heavenly Prince's executioner!"

498

Releasing She-she, the Taipings fled before the woman's far from idle threat. No one knew whence Sai-tin had come, but during the short time Chang had been with the Taipings, she had become a legend. She had proved an exception to the rule of strict segregation within the Taiping army. Accompanying the Heavenly Prince wherever he went, Sai-tin attended to all his household needs and kept his male servants in constant fear for their lives.

"Come with me." Sai-tin beckoned to She-she. "We have part of the river screened off in order that the women soldiers might bathe in privacy. It's cold, but it will liven you up, I dare say."

"Women soldiers?" She-she's hopes rose momentarily. "Is Kau-lin with them?"

"You know her?" Sai-tin looked at She-she suspiciously. "Yes, she is here, but not in this part of the camp."

"Can you get a message to her for me?" She-she spoke eagerly. Too eagerly.

"No — and if you try to speak to anyone at the river I'll have some of the soldiers brought from the camp to bathe you and ensure you behave."

She-she said nothing, but if there was any chance of making good her escape at the river she would take it. Like most Hakka girls from her village, she was a strong swimmer.

Once at the river it soon became clear there would be no opportunity to use her talents as a swimmer. The women's bathing area was screened around with stout linen cloth securely fastened to stakes driven deep into the river bed. It would be impossible for a man or woman to enter the bathing area — or to leave.

Frustrated, She-she bathed and changed into clean clothing. All the time she was constantly aware that guards were nearby.

Her ablutions completed, She-she expected to be taken back to the hut where she had met Chang. To her relief she was taken instead to a large tent — but her relief was short-lived.

The tent was fitted out as a luxurious bedroom, but the clothes hanging in one corner were a man's. They were of such a fine quality that they could belong to only one man . . . Chang, the Heavenly Prince of the Taipings.

"Why have I been brought here?" She-she demanded of Sai-tin.

"You will find out soon enough. It is said the Heavenly Prince led a celibate life before joining the *T'ien Wang*. His virility makes such claims difficult to believe. Perhaps he is working hard to make up for all the lost years. He is almost as virile as the *T'ien Wang* himself."

As the old woman began chuckling to herself, She-she said, "I don't want Chang. I've never wanted him. He knows this."

Sai-tin glared at her. "It does not matter what you want. You are nobody. The Heavenly Prince is a cousin of the *T'ien Wang* . . . " Her voice tailed away to an indignant muttering. Eventually, she said, "It is late, the Heavenly Prince will be here soon. Drink this."

She-she was thirsty. She took the drink from

the woman, but as she put it to her lips breathed in a strange aroma that caused her to catch her breath.

Lowering the beaker, she said, "What is this?"

"It doesn't matter what it is. Drink."

"No, I don't like it."

"You will do as you are told. Drink it." Sai-tin stood in front of She-she, hands on her hips.

"It smells like opium and I will not take it." She-she tipped the beaker and poured the contents to the floor.

"You are a very foolish girl. You are making it hard for yourself."

Going to the flap of the tent, Sai-tin called into the darkness. Moments later a number of guards filed inside the tent.

"Take hold of her." The guards hastened to obey the woman and, despite her struggles, She-she was soon held fast.

Sai-tin spent some minutes mixing a drink. When she was satisfied she carried it to where She-she was secured by the Taiping soldiers.

She-she began struggling once more but the soldiers held her even tighter. They used her struggles as an opportunity to fondle her, until Sai-tin brought their activities to a halt.

"Enough! Hold her head back — and keep it still."

One of the soldiers took a firm grip on She-she's hair and pulled her head back. She still refused to open her mouth, but Sai-tin pinched her nose.

She-she held her breath until she felt she must

burst. When she could hold it no more, she opened her mouth to suck in air and the infusion of opium was poured down her throat.

She-she still struggled desperately, alternately spluttering, choking, and swallowing. She tried to spit out the liquid that was being poured down her throat but most of the infusion was swallowed and the first beaker was followed by a second.

By now She-she was sobbing with a combination of frustration and anger, but Sai-tin had won.

Gradually, in spite of herself, the anger within She-she began to seep away. As it disappeared she experienced a ringing in her ears. She suddenly felt as though her body was caught in an invisible tide, alternately ebbing and flowing. At the same time her eyelids began drooping, trying hard to close.

Sai-tin had been watching her closely. Now she said to the soldiers, "Leave us. Go."

She-she was not aware that she and Sai-tin were alone. She realised the older woman was helping her to the bed but could not resist as Sai-tin laid her down and undressed her, occasionally stroking her body. She felt incredibly drowsy. There was an overwhelming desire to sleep, but sleep would not come.

She did not know how long this feeling lasted. It seemed there was an increasing weight pressing on her brain. At the same time it felt as though an invisible hand was stroking her arms, legs and spine, yet she was sure no one was there.

She-she found she could no longer move, yet neither did she want to. She felt more relaxed than at any time in her life and was possessed of an extraordinary sense of well-being.

While she was feeling like this she became vaguely aware that someone was standing over her. Whoever it was reached down and laid aside the loose clothing in which she had been dressed. The other being was a shadowy, indistinct figure and then it was touching her, removing her remaining clothing.

At some point in this timeless period she realised that the person touching her was a man. She knew because he lay upon her and she felt him inside her . . . moving with a wonderful motion she remembered as though from another life.

Her body moved in rhythm with his and suddenly a name was upon her lips. For a few moments the name remained there, going no further. Then, as her body began to move, independent of her brain, the name escaped.

"Kernow . . . Kernow . . . Kernow . . . !"

She was not aware that as she uttered the name the movement of the body lying upon her ceased abruptly. She was drifting off into a sleep that bordered upon unconsciousness.

She was unaware of the unheavenly curses uttered by Chang, the Heavenly Prince. Unaware of his anger, his frenzied kicking caused her no pain . . .

32

WHEN Kernow arrived at the camp where he had left the Chinese commissioners, he found they were no longer here. If any further confirmation was needed that the Chinese planned mischief, this was it. The commissioners should have been at the camp, preparing to meet Lord Elgin.

Kernow had a dragoon trooper and two Indian sowars acting as his escort. Angrily leaving the commissioners' empty tent, he said, "This is another of the Chinese ploys to gain time. They're hoping that winter will defeat us where they can't. We'll ride back to where we left the colonel and all return to General Grant. There's nothing more for us here."

As Kernow was speaking the Chinese crowded about the four men. Suddenly, in response to a signal given by an officer standing out of Kernow's sight, the Chinese soldiers rushed in and seized them.

"Don't try to struggle!" Kernow shouted the warning, but he was too late. The British trooper fought back violently until he was felled with a blow from the butt of a musket.

The soldier who had knocked him to the ground raised his musket to deal him another blow, but Kernow called, "No!" in Chinese. The soldier lowered his musket, but Kernow received a blow from a pike handle to the side of his head for daring to give an order to a Chinese soldier.

Kernow and his three companions then had their hands tied behind their backs, the cords being pulled so tight that they dug deep into the flesh of their wrists.

Kernow protested volubly, demanding that the commissioners be called to the scene.

The officer who had ordered the seizure of the four men gripped Kernow by the shoulder and spun him around. Then he pushed him in the back, causing him to stumble. Speaking in Chinese, he said, "The commissioners have returned to Peking. That's where you are going. Maybe they will speak to you, but I doubt if you will hear them. You will certainly not be able to reply. Heads on the poles above the gates of the city do not say very much."

The officer's reply provoked much laughter among his men. They followed his example in pushing the pinioned men from one to the other, kicking them to their feet when they stumbled.

This game went on for almost half-an-hour until, staggering dazedly, they started off on the road to Peking.

Proof that this had been a deliberate and planned taking of hostages was provided along the way. The cavalry colonel and his handful of men had been the only ones to make their way back to British lines. By the time Kernow and his party reached Peking they had been joined by some forty French, English and Indian soldiers.

Paraded through the streets, the *Fan Qui*

soldiers were reviled by jeering crowds who threw mud and stones at them.

When the novelty of parading the foreigners palled, their Chinese escorts herded them to the Emperor's Summer Palace. The temple and its gardens were monuments to beauty, but the unfortunate prisoners were given no opportunity to appreciate its wonders.

Herded into an enclosed courtyard they were thrown to the ground and now their captors bound each man's ankles as tightly as his hands.

One of the Indian cavalryman was crying that the bonds left his hands with no feeling at all. Kernow called to the Chinese officer, pleading that he allow someone to slacken off the rope on the cavalryman's wrists.

The Chinese officer's response was to call for water to be brought. When it arrived he ordered that each man be turned on to his face and water poured over the ropes, tightening them even further.

Soon after this the Chinese soldiers discovered a sport that seemed to please them greatly. Lifting a man to his knees they would then kick him on to his back. This game kept them amused until dusk when they went off leaving about a dozen soldiers to guard the bound and moaning men.

Soon after darkness fell one of the prisoners began screaming. Two of the guards went to the man and Kernow could hear the sounds of a beating. Long before it stopped the screams had subsided to a low, uncontrolled sobbing.

When daylight broke over the courtyard, the man who had been sobbing was dead. So too was one of the Indian soldiers who had been beaten badly earlier in the day.

For three days and nights the prisoners were held in the courtyard of the Summer Palace, by which time four more men had died and a number of others were delirious.

No food or water had been brought for the prisoners during the whole of this time. When Kernow lodged a protest through cracked lips, the soldiers' response was to cram earth and dirt into the mouths of their helpless prisoners, treating it as a huge and clever joke.

At the end of the third night the men were wakened by their captors who brought iron shackles and chains to take the place of the cruel ropes. By this time the hands of a number of the prisoners had been starved of blood for so long they would never function again.

When sufficient feeling had returned to the feet of the surviving prisoners, they were divided into four parties and led away, staggering from lack of food and the effect of their bonds.

Kernow and five other prisoners were taken to what appeared to be a small fort in the hills outside Peking. Here they were lodged in an evil-smelling building that had until recently been occupied by the buffaloes used on the fields around the fort.

They had still been given no food and Kernow was very worried about the condition of a young bugler boy belonging to one of the infantry regiments. Kernow pleaded through the high, barred window of the outhouse whenever he heard a sound from outside, but his pleas for food went unanswered.

"We're going to die here, sir, aren't we?"

The bugler's voice was weak and cracked. He was one of those who had lost all sense of feeling in his hands, and much of the use of his feet. He had been supported by Kernow and a Frenchman during the last hours of the journey from the Summer Palace.

"Of course we're not going to die — and you'll outlive us all. One day you're going to be able to spend your days sitting in the sun, surrounded by grandchildren. Then you'll tell them how you were imprisoned by the Chinese and were so brave they promoted you to corporal immediately upon your return to the regiment."

The young boy made a pitiful attempt at a smile. It seemed to drain much of the remaining strength from him. "They can't make me a corporal yet, sir. I . . . I'm only a boy bugler."

"They'll make you a corporal, or I'll want to know why. What's more, I shall personally recommend it to General Grant." Kernow's voice was hardly stronger than the bugler boy's, but he hoped he sounded more convincing than he felt.

* * *

In the middle of the night Kernow awoke from a fitful doze to hear the sound of voices outside the outhouse. For a moment he thought they were part of some delirious dream. Then he heard the sound of bolts being drawn on the outside of the door. The next moment a number of men entered the outhouse, some carrying lanterns.

Kernow was certain he was suffering from delirium when a voice said in French, "Hello, Captain Keats. You seem to make a habit of being taken prisoner by the Chinese." It was Shalonga, son of the Tartar general.

"Have you come to gloat, or to set us free?"

"Neither, my friend. I cannot order your release because you were taken prisoner on the orders of one of the Emperor's commissioners. Even I cannot defy such an order. But I can ensure you are treated better than you have been until now. I have had food and water brought. Which will you have first?"

"A drink . . . but give some to the young boy in the corner first. He's in a bad way."

Shalonga snapped an order in a language that Kernow did not understand. A soldier wearing a shaggy ankle-length fur coat carried a pitcher of water to the form lying in a corner of the outhouse. Another leaned over him with a lantern.

The soldier carrying the water spoke over his shoulder in the same, unfamiliar language used by Shalonga and then straightened up.

"Your young friend is in a bad way no longer, Captain Keats. He is dead. Here, let me help you to sit up. You were unfortunate enough to be taken prisoner by a brigade of bannermen who have seen little fighting. Fighting men understand and respect other soldiers. Men such as these do not."

Kernow took some water as other prisoners about him did the same. He felt it travelling every inch of the way to his stomach. Although he only took five or six mouthfuls it bloated him as though he had drunk a couple of pints.

"Your commissioners have much to answer for. The Emperor too. Lord Elgin is not likely to allow him to forget this."

"The Emperor will not be in Peking to greet Lord Elgin. He has fled to a place many, many miles from Peking. But we can talk of this tomorrow. I am having you moved to more suitable quarters. There will be beds and good food."

One of Shalonga's soldiers had obtained the keys to the prisoners shackles. As they were unfastened, Kernow asked, "What's happening in the war? Has there been any more fighting between our armies?"

Shalonga looked at Kernow pityingly. Battered, bruised and dirty, he looked as though he might drop dead any moment.

"We have much to talk about, Englishman, but it will wait until morning. Come, I will show you and your men your new prison quarters."

★ ★ ★

The next morning, bathed, fed and more confident of the future, Kernow repeated his question of the previous night.

This time Shalonga gave him a reply. "There

510

has been a great deal of fighting, as I knew there would be. Your General Grant and the French General de Montauban are now at the gates of Peking, threatening to bombard the city and take it by storm if you are not released."

"What of the other prisoners? Have you been able to help them all?"

"I am a fighting soldier, not a nursemaid, Englishman. I heard Lord Elgin's soldier-interpreter had been taken prisoner. I thought it must be you and made enquiries. I have found you."

"I am glad you have, Shalonga. We all are but I thought you had been brought from your home to fight the Taiping rebels, not us."

"That is so. My father is still fighting them. I would be too, but the Emperor asked for part of my father's army to come and defend Peking."

"You were a long way from the Taipings and Peking when I saw you dressed as a peasant on the bank of the Pei-ho river."

Shalonga suddenly looked serious. "Landing in such mud to try to take the forts was madness. My men would have turned upon me had I given them such an order. I saw you fall during the battle. I feared you were dead."

"I thought so too, but here I am."

"Yes, here you are, a prisoner — but I doubt if it will be for very much longer."

"I would have been a dead prisoner had you not found me. I will always be in your debt, Shalonga."

"Soon this foolish war between our countries will be over and you will be free, but I fear

China will never be the same again: Missionaries and the long-robed men of the French will be everywhere."

"China couldn't go on for ever pretending the rest of the world doesn't exist. It does, Shalonga, and you're a part of it."

"Perhaps. What will you do when the fighting is over?"

Kernow thought of She-she and the uncertainty of their future together. "I don't know."

As though he had been reading Kernow's mind, Shalonga said, "What of your Hakka girl?"

Kernow started as though someone had fired a shot beside him. Then he remembered speaking of her to this man when they had first met close to the Canton river.

"You have a good memory. She is in Shanghai."

"You still see her?"

"Yes."

The single word explained nothing, yet Shalonga seemed to find it sufficient.

"You will soon see her again, my friend. This war will be over within a week."

33

HOSTILITIES between England and France on the one side, and China on the other, ceased only three days after the conversation on the subject between Kernow and Shalonga.

The Allied armies had fought their way to the north walls of the capital and were now making preparations to launch an attack on Peking itself.

Grant had his men bring up batteries of guns and he set them up in positions from which they could lob shells over the walls of Peking. Around and between the guns his infantrymen were established in a maze of trenches.

The British commander-in-chief's clear intention of attacking the city reaped its reward. The watchers on the city walls were thoroughly alarmed. A high government official was sent to negotiate a ceasefire. He returned to the city empty-handed. Neither Grant nor Elgin was in a mood for negotiation.

Grant set out their views bluntly to the unhappy official. "Return the prisoners you have taken and surrender the great Anting Gate, or the Allied armies will take Peking by storm."

The next day Kernow rode into Grant's camp accompanied by one of the captured Indian soldiers. The welcoming roar of the army's cheers brought Grant from his tent.

"Captain Keats! You don't know how delighted I am to welcóme you back." The commander-in-chief grasped Kernow's hand and winced as he caught sight of the rope burns still angrily encircling Kernow's wrists. His glance moved to the Indian who was surrounded by cheering men of his own regiment.

"Have the others been sent back with you?"

Kernow shook his head, "A trooper and a sowar are being brought in by litter. They are unable either to walk or ride. There were other prisoners, but I fear many will have died as a result of the treatment meted out to us by the Chinese."

Grant's chin came up angrily. "You'd better come inside my tent, Captain Keats, I want to hear all about your experiences."

★ ★ ★

Over the course of the next two days nineteen more prisoners were returned to their armies. The Chinese declared they held no more. When General Grant declared this to be unacceptable, the Chinese returned coffins containing the remains of twenty-one others. Most were unrecognisable.

The mood of the soldiers of the British and French armies was one of simmering anger. There could be no excuse for the brutality of the Chinese towards prisoners they had taken by treachery.

In a bid to take the edge off their anger,

514

Grant decided the dead men should be buried with full military honours. There was a Russian cemetery close to the Anting Gate and the British prisoners were buried here. Conveyed to the cemetery on gun carriages and escorted by infantry and mounted men, they were buried with full military honours.

Kernow had told General Grant about his conversation with the dying bugler. He was deeply moved when he learned that Grant had ordered the inscription on the cross marking the young soldier's grave to read 'Corporal Bugler Cummins'.

Later that evening, Kernow was called to General Grant's tent. He found Lord Elgin there and it was the British ambassador who spoke to him first.

"You know the Chinese thinking better than either of us, Keats. Do you think the impressive funerals we held for the prisoners they killed will prevent them doing it again?"

"I doubt it, my Lord. They will shrug their shoulders and put it all down to the peculiar customs of the *Fan Qui*. They can't understand why we're making such a fuss about a few men whose lives meant little to anyone except perhaps themselves."

"That's rather the way I see it and General Grant agrees. I'm determined to punish them for what they've done, so we've decided to burn down the Emperor's Summer Palace. After all, that's where they took you and the others and kept you for three ghastly days. It would be an appropriate gesture. One that I feel might have

515

a real impact upon the Chinese authorities."

The decision startled Kernow. The Summer Palace was a wonderful building. One of the wonders of the Eastern world. Burning it would be almost sacrilegious. And yet . . .

"I think burning the palace would certainly leave them in no doubt about the depth of our revulsion, my Lord."

"Good. I want you to go and take charge of the burning, Captain Keats. There'll be an Engineer officer to help you. A Captain Gordon."

* * *

The Summer Palace was in the French army's line of march and it had already been thoroughly looted by Britain's allies. However, such was the vast quantity of treasure within the palace, there were still many items of considerable value lying about the pavilions and grounds.

"It seems a criminal act to put a torch to such a wonderful place." Captain Gordon made the comment as he and Kernow gazed up at the golden roof of a pagoda, glinting in the sun.

"It is a criminal act. Unfortunately, only something on such a scale will impress the Chinese enough to make them think twice before ill treating and murdering prisoners."

"You were one of their prisoners, and I appreciate how you must have suffered, but don't you think the experience has biased you against the Chinese?"

The Royal Engineer officer who was to carry

out the destruction of the Summer Palace had earned a reputation among his fellow officers as something of an eccentric. Some said he would have been happier had he come to China as a missionary and not a soldier.

"You can have no appreciation of how I and the others suffered, and I am not biased against the Chinese. I would risk my life for the Chinese officer who saved me . . . and for others."

Kernow's thoughts turned to She-she. She had been on his mind a great deal since his return to the army. The news from Shanghai was that there had been fierce fighting in the vicinity of the city. It was also reported that the suburbs had been destroyed, although there was some confusion about which side was responsible for this.

She-she should have been safe enough in the house of the Strachans, but he could not help worrying about her.

★ ★ ★

The destruction of the Emperor's Summer Palace did all that Elgin and Grant hoped it would. Only days later the ambassador rode through Peking streets lined by British and French soldiers, in a procession that had all the pomp and colour that Elgin could have wished.

At the Hall of Audience, the long-delayed ratification of the treaty between Britain and China was finally signed by Lord Elgin and Prince Kung. Neither man exactly oozed *bonhomie*, but Elgin firmly believed that time would heal the bitterness between the two countries. Meanwhile trade would bring great benefits to both nations.

The following day it was the turn of the French ambassador to sign a similar treaty on behalf of his own country. That night a celebration was held in the British camp with toasts to all three countries and to a brighter and harmonious future.

As the party broke up in the early hours of the morning a very cold wind blew through the tents of the sleeping soldiers.

Standing at the entrance to his own tent, General Grant looked about him. The hills about Peking were silhouetted against the skyline in the bright light of a full moon.

"Back in England there'd be a hard frost on a night like this, Keats."

"There's probably one tonight, sir. After all, it's late October."

"True. Hopefully, we'll all be home in time to see the last frosts of the winter, at least. You'll be looking forward to that, I've no doubt?"

Fortunately, after calling out 'Good night', General Grant turned and entered his tent without waiting for an answer.

The question troubled Kernow. He was not ready to return to England yet. He would need to convince She-she that he really wanted her to go to England with him. It would not be easy. He could not make up his mind which problem was likely to be more difficult: convincing She-she he really wanted to marry her, or persuading her to go to England as his wife.

Walking back to his tent he was comforted by the thought that in only a few weeks' time he should be with She-she once more. They could tackle the problem in the privacy of a shared bed. Thinking about it left him with a warm feeling that chased away the chill of an approaching Chinese winter.

34

ON 8 November 1860 the British and French armies began their withdrawal from Peking. Winter had set in with a vengeance now. It was bitterly cold and there had been snow flurries on the hills beyond Peking. General Grant and Lord Elgin had been right not to allow the Chinese commissioners to delay the advance upon Peking. Another couple of weeks and the weather would have provided the Imperial army with an unbeatable ally.

The treaty had been signed, China, France and Britain were at peace with each other, but there was still an absence of trust between East and West. As the Allied armies marched alongside the Pei-ho river, a flotilla of British gunboats kept pace with them, ready to take a hand should there be any last-minute treachery on the part of the Chinese.

Nothing happened to break the peace. Leaving strong garrisons behind at the town of Tientsin, and at the Taku forts, the victorious armies set sail. Some would go to garrisons in Hong Kong and India, others were returning home to Britain and France.

Kernow arrived at Shanghai with General Grant on 4 December. Lord Elgin had gone ahead, bound for London, where he would receive the warm gratitude of his Queen and country.

When General Grant went ashore to be fêted by the British community, Kernow lost no time in heading for the Strachan home. On the way he saw that rebuilding work was already well under way in the suburbs destroyed by the defenders of Shanghai.

He was relieved to see that the Strachan house had suffered no harm. Nan Strachan was in the garden, hanging out clothes on a bamboo frame. When she saw Kernow the expression that came to her face told him his relief had been premature.

"Where's She-she? Is she inside?"

"She's all right, Kernow, but . . . don't you know?"

"Know? Know what?"

Kernow was confused. Nan had said She-she was all right, but the statement was at odds with her evasive attitude.

"You'd better come inside and talk to Colin."

"Where's She-she? What is it you're trying so hard not to tell me?"

"Come, in . . . please."

Inside the small house, Colin was working at the kitchen table, fashioning a small wooden horse for one of the children for Christmas. He rose immediately and extended his hand.

"Kernow! It's good to see you. We heard about your capture and release. You must have had a bad time. Have you seen She-she yet?"

"I thought she was here. I've been asking Nan where she is, but apparently there's something I should know before I see her."

"That's right. Sit down, Kernow. Nan, fetch

521

something for Kernow to drink."

"I'd rather stand, if you don't mind — and don't *you* start prevaricating now, or I really shall start worrying. What's happened to She-she?"

"She was kidnapped from this house by Chang's men, and taken to his camp. I tried to stop them and was knocked unconscious as a result."

"Where is she now? Does Chang still have her?"

"No. Caleb Shumaker negotiated her release. Esme and I went with him. But she never came back to this house. Sally Merrill took her to the United States consulate. She's been there ever since."

"God! What a terrifying experience for her. Was she harmed?"

When neither Nan nor Colin Strachan replied to his question immediately, Kernow said, "There's something more, isn't there? I'll go to the U.S. consulate now and see her."

"Wait, Kernow! Yes, there is more. I wish there was some easy way to tell you, but there isn't. Chang doped her with opium. Then he beat and raped her. She hasn't fully recovered yet. She doesn't want to see Nan or me, and Sally Merrill says she hardly speaks to her. She-she must dread the thought of having to face you after everything that's happened to her."

★ ★ ★

All the way to the United States consulate Kernow's thoughts and emotions were in a turmoil. The knowledge of what Chang had done to She-she sickened him. The thought of how she must have suffered, mentally and physically, caused him to alternate between anger and anguish. Much of his anger was directed against the French authorities. The Strachan home was on the fringes of the French area, but it was part of the Concession. They had a duty to protect it.

He was angry with General Grant for not releasing him to return to Shanghai; with the Chinese for keeping him a prisoner, unaware of what was happening at Shanghai, even though he could have done nothing to help. Most of all he was filled with a deep burning anger that encompassed the Taiping movement and centred upon Chang.

His anguish was for She-she and the effect her experiences at the hands of Chang would have had. He would need to be both patient and understanding with her. It would not be easy in the emotion of a reunion.

The first person Kernow met at the United States consulate was Caleb Shumaker. The American appeared to have far more confidence in himself than when they had last met. As the two men shook hands warmly, Caleb said, "I saw the ships were in and went down to the anchorage to find you. They told me you were already ashore. I knew you'd make your way here eventually."

"I've come to speak to She-she, but I'm glad

I've met up with you. I want to thank you for rescuing her from the Taiping rebels. It was a very courageous thing to do and could have landed you in serious trouble with your own government. Thank you."

"I brought her back here, yes. As for thanking me . . . I'm not so sure you'll be ready to do that when you meet her again. I never knew her before. I wish I had. She's a beautiful girl, but mentally she's in a mess. She's told Sally more than once that I shouldn't have brought her back. That I should have left her so that she could one day have killed Chang for what he did to her."

Aware that he might have said more than was wise, Caleb said hesitantly, "You do know . . . what happened out there in the Taiping camp?"

Kernow nodded grimly. "Colin Strachan and his wife told me. I can only imagine the torture She-she has suffered."

Accompanied by Caleb, Kernow entered the consulate. Before he was reunited with She-she, Sally intercepted him in the hallway. She too was aware of the return of the fleet from the Pei-ho river and had been expecting him.

Close to tears, Sally gave Kernow a warm and sympathetic hug. Such a demonstration of affection towards him would have angered Caleb Shumaker a few months before, but the rescue of She-she from Chang had given him a new maturity. He had more confidence in himself. As a result his relationship with Sally had strengthened.

"You're a lot thinner, Kernow. We heard about your horrific experiences at the hands of the Chinese. It's wonderful to have you safely back with us." The tears were still in evidence as she added, "Only you know how much you suffered, but Esme and I prayed for you every night. So did She-she. It's the only thing she's put her whole heart into."

"How is She-she? I want to see her, Sally."

"You know . . . about Chang?"

Sally looked to Caleb and received a nod.

"I'm very worried about her, Kernow. Except for the evenings when Esme comes here and we say a prayer for you, she hardly speaks to anyone. When Caleb brought her back from the Taiping camp she'd been drugged with opium and didn't know what was going on around her. I insisted she should stay here with me. I wanted to look after her. It might have been a mistake. Perhaps she would have been better with Nan Strachan. Another Chinese girl might have understood her needs more."

"From what I hear, you've both been very kind — and words can't express my thanks to Caleb. But I want to see She-she now. Where is she?"

"Where she spends most of the time. In her room. I'll take you there."

"I'd like to see her alone, Sally."

The American girl hesitated for only a moment. "Of course."

Sally led Kernow upstairs and at the end of an airy corridor knocked at a door. When there was no reply she opened the door. Looking inside she said, "She-she? There's someone to see you . . . "

"It's all right. I'll go in."

Sally was still not certain she was doing the right thing, but Kernow moved past her and went in the room, closing the door behind him.

She-she was seated at the window. From here she could see across the front garden of the consulate to the ships in the foreign anchorage. She must have seen him arrive at the house.

When she did not turn around immediately, he crossed the room and dropped to his knees beside her. She had always been slightly built, but now she appeared so fragile he was almost afraid to touch her.

"She-she, I've been told what happened. Forgive me for not being here to protect you."

The faraway expression on her pale, drawn face made him wince in anguish. "I love you, She-she." Putting his arms about her he pulled her gently to him.

For a moment she leaned into him. Then, as though something had triggered in her mind, she went suddenly rigid. It was like holding a statue and he could feel the explosive tension in her.

Without releasing her, he said, "I'm back now, She-she. Everything is going to be all right. I want you to come back with me to the Strachans' house. I've been there to see them. They'd like to have us living with them again."

When she made no reply, he said gently, "I know everything that happened to you at the

526

Taiping camp. I want you to put it behind you. To forget it ever happened. Nothing bad matters any more. Not now I'm with you."

"Does matter. Matter too much." She spoke in English, her voice even softer than his. But at least she was speaking to him.

"No, She-she. You're safe, and I'm safe. We've both been prisoners. When I was trussed up in the Summer Palace, expecting to die, I realised that life is too precious to waste in bothering about foolish matters. I love you and you love me. That's all we ever need remember."

Without looking at him, She-she said, "I happy you safe. Every night I pray with Esme to your God to make you safe. He listened, but even He cannot change what happened to me. Cannot forget. Will never forget."

"You can, She-she — and you *will*. Chang only abused the parts of your body he could touch, nothing more. He couldn't touch your mind, which is yours, or your heart, which is mine. Last year a Chinese shell shattered my body and left me permanently scarred. Must *I* be held to blame for that? Of course not, any more than you are to blame for what someone else did to your body."

She-she was quiet for many minutes while she thought of what he had said, then she replied, less certainly, "Not the same."

"It *is* the same. Exactly the same. Think about it."

"I don't want to think about what happened."

"After today there's no reason why you

527

should, but we've got to clear it out of the way now if we're to make things right between us again. Once we've done that you can forget it for always. It's very, very important to you and to me. Chang tried to take you from me and he failed. Don't hand him victory now."

She-she pulled away from him and looked out of the window again. With increasing desperation Kernow realised he had failed to break through the barrier she had built about herself. She had become one of the 'inscrutable Chinese', as seen by those with only superficial knowledge of her people.

"She-she, more than anything else in this world I want us to be together again, as we were before I went away. For you to love me as I love you."

He detected uncertainty in her stance and for a few breathless moments thought she was about to come back to him.

"Please, She-she. I need you."

"I would like you to leave me alone now."

"I can't leave you like this, She-she. Let's talk some more. Until we work things out between us."

"No talk. Please, you leave me now."

Kernow felt torn apart by She-she's attitude towards him. Although he realised she was very close to breaking point at this moment, he did not want to leave her without having matters settled between them.

"I need to think, Kernow. I must think. English girl not need to think, maybe. I *Chinese* girl. If can't think here I should go live in city, perhaps."

"You know I don't want that. All I want is for us to be as we were." He took her by the shoulders and turned her towards him, but when she looked up at him it was as though she had shrivelled inside. He dreaded to think what might happen to her if she were suddenly thrown upon her own resources inside Shanghai city. He would probably lose her for ever.

"All right, She-she. I'll leave you alone to think. I'll be back to see you again soon because I intend that one day we'll be together, loving each other for the rest of our lives. Think about that too, I beg you."

35

KERNOW would have only one meeting with She-she before he was unexpectedly sent from Shanghai once more. When he reached the waterfront to board a boat that would take him back to the ship, a soldier was waiting with a message from General Grant. The commander-in-chief was at the British consulate. Kernow was to go there immediately to meet him.

Shown into a room where the air was thick with cigar smoke, Kernow found Grant with a number of other senior officers. He was in an unusually jovial mood.

"Ah, there you are at last, Captain Keats. I was beginning to think you'd gone off on another of your mysterious jaunts."

The commander-in-chief had just been congratulated by the British consul and shown a copy of a letter sent to the British government in London by Lord Elgin. The British special ambassador had been extremely complimentary about the commander-in-chief of the land forces.

"I've just received a most unusual request, Keats. It's come from one of the Chinese generals we were fighting on the way to Peking. The chap you mentioned to me. The civilised one who improved things for you when you were a prisoner. Son of a war lord or some such, isn't he?

"As you know, now we've finally ratified the treaty with the Imperial Chinese there's only one thing standing in the way of permanent peace and increased trade. I'm talking, of course, about the Taipings. They are straddling the Yangtze river, the lifeline to the heart of China. If we're not careful they'll destroy all we've fought for. This Chinese officer has asked if we'll loan you to the Imperial army to help train a few regiments of Chinese. They've already mustered a company of European irregulars — mercenaries, and a cut-throat gang they are too, by all accounts — but they'll fight, at a price. He's suggested that you select any men you need to help you from among their number."

General Grant coughed as though embarrassed. "It's all highly irregular, of course, but not without precedent. I spoke to Lord Elgin before he left. Rather surprisingly, he thinks it's a good idea. He suggested the post might have been made for you. I agree with him. You speak fluent Chinese and have an understanding of the Taipings. It seems this Chinese chap who rescued you will be in overall charge of things, so he'll be able to keep an eye on you.

"I've made a few stipulations, of course. You're not to be used in a combat role — unless you personally feel it to be in the best interests of Great Britain. In order to prevent any repercussions at home about serving British officers fighting with a foreign army, you'll be taken off the active duty list. Placed on half pay — with the rank of brevet major, I might add. The Chinese have promised to more than make up the rest. What I'd particularly like you to do is see if you can't persuade the Chinese to maintain some sort of control over this hotch-potch army of mercenaries. At the same time I hope you can build up a good relationship with them. It's a tricky job, Keats, but I have every confidence in you. What do you say, eh?"

A vision of Chang's face rose up between General Grant and Kernow.

"I'll be delighted to take on the task, sir. When do I begin and where?"

"Good man. I thought that's what you'd say."

The general had the grace to looked mildly embarrassed as he continued. "Your duties begin right away. This Chinese general chap seemed so certain everyone would agree to his request that he sent an escort along with it. I've told them you'll be ready to go off with them tomorrow. That suit you?"

It did not suit Kernow, but having said he would accept the task he was obliged to agree. "I have a few things to settle first, sir, but I'll be ready to leave in the morning."

"Good man! I trust you'll be discreet in all you do. We don't want to provoke any awkward questions in the House of Commons about Royal Marine officers training Imperial Chinese troops in their war against the Taipings. Before you go kit yourself out well with whatever you need. I doubt if you'll get much from the Chinese. Take your pick of the cavalry horses and requisition anything else you think you'll need. When you eventually get back to England come and see me. I'll find a place for you on my staff. You've done a sterling job out here."

* * *

Kernow broke the news of his imminent departure to She-she that night. It shook her out of her apathetic state as nothing else had been able to do.

Seated on a chair by the window in the United States consulate she swung around to face Kernow and a succession of expressions chased each other across her face. Fear, distress, unhappiness, uncertainty. All were there.

"You go away to war again? Why? Because of me? Who you fight now? I thought your country had made peace with the Chinese?"

"We have and I'm not going to fight anyone. Shalonga has asked for me to help train Imperial Chinese troops. I couldn't refuse. He has saved my life twice."

"So you will help him defeat the Taipings? Defeat Chang?"

"Yes." Kernow hesitated before saying, "Have you thought any more about what I said? About us?"

She-she nodded. "Much of what you say is true. Not all. What happened to your body brought you honour. For me there is only dishonour."

He would have interrupted her at this point, but she silenced him with a movement of her head. "No, hear me, please. I believe you speak the truth when you say 'no matter'. I think maybe you love me enough. I was going to ask you to give me time. Time to stop thinking all time like Chinese girl. To learn more how *Fan Qui* girl thinks."

It had been a long time since Kernow had heard She-she use the expression *Fan Qui*. It showed him how far her mental attitude had reverted since she had been taken by Chang's men.

"I have time now. I will try hard, Kernow. It would be easier if you were here with me, but I will try. You will never be ashamed of me, I promise."

Suddenly She-she began to cry. When he held out his arms she came to him and there was no holding back now. No tension in her body. He knew then that the hardest part of the battle to make She-she come to terms with what had happened to her had been won.

★ ★ ★

Kernow left Shanghai in the company of Shalonga's escort a much happier man than he had been twenty-four hours earlier. She-she was on the road to recovery, of that he had no doubt. It might prove to be a slow progress, but she had friends about her to help. She was also aware now that nothing of her relationship with Kernow had been destroyed by what had happened to her.

It would take time before She-she could put

the kidnap and rape behind her, but she had made a start. Kernow had spent much of the night in her room either talking with her or content just to hold her in silence.

Now Kernow was on his way to the town where Shalonga was camped, no more than sixty miles from Nanking. The commander of Kernow's escort was a knowledgeable man who was able to talk about the progress of the war. He claimed that the Taiping rebels guarding the road between the Imperial Chinese camp and Nanking were commanded by Chang, the Heavenly Prince himself.

Kernow hoped this was so. He had been forbidden by General Grant from taking an active part in the battles between the Taipings and their Imperial Chinese enemies, but if Chang were involved . . .

On Kernow's arrival at his destination, Shalonga introduced him to some of the officers of the mercenary 'Ever Victorious Army'. Kernow was not impressed with any of them.

He was even less impressed when he accompanied the irregular unit in a small battle to take a poorly defended town, only five miles from Shalonga's camp. They conducted much of the battle at long range, where their superior weapons gave them an impressive advantage over their opponents.

There was nothing wrong in this, but once the town was taken the men, most of whom were Europeans, went on an orgy of rape and pillage.

When Kernow tried to prevent this happening he was warned to stay out of the way or he would be shot. The men of the 'Ever Victorious Army' were deadly serious in their threat.

When Kernow reported the matter to Shalonga, the Tartar commander merely shrugged his shoulders, saying in French, "To the victor goes the spoils, my friend. It is a reward given to every victorious army in China. Even the Taipings, now."

"It will be their downfall, as it might well be yours. A defending army will fight to the last if death and the rape of their women is the only reward for surrender."

"How else would you reward men who risk their lives in battle?"

"By paying them far more than they would receive in other occupations and by putting towns out of bounds when they are captured. Give them instead a pride in winning. Pride in themselves."

Shalonga smiled. "It is a unique solution, my friend, but I will give it a try. Do you have any further ideas for improving the efficiency of the Imperial army?"

"A great many. Let it be known that you are recruiting men for a special unit. A unique unit, whose pay will be far higher than that of their fellow soldiers. Let them understand that every volunteer will be interviewed and only the very best will be accepted. I believe you'll have more volunteers than you need."

★ ★ ★

Kernow's predictions were proven to be correct. They were overwhelmed with volunteers but initially accepted only one hundred men.

Even more surprising, three officers serving with the Ever Victorious Army volunteered to join, at a reduced salary. Kernow accepted two of them and had no cause to regret his decision.

He now commanded a company of men of whom he was very proud. As part of his policy of making them feel special, they were given a red sash to wear, similar to the one made for Kernow by She-she.

His elite company became known as the 'Red Sash soldiers' and good men were clamouring to join. His soldiers were well paid and, what was more important from the men's point of view, their pay was received regularly, something that Kernow insisted upon. They were better fed too.

Before long, the discipline of Kernow's company was such that, even though they were still a training company, when a town was captured from the Taipings, they were detailed to police it, in order to keep their more rapacious companions out.

They did not lose by their discipline. What they had not taken by force was freely given to them by a grateful population.

Soon Kernow was able to raise a second company, then a third. He set his standards even higher, but still men flocked to join him.

Meanwhile, the battles between the Taipings and the Imperial Chinese army were fought on a very wide front, and neither side could claim absolute victory. The Taipings would win a battle here, the Imperial army there.

The battle front resembled hot fat in the bottom of a cooking pan, moving this way and that, constantly changing shape, forever in danger of erupting into flames.

36

SOME months after taking over the training
of troops for the Imperial army, Kernow
was in his headquarters tent, only three
miles from Taiping territory. He was reading a
letter for the third or fourth time.

The letter was from Esme Pilkington.
Crumpled and grubby, it was three months
old and had undoubtedly travelled in a great
many pockets and pouches before arriving at
its destination. The letter contained much of
importance to him, providing news of She-she.

The missionary assured him that She-she had
almost fully recovered from her ordeal at the
hands of Chang. This was fortunate because
she would soon be obliged to move out of
the consulate home of the Merrills. War had
erupted in the United States of America. The
Southern States had seceded from the Union
and battle lines were being drawn. Even more
than in the war between the Imperial Chinese
and the Taipings, it would be a conflict where
brother would fight against brother.

The Merrills were from the South. Consul
Merrill felt he could no longer represent the
interests of the government of the North. Caleb
would return with them. He too was from the
South and felt obliged to offer his services to
the armies of the secessionist States.

However, Esme assured Kernow he need not

worry about She-she. Esme had accepted a new post at the missionary station at Ning Po and was taking She-she with her. Esme informed Kernow that She-she was working hard to learn about Christianity. She was, declared Esme, a 'good girl', adding, "If ever good is seen to come from evil, this is it. After all that happened to her I despaired for a long time of health and reason being restored to her. I am convinced that God has taken a hand in her recovery, although credit must also be given to the faith she has in you. It is a great responsibility, Kernow, but I trust, I beg, you will not let her down."

His deep thoughts were interrupted by a commotion outside as a Tartar horseman, riding hard, galloped into the camp, arms and legs urging his horse on. The animal seemed to have captured the excitement of its rider and caused havoc among the men who were sitting down for a meal. Without dismounting, the Tartar shouted for Kernow.

He hurried outside. When the horseman saw him, he shouted, "You must come quick to the valley over there. The Taipings have made a surprise raid. Shalonga is in trouble."

The Tartar did not stay to tell Kernow what he needed to know about the strength of the Taiping force and the exact position of Shalonga's camp. Wheeling his lively pony about, the wild cavalryman galloped back the way he had come, scattering Chinese soldiers along the way.

Many of the men in the training camp had heard the news shouted by the Tartar horseman and it was quickly passed on to others. Kernow knew they waited to see what his reaction would be. Having received extensive training under his guidance they were fit and ready to fight the Taiping rebels. They were also fully aware of the restrictions placed upon Kernow by his government.

He hesitated for only a moment. "Sound the bugle for the men to fall in prepared for battle. Break open the ammunition boxes. N.C.O.s, get the men moving the moment they're ready. Officers, come and see me as soon as your companies are formed up. We'll talk on the march."

The trainee soldiers fell over themselves in their eagerness to be among the earliest to move off. The first company was on its way in a matter of minutes. The remainder were not far behind.

Kernow had more than three thousand men under his command. The majority had never been tested in battle, but he hoped surprise would prove a decisive element in the fight that lay ahead.

He had not gone far before the sounds of conflict came to him. He realised he and his men had been fortunate. Had the Taiping rebels not fallen upon Shalonga and his men, they might have stumbled upon the training camp and taken them by surprise. The slaughter would have been horrific.

Taking his men at a trot through a copse of tall, spindly trees, Kernow suddenly came out in the valley where the battle was taking place.

It was a desperate fight.

The Taipings had managed to surround Shalonga's Tartars. During the initial engagement they had succeeded in driving off a great many of the horses. Those men who had kept their mounts were so hemmed in by the enemy they were unable to make use of them.

Fortunately, there was a small hamlet beside the Tartar camp and Shalonga had managed to rally most of his men here. Nevertheless, when Kernow and his men appeared on the scene the Tartars were engaged in a desperate hand-to-hand battle for survival.

The arrival of three thousand Imperial reinforcements took the Taipings by surprise and Kernow launched his men straight into battle where the fighting was most ferocious.

The move threw the Taipings into a fatal confusion. While some continued the attack against the Tartars within the hamlet, others turned to meet this unexpected threat.

Shalonga was an experienced general. Realising that the advantage had shifted heavily in his favour, he ordered his men to charge from the hamlet and take their revenge upon the Taiping attackers.

Caught between the two Imperialist forces, half the Taiping army broke and ran, causing the attack of their colleagues to falter.

The Taipings fled, some up the slopes of the surrounding hills, others along the far side of the valley itself. The mounted Tartars galloped after them, cutting the rebels down as they overtook them. Kernow feared his own men would also take part in the disorderly pursuit. But the many tedious weeks of training insisted upon by him now bore fruit. Flushed with the excitement of their first battle, and their first victory, some did continue to chase the Taipings, but the great majority returned to where he waited. Some even brought prisoners with them. As the Chinese custom was summarily to execute any prisoners taken in battle, Kernow knew beyond all doubt that his training methods had been successful.

"Hello, my English friend." Shalonga reined in his pony beside Kernow. Hot and black-faced from gunpowder smoke, he grinned as though he were enjoying himself. "I think I owe my life to you and your training regiment. Another half-an-hour and we would have been overwhelmed and annihilated."

Shalonga jumped from his pony and embraced Kernow warmly.

"It seems I've paid back at least part of the debt I owe you. I hope there will never be another occasion as closely fought."

"It was a brief but glorious battle. Unfortunately, I had only my advance guard with me when the Taipings attacked. My headquarters and my main army will be here by evening. You must come and eat with me."

★ ★ ★

That evening Kernow made his way to the Tartar camp and found Shalonga relaxing in a huge tent. Hung inside with expensive silks, it was more reminiscent of an Emperor's pavilion in its splendour than the tent of a general in the field.

Kernow was also surprised to find a great many women in the tent, all obviously belonging to Shalonga. When he expressed his surprise the Tartar general looked at him quizzically. "It appears unusual to you? Why? Because a soldier spends most of his life fighting it does not mean he should forego all the things other men enjoy. No, my friend. Women are attracted to men who go to war. Why should I deprive them of their simple pleasures? You ought to have your own women too. Would you like one . . . or more? There is an attractive Korean girl who came to me the other day. I have had no time for her yet. Take her."

"No thanks, I don't need one at the moment."

"Ah, yes, your little Hakka girl. Where is she now?"

"I thought she was in Shanghai, but I received a letter this morning telling me she has gone to Ning Po with a missionary woman who has befriended her."

"When did she go?"

The question came back so swiftly that Kernow felt a sense of alarm. "About three months ago. Why do you ask, is the timing significant?"

"I was curious, that is all. I was myself in Ning Po a few months ago. However, it would have been before your Hakka girl and her friend arrived there."

Shalonga switched the conversation and for

the remainder of the evening the two men discussed the fighting of the day and the need to train more men.

The next morning Shalonga went off without saying goodbye to Kernow or leaving word of where he was going. With him he took only a couple of hundred men. Kernow was a little surprised, but Shalonga was an autocratic general. He was not in the habit of discussing his movements with anyone.

Kernow soon stopped wondering where Shalonga might have gone. He was very busy. The soldiers he had been training had proved beyond all doubt that they were ready for active service. As soon as it could be arranged they would be sent to fill the ranks of other regiments. He had to interview and commence training a few thousand more.

★ ★ ★

Kernow did not know Shalonga had returned until he sent Kernow an invitation to go to the young Tartar general's camp for an evening meal once more. At first, Kernow was inclined to turn down the invitation. He had a great deal of work to do if he was to organise another training course. Thousands of volunteers had turned up at the camp in the last few days. They were fired with enthusiasm by the victory won by the training regiment. They too wanted to join the *Fan Qui*'s victorious army and fight the Taipings.

The recruits would wait until tomorrow.

Kernow always enjoyed Shalonga's company. He put down the work on which he was engaged and took himself off to the Tartar general's camp.

"Ah! There you are, my English friend," Shalonga greeted Kernow at the entrance to his tent. "I was beginning to think you were not coming."

"I very nearly didn't," Kernow confessed. "We have enough volunteers to form two training regiments and I think we should take them on while they're still keen."

"So we shall, but we will talk of this later. I have a number of plans I wish to discuss with you. First I have some guests I would like you to meet. They have been awaiting you eagerly."

Puzzled Kernow followed Shalonga inside the tent. The Tartar general had introduced him to some of his colleagues on other occasions, but few could have been said to be eager to meet him.

Once inside the tent, Kernow's puzzlement turned to utter disbelief. Here, seated at a low table filled with food, were Esme — and She-she!

"What . . . ? How . . . ?" Kernow's amazement at seeing She-she was so great he was lost for words. He could not shift his gaze from her. She looked well, much improved from the last time he had seen her. He wanted to touch She-she. To hold her. Yet he dared not while others were present. He would not be able to control his emotions. Her expression of sheer joy told him she felt the same way. But it was Esme who heaved herself up from the table first. Hugging him to her, she called him her "Dear boy! Very dear boy!"

She-she was slower to her feet. She would have bowed low before him had he not taken hold of her shoulders and drawn her to him. She yielded for only a moment and then drew away, her face more flushed than he had ever seen it. He would never know that inside she was singing. Kernow had acknowledged his feeling for her in front of Esme and the Tartar general. It was a moment she would cherish forever, whatever might happen in the future.

"What are you doing here? I thought you were at the mission in Ning Po."

"General Shalonga brought us here. He was only just in time. The Taipings were within a mile or two of the town."

When Kernow looked accusingly at his friend, the Tartar general shrugged. "You can thank your training methods, Englishman. Your men took prisoners and mine questioned them. One captive was a senior Taiping officer. He told me that the great Taiping army of the East, led by Chang himself, was advancing upon Ning Po. He boasted they would have the town within the week. He was not wrong. We were only just in time."

"You knew of this the last time we met, yet said nothing? Why?"

"What would you have done had I told you? I will tell you. You would have jumped on your horse and galloped off to Ning Po. Along the way you would have met up with Taiping soldiers and they would have killed you. My army has need of you. It was better that I go instead."

Smiling at the expression on Kernow's face, Shalonga said in French, "Now I have met She-she I understand why you think so much of her. She is exquisite. I almost understand too why you would not accept one my girls."

"I am sure She-she will be pleased to hear that." Esme's French was excellent, if halting.

"You speak French!" Shalonga was delighted and not at all embarrassed. "It is my favourite language. Come, we will leave Kernow and She-she together. You can speak to me while I show you where your quarters are to be. I have given you a room in the house where my own women are living. I have no doubt you will be a good influence upon them. If you wish to promote Christian ideals while you are there I have no objections."

As he spoke, Shalonga guided Esme towards the door of the large tent. Suddenly excusing himself, he returned to Kernow.

In a low voice he said, "I have taken the liberty of having your things moved to new quarters. The District Magistrate has had to make an unexpected journey. His family has travelled with him." Shalonga smiled warmly. "He has kindly placed his home at your disposal."

Switching to French once more, he added, "Do not concern yourself with the formidable Esme. She will be quite content in her new quarters. Besides, I find her quite charming. We will no doubt still be discussing the merits

548

of the various religions when the sun rises. Relax for a few days with your She-she. After that we will discuss the plans I have for your future."

When the young Tartar general had gone, Kernow felt slightly embarrassed as he explained to She-she, "Shalonga has assumed you will be staying with me. He has given us the District Magistrate's home."

After a few moments' silence, She-she said, "Is this what you wish?"

"It is what I've always wanted. For you to share your life with me. But when we last met . . . " Kernow shrugged without completing the sentence.

"When we last met I was very unhappy. I was also confused and frightened. You said many things to me. Kind things. It made me think a great deal. You remember?"

"I remember."

"Do you still feel the same? You have not changed?"

"I'll never change the way I feel about you, She-she."

"That makes me very happy, Kernow. Esme has taught me much about Christianity. The love of God fills her life. She needs nothing more. That is good for her. It would be good for me too, perhaps, but to fulfil my life I need *your* love too. I think I have always known this, but I am more certain now. If you love me and want me, I will stay with you wherever you go. We will be very happy together. If one day you say you have to go back to your own people it will not matter. I will be happy with my memories then."

Almost too choked to speak, Kernow said, "You will never have to rely on memories to find happiness, She-she. You say you love me and I know I love you. I think I always have and I know I always will. Everything will work out for us, you'll see."

Reaching but almost shyly, he took her hand. "Come, let's find the way to our new home."

37

THE next few days were very happy ones for Kernow and She-she. The departed magistrate had left behind a beautiful house and gardens at their disposal. The servants were falling over each other in their eagerness to please the *Fan Qui* war lord who had defeated the Taiping rebels on their very doorstep.

It did not matter that the unexpected journey of their master had not been entirely voluntary. In fact, it added to their pleasure at serving the *Fan Qui* and his lady.

Such an idyllic existence could not last forever. Five days after their taking up residence, a Tartar officer called at the house. He found them in the garden feeding giant carp in the absent magistrate's pool.

The message for Kernow was that Shalonga wished to see him. At that moment She-she knew that their brief carefree period was over. It had served its purpose well. They had learned to know each other again and it was even better than the weeks they had spent with the Strachans.

Kernow was aware of this. When they were staying at the Strachans' house his relationship with She-she had been a clandestine one, kept hidden from the view of his fellow Europeans. Here, among the Chinese people, such a relationship was accepted without question.

The realisation disturbed him. He wondered whether such disapproval would be restricted to the European colonies in Hong Kong and Shanghai, or whether he and She-she could expect the same in England. It disturbed him because he wanted everything to be right for them. He did not want She-she to have to face the disapproval of his fellow countrymen and women.

He would dearly have liked to discuss his feelings with Esme, but the missionary had thrown herself into the serious business of teaching Christianity to the women of Shalonga's harem with her customary enthusiasm, oblivious of all else that was happening around her.

★ ★ ★

When Kernow entered the meeting hall it was immediately apparent that this was to be no friendly chat between himself and Shalonga.

It was being held in the building where taxes were usually gathered by the Imperial government and Shalonga was not the most senior soldier present.

At the head of the long table sat a thickset man who exuded an air of great natural authority. He was surrounded by army officers who wore Mandarin buttons denoting impressive ranks.

Shalonga was seated beside the authoritative man, whom he introduced to Kernow as his father, General Tingamao, the great war lord who ruled China's borders with Vietnam.

General Tingamao fixed Kernow with his dark

552

eyes and did no more than incline his head. It was enough for the senior officers present to defer to Kernow and move up to make room for him at the table, alongside the war lord's son.

When Kernow was seated, a conference of war was convened. It was immediately apparent that the war lord possessed an impressive grasp of the situation affecting the whole of China. As details were unfolded realisation dawned on Kernow that the men in this one room commanded all the armies of China.

The war lord did not 'discuss' strategy. He dictated to his fellow officers what he proposed, and what he expected from them. Only when they had been told where they and their armies would operate were the commanders allowed to speak.

In the main, they all spoke of the need for more men. In only one case did a speaker with local knowledge of the country in which he would be fighting suggest alternative routes. He also asked for more time to move men to the objectives he had been given.

Unfortunately for the commander, the war lord possessed an equal knowledge of the area. He agreed to the alternative routes, but declared that by taking them the commander could arrive a day *earlier* than had been proposed.

During the briefing, Kernow listened carefully to hear the orders for Shalonga. They did not come until the very end.

"You, my own son, will take ten thousand of my men to fight the Taiping rebels' Eastern Army. They have taken Ning Po and we have received many complaints from the *Fan Qui* authorities about disruption to their trade. You will drive the Taipings from the port."

Shalonga bowed over the table, "I hear your orders and I will do as you ask. But I too would like to take more men with me. I have in mind the three thousand men of the training regiment. They have proved their worth in battle and will do great credit to the Emperor. I also wish to have the Englishman, Major Keats, to lead them for me."

Kernow was startled by the suggestion. "I have authority from my commander-in-chief only to train your troops, not to lead such a brigade into battle."

"I am thankful you did not remember that when I was so hard pressed by the Taiping rebels, Englishman. I would also like to point out that the rebel Chang is in personal command of the Eastern Army. I think you would like to have a hand in his defeat?"

As Kernow hesitated, Shalonga said, "I seem to remember you telling me you are sanctioned to take part in the fighting if British interests are at risk. Your country has much trade through the port of Ning Po and a European community is resident in the town. There is every excuse to involve yourself in the fighting should you so wish."

The offer tempted Kernow greatly. He was a professional Royal Marine officer who had been trained for warfare. He had enjoyed leading his training regiment into battle. To command such an army of men in the field would give him the power and responsibility usually reserved for a brigadier, or even a major general. Then there was Chang . . .

"The *Fan Qui* is too young to command so many men in battle." The comment was made by Tingamao, as though Kernow were not present.

"Was I any younger when you sent me with the whole of your army against the Vietnamese war lords?"

"You are my son. You were born to command fighting men and I knew you."

"Major Keats is a friend who has saved my life and the lives of many of your own men. I have seen him in battle, fighting both for and against us. I know him."

Tingamao's glance rested briefly on Kernow. "Very well, Shalonga. You are to be in supreme command of the army. The decision is yours to make — but I have not yet heard him agree to do as you ask."

"I'll come with you," declared Kernow, speaking in Chinese. He added, in French, "What is to happen to the women?"

Shalonga was pleased with Kernow's acceptance and he replied to his question in the same language. "What you really mean is, 'What is to happen to She-she?' You need have no fear for her safety. The women will travel with us when we are on the move. When a battle is imminent they will be escorted to safety and guarded well. I have not lost a woman to the enemy yet. I have no intention of doing so now."

It was rudeness to speak in another language

555

in front of others, but now Tingamao spoke in a language that Kernow had heard before but did not understand. He guessed correctly that the war lord was speaking in a Tartar dialect.

Those in the room who understood what he was saying smiled suddenly and approvingly at Kernow before Tingamao rose abruptly from his chair. With a brief nod in Kernow's direction he left the room, closely followed by the other generals.

"What was all that about?" Kernow asked of Shalonga.

"My father was honouring you, Englishman. He said that to commemorate your success in saving his son, the red sash worn by the men under your command will henceforth be worn with pride by all the men you have trained, wherever they are sent to serve. He also gave orders that the banner you will carry into battle will have a red band running from corner to corner. You are now the commander of your own brigade, with your very own banner. I am well pleased, my English friend. We will fight well together, you and I."

38

SHE-SHE was apprehensive about Kernow becoming involved in full-scale fighting between the Imperial army and the Taiping rebels, but there was never any question of her not accompanying him into battle. She was Kernow's woman. She would go with him anywhere for as long as he wanted her to be there.

Esme decided she too would go along. She was giving religious instruction to Shalonga's women and enjoyed the hours-long discussions she frequently held with the young Tartar commander.

Of them all, Kernow had the most self-doubt about the wisdom of going into battle with the Imperial Chinese army. He was aware of the embarrassment it might cause to the British government if word got back to London.

Before Shalonga's army set off, Kernow sat down and wrote a long letter to the commander-in-chief in Hong Kong. In the letter he explained what he was doing and gave his reasons for the action he was taking. He was convinced, he wrote, that it was in the best long-term interests of Britain to drive the Taipings from Ning Po and re-establish normal trade between Europe and China in the treaty ports.

He sent the letter off in the certain knowledge that it would take many months to reach

Hong Kong. By that time anything might have happened. If the Imperial army's campaign ended in a decisive victory it was fairly certain his explanation would be accepted. Only if Shalonga's army were to be defeated would there be any serious recriminations from the government in London.

★ ★ ★

Shalonga's army made slow progress through the Chinese countryside. There was an occasional skirmish with Taiping rebels, but only twice were they called upon to fight anything resembling a full-scale battle. On both occasions Kernow's 'Red Sash' Brigade acquitted themselves well. Their morale was high and Kernow would have happily matched them against the troops of any nation in the world.

The slow progress of Shalonga's force was a deliberate policy. He wanted to put off having a decisive battle with the Taipings until winter was about to set in. If he could prise the rebels from Ning Po then they would be driven into the countryside. It would be quite impossible for such a large force to feed themselves from the land and they would be forced to retreat to a Taiping-held town, throwing a strain on resources there too.

The Taipings did not make a stand until Shalonga's army reached the very walls of Ning Po but the battle here was fierce. It ended with Kernow's brigade taking many prisoners. From these, he learned with disappointment that

Chang was no longer with the Taiping garrison inside Ning Po.

He also learned that the commander of the Taiping garrison in the treaty port was Peng Yu-cheng, Kau-lin's brother. She and her women's regiment were also part of the town's garrison.

Kernow had always been very fond of Kau-lin and the last thing he wanted was to fight against either her or her brother if it could possibly be avoided.

Before he could discuss his predicament with Shalonga, a company of Tartar horsemen arrived bearing dismal news.

Tingamao, great war lord of the Vietnamese borders and veteran and victor of more than a hundred battles, had been stricken down with a battlefield disease. He was lying seriously ill in a town not more than fifty miles from the Taiping capital of Nanking.

They brought other momentous news. Hsien-Feng, Emperor of all China, had died in the palace to which he had fled when the Allied armies closed in on Peking. His successor was a five-year-old boy, son of one of his secondary wives.

The secondary wife, Tsu-Hsi, to be known as the Dowager Empress, had been appointed co-regent of her son, together with the first wife of the late emperor. However, said the messenger, Tsu-Hsi would be the real power behind the Imperial throne, and likely to remain so for very many years to come. She had already foiled a coup. Supported by the Prince Kung, she had a firm grip on the reins of power in the Chinese kingdom. She had appointed her own supporters to key positions throughout the land and was likely to continue the purge.

Among those appointed was a new Viceroy for Chekiang, the province where Ning Po was situated. Li Chau was the name of the new Viceroy and he was reported to be on his way.

All this news was told to Kernow by Shalonga as the Tartar general dressed for the long journey he intended making to be with his sick father.

The weather was turning cold and Shalonga's coat was of bearskin, as was his hat and the leggings that a servant bound around his legs.

"Li Chau is not known to me, but as he has been appointed by the Dowager Empress with such great speed he is undoubtedly loyal to her. It stands to reason therefore that he has been sent to the province for a purpose. I wish I knew what it was."

Shalonga fastened the clasp of the coat about his neck. He needed to be warm and was not concerned about the difficulty he might have in removing his clothes. He would ride day and night to be with his father, pausing to sleep only when he was ready to drop. He would not remove his clothes until he reached his destination. This was his way.

"Should Li Chau arrive before my return, treat him with extreme caution. My father's clan is too powerful for the Dowager Empress to risk our displeasure, but we are not beloved by her people. She also has a dislike of Europeans and will never forgive you for forcing her and the Emperor to flee from Peking during the recent war."

"I'll do my best to keep out of the way of this Li Chau, should he come to this part of his province."

"It may not prove easy, Englishman. I am giving you command of the army in my absence. Don't look so surprised. You are familiar with the conduct of a campaign and have a natural caution which is important in a leader if he is to win wars as well as battles. My men will fight for you — and fight better than any other warriors in the world — but they are headstrong. In the heat of battle they cease to think of anything but killing. However, they will die for you, should the need arise. Remember this before you send them into battle, Englishman. I do."

Pulling the dark-furred hat down over his ears, Shalonga strode from the tent to where an escort and a string of ponies awaited him.

★ ★ ★

That evening Kernow discussed the unexpected situation with She-she and Esme. The missionary had only just heard of Shalonga's abrupt departure and had come to Kernow's tent to learn what was happening.

"I'd like to resolve the situation with as little loss of life as possible," declared Kernow. "All our intelligence reports suggest the Taipings have very little food in Ning Po. If I maintain a tight cordon about the town I might starve them into submission before Shalonga's return.

It's certainly worth a try."

"I have a better idea," said She-she unexpectedly. "Why don't Esme and I go into Ning Po and try to persuade Kau-lin and her brother to surrender? We can be certain that Kau-lin will see us and she has influence with her brother."

The suggestion startled Kernow and he had doubts about the likelihood of its success.

"It's not likely that a general like Peng Yu-cheng will take any notice of what two women have to say over a matter like this."

"Then make us your official messengers," said Esme. "I think She-she's idea is a most sensible one. I've met Peng. He's an intelligent and courteous man. I know he'll listen carefully to anything we have to say to him. I also know he has been disillusioned with the *T'ien Wang* and his increasingly erratic behaviour for some time now. The war is going against the Taipings, there is now no hope they will ever win. The opportunity for victory was lost a long time ago. If Peng fights on to the bitter end he will forfeit his life and the lives of all his family and followers.

"It's my opinion that if anyone offered him a means of bringing his own war to a satisfactory conclusion he would take it. Write him a letter, Kernow. Offer him honourable terms for surrender. I and She-she will take it to him. With God's help I'll persuade him to lay down his arms and so avoid the bloodshed that will follow if he decides to fight."

Kernow spent much of that night composing

his letter to Peng Yu-cheng. He called in Shalonga's senior officers and explained to them what he was doing. Not all agreed with him. There were spoils to be taken in Ning Po, and women.

After a long discussion, Kernow won a majority of the Tartar officers over to his side. They had a great respect for the Taiping general who held Ning Po. He and his men would defend the town with fanatical zeal. The weather would be on their side if they could oust him from Ning Po. It would work against them if they did not. They agreed that Kernow should attempt to negotiate the surrender of the town.

She-she and Esme took Kernow's letter to Ning Po the following morning. Kernow was greatly relieved to see Kau-lin leading the party who came out from the gate to meet the two emissaries and escort them in through the gate. Now he had the difficult task of waiting for their return, wondering and worrying about what might be going on inside the high walls.

39

FOR two days Kernow sat outside Ning Po, gradually convincing himself it had been a disastrous mistake to place She-she and Esme in the hands of the Taipings. He had actually sent out a message for an emergency meeting of the senior Tartar officers to discuss his next move when a messenger bearing a white flag emerged from the encircled town.

The messenger carried a letter to Kernow from Esme. The two women had spent most of the two days talking with Peng Yu-cheng. He had held a meeting of his officers and was now ready to meet Kernow.

The meeting would take place on open ground halfway between the main camp of the besieging forces and the main Ning Po gate. As added insurance for Peng's well-being, the two women would remain within Ning Po until a conclusion had been reached in the talks between the two men.

Esme explained this by saying that while Peng had full trust in Kernow, he did not have the same confidence in the Tartar army. For this reason, neither man would be accompanied for the preliminary discussion between them.

Kernow agreed to the Taiping commander's conditions. An hour later he crossed the open space between Tartar and town, feeling extremely vulnerable and alone.

Not until he had reached the allotted place did the town gate swing open to allow Peng to come out. The two men met and shook hands and after exchanging the customary pleasantries, Peng said, "Your offer of a conditional surrender interests me, *Fan Qui*. What are your conditions, and how will you be able to guarantee that the Tartars of General Shalonga will accept them?"

"The Tartars are under my command at the moment. They will do as I say. You have my word. As for conditions — all I ask is that you leave Ning Po and hand in your arms. If you wish I will arrange transport to take you and your men back to Canton."

"Our lives would not be safe there. We would be hounded by both the Imperial authorities and those of our own people who resented our return. No, *Fan Qui*, we are fighting men. I will surrender to you on condition we are taken into the Imperial army as a fighting unit. Not to do battle with our fellow Taipings, you understand, but sent to one of the northern provinces to fight rebel tribesmen or the Mongols."

"I will need to consult the new Viceroy of the province before that can be agreed. It might take time."

"We have sufficient food in Ning Po for our present needs. Time is of more consequence to you than for us."

Kernow did not know whether the other man spoke the truth, but if bad weather set in it would be the Tartar army that would be hard-pressed to find sufficient food to survive. "Very well. You'll release Esme and She-she in the meantime?"

"Of course. It was courageous of them to bring your message to me and both are friends of Kau-lin. They will be with you by this evening."

* * *

She-she and Esme arrived at the Tartar camp before dusk. They were accompanied by Kau-lin who intended staying with them for a few days. Kernow was not at the camp. He had gone to the capital of the province, to find Li Chau, the new Viceroy and discuss Peng's surrender with him.

Hangchow was a two-day ride to the northwest, but Kernow and his escort had travelled less than half the distance when they met with the new Viceroy. He was on his way to see for himself what was happening at Ning Po.

Kernow was kept waiting by Li Chau for more than two hours before the provincial Viceroy sent for him.

Matters were not improved when Kernow refused an order to kow-tow to the new Viceroy. His anger showing, Li Chau snapped. "I am told you come with a message from Shalonga. Deliver it and you may go, *Fan Qui*."

Kau-lin's brother had also called Kernow a *Fan Qui*. Kernow had found it far less offensive than the same words from the tongue of this man seated in splendid robes in front of him.

"Shalonga has gone to the bedside of his sick

566

father. I am in command of the Tartar army besieging the town of Ning Po."

Before the Viceroy had recovered from the shock news, Kernow continued, "I have spoken to Peng Yu-cheng, Commander of the Taiping army occupying the city, and discussed his surrender. He is willing to lay down his arms if you agree to take him and his men into the Imperial army and send them to fight rebels in the north of the country."

"Peng is in no position to demand terms. He will be treated as would any other rebel commander who surrenders to the Imperial army. He will write his confession and then be beheaded as a traitor to the throne."

"Then he will refuse to surrender and is likely to hold on to Ning Po for the whole winter. I doubt if that will please any of the traders, Chinese or European."

"You will not allow him to remain at Ning Po. You and your army will attack him immediately."

"I have ten thousand men outside the walls. Inside Peng has at least twice that number. I think he will also have the weather on his side. If there is snow it will favour the Taipings."

"You fear what will happen to you if you storm Ning Po? What sort of soldier are you?" Li Chau spoke contemptuously.

"I am an *experienced* soldier. However, should you wish to lead an assault yourself, I will place the army at your disposal. I will also ensure you are buried with all the honours due to a Viceroy of his Imperial Majesty."

Li Chau looked at Kernow in silence for a very long time before saying, in a much less arrogant tone of voice, "This offer made by Peng to surrender and serve the Emperor — do you believe he will keep his word?"

"I am certain of it. Peng is a man of honour."

"He is a rebel!" Li Chau spat out the word. "However, since you refuse to attack the town it would seem I am left with no choice. Very well, tell him I accept his terms."

Kernow should have been delighted by the Li Chau's words, but he was not. The Viceroy had capitulated too easily.

"If I persuade Peng to surrender I will be giving him my solemn word that he and his men will not be harmed in any way."

"So? Is your word more sacred than the promise of a Viceroy of Imperial China?"

So indignant was the Viceroy that Kernow thought he must have misjudged him. After all, Li Chau had only recently been appointed to his position. He was not yet used to taking such decisions.

"I will go to Yaugang to await the surrender of Peng Yu-cheng and his men. He will come to me there and sign a declaration that he is willing to serve the Emperor."

Yaugang was a small and ancient walled town some four or five miles along the coast from Ning Po.

Without a word of farewell, Li Chau waved his hand in a gesture of dismissal and Kernow was escorted from the Viceregal presence.

568

40

NEWS that Li Chau had accepted Peng Yu-cheng's surrender were conveyed to the Taiping leader inside Ning Po by the second senior Tartar officer serving with the Chinese army. After discussions between the two, Peng agreed to evacuate the sea port town at noon the following day.

Kernow was not there to oversee the departure of the Taiping rebel leader and his men. He had returned from his meeting with Li Chau to find a fleet of British warships lying at anchor off Ning Po. On board the flagship was Sir Frederick Bruce who, in addition to being the brother of Lord Elgin, was the current British ambassador in Peking.

The arrival of the warships at the time of a possible battle for the possession of Ning Po was no coincidence. There were British interests to be protected in the treaty port — and Bruce also wanted to speak to Kernow.

A message was waiting at the Tartar headquarters for him to repair on board the flagship immediately.

Kernow knew that such a peremptory message boded ill. Bruce did not want him on board the flagship to congratulate him on the victories he had gained fighting with the Tartar. Kernow delayed obeying the summons until he had seen Peng and his men march from Ning po unmolested by the Tartar soldiers. Then he hired a fisherman to take him out to the anchored warships in a tardy response to the British ambassador's call.

The twenty-four-hour wait had done nothing to improve Bruce's temper. As soon as Kernow stepped on board he was hurried to the admiral's cabin where Sir Frederick Bruce and Admiral Sir James Hope were present with a number of other senior officers.

Only Admiral Hope offered him a greeting and this was so uncharacteristically subdued that Kernow knew he was in trouble.

"Major Keats, I summoned you yesterday, leaving a message that you were to report to me *immediately* you returned to the Tartar camp. Am I to understand you returned there only today?"

"No, Sir Frederick. I came back yesterday, but I have been arranging the surrender of the Taiping garrison in Ning Po. I wished to see it through."

It was quite apparent to Kernow that his words had taken everyone in the room by surprise. Admiral Hope's face broke into a delighted smile.

"You've done *what*?"

"I met with the Taiping leader some days ago and worked out terms for his surrender. Then I travelled to see the new Viceroy for Chekiang Province and persuaded him to accept the terms. I have just watched the Taiping rebels march out of the town, leaving their arms behind."

"What right have you, a British Royal Marine

Officer, to interfere in the war between China and the Taiping rebels? It is an internal matter, not one to involve British citizens — especially those wearing the Queen's uniform."

Kernow was puzzled by the ambassador's anger and stung by his line of questioning. "I was asked by General Grant to accept secondment to the Imperial Chinese army. It was an arrangement that met with Lord Elgin's approval."

"The arrangement was for you to accept attachment to the Chinese army in a *training* role. It was not intended you should become involved in their battles. Do you deny you have fought against the Taipings on behalf of the Chinese?"

"I deny nothing. The commander of the Tartar army in this area is a friend. He was in danger of losing his life at the hands of the Taipings. I took my training regiment to his rescue."

"And you have continued to play an active role in the war between the two sides, I believe?"

"I travelled with General Shalonga to Ning Po, yes," Kernow prevaricated.

"Ah!" Frederick Bruce looked from Kernow to Admiral Hope triumphantly. "Do you realise, Major Keats, that by your actions you could have placed the lives of every European in Ning Po in jeopardy?"

"On the contrary, Sir Frederick. By arranging for the surrender of the Taipings I have undoubtedly resolved a very dangerous situation.

571

Not that they would have come to any harm at the hands of the Taiping commander. I know him for an honourable man. The danger would have come during a battle for possession of the town. I have removed that danger."

"Nevertheless," Sir Frederick Bruce persisted doggedly, "in my opinion you have far exceeded any orders given you by General Grant. I have very strong views about British nationals becoming involved in any dispute of this nature. It is essential that we not only remain neutral, but are *seen* to be neutral."

"I trust you were able to explain this to the satisfaction of the Taipings who were driven back from Shanghai by British and French troops manning the walls of the city, Sir Frederick?"

"That is an impertinent remark, Major Keats. Whatever happened at Shanghai has no bearing on the matter in hand."

Turning to Admiral Hope, the ambassador said, "Sir James, you are the commander-in-chief of the Far East Station. I strongly recommend that in order to avoid future censure you relieve this officer of his duties immediately. I also recommend that steps be taken to return him to England at the first possible opportunity."

Admiral Sir James Hope appeared shocked. "With all due respect, Sir Frederick, this young man has served his country well during long service in China. To send him home in disgrace would be grossly unfair."

"As I said, Sir James, I strongly recommend that you act upon my advice. Whether or not you do is entirely up to you. I will show you a copy of my report before it is despatched."

"Then I shall also be forced to place on record my protest at your unduly harsh recommendation. In my view it goes against all the known facts. I will send a copy to Lord Elgin who has first-hand experience of Major Keats' value to the service of his country. With all due respect, Sir Frederick, you cannot say the same."

"Please don't jeopardise your future career for my sake, Sir James. I am on half pay at present, so I can't be removed from active duties, and I have no wish to return to full service. I will put my resignation in writing. In the meantime you have sufficient witnesses here to verify my stated intentions . . ."

At that moment there came an urgent knocking at the door. It opened to admit the officer-of-the-watch. Addressing the admiral, he said, "Begging your pardon, sir, I think you should come up on deck. There appears to be something happening along the coast at Yaugang. There's a whole lot of shooting and what sounds like screaming."

There was a swift exodus from the admiral's cabin but while the other officers hurried aft to the quarter-deck to listen to the sounds coming from Yaugang, Kernow hurried to the boom where the duty boat was manned.

"Coxswain! Take me ashore to Ning Po — and be quick about it."

The coxswain hesitated. "Begging your pardon, sir, but are you one of our officers?"

"Damn you, man! Do you want to lose your

rank? This is an emergency. Can't you hear the shooting on shore? Get me to Ning Po immediately or you'll be in irons for the rest of your Far Eastern service."

The coxswain was used to the threats of officers — but this one sounded deadly serious. Moments later the ship's boat had been cast off and the coxswain was berating his men for not pulling harder towards the shore.

★ ★ ★

Kernow found the Tartar camp in a state of confusion. They had heard firing coming from the direction of Yaugang, but without Kernow to direct them they were not sure what they should do.

They were restraining Kau-lin too. When she had first heard the sound of shooting coming from Yaugang she had tried to seize a Tartar pony to ride off and learn what was happening. When she saw Kernow she screamed at him, "You've sent my brother to his death. The Viceroy has killed him."

Ordering that she be detained until he returned, Kernow gathered at least half the Tartar army behind him and galloped to Yaugang.

The sounds became frighteningly louder as they drew closer, but the gates in the high wall were closed against them.

Kernow called upon the men inside to open the gate, but there was no response. Not until he ordered the Tartars to fire a volley at the gate did a town official appear on the battlements above the gate. Kernow called to him, demanding to know what was happening inside.

Kernow repeated the question three times before the decidedly nervous official replied, "It is said the Taiping prisoners tried to seize the weapons from their guards. They were overpowered and are now being executed."

"Those men surrendered because I gave my word they would not be harmed. They are *my* prisoners. I demand you open this gate immediately."

The official disappeared hurriedly from the wall and ten minutes later his place was taken by an officer of one of the Imperial bannermen regiments.

"What is it you want, *Fan Qui*?"

"Where is Viceroy Li Chau? I demand that the Taiping prisoners be released immediately."

"You *demand*! I fear you have taken leave of your senses, *Fan Qui*. Remain there and observe. You will soon be able to pick out the heads of those you seek among the crop to be planted above the gate."

"If you don't open the gate I will bring up cannon and blow the gate open."

It was an idle threat. The Tartars were cavalrymen. They possessed no cannon. It seemed the officer on the wall was aware of this too.

"Go and fetch your cannon, *Fan Qui*, but I doubt if it can match this."

There was a loud report from the ramparts of the wall and a cannon ball carved a path through the Tartar cavalry, knocking horses and riders to the ground.

There was a roar of anger from the Tartars, but Kernow knew the Viceroy would not be influenced by the anger of horse-warriors from the Vietnamese border region.

He waved the men back from the gate, out of range of the cannon. Leaving a thousand men to picket the gate, he rode back to the main camp with the Tartars who carried their wounded men with them.

41

WHEN Shalonga returned to the Tartar camp a week later the siege of Yaugang was still being maintained. The Tartar general was in a mood of deep sorrow. His father had died within hours of Shalonga's arrival. Despite his grief, he listened to the story of Li Chau's treachery with growing anger.

"It is no more than one would expect from a man of his clan," said the Tartar chief. "Come, we will find Li Chau."

"I doubt if he'll speak to you," said Kernow. "He's not showed his face on the walls since the Taiping prisoners were executed."

"He will open the gates to me, or within a week he will be on his knees, begging the executioner for mercy. Come."

At the gates of Yaugang, Shalonga refused to speak to anyone but the Viceroy, insisting that he come to the wall above the gate. Much to Kernow's surprise, within fifteen minutes of their arrival the yellow-robed Viceroy stood on the walls above them.

"Open the gate, Li Chau."

"A Viceroy does not take orders from the son of a war lord, no matter how exalted that war lord may be."

"My father is dead, Li Chau. I am the war lord now. The remainder of my army will be here by tomorrow night. We will then be fifty

577

thousand strong. We may not have cannon, but we can obtain gunpowder from other towns. If it is necessary to blow down the doors of Yaugang I will allow my men to sack the town. Your execution of the Taiping prisoners will be as nothing compared to what my men will do. Tell me, Li Chau, are your family with you? I trust they are well . . . "

In another fifteen minutes the gates of the small town of Yaugang swung open. When Kernow, Shalonga and the soldiers of the Tartar army passed through the gate into the streets, there was not an occupant to be seen.

Shalonga gave orders for his men to commence a search. They eventually found a house in which almost a hundred surviving Taiping rebels were being held prisoner.

They were brought to the garden of the magistrate's house where Shalonga, Kernow and Li Chau sat in silence.

Choosing one of the Taipings who appeared to have some authority, Shalonga asked, "What happened?"

The Taiping was frightened but defiant. "We came in to Yaugang because the *Fan Qui* had promised Commandant Peng we would be safe. Suddenly we were rounded up and the executions began."

"Li Chau has said you tried to seize guns from his soldiers."

"There was no uprising. Why should there be? We had been promised our freedom."

"What of Peng Yu-cheng?" Kernow put the question.

"He was beheaded because he refused to sign a 'confession'."

"Very well," Shalonga nodded to the man. "You have told us what we wished to hear. You and your men are free to go."

The Viceroy's protests were cut short by Shalonga. "Do not tempt me to separate the evil that is in your heart from the lies that come from your mouth, Li Chau. By your treachery you have brought dishonour upon the Dowager Empress's name. She is slow to forgive matters of honour."

"You overstep your own authority, Shalonga. You will hear more of this."

"You will need to send your messages a long way, Viceroy. Now my father is dead I have no stomach to stay in provinces ruled by men like you. My soldiers have been away from their homes for too long. I am taking them home. Come, Englishman. We will leave Yaugang to the dead and those like Li Chau who feed on carrion."

Escorted by ten thousand Tartars the two men were safe from any treachery Viceroy Li Chau might plan. Soon the other forty thousand Tartar warriors would arrive. There was not an army in the whole of China would dare oppose them.

"What will you do now, Englishman, you and your She-she? I fancy you have no further stomach for the Imperial cause. Will you return to your own armies?"

"I am no longer part of either the army or the navy of my country. I was called before the British ambassador soon after you departed from your camp. I have resigned my commission."

"Why?" Shalonga looked at Kernow sharply.

"Because I led the men of the training regiment into battle. It doesn't matter. I have no wish to fight for the Chinese any longer."

"Nor I. The Dowager Empress came to the royal household from a clan that does not look favourably upon me and mine. It is best that I return to the border country. There I can raise four times as many fighting men as my father brought to fight the Taipings. I will be safe from the treachery of the court there."

★ ★ ★

Kernow spent a week at Shalonga's camp. It was an unexpectedly relaxed period. He enjoyed the company of She-she and they both tried hard not to think of what the future held for them. Kau-lin remained here too, mourning her brother, and spending most of her time with Esme in the quarters of the women.

One evening, as the camp was preparing itself for the long march home, Shalonga called a meeting of his leaders. It was late in the night when Kernow was summoned from the house he shared with She-she. He was told she must come with him to the meeting too.

Arriving at Shalonga's huge headquarters tent, Kernow and She-she walked in to find the officers of the war lord's army seated in a circle around their leader. They were a ferocious-looking group of men, tough fighting warriors with a fierce pride in their prowess.

Shalonga looked tired, but smiled up at them as he addressed his words to Kernow. "I have done much thinking since my return, Englishman. Before I could put my thoughts into words for you I needed to be confirmed as war lord in my father's place by all those who served him. It is now done. I am truly war lord of the Vietnamese border lands and as such I put my wishes to them.

"You have saved my life and the lives of many men here. Your actions found disfavour with your own people and you have sacrificed your future for us.

"I offer you a new future among our people. You will be given your own lands." Shalonga smiled. "More than your own ungrateful country would give you. As much as the country you call Wales. There you would be emperor, king, war lord . . . you may call yourself what you will. All I ask in return is your loyalty and your assistance should someone be foolish enough to wage war against me. I will do the same for you, should you make enemies.

"It will mean breaking with your own country, your own people, but it will not be without compensations, I think. You will have your She-she and be able to live in a community who will accept you both as their rulers and your sons as your heirs. Indeed, you will be passing on an inheritance that would be impossible in your own country."

Shalonga was silent for some time but when Kernow looked at his face he realised how much it meant to Shalonga to have him accept his offer.

If Kernow had any doubts about what he should do, one glance at She-she was enough to drive away the last vestige of hesitation. She looked as though she might burst with the joy she felt.

Reaching out, he gripped Shalonga's hand. "I thank you, my very good friend. I thank you from the bottom of my heart. When do we go home?"

THE END